EM'S WHEEL

A NOVEL

KRIS HEYWOOD

EM'S WHEEL

Copyright © 2011 by Kris Heywood

This is a work of fiction. All the characters, names, incidents, organizations, and dialogue in this novel are either the products of the author's imagination or are used fictitiously.

Cover Art by Leanne Zinkand, Silverlining Designs

Library of Congress Control Number: 2011913132
ISBN: 0615517714
ISBN-13: 978-0615517711
Siskiyou Press

ALSO BY KRIS HEYWOOD

VOID

MARIA

PRIVATE WALLS

SAVING FOR ATLANTA

WAKING UP SCARED

GROWING AROUND
THE WOUNDS

For Abraham, Michael and Seth

CHAPTER 1

THE ROOM WAS A SOMBER BLACK, the dying embers providing only the faintest glimmer of light. It gathered on the shape of a red dog napping on a braided rug and the six pairs of bare human feet that rested lightly against the dog's luxurious fur. As usual, the feet were split into two distinct sections. Odasan and his wards, Lupe and Brendan, had theirs on one side of the dog. Alden and his most loyal follower, Hertha, had theirs on the other, matching ankle to ankle.

Anckar's feet lay all alone at the dog's tail end—also as usual. Six pairs of legs rayed outward, blending with the parlor's gloom. The door to the yard was open, allowing the shrill chirrup of crickets to stream inside.

"We've done as much as we can by ourselves," Alden's dreamy voice said from the shadows. "To go on, we need the girl and her friends."

Lupe's question was timid and stubborn at once. "Why should we go anywhere when we have paradise right outside this door? There is no place better than this. No one below knows we're here."

Anckar gave an indignant sniff. "They know exactly where we are. It's only because this is such an inconvenient location that they

1

haven't come after us—yet. Have you forgotten what happened to the original freaks?"

Brendan stirred uneasily, as he always did when Lupe was under verbal attack. "This time she's right, Lupe," he said gently. "They put that sign in the store window. That's not exactly a peaceful act."

There was a long pause, and then Hertha added in her rich tone, "I don't know how much longer the store will take our stuff for trade. Tilden's wife is finally getting to him. What will we do without lamp oil? Without matches? Without grain?"

The dog sighed and shifted, causing the six pairs of red-tinged feet to rise and settle again. From the edge of the mountain forest, an owl screeched a high-pitched "Whooo!" A warm breeze blew faint life into the coals, shifting deep shadows.

"Alden, tell us about the girl." Odasan's calm voice invited reasonableness. "Why won't she come?"

With a rueful laugh, Alden said, "She reminds me of how it was for me. She lives in the same kind of small, dying village where the farmers are losing their fight with the drought. Every dream I send her she manages to forget the moment she wakes. She's so used to her miserable life that she thinks there's no other way to be."

"And her companions?"

"I think there are three. One is an old friend content in solitude. The second is a man she has yet to meet. I haven't been able to form a clear link with the third but I do know none of these three will come without Em, and without her, we can't proceed."

Somewhere downslope, a second owl boomed a resonant reply to the call of the first. Twice more did one owl ask and the other respond before Odasan said softly, "If we could fetch her somehow." It sounded almost like a suggestion.

The dog sat up, toppling their feet onto the plank floor, and apologetically licked Brendan's heels, spending a few extra seconds on the misshapen one. Then she went to stand in the dim rectangle of the doorway, gave one decisive bark, and was gone. "Nada!" Brendan cried sharply. There was no reply. "You don't suppose she'll—"

"Why not?" Odasan said. "Didn't we agree, when she first came to this clearing, that she is no ordinary dog?"

The boy, who had never shown the slightest inclination to contradict his sensei outright, replied respectfully, "True. And she's always been good at retrieving."

Abruptly, the crickets ceased fiddling. Deep silence spread over the steep, inky hillside. A cold draft invaded the cabin, bearing the scent of autumn and frost.

CHAPTER 2

Em woke with her long legs dangling over the end of her mattress. She fished for the stool she always used as a bed extender but could not find it. Most likely she had kicked it out of reach during that last vivid dream, already fading. Keeping her eyes closed, she took a deep breath and was almost sure she could smell a mouth-watering blend of vanilla and butter.

No doubt her birthday cake was already cooling on the kitchen sill directly below. Last year it had been rich with cream from their own cow, who had since died of heat and starvation. But there'd only been one candle stuck on top instead of the fifteen she had expected. She hadn't seen as much as a cake crumb since but her taste buds still recalled every nuance of flavor.

The tantalizing aroma of her new cake catapulted her out of bed and into her rough, hand-sewn summer dress, already too short and too tight. She smoothed her hair, scooped up her oversized sandals, and ran out to the landing for a better whiff but all she could smell was yesterday's stale heat. She leaned over the banister to look at the kitchen door, which was always kept open. This morning it was shut. From behind it came a mute scraping of chair legs, a plate set down unnecessarily hard, the sparse murmur of her parents' cheerless voices.

They were waiting for her.

She took the stairs three at a time, sliding a hand along the banister and hesitating at the bottom just long enough to yank the unevenly stitched dress hem toward her knees. Then she opened the door. A reflection of dawn colored the kitchen walls a festive pink, but there was no cake on the sill and the counter was equally bare.

The table was set for three with the unmatched everyday dishes, the usual rosehip tea and a dark loaf of rough-milled bread. Her father sat stooped over his plate on one side of the table, her mother over hers at the other. Both were tenaciously chewing.

Em dropped her sandals. Her mother turned to face her, twisting her mouth into a stingy smile. "Land's sake," she said. "You got up by yourself today. Must be a special occasion." It was plain that she didn't realize what day it was until the last word was out. Then a shadow of discomfort crossed her lined face.

"Don't tell me you forgot," Em said, as if it wasn't entirely obvious.

Her father slurped tea to wash down his last bite. "And a good morning to you, too," he said with his usual gruffness, not bothering to look up. "Forgot what?"

"Oh, nothing." Em made an effort to sound calm. "Just my sixteenth birthday, is all." She glanced hopefully back at her mother. "Did you . . . bake me a cake?"

"Foolishness," her father answered instead. "Waste. When flour's so costly right now. Sixteen, you say? Old enough to know that money doesn't—"

"—grow on trees," Em finished his favorite sentence for him, just to get it over with. "Mom? A present? Just one?"

Her mother got up to rinse her plate in the sink. "We're heading out to the fields, Emma. Before the heat comes on. You'll have to eat your bread while we're walking. No money for presents this year. Times are—"

"—hard," Em supplied, still at the door. "But Mom, I gave you something for *your* birthday."

"What, that bunch of dried weeds?" her mother scoffed. "Tell you what—I'll pick you one just like it, soon as we get to the—"

"—fields," said Em, retrieving her sandals. "You'll have to bring it back here then, because I'm not pulling a single thistle today. I'm staying home, and if nobody's willing to celebrate with me, I'll do it all by myself." She whirled out to the hall and slapped her big feet across the tiled floor and up the sagging stairs. Her exit would have sounded more impressive if she had worn shoes.

"I'm sleeping in!" she yelled from the landing. "For as long as I want! And when I wake up, I'll bake my own cake. And I'll find my own self a present—just see if I won't!" She slammed her door and hooked the latch, expecting immediate retribution, but neither of them came after her. Maybe it was the one thing they were willing to give her on her sixteenth birthday—the once-only permission to be rude without getting punished for it.

Soon after, she saw her parents walk away on the dirt road. They looked stunted from her angle, both short, stiff backed, and shabby. Her father balanced a shovel on one bony shoulder, a hoe on the other, the lunch sack swinging from its sharp blade. Her mother carried both rakes and a water skin. They walked four feet apart, framing the space Em usually filled. Had always filled until now.

Part of her wanted to catch up and fill her old space, keep everything as it was, ease one of the rakes off her mom's shoulder and work extra hard in the furrows between them until they would pardon her lapse into defiance. Some other part of her jerked the curtains shut, gulped air already too warm, and knew she had finally breached a line that could not be mended.

An hour later, in a kitchen sweltering from the cook stove, she put something lopsided and lumpy on the sill. The counter was a sticky mess. She was tempted to leave it but didn't quite dare. While it was true that a girl shouldn't have to wash dishes on her birthday, it was also true that a mother shouldn't have to come home to the aftermath of a cooking disaster.

She scrubbed everything clean. Then she fetched her latest book and carried it out to the yard. In the shade of the carob tree, she gathered a handful of pods that had fallen during the night, sat with her back against rough bark, and examined each pod for worms. She kept only the best and nibbled on them while she scanned the book in pursuit of her favorite word, the one with the promise of accelerated action. It was *suddenly*.

There were two reasons she found it hard to keep her eyes tracking the page. The first was the quick mental glimpse she kept getting of that one last dream she'd had during the night, complete with patterns of pulsating light, a strange haunting song, and a quiet voice that had whispered incredible secrets into her ear. She could still hear the words though they'd stopped making sense right after she woke up.

The second reason was guilt. It made the carob pod she was gnawing bitter in her mouth. How selfish could she get, using the last of the sugar and eggs and spilling costly wheat flour while her parents crouched over a nightmare of thistles and weeds, the sun sweating the lives out of them drop after salty drop? And surely it was wrong for her to read in the middle of the week when the book could have waited for Sunday.

If only they would admit how senseless their labors were in this endless drought, under a sky of merciless blue empty of the smallest hint of a cloud. Sitting in the shade of the carob tree, she wished she could do something, anything, that would make a difference.

"You're about to get your wish," the voice from her dream seemed to whisper inside her ear.

"Oh, hush," Em said, jumping up. "You're not even real!" The book dropped onto the hardpan, slamming shut.

And then, suddenly, the world went still.

It was as if every sound had been sucked right out of it. Her eardrums fluttered. She slapped her ears, expecting the pop that sometimes came with a yawn, but it didn't come. No crows, screeching. No hens, cackling. No village noises at all. Even the silence in Bena's old woods was louder than this, with the conifers rustling in the breeze, making green waves.

A wasp swooped close and hovered in front of her nose, its wings vibrating without the usual hum. If wasps got thirsty enough they would land on bare skin, wanting the sweat. She backed away from it and walked around the big tree, staying in its circle of shade. When she returned to her starting point the wasp was gone. She stooped for the book at her feet just as the voice in her ear said,

"Now listen!"

Sound rushed back in—first the din of crows and the shrieking of hens, then the shrill neighing of a stallion, followed by an incoherent, terrified scream. It pierced clear through her. Something nearby was hurting. She ran, letting her heart pull her down the same road her parents had walked, around the same two curves, toward the fields. She could hear boys hooting and wasn't surprised to recognize Nev's voice among them. It had been his stallion, trumpeting—Thunder, who had taken Em's place in his affections, for whom he had so easily betrayed her.

She was rounding the second curve when the scream rose again, tearing through excited male laughter.

"Bull's eye!" Sean shouted. He had made fun of Nev all of last year for playing with Em, who was growing not by inches but by feet, looking more grotesque with each passing month. On the day Nev finally saw her through everyone else's eyes, Sean had promptly slipped into the best-buddy role she had to relinquish.

"My turn. Watch this!" yelled Tim, the sheriff's son.

And then she saw everything—Thunder rising, Nev proud in the saddle, his two friends on either side of the horse. Tim was aiming a stone at something too close to miss, something trying to hide between two low furrows. It was red, dusty, and utterly defenseless.

"Hey," Em yelled, outraged. She snatched up a crumbling piece of fence post. "Hey!"

Tim dropped the stone. Thunder's hooves came down. Nev shrank in the saddle.

"Well, if it ain't your old sweetheart, the giant," Sean drawled. "The cavalry to the rescue. Or is it *Horse-Face* to the rescue?"

"Neither," Tim sneered. "It's *Spider-Legs*, wearing a dress for a change. Not that it does her much good. Homely is homely."

Nev shrank some more. So did Em, but on the inside, where it didn't show. She ran on, wielding her stick. The thing in the furrows raised its head and looked hopefully in her direction. As she closed the last few yards it tried to crawl toward her. A dog?

"Careful," Nev said. "She's got the mange. Don't touch her. We're trying to chase her away before she passes it on to the village dogs."

Em glared. "No reason to use her for target practice!"

Nev looked away.

Em dropped the fence post, sank to her knees, and stretched out a hand. A red muzzle bridged the gap left between them. The instant that hot, dry nose touched the back of her hand and the dog's round red eyes locked onto hers, a shiver of pure recognition passed through Em, even though she was quite certain they had not met before.

"Leave that sick bitch alone," Nev warned. "She doesn't belong here."

"She does now. She's mine." Em rose, one hand under the stray's scabby chest, the other supporting the hind legs.

Tim made a puking sound.

Sean said, "Ugly giant, ugly dog. You two deserve each other!"

But Nev wanted to reason with her. "Put her back down, Em," he said as Thunder nervously danced sideways. "If we don't chase her away the sheriff will shoot her."

Em clutched the dog to her chest. "Today's my birthday, remember? And this is my present, the way Thunder was yours. You know I always wanted a dog."

Nev twisted the reins and looked to where the fields met the forest as if wishing himself far away. "What's the matter, Nev," Sean said. "You're not still sweet on the freak, are you?"

"You kidding?" Nev kicked Thunder in the ribs and the horse reared again, drumming air. The boys jerked away from the hooves, scowling at Em to hide their lapse into panic.

She turned her back on them all, retracing her path to the road, around the curves, and to the house. The dog in her arms was as light as skin, bones and an empty belly could get. The longer she held her, the more she felt a bond growing between them, like the one she used to have with Nev. He had been more twin than friend until the day his father took him aside and told him he was getting too old to hang out with girls, especially gawky ones who made him look like a midget. He'd offered him Thunder instead and Nev cut her loose and accepted the bargain without thinking twice.

Funny how the stray in her arms could almost make it stop hurting.

CHAPTER 3

Em CARRIED THE DOG BEHIND THE BARN and put her down in the coolest part of the shade. "Don't move," she said. "I'll bring you some water." The dog's tail twitched in response as she obeyed. But her red eyes anxiously looked after Em, who glanced over her shoulder twice before she rounded the barn corner. Turning to peek, she found the eyes still trained in her direction.

In the kitchen, she filled her mother's oldest pot with water and grabbed some meat scraps out of the cooler. She laid her offerings before her new friend who drank in great gulps, ignoring the food. Then Em took her first close look at her one and only birthday present. The dog's hide was flaky and raw, hanging in loose folds. Em's dress was stained with rust-colored blood from carrying her. Since it was already dirty she used the hem to wipe pus from the dog's runny eyes. "You're a mess," she said. "Good thing I found you. But don't worry. I'll fix you up somehow." There were certain weeds, much as her mother scoffed, that held the power to heal—but she wouldn't know which to pick until she had an idea of what ailed her new friend.

Then she noticed a leather strap around the thin neck. It was crusty with dirt, but somebody must have cared enough to fasten it on her. Someone she lost, maybe weeks or months ago. Em tried to

11

work the tight knots, stopping when a fingernail split. "Maybe I can't help you get home, wherever that is," she said. "But I promise to take good care of you here." She eased herself on to the ground beside the dog and stretched out full length, crooking one arm for a pillow, resting the other on a red flank. "Red," she said. "That's what I'll call you. Now let me think this through."

The dog put her muzzle trustingly on Em's chest, right over the diaphragm, where it moved up and down with Em's breathing. The food scraps attracted a fly that proceeded to buzz loudly in wide circles. An ant climbed over Em's ankle and traveled up her shin. A wasp landed on her big toe and squeezed itself into the valley between it and the second toe.

She held her foot still. The wasp's tiny feet tickled. Then it rose to investigate the fly's treasure, adding its drone to the buzz. The fly retreated to land on one of the dog's oozing sores. Red twitched her hide, sending it back into the air. Em yawned, closed her eyes, listened to the buzz and the drone, and felt the ant tickling her knee. She thought about flicking it off—but what harm did it do?

Her mind floated and sank. *Catnap* was her next-to-last thought. She changed it to *dognap* and slept.

Her rumbling stomach awoke her. Lying sweat-drenched in a patch of bright sun, she felt too heavy to move. Her lids seemed glued shut. It took her forever to put a hand over her belly. As soon as she managed the feat, an array of faces appeared on the screen of her mind, each smiling at her with prompt recognition before making room for the next. If she had seen any of the faces before it sure wasn't in this life. She rarely left the confines of Oren except for an occasional secret trip into the wildest part of the forest and her monthly hikes to the used-book store in Clydestown.

She answered each of the smiles with one of her own. What could it hurt? The last face to appear belonged to a pale, long-haired man wearing a red bandana tied over his brow. He looked drowsy and daft. "I'm Alden," he said without moving his lips. "Welcome to the fiery hill."

Startled, she jerked her hand off her belly, whereupon his image disappeared. She must have been out in the hot sun too long; it was baking her brain. Red raised her head, panting. The water dish was dry. The food scraps were gone. So were the bugs. "I know where to take you," Em told her. "To Clydestown. There's an animal hospital across from the bookstore."

The dog cocked an ear as if considering the suggestion.

"The vet will know if you've got the mange or not," she explained, turning over one of Red's paws. The pads were worn raw. On her other feet, too. "You can't walk on these for two hours, but light as you are I can't carry you that long."

Red wagged her tail, waiting for Em to work it out.

"I know," Em said. "We'll borrow Pop's handcart. I'll be back in a minute."

She thundered upstairs to her sweltering room, snatched the hot piggy bank off her dresser, stuffed it in a bag along with an old blanket and the aluminum flask from her closet shelf, and carried everything to the kitchen to add more leftovers from the cooler. While she filled the flask and Red's dish she briefly considered the collapsed cake on the sill. With a shudder, she decided to take along a few slices of plain bread instead.

It wasn't until she came out into piercing sunlight that she remembered the dismal state of her dress. Running up to her room again, she changed into a loose pair of shorts and the sleeveless blouse she'd helped her mom sew, shed the sandals in favor of socks and her sturdy walking shoes, snatched her wide-brimmed straw hat from its peg behind the door, and was ready to go.

The trick was to leave the village unseen, especially by her parents, who couldn't refuse permission as long as they were conveniently absent. Em avoided asking herself how they would like the new family addition. When she's made sure Red was comfortable on the folded wool blanket inside the cart, she took off at a brisk pace, thankful her father kept the wheels so well oiled. The Clydestown vet would prove Nev wrong, of course, and then Red would be safe anywhere in Oren.

TWO HOURS later she slumped on the bench in front of the bookstore, dejectedly wiping her brow with a sunburned arm, frowning at the small sign across the street, tacked to the hospital's door. *Closed until two.* It was barely one—the hottest time of the day. She wanted to browse in the store but dogs weren't allowed. Clydestown seemed to have run out of shade and Red was panting again.

"More water?" Em asked, stooping to push the dish under the dog's nose. She straightened in time to see an oddly shaped horseless black wagon roll up the street toward her. It had fat black wheels that moved soundlessly, as in a dream. When it drew nearer, she noticed a thick sheet of glass in front of the young man sitting inside, and the tops of plush seats finer than any Nev's mother kept in her parlor. The driver seemed as startled by her as she was by him. He nodded at her when the wagon drew level. Then he veered the contraption into the alley that went to the rear of the clinic.

Without a thought in her head Em grabbed the cart handle and clattered in pursuit, catching up to the thing just as one of its doors swung wide. Out came a knee, followed by an oversized foot in an extremely large shoe. Then the rest of the man emerged, unfolding one limb at a time. She could hardly believe someone that tall had fit inside.

His hair flamed in the sun. A trim beard, equally red, spread in jaunty curls over and under soft lips still trying to leave boyhood behind. From the cart, Red gave a deep-chested purr, like a contented cat. Scrambling out, she limped as fast as she could to throw herself belly-up at the man's feet. He crouched, letting the wiggling dog lick at his beard.

Em's eyes pricked with jealous tears. "That's one of those old-timey cars, isn't it?" she said crisply. "I'm surprised no one's set fire to it. They're illegal in these parts."

"Not this one." He rubbed the dog's back, carefully avoiding the sores. "It's a Doble. Runs on steam. I've just about convinced all of Clydestown that it's entirely harmless. You're not from around here."

"We've come from Oren," she explained, wishing Red would show a bit more restraint. "To see the vet. I need to find out what's wrong with my dog."

He tightened his mouth. "You've left it overly long, don't you think?"

"I just rescued Red this morning," she sputtered, offended by his critical tone. "Some boys were torturing her. They claimed she has the mange. What's it to you?"

Rising to his full height, he was an amazing head taller than she. "I get upset whenever I see someone mistreating an animal," he said instead of apologizing. "As it happens, I'm Dr. White's new assistant. He's out to lunch. Anything *I* can help you with?"

He was obviously too inexperienced to do Red much good. If she was going to trade her savings for an examination she'd rather take her chances with a real vet. "Out to lunch?" she repeated dully, wiping sweat from her forehead. "I don't know. Another hour in this heat . . ."

He jiggled some keys. "I was about to suggest you come inside where it's reasonably cool. I have to tend to my patients but you can skip to the head of the line. Shouldn't take long just to check for the mange." He unlocked the back door and ducked on his way in.

Em fervently hoped she had reached the end of her growth spurt—*she'd* forget to duck. Steel cages lined the dim corridor walls. Inside them, dogs barked, cats yowled, and one lone brown hen, her neck feathers plucked, red goose-bumpy skin full of stitches, tilted her head from side to side and crooned a soft question.

"Patience, my friends," he said. "You'll get my full attention as soon as I'm done with the ladies of Oren."

Em and Red followed him to the far end of the corridor where he opened a door and beckoned them in. "Our examining room. If you put Red on the table I'll take a look." He busied himself at the sink. Em lifted the dog up and stayed close to keep her from jumping back on the floor. The young would-be vet pushed the dog's rear into a sit before scraping a knife over several lesions. Then he smeared the samples on a clean rectangle of glass and slipped it under a black tube, nodding at the wall switch. "You can click off the overhead light."

Clydestown was bigger and richer than Oren, entitling it to longer bouts of electricity, although oil lamps stood on a nearby shelf to take over the next time the electric lights failed. Em flicked the switch. After a long, silent minute in the dark, he pronounced, "No sign of the mange." He flashed something violet. When he turned the ceiling fixture back on he was smiling. "Nor is it a fungus. Now that's the kind of news I like to tell."

"If it isn't the mange, what is it, Doctor?" Em asked. "Or do I call you Assistant?"

"My name's Driscoll."

Deciding he didn't need to know hers, she wondered out loud, "Why is she going bald?"

He stroked his short beard. "It could be a flea allergy. Or malnutrition. She looks as if she ran a long way. Probably couldn't find much to eat. Not much water, either." He peered at one of Red's pads, shaking his head. "She ran a *very* long way. Her nails are worn to the quick. Aha!" He had discovered the collar. "Obviously she belongs to somebody. Shall we look?"

Em didn't like the direction the exam was taking. "Red belongs to me now," she said firmly. "She's my birthday present to myself."

He worked the knots, broke a fingernail, and gasped, "Ouch!' under his breath.

"Tough knots, aren't they?" she said with satisfaction.

"Not tough enough." He sliced the leather with one of his blades and gently pulled it away from the dog's neck. "It grew right into her skin," he grumbled, shaking his head. "Made a groove."

"She must have belonged to a very thoughtless person," Em said. "I would have checked the collar regularly to make sure it stayed loose."

He held the piece of leather up to the light. "There's something stenciled inside. *Brendan's Nada. Fiery Hill.* Odd."

"Peculiar," she was quick to agree. "And not very helpful." Then she remembered her half-dream behind the barn. That man with the bandana—hadn't he said something about some place called Fiery Hill? "But his name was Alden," she muttered to herself.

Driscoll cocked an eyebrow. "Whose?"

She shrugged, feeling self-conscious. "I had some kind of dream before we came. There was a man in it with a rag tied around his head. I thought he said, 'I'm Alden. Welcome to Fiery Hill.' The dream sounded absurd, even to her. "I must have got sunstroke. I fell asleep in the shade but it moved."

His eyebrows arched higher. She felt her cheeks go hot with a blush. But he was no longer looking at her. He was staring right through the wall as if he could see what was on the other side. And then he grinned, fully present again. "I hate to admit it, but I had a similar dream. Just last night. A rolled up kerchief, tied on his brow. Unusual, shimmering eyes."

Red heaved a sigh and looked first at Em, then at the floor. She put out a restraining hand to keep her from jumping off. "There's no town named Fiery Hill anywhere around here, is there? Clydestown is the farthest I've ever walked. I like to come to the bookstore."

"I know," he said, his voice growing warmer, "I've seen you go in. Once a month, is it? I asked the clerk about you. Made up my mind to say hi the next time you came. You beat me to it. I believe you're the tallest girl in this desert of dust. Hard to miss." She frowned, finding the observation less than endearing, but he failed to notice her reaction, for the faraway look had returned to his eyes. "As a matter of fact, I think I might know where the fiery hill is," he said slowly, as if he were trying to recall something he once read.

"It's not a town. It's a mountain. I always planned to go there someday."

The last thing Em cared to see was a burning hillside. "Oren is as hot as I can stand it, thank you," she told him. "And if you have some medicine for my dog we'll leave you to your regular patients and be on our way."

He fingered one of the lesions. "I only told you what it isn't. I don't know what it is yet. We should do some tests. When can you come back?"

"That's okay." Clearly, he had no idea how long a two-hour walk was, especially if you had to do it twice in one day. Em pulled the piggy bank out of her bag, pried out the plug, and spilled her paltry coins across the steel table. "You told me what I needed to know. I think I'll take her to somebody I know who doctors deer and rabbits and such. I've never seen her work on a dog, but how different can they be? Skin's skin. She's got all kinds of salves. She's a—" She managed to stop herself before she could say 'witch.' To hide her confusion, she gathered Red in her arms.

". . . healer," he finished the sentence for her, waving her savings away. "There's no charge. Any friend of Bena's is a friend of mine."

"You've met Bena?" In Em's surprise, she almost dropped Red "She speaks to no one but me. She lives all alone in—" But that was a secret, and none of his business.

". . . the middle of the old forest," he said, raising his hands when he saw her alarm. "Let me explain. Recently, I followed a wounded doe through a blackberry tunnel. Quite by accident, I thought then, but now I wonder . . ."

"Wonder what?" she asked sharply, stung that he'd found the well-hidden entrance to Bena's little clearing. What had he been up to, anyway, snooping in that inaccessible, forbidding part of the forest?

With an embarrassed shrug, he said, "Some people say there's no such thing as an accidental meeting. Take us. We seem to have more than one thing in common." He swept the coins into his cupped palm and returned them to the pig's belly. "Bena. The dream. Our height . . ." He busied himself with the plug.

"You are mistaken," she said coolly, "We have nothing in common at all." She held out her hand. "It's been nice meeting you, Dr. Driscoll. Thanks for your time."

17

His eyes gleamed with amusement. "Just Driscoll," he said with a firm shake. Then he pressed a small jar at her. "It's a long walk through those woods. This is the best salve we have to offer. Use it until you can take her to your friend."

He got that right—*her* friend, not his.

She put Red on the floor and stuffed the bank in her bag.

He waited until she had taken the first hesitant step toward the door, then he asked, "If you lost *your* dog, wouldn't you want to know that she's safe? Wouldn't you pray somehow she'd find her way home?"

Sticking his nose where it didn't belong seemed to be an habit of his. "I'd pray that whoever found her would take good care of her. And I will," she said, making her second step more determined. Without Red, she would have nothing—which was exactly what she'd had when she woke up this morning.

Somehow, he managed to get to the door before she did, standing there with his arms crossed as if meaning to block her from leaving. Every trace of his friendly smile had disappeared. How could she explain to this disapproving stranger that Red was already the best part of her? "I'll send a letter to that Brendan on the fiery hill," she conceded, hoping her words could get him away from the door. "In case he actually cares. And now I'd thank you to get out of my way."

He only moved a couple of inches. "Here's an idea," he said in a patient voice, as if she'd missed the main point. "I have tomorrow off. I can take you there. It's no more than a day trip by car." She reached around him to push at the door and found her gaze caught by his intent green eyes. "An easy day trip," he went on. "We'll eat a picnic lunch under a tree. By a creek. I'll bring fresh bread from the bakery. The white kind. Cheese too. And cherries."

Slowly, the door swung open. But as it happened, she wasn't quite ready to go. "Cherries?" she repeated weakly. "White bread?" Wouldn't find either of those around Oren.

"Why not let Nada decide for herself?" he said, stepping aside, knowing he'd won.

"What if we can't find that Brendan guy?"

"*She* will." He nodded at Red who sat between them, watching them both as if she understood every word.

"You want us to go?" Em asked her directly.

Red barked once, loud and clear. Wincing, Em brushed past

Driscoll out into the corridor. "Tell me," she said bitterly, turning, "That hurt deer—were you going to fix it up or put it out of its misery?"

He flinched as if she'd slapped him.

Instantly, she felt ashamed. "Sorry," she said. "I just had to be sure."

He glared at her for a small, uncomfortable eternity. Then his face softened. "I hear your name's Em. Can we be friends?"

It wasn't as if she had an overflow of those. He did say he'd stumbled upon Bena's tunnel by accident. And who else would offer her store-bought white bread and cherries out of season? "I guess we can try," she said grudgingly. "Why not?"

They shook on it.

Counting Bena and Red, it would make three. Two more friends than she had started the day with—this very strange day, which seemed like an ending and a beginning at once.

CHAPTER 4

WHEN SHE GOT HOME SHE PARKED the cart behind the barn near the old well and filled the pull-bucket with brownish water, plunging her head in until her brain stopped cooking. Then she emptied the bucked down her back, filled it again, and doused Red right in the cart, blanket and all. The dog rolled in the puddle, jumped out, and gave herself a hard shake.

"I wish we could just go up to bed," Em said. "But my room's an oven." She flopped on to her back on the wet ground in the barn's shade, her feet throbbing from four hours of walking. Too tired to kick off her shoes, she focused on the pulsating pain until both feet began to feel lighter. So did her calves, her knees, and her thighs. It was as if her legs were filling with air. By the time Red had wiggled close enough to put her chin on Em's hip, that hip didn't seem to belong to Em anymore. She barely managed to lift a rubbery arm to the dog's sodden flank before the floating sensation overtook the rest of her body.

The next thing she knew, Red rose into the air. A second later so did she. They floated straight up the rear wall of the barn like a couple of birthday balloons. Looking down, she noticed their bodies still asleep on the ground. For some reason this did not worry her. At first she and Red merely hovered over the corroded barn roof, but soon they drifted over the sagging eaves of the house. On their way to the chimney they got a bird's eye view of a patchwork of dust-covered roofing tiles. Red spun around like a weathervane, stretched herself into an arrow, and zoomed toward the haze at the horizon. Em followed close behind.

They flew over the village fields and the forest. On its far side they passed endless miles of furrowed dirt, tinted yellow by the star thistle plague. Tiny stick figures hacked at the spiked flowers as if it would do any good, when everybody knew they'd just grow back next year, in greater numbers.

Gradually, the land rose to form hills scarred by dry creek beds. Here and there a lone oak stubbornly clung to life, spreading its umbrella shade over a frail ring of grass. Farther up, the parched soil was dotted with clusters of low-growing shrubs, then gradually a few conifers began to grace the slopes. The yellow hue of thistles thinned and then disappeared, leaving the meadows below Em almost as green as nature intended. Halfway up the first mountain she'd ever seen the forest grew denser. Clouds darkened the trees, creating beautiful patterns of light and shade. The air was scented with pine.

The red arrow aligned itself with a steep, winding path and traced it uphill to where it dead-ended against a pileup of boulders. They looked as if some prehistoric monster had flung them together in a fit of violent rage. Red flew over the heap, the plot of small firs behind it, a second stone pile, and then an expanse of knee-high pine seedlings. They were framed by two chaotic blackberry hedges that seemed determined to merge and choke off all other vegetation. This vast bramble sea lapped around the base of a third collection of boulders.

A man sat on the top slab, legs crossed, eyes shut. An errant strand of flaxen hair had escaped the cloth tied over his brow and was playing with the breeze. The red arrow hovered beside him, shape-shifted into the dog, and nuzzled one of the man's bony knees. He opened his languid, fog-gray eyes, looked down at Em, and said, "Oh. Hi there. I see Nada has found you at last. Now we can—"

Something inside Em snapped. She shot back the way she had come at an impossible speed, plummeted from a great height into her slumbering body, and spasmed awake. Jerking to a sitting position, she flailed until her hands could feel solid ground beneath her. Red's head was still resting on her thigh.

Desolate, she gathered the waking dog in her arms. "Driscoll was right," she sobbed. "Your name really is Nada, and you do want to go home. Can you wait one more night? I doubt we'll fly but a ride in his Doble is bound to be the next best thing. This time tomorrow you'll be with that Brendan of yours—if that's what you want."

Nada's delighted woof made Em weep into her scanty ruff as she tried to let go, inside and out. What she wanted more than the dog was the dog's happiness. In her distress she missed hearing the approach of footsteps.

"So there you are!" her mother said, coming around the barn corner. "We've been looking all over for you and that cur. What a hideous old beast. The sheriff stopped by twice to haul her away. Where have you been?"

Em felt Nada stiffen in her arms. "In Clydestown," she said. "At the vet's. He says it isn't the mange. Nothing catching at all. He says she's just worn out from being lost."

Angry red splotches spread over her mother's cheeks. "You'll lie to get what you want. The sheriff's fixing to shoot her. We'll let him decide what she's got. Stay with her while I get someone to fetch him. Afterwards, don't come in the house till you've scrubbed yourself clean."

Em was shocked. 'I don't lie to you! Never have. If you don't know that you don't know me at all."

Her mother put her hands to her hips. "Fiddlesticks! All children lie!" She narrowed her eyes. "I can read you like one of them fool books you've always got your nose in. No use trying to argue your way out of it, Emma—you can't keep her, no how and no way. The sheriff will tow her off and that'll be that. What happens afterward is none of our business."

"Please let her stay for the night," Em pleaded in the most endearing tone she could find, to buy the dog time. "Just give me a few more hours with her. We'll sleep outdoors. It's too hot in the house anyway." Now she was grateful Driscoll was coming for them before dawn.

"Nothing doing. This is your pop's farm and mine. You want to live here you best do what we say. From now on. No more of your sass, understand?"

Em opened her mouth for a brilliant reply, but decided to shut it again, nodding instead.

Her mother let her hands drop to the sides. "All right then. Hold on to her now. Won't be long."

As Em watched her shuffle off she realized that she didn't want to live on the farm anymore. Not another day. Not even a minute. There had to be someplace better than this. Peering around the corner, she saw her mom cross the yard and start up the road to where a few small boys were listlessly kicking at a ball. Hailing the nearest, she waited for him to come to her and then said something to him. From the way he nodded and bounded off, Em suspected she'd offered some small tip—or maybe the excitement of witnessing an execution was reward enough for someone his age.

After her mother had gone into the house Em ran back to Nada, whispering, "We have to leave! Right now!" She scooped her up, abandoned the cart and everything in it, and carried her to the far end of the barn and across the dirt road. The dog's front legs clung to Em's shoulders; her hind quarters sought purchase on the girl's hips. Passing from field to field, Em aimed straight for the forest, hoping to disappear into its depths before anyone behind her thought to look in this direction. Every time her burden slipped she hoisted it higher. At last she stepped in among trees and let Nada slide onto a cushion of old pine needles and leaves. "We made it," she panted, her heart pounding. "Now we'll go straight to Bena. I hope you can walk for a while. My arms feel like lead and these wet shoes are rubbing my heels raw."

Both of them limping, they turned away from the relentless sun, village noise and village law, to wander into the woods. Overhead, a squirrel chattered a shrill alarm. Nearby, a bird whistled in reply. A draft moved lightly from crown to crown and soft fir branches brushed against Em's cheek. Latticed sunlight and shade sketched intricate patterns onto the forest floor. Deeper and deeper into the shadows they went, aiming for its heart, for the black witch.

How old had Em been that long ago summer when she'd gone berry-hunting all by herself and gotten terribly lost? Four or five? She had circled around the same section of trees until daylight waned and night closed in all around her. Then she'd sunk to the foot of some great pine and wept. A figure had stepped out of the dusk, cloaked in black, and a hoarse voice said, "Don't be afraid. I can help you find your way home."

"You're the black witch!" Em had cried, shielding her face. "The one who eats children!"

The witch laughed and pushed back her hood. Her eyes were an intense violet, even in the near dark. She slipped the cloak off her shoulders to reveal an elfin figure wearing a shapeless sack dress. Black hair, threaded with silver, fell to her waist. "I'm Bena," she said, holding out a diminutive hand. "I've lived here forever, I think, and gave up eating flesh a long time ago. Come, I'll take you to the path that goes to Oren—or is it Clydestown?"

"Oren," Em told her, taking the offered hand and trusting it to lead her to safety, although the witch wasn't much taller than her. And as Em stumbled on a faint trail, Bena said,

"I know every tree and bush, every squirrel. Next time you come I'll show you where the best berries grow. Bring a bucket. We'll fill it."

Tugging at the witch's delicate hand, Em asked, "Will you invite me to tea?"

With a quiet smile, Bena said, "If you want."

"How will I find you?"

Bena gave Em's fingers a squeeze. "You just come. I'll find *you*."

And so it had been. Em returned the next weekend clutching a pail that contained a sack of stale biscuits. Bena stepped out from behind a bush and led her farther and farther from Oren until they arrived at a stand of immense trees and then at the bramble thicket behind it. They passed through a tunnel of blackberry vines into mild sunshine and stood in a clearing just big enough for a little house and a small garden. Nearby, a creek snaked over brown stones, bubbling into a shallow pool and out again.

Just thinking about that long-ago day made Em glad. "You'll like Bena," she promised Nada. "And she's sure to love you."

Eagerly wagging her tail, Nada pulled ahead in spite of her sore paws. Each time the deer trail divided, she unfailingly chose the correct fork, and when at last they reached the old-growths and the adjacent brambles, Nada found the tunnel before Em did. It must surely be true that a dog's sense of smell was many times finer than that of a human.

The sixteen-year old Em found it much harder to squeeze through the tunnel than the five-year-old had, but she managed to avoid the nastiest vines. She was greeted by a cathedral-like hush when she emerged inside the clearing. It its center stood Bena's hut. The old woman called it a *yurt* because it was round, but Em had nicknamed it *mushroom house.*

Long ago, a massive cedar fell, leaving a huge hole in the forest canopy. Bena had built her yurt against the gradually decaying trunk. She liked to sit on it in the mornings while she waited for the sun to rise. At night she counted the stars twinkling between conifer tops.

Over the decades the yurt's pole walls had weathered to the same shade of silvery gray as the old trunk so that it and the house seemed hewn from one piece. That was where Bena was sitting now, head bowed, ankles crossed, as if she, too, was a part of the carved set.

One of the unspoken courtesies between her and Em was that the girl would not interrupt her friend's meditations. Em pointed the dog to the narrow porch Bena had built of poles lashed together with vines. They settled quietly on its floor for what might be a long wait. Em worked Driscoll's salve out of her pocket and applied it to the dog's sore pads, rubbing it deep into each crack.

He would drive to Oren before sunrise and park at the crossroads, as they had arranged. How long would he wait before deciding she had never meant to keep the promise she made? There would be no one to tell him it wasn't her fault. But the change in plans had its advantage, for if she never saw him again she would get to keep Nada. She smiled at the comforting thought and leaned against the curving pole wall. A few minutes later she yawned and slid to the rough deck next to Nada. As her breathing slowed and deepened, she asked herself one last question: what would be worse, losing Nada or never seeing Driscoll again? She claimed the dog with her arm, sank into sleep—and had the strangest dream. About Bena.

CHAPTER 5

IT WAS THE MOST VIVID DREAM EM EVER had. Once second she glimpsed a diminutive black-haired girl with violet eyes who was grimacing at her own doll-like reflection in a gilded wall mirror. The next, she *was* that girl, tying her long black hair up with a ribbon and then letting it down again.

"Bena, they're here," her mother yelled from the kitchen.

"Coming!" she called back, straightening the white fringe on her bedspread, grabbing her jacket, stepping into her shoes. She skipped down the stairs graceful and light, her rose-patterned skirt swinging out behind her. The picnic basket she'd helped pack sat on the table next to her mother, who was in the process of raising a cup of hot peppermint tea to her lips. "Mmm, that smells good," Bena said, kissing her mother's round cheek.

The woman reached out to smooth Bena's hair into place. "I poured yours in the thermos, with honey and milk. If you wore your hair in braids it wouldn't tangle so."

"Yes, Mother," Bena laughed. "I know."

Her mother cupped the girl's chin, wiped at a smudge, and said with an odd little catch in her voice, "Really, you have the most beautiful eyes. I still wonder which side of the family you—"

"Bena! Yoo-hoo!" Adra cried from somewhere outside.

"Go on," Bena's mother said, her hand shooing now. "Don't keep them waiting. They tend to get loud."

Bena picked up the basket, snatched a folded blanket from a chair, and ran out, slamming the screen door behind her. The old hay wagon at the curb was full of her friends and their picnic supplies. Adra, up front in the driver's seat holding the reins, scooted aside. "Hop on, birthday girl," she said, patting the seat next to her ample hips. "Here comes Val. Let him squeeze in with the others."

Bena tossed her things into the wagon.

"You bring your new ball?" Val asked, struggling to climb over the tailgate while clutching a homemade kite, a bag, and his sweater.

"Not yet," Bena said and ran back inside to rummage in the hall closet. When she went out this time her mother managed to grab the screen door, closing it gently as she followed Bena into the yard. Her father emerged from the woodshed, leaned his axe against the wall, and massaged alongside his spine, waving. Bena made a quick detour to give him a peck on the nose and was already out of reach when he spread his arms for a hug. She threw the ball to Val, who'd squeezed himself into the least crowded corner in the cart. He let go of his kite to catch it.

"Ready, Bena?" Adra asked from her perch. "Climb up or in; we're on our way."

Bena stood undecided. "Maybe I'll walk," she said.

Adra gave a non-committal shrug, tugging the reins. The mule turned his head and gave her a cold stare. "Go, lame-brain, go!" Adra shouted, jerking the bit. The mule blew, flicking his tail.

"The wagon's too heavy for him," Bena said. "Get off, you guys. Walk with me. It's much better for you anyway." She rubbed the mule's velvety nose, murmuring, "And for you."

"I wouldn't be surprised if she picked him up and carried him just to save his feet from wear," her father chuckled, coming to stand with his wife.

"If she were just a bit bigger she probably would," Bena's mother said, chuckling along.

"Down, guys," Bena repeated, already lowering the tailgate. "You've all got strong legs. Use them."

"Aw, Bena," Adra said, dropping the reins.

The boys and girls in the cart complained loudly as they climbed out and started to push. "Who needs a mule?" Val grumbled. "Now that the wagon's so light we can move it all by ourselves."

"Bite your tongue," Adra said, jumping off her high seat to land next to Bena. They walked together as they so often did—small, dark-haired Bena lengthening her stride to keep up with her taller, chunkier friend. Mule and wagon followed with ease. The red ball rolled off the open tailgate straight into the ditch. Val's father fished it out and tossed it to Bena.

She smiled at him. "Thank you, Mr. Frenn." He gave a small bow and watched her catch up to her friends.

"Stay on the road. Don't get lost," Adra's mother yelled from her porch.

"Really, Mother. I'm not a child," Adra yelled back.

"No monkey business," Val's father put in. "Be home before dark."

"We promise, Mr. Frenn," Bena said.

He went to stand with her parents. "Val thinks Bena's the prettiest girl in the flatlands. I think he's right."

"Beautiful inside and out," Bena's father agreed with a proud grin. He put an arm around his wife and the three of them looked after the creaking cart until it was out of sight.

An instant later Bena's mother burst into tears. "She was always such a good child," she wept. "Never caused us a moment of grief !"

"That's nothing to cry about," Val's father said. "You're luckier than most. Whatever she's got, I hope it rubs off on my dear, exasperating boy."

Bena's mother wiped her cheeks dry and gave another sob. "Excuse me," she cried. "I don't know what—" Turning, she fled into the house.

Bena's father found her huddled against the sink, her apron over her face. "What is it?" he asked, putting his rough farmer's hands on her plump, heaving shoulders. "What's wrong?"

She shook her head, as bewildered as he. "Nothing. Nothing's wrong." Rubbing her eyes pink with the apron, she tried for a smile but leaked more tears instead.

"Women!" he said, pouring her a fresh cup of tea and stirring in a heaping spoonful of sugar. Then he went back to the shed to get on with splitting his logs.

THE ROAD dipped and rose many times before they reached the meadow they'd aimed for. They unhitched the mule at the old oak and Bena led him to a lush patch of grass near the creek. "Eat all you like," she told him. "Don't go too far, though. If you're good I'll bring you my juiciest apple for dessert."

Meanwhile the others had unloaded the wagon and spread their blankets under the tree. Adra tuned her guitar and soon everybody joined in her songs. They sang and ate, talked and ate, gossiped happily about friends left behind, and ate some more. The shadows grew long. Clouds drifted over the horizon. A small breeze stirred the branches above.

"Bena," Val said, "the wind's picking up. Want me to get our kite?"

She nodded. When he came off the wagon, a harsh gust blew out of nowhere, ripping the kite out of his hands. The old tree moaned; something big snapped overhead just as Bena reached for an apple. A huge limb slammed her to the ground, covering her with quivering leaves. Adra covered her eyes and screamed. The others jumped up and ran aimlessly from blanket to blanket, shouting, stepping on grapes, berries, bread and cheese. Bena's red ball started to roll toward the creek, picked up speed, and bounced against one of the mule's haunches. He kicked out and fled.

The branch hid Bena completely, Only a few ends of black hair showed through the foliage.

"Bena, are you all right?" Val asked.

There was no answer.

Adra pulled at some twigs, wailing, "Help me!"

The boys carefully lifted the branch and set it aside. And there sprawled Bena, still holding the apple, her face white as chalk, her lids a bruised purple. A small bump shone high on her forehead. With trembling fingers, Adra touched Bena's cheek and wept.

THEY DIDN'T keep the promise they'd made. It was way past dark when they came home. Lightning flashed, thunder growled, and rain poured, flooding the street. Their parents hovered behind closed windows until they heard the eerie pitch of their children's laments in the lull between peals. Then they rushed out without umbrellas or coats. Drenched, they waited at the curb until the unhitched wagon rolled out of the night, four boys pulling on the shaft, three girls pushing the cart from behind. And in it, on a grape-smeared jumble of blankets, covered by soaked jackets, lay the still, pale form of Bena.

Her father carried her inside and laid her on the parlor couch, straightening her limbs, holding her slack hand while her mother put cold compresses on Bena's bruised forehead. On the first night the swelling turned a bruised purple and grew to the size of an egg. On the second it had taken over half of her face. On the third her features were no longer recognizable. The next morning, before dawn of what would have been her sixteenth birthday, she died.

Adra had been invited to attend a surprise party but came to a wake instead. Bena was still on the couch, covered with a crisp linen sheet, white hands folded serenely over her chest, her face hidden under an immaculate lace handkerchief. Adra thrust a bunch of garden-fresh carnations at Bena's mother and gave the couch a wide berth. She followed the woman toward the sound of low voices coming from the kitchen, closing the parlor door firmly behind her.

The table was crowded with food, the room with villagers, all claiming they'd been close friends of the dead girl. Young and old mingled easier than usual to pay their respects. With their plates piled high, they murmured Bena's praises in between bites.

"I'm not hungry," Adra claimed unconvincingly.

"You?" Incredulous, Bena's mother thrust a filled plate at the girl. "She'd want you to eat," she said, almost pleading, "She loved your good appetite." Adra studied the generous samples of various casseroles and salads on her plate and then let the scent of hot apple pie draw her gaze to the table. Val's mother poured her a tumbler of lemonade and began to score the pie.

Bena's father sat next to the only empty chair, staring at the nearest wall. His wife pulled the chair out, saying, "Adra, come sit in Bena's place so we won't be tempted to wait for her to fill it again. Is there something you wanted to say?"

Adra sat. "She was my best friend," she began.

Bena's mother nodded, waiting for more.

"We did everything together," Adra went on, finding her pace. "We played together, started school together, did our homework together. She was like a sister. I remember one day we were walking to the store and she saw a bee drowning in a mud puddle. I hardly noticed it, busy talking, as usual. But Bena found herself a twig, knelt in the dirt, and rescued the bee. She didn't just put it down on the ground somewhere either—she carried it to a tree and set the twig with the wet bee on it on a high-up leaf so that the breeze could blow its wings dry and no one would accidentally step on it while it recovered. Bena was always doing things like that."

"Always," Bena's mother said fondly, pushing the plate closer to Adra. "Don't let it get cold." Val's mother added a generous wedge of pie and Adra picked up her fork and stuffed a big piece of golden-brown crust in her mouth.

Something scratched at the other side of the parlor door. The knob turned and the door slowly swung wide. Bena stood in the frame, dressed in her best ruffled nightgown, trailing the sheet that had covered her. All conversation ceased. Bena was beautiful no more. Her hair was dull with caked blood, her face the bluish mask of a cadaver. She lurched to the table, groping its edge. "Adra," she croaked. "You're sitting on my chair."

Adra spat out her cursed bite, vacated the chair so fast that it bounced off the wall, and ran screaming into the garden, followed by a stampede of villagers racing for home. Only three living people were left in the kitchen—Bena's parents, backing away until they were stopped by the counter, and Val's mother, clutching the lemonade pitcher tight to her chest. Then Bena's mother moaned and slumped to the floor. Her father swayed on his feet, staring in horror at what had become of his daughter.

"Father?" she whispered, "Mother?"

The pitcher dropped and broke. Val's mother fled out of the door, crossing herself. With a half-strangled cry, Bena's father rushed past the specter to glance at the parlor couch. It was empty; the lace square that had covered her face lay on the rug; a stained sofa cushion still held the indent of the head that had so recently rested upon it. He turned to Bena with the look of someone betrayed. Had she come back from the dead to haunt him for old slights, words left unsaid, things left undone? He knelt to embrace his unconscious wife, leaving his child to stand all alone. It was the first time she had caused her parents deliberate pain.

By and by, the villagers might have begun to tolerate what she had become. Maybe after a few years they would all have laughed together, remembering the day they held Bena's wake while she recovered in the next room. It was Bena herself who made everything worse. With her customary honesty she insisted on describing her passing. How she had left her body to float through some dark tunnel toward a beckoning light; how when she was forced to return she'd hovered just under the kitchen ceiling, listening to all the wonderful things everyone said about her, watching her mother fill Adra's plate, hearing Adra talk about the bee in the puddle.

There was only one thing to be done by decent folk when one of their own refused to stay properly dead. One evening, the villagers met and decided. The next day it began: the shunning of Bena. That morning at nine she saw three of her friends walk down the street together. When she hailed them they immediately crossed to the other side, pretending they didn't hear her. At ten she went to visit Adra, who sat on her stoop balancing cookies and milk on her pudgy knees. Plate and glass shattered as Adra fled inside, slamming and locking the door.

On that day and those that came after no one would talk to Bena—not Val, not the ever-friendly Mr. Frenn, not even her own parents. Her father who would have given all he owned to keep his daughter alive as she lay dying refused to come anywhere near her. He worked in the far fields from dawn to dusk. In the evenings he went straight to bed. Bena's mother saved no chores for her, gave her no errands to run, set no place for her at the table.

Soon Bena understood clearly that she was not welcome among the living. Day by day, she felt herself diminish. Her eyes grew dull. She gave up trying to talk and became as silent as a shade. The unspoken thought coming at her from every direction was that the villagers would consider it a kindness if she'd just get on with her dying so they could get on with their lives.

More and more, she stayed in her room behind drawn curtains to watch Val's mother pull weeds from her flowerbed while Val was outside playing with his dog. If Bena as much as put a hand on her curtains all three would bolt for their back door. Before long Bena slept the days away, her sheet soaked with her tears. At night she waited until the last light was extinguished in the house before she tiptoed to the kitchen in search of food. The pantry was locked against her. The refrigerator was left almost bare. She grew ever thinner. Although the autumn was hot she felt increasingly cold as if they were right and she really did belong in a grave.

From her bed she watched the gauze curtains blow in and out. They reminded her of how it had felt to be lighter than air in that dark tunnel. She had emerged into a bright world, on to a field of tall, waving grasses, silver and green. She'd lain in a sun-dappled hollow ringed with long-stemmed white flowers and gazed up at a flawless sky. The high grass all around her made her feel as safe as a newborn. At last she had started to rise but an ancient woman's face appeared over her, blocking the sky. "Bena, you must go back," she said. "You can't belong to us yet. You have a lifetime still to live, little one, and much to learn before you come here to stay."

Bena had no wish to return to the heavy world she had left behind, but when she opened her mouth to say "No!" grass, sky and old woman disappeared, the ground dropped away, and she fell back to a place no longer her own.

Curled on her sheet, under her winter quilt in the hot afternoon, she longed only for the silver-green world and knew she would never cease longing. One day she'd go there again. The old woman had said so. Meanwhile, this was what she had already learned: If a town full of people thought she must be punished for being alive, it could only mean that a town full of people were wrong about her, for she was as good as she'd ever been, even if she was the only one left to know it.

The morning after she learned it, her mother got up to cook her husband some breakfast and saw that Bena's room door was open, with no one inside. The closet was open too, emptied of clothes, shoes, and traveling bags. Gone was the goose-down comforter, the blanket, the wood-cart that was usually parked in the shed. The woman sat on the bed Bena had so thoughtfully stripped for her and ran her palm over the blue-flowered mattress until the tears she'd kept shut deep inside loosened and welled in her eyes. When her great mourning cry tore through the walls the villagers knew that the shunning had ended.

CHAPTER 6

"WHAT IS IT, CHILD," A FAMILIAR VOICE was asking from nearby. The girl opened her eyes and saw an older version of herself hover above, with the same violet eyes but with silver strands in her hair. Em stared in confusion. Was she the girl who had been dreaming, the girl she had dreamed about, or the old woman that girl had become, asking again, "What is it? What's wrong? Why are you here?"

"What color are my eyes?" Em finally asked, only then realizing that she had been crying in her sleep.

"Hazel, of course."

"Then I am Em," she said with relief.

"For as long as I've known you," the woman confirmed.

"And you are old Bena," Em ventured to guess.

"So it would seem." Bena's smile was patient and wry.

"I dreamed that I was the *young* Bena," Em hastened to explain. "I dreamed about the shunning."

Bena stopped smiling. "That Bena died," she said briskly. "The day I left home I was a child with no place to be except here. I stayed because I learned to belong. I've grown old with the trees, measure time only in seasons, and sit for hours watching a single flower unfold. I see eternity in it."

"Happy?" Em asked, carefully studying the dear face.

"Elsewhere, I was happy," Bena said. "In this world, I am content. And thankful for all that I have, including your visit and the friend that you bring."

"Oh. You mean Nada. She's my birthday present to myself." Em stroked the watchful dog lying beside her. "I've decided that from now on I'm providing my own presents. That way I'm sure to get exactly what I want."

"We met yesterday." Bena offered the dog the back of her hand. Nada sniffed at it politely.

"Then she must have come here before she wound up in Oren."

"For a short visit." Bena ran a finger lightly over Nada's lacerated back.

"On her own?"

"Alone, yes," Bena said. "I'd been foraging at dawn. She might have followed my scent through the tunnel. At first I mistook her for an odd-looking coyote. It's been years since I saw a dog, you see. Then I assumed she came for a healing, the way the forest creatures do. But she just circled the clearing twice with her nose to the ground and ran out again. Toward Oren, it would seem. She must have been looking for you."

Em pulled the salve out of her pocket. "The vet in Clydestown gave me this for her cracked paws. Do you think it will work?"

Bena sniffed at the jar. "That would be Driscoll you saw. He got it from me. I have more in the house. We'll put it on her back. I'll make a soak for her paws later."

Em rose and followed Bena inside. "He did say it was the best medicine he had to offer. Why didn't you tell me about him before? I thought I was the only one who ever came here." She winced at the reproach she heard in her own voice.

Bena shrugged. "He crept through the tunnel a couple of times. First he wanted some of my herbs and paid for them by fixing a leak in my roof. Last week be brought me these." She nodded at the counter, where butter, flour, eggs and a box of candles were lined up in a row. "He wants me to teach him all that I know."

"But you were going to teach *me*!" Em reminded her in a peevish tone.

Bena nodded. "And I will. I told *him* I'd have to think about it. I'm certain he's a good man, though his butter does make me bloat. I'm not used to rich food. We've got all the makings for pancakes right here, to honor your birthday. We'll stick one of his candles on top of your stack."

Em laughed. "It's bound to be better than the deformed cake I baked this morning."

Bena reached for a wooden bowl. "I'll stir up the batter. You can gather blackberries down by the stream for our syrup. And please dip this bucket while you're so close." Like magic, Em found a basket hanging from one arm, the bucket from the other. Then Bena cradled Em's hands in her own, a smile lightening her eyes. "I'm so glad you are here. Every one of your visits is like a birthday for me."

Em's mother had never said anything half as nice in the entire sixteen years they had lived together. Impulsively, Em put Bena's small hands up to her cheeks. "I love coming to see you. If only it wasn't so far."

Bena patted her face. "The distance serves," she said. Then she kindly told Em to get on with her errands. When Em returned with the berries and water, Bena stopped stirring the batter and poured the first batch into a pan. Em's stack turned out to be astoundingly high, doused with a small lake of butter and newly made blackberry syrup, and crowned with a fat white candle. She watched its flame dance before she dripped hot wax on the plate rim and stuck the candle upon it. Then she proceeded to eat her way through the tiers. Bena gave most of her stack to Nada, who shared Em's enthusiasm for the lavish meal.

Toward its end Em had to undo the top button on her shorts. "I think I'll pop," she sighed, scraping her plate clean.

"You didn't have to eat to the last bite," Bena said from the stove, where a kettle was boiling. She measured some herbs into a white porcelain pot. "These will be bitter, but they'll soon settle your stomach."

Em rubbed at her belly. "The last bite was too good to leave. Oh!" She jerked her hand away. "I almost forgot—something strange happened this morning when I touched myself there. I had some very odd dreams."

"How odd?" Bena asked, pouring steaming water onto the pot. Em described the flight to the mountain, the trail, the three boulders, and the man sitting on top of the third.

"I thought he said, 'Welcome to Fiery Hill.' When Driscoll sawed the collar off Nada's neck those very same words were etched inside, along with her name. Driscoll wanted to take me there in his

Doble machine. In the morning. Did you know he has an old-timey car?"

"He mentioned it."

"I was supposed to wait for him by the crossroads. At first light. But now I won't be there because I've come to spend the night with you, Bena. If it's all right."

"You're always welcome here," Bena said.

Em scraped the last bit of syrup from her plate with her finger. "He dreamed the same dream."

Bena's face grew taut. She leaned forward. "About a man with a red scarf tied around his head?"

Em stared. "You, too?"

"Compelling, light-colored eyes."

Pensive, Em licked her syrupy finger. "Three people sharing the same dream. Isn't that weird?"

"I've dreamed weirder." Bena pointed at the small bit of sky directly overhead, framed by tall conifers. "Look, birthday girl. Thunderheads, just for you."

"They never amount to much. At least not in Oren."

"They do fine here. The trees pull them down. There'll be a cloudburst tonight. Birthday rain. As for Driscoll, he'll find his way to me and then he'll find you."

Em felt her cheeks grow hot. How strange, to blush in front of Bena, the one person in the whole world who had always been able to see straight into her heart. What was in her heart, about Driscoll? Gravely, she said, "But if he finds me he'll find Nada."

The laugh-lines around Bena's eyes crinkled. "She's already adopted you. No one will pry her away."

Nada lay at Em's feet, her round eyes, fixed on the girl, oozing devotion. Em stroked the dog's domed head and vowed, "I'm never going back to Oren. Not with Nada, not without her. I'm done with that place and everything in it." She looked pleadingly at her old friend. "Can we stay here with you? Forever?"

Bena showed no surprise. "Didn't I just say you're always welcome here? Stay as long as you like. Just make sure it feels right inside. Come, let's gather rushes and ferns for your bed while we can still see." They found plenty near the creek. Heaping them on the yurt's floor, they spread half of a large quilt over it, folded in half to make a sleep sack. When Em asked her why she had so many quilts, she said, "You've never been here in the middle of the winter, have you? When the sun never shines? Winters are much more pleasant in Oren."

Em rolled up a wool blanket to make a pillow. "I don't care. I'd rather be too cold here than comfortable there. It's been a long day. Do you mind if I drop off to sleep early?"

After a short pause, Bena asked lightly, "And who's going to wash our dishes?"

For just a moment Em heard the echo of her mother's voice. Then she laughed. "What dishes? We used two plates and Nada licked them both clean."

"Not quite." Bena pointed to the mixing bowl filled with rinse water, the two cups, the forks. "I'll wash up tonight, since it *is* your special day. But from now on—"

"—I'll do half of all the work," Em said. "And more. Starting tomorrow." In her unspoken opinion that wouldn't amount to much, not like the tough field labor she'd had to endure in Oren. The only things from there she'd miss were the carob tree and her books. "I'll do whatever you say, Bena." She shielded her mouth for a wide yawn. "You'll see." Her lids grew heavy. It took effort to make her voice sound indifferent. "Did Driscoll mention how old he is?"

"Twenty, I think."

"Oh." Em's hands slackened, plopping on the pallet, a sign Nada interpreted as a definite invitation. She crawled on the quilt and, with a sigh of contentment, wedged herself between Em's legs and the curving wall. Porcelain clinked softly in the distance. Em slept.

Side aching, heart pounding, she ran like a pursued deer up the dark trail. All around her the air stank of fear and of death; from down below came wave after wave of black hate. Conifers laced against spectral, sulphurous clouds. Brendan hung onto Alden. On the boy's other side, Odasan supported his waist, keeping as much weight as he could off Brendan's poor feet. Lupe, in front, clutched at his belt, propelling him onward. "I can't go on," he whimpered.

Or was that Bena's weak voice, her face close one instant, gone the next? There was a rifle shot, a low cry cut short. They all froze, swaying with exhaustion.

"Leave me," Brendan begged Odasan, who nodded and rushed back down the trail.

"No one gets left!" Em hissed into Brendan's ear when she took Odasan's place. "No one!"

Then came a split second glimpse of Driscoll, gasping for air, and

39

another of her, pointing at a large boulder while lightning flashed from her fingers and the earth trembled under her feet. There was a loud crack of thunder—or was it a shot?—and the rock burst, taking the mountainside with it.

"Bena!" she screamed. "Bena!"

Bena bent over the pallet, her face eerily lit by what was left of the candle. It cast a grotesque shadow of her on the pole wall. "You had a nightmare," she said. "Made of thunder and indigestion. What was it about?"

"You were shot." Em sat up, her hair wild. "You fell. I heard you cry out."

Bena lowered herself to kneel on the quilt. "Again we share a dream," she said. "Only I like my version much better than yours. But then I ate far less than you did. There was a shot and I fell, true enough. And then I felt myself rising, light and warm, safe in strong arms that carried me higher and higher to some wondrous place. There was love all around me, bright as spring air. And so I've decided to come along with you in the morning."

"To where?"

"To the fiery hill."

A feeling of absolute dread washed through Em. "You can't. I'm not going."

"It's waiting for us, Em."

"Let it wait. It can hardly come get us, can it?"

"It can," Bena said drily, indicating Nada. "And it has." She patted Em's hand. "You slept through most of the storm I promised you, even with thunder cracking over our heads like the wrath of God. Just before you started yelling my name trees were bending in half out there. But listen—what do you hear now?"

Em heard silvery sounds. It was the music of raindrops striking wet leaves. "Never does that in Oren," she said.

"Because they cut down their trees. Trees are cloud magnets, Em. They bring on rain and hold it in the ground." They listened to the fading growl of some god appeased, and to the symphony of water and wind. Bena held a candle high to examine the pole ceiling. "It's a good thing Driscoll fixed that leak. It was right over your bed. I must thank him again tomorrow." From her roost by the wall Nada watched them as if she understood every word.

"What could possibly be there for you at the fiery hill?" Em asked, lying down on her pallet, still hoping somehow to dissuade her.

"I'll know it when I see it," said Bena, holding firm. "And I will see it." She rose, calling the dog, who followed her to a bowl waiting by the sink. "Careful," she murmured. "Let's just dunk in one foot at a time."

Em turned to the wall, crooked one arm under her woollen pillow, and hooked the other hand firmly onto the bent elbow. No more hands on her belly. No more bad dreams. At least not tonight.

CHAPTER 7

THEY ATE BREAKFAST ON THE WET PORCH, balancing their bowls on their knees. Bena wore her witch's cloak against the chill and Em wrapped herself in the rough wool blanket that had serves as her pillow. The plants in Bena's small garden sparkled with raindrops reflecting the early morning light, looking greener and more satisfied since the storm.

Em rubbed at the goose bumps that had appeared on her arms. "I can't believe how cold it is."

Raising the teapot she'd been cradling on her lap for the warmth it provided, Bena said, "It's always cold here until the sun clears the treetops. Have some more tea."

Em held her replenished mug first against one cheek, then the other, heating both her hands and her face. Nada, sprawling inside Em's voluminous blanket, abruptly lifted her head and gave a low growl. In the next instant she burst out of the blanket, leaped off the porch, raced over soaked grass, and hurled herself into the bramble tunnel. Almost at once she backed out again, tail wagging. A man's voice murmured a few friendly words. Leaves rustles. Driscoll crept out and got to his feet. There were purple stains on his white shirt and twigs in his hair. Em peered around her mug to watch him brush himself off.

"Driscoll!" Bena cried. "I knew you would come!"

He smiled, looking directly at Em. She felt a heat wave travel up under the blanket. "I believe I destroyed some poor spider's life's work," he said, pulling sticky threads out of his hair and wiping then on the grass. Nada threw herself at his feet just as she had the first time they met, soliciting another belly-rub. He stooped to oblige. Em gulped some tea, hardly noticing how it burned on its way down her gullet. If Nada had one fault it was that she was too friendly with strangers.

Bena raised the pot. "Will you join us for tea? There's an extra cup on the shelf."

"That would hit the spot," he admitted. "I got soaked on my hike through the woods in spite of my best efforts to keep my clothes dry. What did you put on this dog? She's looking much better."

"You mean besides the salve you gave Em in Clydestown? That would be Calendula. It's a good wound healer."

"So I see," he said, examining Nada's paws. "And it comes from what miraculous herb?"

"It's related to Marigold. A common garden flower. Are you hungry? There are blackberries and hazelnuts on the counter."

"Excellent." Driscoll walked through the morning's first sunbeam, which gilded his hair and his beard. "I was just getting hungry." He paused in front of Em and said, "I waited where you told me to. Just when I decided that you had stood me up, a boy rode by on a black horse. He said you'd gone to the witch and that I should pass on that your mom is looking for you."

"Why? It was she who made me choose between her and the dog."

"And so you chose the dog?"

"Yes." Even now, she realized it was the only choice she had been capable of making. "They were planning to kill her. I told my mom that you were sure it wasn't the mange, but they were still going to shoot her. That boy on the black horse was Nev. He often goes riding real early, before it gets hot. How did he know you were waiting for me?"

"Was it a secret? I told him." Driscoll came up the stairs. "Looks like it rained hard here. In Clydestown it just thundered. No lightning, though. Not that there's much left to burn." He touched Bena's shoulder and she squeezed his hand.

"It rained buckets," she said cheerfully. "And the ceiling stayed dry through the worst of it. Thanks to you."

"The storm was awesome." Em had already forgotten how frightened she'd been. "I wouldn't have missed it for anything." Furtively, she checked her hair for tangles. There was no telling how gruesome she looked. "I hope we have another one soon."

Driscoll raised a brow. "You mean to stay here? With Bena? Is that wise?"

She pulled the blanket up to her chin. "I'll be her apprentice, help gather herbs, and work in the garden. I'm good with a hoe." She had the distinct impression he wasn't happy with the news. Jealous, no doubt.

"You *are* still coming with me, though? Once we take Nada home your mother will have nothing to quarrel about."

"Then you don't know my mother!" She crossed her legs to give herself time to think. Most likely, he was counting on Nada's desire to return to the fiery hill. Bena had seemed so certain the dog would prefer remaining with them in the yurt. Could she be wrong, and Driscoll right? "I'm sorry," she told him, "but things have changed. Nada wants to stay with us. She's quite happy here, as you can see." The blanket slipped and slid apart, revealing her impossibly long legs and upending the bowl on her lap. Berries and nuts spilled over the porch floor. Nada disposed of them as fast as she could.

Driscoll stared at Em's legs and then at a couple of berries Nada had missed. "They look good," he said, turning scarlet. "The berries, I mean. I guess I'm even hungrier than I thought. I'd better get myself that bowlful. You want a refill, Em?"

"No, thanks," she snapped, rearranging the blanket. As soon as he disappeared inside the yurt she fluffed out her hair and brushed her eyebrows with a spit-dampened fingertip.

Bena watched and smiled to herself. "I've packed us a lunch, Driscoll," she said, raising her voice. "I've decided to come with you. As chaperone."

Mortified, Em shrank down into her blanket. "He won't need one, Bena, because I'm not budging. You go right ahead, though. Have a ride in the Doble. Nada and I will catch up on the chores while you're gone."

"What did you say?" Driscoll called from inside the yurt.

"She's afraid of losing the dog," Bena called back. "But I have assured her that it isn't possible." He ducked outside with his bowl and a cup, which he held under the spout. Bena poured, giving him a significant look. "We'll do it this way: I'm coming with you, Em is coming with me, and Nada will come with Em. We will pay our respects to the people on the mountain, tell them that Nada is safe, and then we'll return. You, me, Em, and Nada. Is that all right with both of you?"

"Quite all right with me as long as they won't object," he said, settling himself between their stools to eat.

"I suppose I might as well go," Em muttered darkly. "Even though it will be for nothing. And I don't care what will or won't be all right with Driscoll and what he can or can't understand—Nada most certainly *is* coming back here with me."

He contemplated his cup. "I understand more than you know. I nursed a stray or two when I was a boy." He shook his head, lost in a private memory, and said, "I forgot to tell you, Em—it might be colder in the high elevation. Especially toward the evening. Did you bring warm clothes and socks?"

She gave an exasperated sigh. "Didn't I just say I had to run for it? I never even had a chance to change out of my shorts."

"Maybe Bena has something that will fit you. A spare cloak ?"

Bena shook her head no. "I only have the one. She can bring the blanket."

"I *like* being cold," Em insisted. "Besides, we won't be on the mountain long enough for it to make much of a difference. Now can we please talk about something else?" There was no doubt about it, he had a tendency to be overbearing. She'd noticed it at the clinic yesterday. As if she were a child who needed looking after. When she was sixteen!

"Of course we can," Driscoll said, his tone deliberately cordial. "About that boy. Nev. I can't decide whose side he is on."

"Neither can he. Since he got Thunder he's mostly swagger and scowl. Before, he used to be my best friend. Except that he didn't like me to read. And he never cared for dogs."

"Magnificent stallion." Driscoll stared into his cup as if he could see pictures on the bottom. "A bit much for the boy."

"Better company than an ungainly girl," Em said. "His father expects him to grow into the saddle. Manly and tough."

He was looking straight at her again. "Those two words don't have to go together, Em. And you're far from being an ungainly girl."

She wanted to ask how far but didn't quite dare. And then she realized she was no longer angry with him for making her do this thing. Because, at the end of the day, it would be Bena who was right. She always was.

Chuckling, Bena set the empty teapot down on the deck. "We'll make peculiar traveling companions. You two are by far the tallest people in these parts and I'm probably one of the shortest—not to mention the most reviled. From far off the people on the fiery hill will think I'm your little girl. On closer inspection they'll think I'm a dwarf."

Driscoll chewed and swallowed a mouthful of berries, and said, "I've found it's best not to care what anyone thinks. When we come back the three of us should form our own club. We'll call ourselves *The Outsiders.* Or how about *The Plains Freaks?* Em, which will it be?"

She folded the blanket, stacked the dishes, and rose. "You and I are the freaks. Bena's still the most beautiful girl of the flatlands. Any fool can see that. I'll wash up so we can leave."

Bena and Driscoll exchanged one of those irritating grown-up glances. "Why don't you go ahead to the car when you're done, Em?" he suggested a bit too casually. "I parked where the last field ends. Right at the edge of the forest, behind a thicket, hopefully out of sight of anyone looking from Oren. If you need warm socks there are spares in my satchel, on the back seat. Bena and I won't be long. I've got some detailed medical questions to ask first."

Em could hardly keep herself from rolling her eyes. It was obvious he wanted her out of earshot. As if she cared. True to last night's promise, she rinsed and dried every dish. For good measure, she put them where they belonged on the shelf. Then she grabbed the picnic basket, picked up the blanket on her way off the porch, signaled Nada, and strolled across to the bramble tunnel. Driscoll and Bena were standing by the garden gate, facing the orchard and murmuring to each other. They didn't even see her leave.

The tunnel was hewn to fit Bena's delicate shape. Creeping through it on hands and knees, Em snagged her hair and the blanket. Yet it was beautiful in there, the green walls shimmering in the early light, golden specks filling the occasional gap between leaves. She sat on her heels for a while, appreciating the combination of colors before moving on.

She was glad to walk through the heart of the forest again, with its regal conifers and the dim, filtered light. The deep silence was pierced by occasional bird song. Damp ferns brushed her ankles. The air smelled of leaf mold and soil. Where giant trunks had fallen to rot on the ground, spindly seedlings were striving to close the holes their elders had left in the canopy. Crowding together, their roots competing for the same clumps of dirt, they were stunting each other's growth. They snapped like toothpicks at the faintest excuse of a wind, and often just keeled over for no reason at all, roots up, leaving shallow pits in the ground. In some spots dead trees lay every which way, piled like a badly tossed hand of pickup sticks. Long ago Bena had shown Em the life in the rot, each crumbling log home to countless insects and fungi busy turning wood fiber into nourishing soil.

At last Em and Nada reached the rim of the forest, where shadows gave way to heat and glare. Nada spotted the car first. It was parked in the shade, its top folded back. It looked more like a wagon that way, even if it was much too fancy inside. Something else was different this time—there was a trailer hitched to it, painted black to match. While Nada thoroughly sniffed at each tire, Em walked around the addition, wondering if it held something of interest. She discovered a tank of water, a box filled with firewood, a metal container that smelled of kerosene, a heavily padlocked strongbox, and compartments that housed unfamiliar tools, spare parts, and extra tires. Driscoll was leaving nothing to chance.

She opened the passenger door and let Nada squeeze in first. They sat on the back seat together, which had springs like a couch and was covered with a soft rug. Em searched Driscoll's satchel for the socks he had offered. They were too large for her feet. She pushed them aside and found more interesting stuff: three books and a fancy new flashlight, along with a box of batteries and spare bulbs. She put her hand over the lens and turned the light on, making her fingers turn pink. Then she laid the flashlight aside, occasionally stroking its smooth metal while she browsed through the books.

One was a slim volume of verses without a single picture among them. The second overflowed with photos but they were all of black cars so much alike that she couldn't tell them apart. The third, to her delight, was a musty volume of fairy-tales with feathery ink drawings. She kept it, repacked everything else, leaned into a corner, and started to read. She was just getting to the end of *The Girl Without Hands* when Bena and Driscoll stumbled out of the woods,

loaded like a pair of pack mules. For some reason Bena had decided
to bring her entire stock of baskets, fitting as many into each other as
she could. Her backpack overflowed with seed packets and dried
herbs. Driscoll was straining under her best quilts, which were rolled
up together like a carpet and tied with twine.

Puzzled, Em asked, "All this for a day trip?"

Strangely colorless, Bena muttered, "For trade. Just in case,"
and pinched her lips shut.

Before Em could ask another question Driscoll frowned at her,
shaking his head, although he stayed silent as he stuffed his load
around her and Nada. Then he gently relieved Bena of everything
else. Soon baskets of all sizes and shapes crowded Em's feet.

Squeezing her eyes shut, Bena stayed in the shadows until
Driscoll took her arm and escorted her to the front passenger door.
"The sun is too hot out here. There's no place to hide," she
murmured, clutching at the door.

Driscoll helped her onto the seat. "It will cool off as soon as we
start moving."

"We're squashed back here!" Em complained. "I can't even
stretch my legs. How long am I supposed to sit like this?" It was the
first time she had seen Bena outside of the forest. In glaring daylight,
she looked as white as a grub. "Bena, what's wrong," she asked with
growing concern. "Are you sick?" Bena sat as stiff as a china doll,
her small bark-shod feet sticking straight out in front. When Driscoll
shut her in, she covered her face with trembling hands and gave a
low moan. "Hey. Wait a minute," Em said as he started to fold
himself behind the steering wheel. "Can't you see how miserable she
is? Let's call this trip off. I'm taking Bena back to the yurt."

Calmly, he said, "You're going to have to trust me, Em." Then
he shut his door and started the engine, trapping his three passengers
inside.

CHAPTER 8

HE PUSHED A LEVER AND THE AIR-FILLED tires yielded with a soft whoosh. It was followed by the novel sensation of being adrift on a cloud. The car rolled out of the bushes, bounced across the bumpy field, and merged on to the road winding away from Oren. Em forgot all her objection. "It's not making any noise at all," she said, more impressed than she cared to admit.

"The ones I knew made plenty." Bena looked longingly at the receding trees.

Driscoll sat proud. "They used to smell bad, too. That's because they ran on gasoline. This is a steamer, or at least it was before my dad modified it. No noise. No pollution."

Em couldn't resist craning her neck for one last glimpse of the village. Then the road curved and the village was gone. "Are you feeling better now?" she asked Bena, who had stopped trembling.

"A little."

"What's wrong with you, anyway?"

Bena attempted a smile. "I'm suffering from a very unreasonable fear. It comes from living in the woods too long."

"Fear of open spaces, it's called," Driscoll supplied in a lecturing tone. "Picture the size of the sky as seen from Bena's clearing—a mere patch of blue or gray, always reliably framed by protecting trees. Then this." He motioned to the vast dome stretching over an endless expanse of wide-open country. "The villagers suffer from the reverse. They are afraid of the silence inside the woods, the towering trees, the green gloom. Two very different worlds, separated by a profound sense of discomfort and fear."

"It's not like that for me," Em said, but then she remembered her five-year-old self, lost in the forest and sure she would die from sheer terror.

Bena turned around, taking the trouble to broaden her smile. "Don't worry about me. It will pass. Now—do you want me to trade places with you? It would be a much better fit for us both."

Even Driscoll could see the logic of it. Em went to sit beside him and Nada soon followed, climbing over the back of the seat and scrabbling over Em's lap to get to the window, thereby forcing the girl to scoot closer to Driscoll. That's when she realized she was suffering from a fear, too—of bodily contact with a near stranger. Afraid of accidentally grazing his arm, and of the peculiar heat that seemed to radiate from his skin, she almost wished she hadn't traded with Bena.

For a while she kept her face averted, pretending to look out of the passenger window to admire the view. Then she became curious about the knobs and dials on the dashboard. He kept glancing at them, although his main focus was on the road ahead. His hands were wrapped around a wheel, making continuous small adjusting motions. They seemed to keep the car centered on the rutted road winding between fields from village to village toward the distant horizon.

How had he learned to do so many things at once? Could it be that he was just naturally smarter than she? Perhaps all those people of the past who had driven cars were born brighter than her kind. Or maybe their lives had merely been easier.

"What smells so good?" she asked.

He nodded to a bundle on the floorboards. "It comes from inside that bag. Go ahead, open it."

She did, inhaling the fragrance of fresh-baked bread. "For our picnic?" She didn't want to admit it to Bena but she was already getting quite tired of blackberries and nuts.

"I bought in on my way out of Clydestown," he replied. "The baker and I were the only two people awake but *he* gets to sleep once his shift is over and I don't."

"And whose fault is that?" she said, groping past the warm loaf to see what else was hiding inside. "Nobody asked you to drive all day. It was your idea." That firm, square, paper-wrapped slab must be the promised cheese, and those little round things could only be— "Cherries!" she cried in wonder, casting aside every doubt she'd held. But when she pulled her prize out of the bag the fruit was green instead of red and clumped on a vine rather than separate on elegantly long individual stems. "Hey, these are grapes," she said, letting her disappointment show. "I hate grapes, especially this kind. They're always sour."

He shifted in his seat. "Yes. Well. I tried every fruit stand in town after work yesterday. There was not one cherry to be found anywhere. This is the best I could do. After countless taste tests, what you hold in your hands is the winning bunch. Try one. You might be pleasantly surprised."

She didn't feel like being pleasant or surprised. "I think people should keep every promise they make," she huffed. "And you promised me cherries." Stuffing the grapes out of sight, she passed the bag on to Bena, asking, "Don't you agree?"

Bena tried a grape and agreed with Driscoll instead. "They are tasty, Em. And the loaf feels like it came out of the oven no more than five minutes ago."

"Then I hope it will cook the grapes and melt the cheese," Em muttered under her breath.

"I brought the rest of my butter," Bena continued serenely, sounding more like her usual self. "What a treat it will be, dribbled on one of the heels. I love the aroma of fresh bread. It takes me all the way back to my mother's kitchen. We used to make brown wheatberry loaves twice a week. The whole house would be filled with the smell."

For some reason she could not understand Em felt a recurrent need to glower at Driscoll, like an itch demanding to be scratched. "Is it the white kind, at least? Like you said it would be?"

His eyes sparked in response. "Yep. White, store-bought, and fresh. And the cheese is better than anything you can get in Oren. You see, at least *I* kept all the promises I was able to keep."

She supposed he was implying that she hadn't kept hers. "I'm here, aren't I?" she said sharply. A minute later she asked, in a more conciliatory tone, "Can I have the other heel?"

His mouth softened. "The crunchy crust? Absolutely. That

leaves me with the middle, which is the best part." He offered her the guarded kind of smile some grown-ups reserve for difficult children.

"And when do we get to eat it?"

"We'll let Bena decide."

Bena said, "As soon as the car stops casting a shadow."

"But I'm hungry right now!"

In response, Bena handed Em a bowl filled with berries. "Have these. They're beginning to weep. Driscoll helped me pick a pail of the juiciest ones. It will make a nice gift for Nada's people. The name 'fiery hill' suggests rocks and ashes. I expect those vines you saw in your dream produce tasteless small berries, if they grow any at all." Em accepted the fruit with good grace and an appetite to match, but by the time she'd chewed the last berry and wiped purple juice from her hands she had to admit Driscoll's grapes might be a welcome alternative.

Gradually, the flatland began to undulate. Thistle-infested fields yielded to scorched pastures that rose and fell along with the road and were graced by sparsely placed, drought-toughened trees. Pastures became hillocks. Hillocks grew into hills. Trees grouped together, and the grass freshened from dun to pale green. The shadows grew shorter and shorter. Then they were gone.

Em's stomach gave a ferocious growl just as the Doble came over a rise into a landscape strangely familiar. Rolling meadows met a meandering creek. Noon light flashed on clear water. The banks were bordered by stool-high white rocks and clumps of tall swamp plants. Nearby, a magnificent oak spread its generous shade-umbrella over a carpet of deep, satisfied green.

"Stop!" Bena and Em said at the same time.

Driscoll parked at the side of the road even though they had not seen a vehicle of any kind on it since they began their journey.

Bena climbed on her seat and looked back the way they had come. "Did we pass a village a while ago?"

"You mean yours?" Em asked. "Is this where it happened?"

Bena studied the old oak and the creek. "I think so. But it's been a long time."

Driscoll seemed puzzled. "You want me to turn around? Why?"

Bena looked back the way they had come and slowly shook her head. "Never mind. Nothing I loved would still be there. No one would know me or care. But if it's all right with you I'd like to have our picnic under that tree." Nada tumbled out as soon as they opened the first door. Barking, she ran a wide loop around the oak. Then, scenting the water, she aimed for the creek and splashed in. "She's got the right idea," Bena said. "I think I'll join her after we eat. We might not pass another creek for the rest of our trip."

Driscoll and Em spread out the blankets and Bena unpacked their feast. The butter had long since turned liquid but lubricated their slabs of bread splendidly. The three travelers savored every bite. "Don't get used to this," Bena told Em. "Living with me, berries and nuts loom large in your future."

"At least you have a good garden," Em was quick to point out. "At home, we ate cardboard and washed it down with sour tea."

"Amazing that you're not all skin and bones," Bena chuckled. "And no wonder you once risked getting lost in the forest for a handful of sweet berries."

Driscoll cut himself a generous portion of cheese. "I don't eat this way at home either. My mother used to say white bread's a crime. The price certainly is." He gestured at the horizon. "That jagged band—that'll be the mountains. More than you've ever seen, Em. Whole chains of them."

She couldn't picture what mountains and chains had in common. "I've never even seen one. Not with my own eyes. Water?" She offered the flask to Bena, who took a sip before passing it on to Driscoll. He drank deeply, tipping his head, his Adam's apple bouncing. When he handed the flask back to Em she recklessly put it to her mouth without wiping it first. It was like getting a delayed kind of kiss. Vexed by the impulse, she began to dig at her hair, muttering, "I bet it's standing on end."

"It's a bit wind-blown," Driscoll admitted. "But it's supposed to look like that after you've been riding in a convertible for half a day. I think it suits you."

She was sure he was just being polite. "Then why isn't Bena's hair mussed? It's much longer than mine. By all rights the wind should have tangled it more."

"I leaned against it while I was napping," the old woman said. "If you're bothered why don't you dunk your head in the creek? I'll weave your hair into braids while it's still wet. That way it'll hold together better. Come when you're ready." She broke off a cluster of grapes and rose. "I'm going to soak my feet and keep Nada company."

The dog had found some shallows to lie in, obviously enjoying the current swirling around her. As Bena settled on a rock at the water's edge, Em said to Driscoll, "She's feeling better now. But tell me—why were you helping her bring all those quilts? On a day-trip?"

He started to speak, then thought better of it. Yawning, he lay back on the blanket. "I've got to catch up on my sleep. No telling when I get my next chance. Hey, here's an idea—when we're on the road again I'll teach you to drive. It's easier than it looks. Then we can take turns."

Astonished, she said, "Me, drive? You must be kidding. My brain doesn't work that way."

"Why not give it a try?"

"And land your one-of-a-kind Doble in the nearest ditch? I think not." Secretly, she was pleased he'd thought to suggest it. He dropped off as soon as he closed his eyes. Em waited several minutes, watching his chest rise and fall, before she dared to stretch out beside him. After she lined up her feet with his, the top of her head went no higher than his chin. It made her feel almost short. It was a delicious sensation. Wouldn't it be awful if she outgrew him too?

Letting her gaze climb past him up the massive tree from low branches to high she eventually found the old puckered scar of a long ago torn-away limb. Oaks were deceptive that way. The sturdiest, healthiest branch might suddenly snap under its own weight. She considered the scar, wondering if what happened to the young Bena could happen to her, and decided that even without a treacherous gust she would rather spend the remainder of their lunch break elsewhere.

Mindful not to disturb Driscoll, she rolled off his blanket and padded across the grass to sit beside Bena who was dangling her feet in the water. With color restored to her cheeks and the sparkle returned to her violet eyes, Bena looked almost as young as she always had in the twilit forest. Em dunked in her feet too. "I see you are yourself again. You had me scared there for a while."

Bena directed a playful splash at her. "I *feel* like myself again, Thanks, but it did show me that I've let the forest fence me in far too long. A person who lives all alone for a most of her lifetime can lose the ability to adapt to changes. Lately, I have been stagnating in my forest, Em. Maybe it's time for me to dare mingling and expect a good outcome."

"Oh," Em said, nodding sagely. "I think I see what you mean."

Bena laughed. "How could you? You've lived the whole of your short life with other people, always having to cope and adjust and hold your own whether you liked it or not. Now go stick your head underwater."

"I think I'd better." Em hankered down in the stream and dipped. The water was deliciously cool. When her lungs ran out of oxygen she came up gasping, wrung out her hair, and reclaimed her rock on the bank.

Bena stood behind her with a sharp twig and drew a straight line along Em's scalp from the center of her forehead to the back of her neck. Then she started weaving. "It's not every day you get your braids done by an old basket maker," she said. "Pick us up a couple of those little reeds by your feet. They'll serve as twine. By the way, cherries have been out of season for months, as you well know. Not even a witch could have found any for our picnic today."

"Then he shouldn't have got my hopes up!" Em bristled, but Bena's sure, soothing hands, busy dividing, pulling and plaiting, soon lulled her into a more cooperative frame of mind. When Bena had finished winding the reed stems around the bottom of each braid, tying sturdy knots, Em silently vowed to try a bit harder to be nice to the young vet. But considering what he expected of her at the end of the day she doubted that she could keep it up for long.

CHAPTER 9

IN THE CREEK BED BELOW, SWIFT WATER danced over slippery rocks. High in the sky, two hawks sailed the updrafts. A dragonfly whirred forward and backward equally fast over some rotting leaves, its wings like glittering glass. Em scanned the creek bottom for a small disk-shaped stone, found one, plucked it out, and rubbed it dry on her blouse. Then she asked, "Why did you bring everything you own?"

Bena replied lightly, "I'm hoping to make some good trades. Are you going to skip that rock? I used to be good at it when I was your age. My friends and I probably skipped half of this creek bed between us. Look at Nada. She's ready to play."

The dog's eyes were trained on the rock. Em dropped it from one hand to the other. Nada shifted her weight in preparation for a quick takeoff. "Ready?" Em said, throwing the stone low over the surface. It bounced twice and sank with a musical *plunk*. Nada was on it the next instant, snatching it before it could settle on a layer of look-alikes. She dropped it expectantly on Em's lap and began to shake off the water streaming from her fur. Quickly Em threw the stone again. This time Nada caught it just as it started to sink, but instead of bringing it to Em, she raced past the girl toward the oak and shook herself next to the blanket, dowsing Driscoll with a sparkling cascade of droplets.

He sat bolt upright, wiping the deluge from his face. "Thanks for waking me up. I'm glad somebody did." Nada dropped the stone at his feet and crouched, ready to chase it in any direction. But he pocketed it, saying, "Oh no, you don't. This is a vet you're playing with. I've seen too many chipped teeth to join in your game. Here, have some cheese." He tossed her a scrap, which she gulped without chewing. "I'm good for a few more hours of driving," he called to Bena and Em. "Shall we go on? The sun's moving faster than we are!"

While Bena and Em cleared the site Driscoll towel-dried the dog, spread a second towel over half of the Doble's back seat, and motioned the dog to lie on it. "Stay there till your fur dries. And don't lean against Bena."

Happily, Nada curled herself into a ball. Bena and Em stashed the picnic things and got in, but Driscoll spent some time poking at the car's innards, front and back, checking dials and topping off tanks. Unlocking the strongbox Em had noticed earlier, he showed them a wafer and said, "I only use these on special occasions. My dad made them. They change regular water into fuel. Only trouble is, I'm almost out and can't find his secret formula." He dropped the wafer into one of the tanks and watched it dissolve. A few minutes later they were heading toward the horizon.

The road rose at a slow but steady pace. Once, they saw the remains of an old city off to the side, conquered by vines. Driscoll pointed to a sagging wire fence containing heaps of unrecognizable metal objects, rusting along with the mesh. "A wrecking yard. Every old city had some. My dad loved to comb through them for parts. He was never happier than when he was grubbing in one of his engines, clothes smudged, black grease under his nails. He was a genius tinkerer. Took the best vehicle ever built and made it better. He used to work in a museum. A place full of old-timey cars, Em. Imagine a hall filled with Stanleys and Dobles."

But she couldn't. "Used to?" she probed.

There was a long pause and then Driscoll said, "They caught him. In a junk yard like the one we just passed. Inside the fence."

"They? Who?"

Bena coughed discreetly from the backseat. Trying to switch topics, Em asked, "And do you like to grub in engines, too,

Driscoll?"

"Not nearly as much as he did," he answered. "I believed it was a disappointment to him until he sat me down one day and explained. He said we lived at the end of the age of machines. Used to be, every man could work on his own car That all changed after the rains. The old men forgot what they'd known and the young never wanted to learn . . . *couldn't* learn anymore."

He slowed to maneuver around a big pothole. "Some strange twist of the brain, is how he put it. He said a new age was coming whose purpose was not yet clear, and that I would fit into it much better than he." He adjusted a mirror. "I think he was right. Every now and then, someone comes along who can still think in the old way, but fewer each year. Even with a tinkerer father, I had to work hard to understand what seemed simple to him. He taught me all I know, which is a whole lot less, I'm sorry to say, than he set out to teach me. I like working with living things better." He turned to smile at Bena, who was applying a new layer of salve to the dog's feet.

She smiled back, saying, "That's where we're alike."

"We always had a lot of animals around," he went on, glancing briefly at his gauges. "Wild ones and strays. I doctored them the way he doctored machines. My mother encouraged it after he died. Apprenticed me to our vet, who had connections. He found me the spot in Clydestown. So here I am, an assistant veterinarian and still learning."

Em thought of her own meager village schooling, the thankless work in the fields, her joy in reading, strongly discouraged by her parents. "I'm still learning too," she said, hoping her future lessons would be more interesting than hard.

"I know you are, Em. After we get back I'll show you my books. The walls in my room are covered with them. You can borrow any you want, though a lot of them are about cars. During the riots my dad started to move the rarest books and the most antique cars out of the museum. He managed to hide this one and two other Dobles before the mob burned the museum down with everything that was still in it." His face clouded. "The first thing to learn, Em, is that when people get real angry they are transformed into packs of wild beasts. Then they do all kinds of horrible things they won't remember once they become human again."

"Like what?"

"Didn't they teach you about the riots in school?"

"What, boring history? Lists and dates?"

Driscoll looked at Bena in the rear mirror. "You must have lived through the rains from beginning to end. What was it like?"

She raised one of Nada's damp, drooping earflaps and peered down the ear canal. "I was extra careful to keep to myself in those days. Deep in the woods. My main problem, as I recall, was fencing an ever growing herd of deer out of my garden. And then, for a long time after, nobody had enough money to buy my baskets and nothing to barter for them. Good, old-fashioned seeds became harder to get. And it kept getting hotter and drier each year. That little stream of mine was much bigger when I first came to the forest."

"You mean you weren't actually *in* any of it? You lived outside of history?" Driscoll seemed upset at her missed opportunity but she just chuckled.

"What is history but a record of past mistakes? The more you focus on them the more likely you are to repeat them."

He gave an uncomfortable laugh. "I have to disagree with you there. The real lesson of history is precisely that once you *are* aware of past mistakes you *won't* have to repeat them."

Bena leaned toward him, gripping the back of his seat. "If that were true, greed and warmongering would be extinct by now, don't you think?"

"Some lessons are harder to learn than others. We're still working on those."

"I'd say the first step would be to throw out all guns!"

After a guilty glance at his feet, he said, "It's not guns that kill. It's people."

She snorted. "Not that again. Spare me. You have to admit guns make it easier."

Em scooted toward the window, asking, "Are you having an argument?"

"A discussion!" they shouted together. Then they laughed.

"We're on the same side, Bena, remember?" Driscoll said.

She gave a heartfelt sigh. "Words. Life is much simpler without them. If you don't mind, I'm going to take a quiet little nap. I'm all talked out." She moved the pile of quilts around to get more comfortable and dozed off.

Eventually, Driscoll said, "This is a good time for you to start driving, Em. You'll love it. I swear."

"I already said no. And I'm tired too." She yawned to prove it. "Tired of looking and sitting and listening."

He cocked a brow at her but remained silent. She glanced out of the window and rested her eyes. Once she woke briefly to find her cheek on his shoulder and made an effort to sit straight. But when she felt herself sliding toward him again, she gave up and let her head lean where it would. The next time she came awake the Doble was parked in the middle of the road and Driscoll was outside, pulling the roof up toward the windshield from Em's side of the car.

"Look over there," he whispered. "The fiery hill."

Before them rose a mighty mountain, its symmetrical top covered by a cap of brilliant snow and surrounded by a circle of clouds. She squinted. "I don't see any fire. Are you sure this is the right peak?" Although the mountain looked tranquil, a chill was wafting straight through her. For an instant she seemed to sense something vile under the pristine cone, something that had cast a hook deep into the flatlands to reel in three hapless fish. Was there still time to break loose?

"What do you think it would be like to stand on the very tip?" Driscoll whispered.

"Cold," said Em.

"The view must be spectacular from up there."

"I guess." She scanned the gray rocky heights and the snow. "Can't you feel it?"

"Feel what?"

"*It*. Crouching. Watching us."

He grinned. "Spoken like a true flatlander. Do you realize how many poems and love songs have been dedicated to mountains? Nearer to God, and all that? I bet Nada's people revere it."

At the sound of her name Nada scrambled to the front, hooked her paws over the window, jumped out, and eagerly inhaled the tangy air, tail wagging.

"*I* don't revere it," Em said.

He put a soothing hand on her arm. "You're afraid Nada will want to stay on the mountain."

"I'm not," she said, shaking it off. "She won't."

He studied the darkly forested slopes. "There's absolutely nothing up there to be afraid of. But whatever happens I'll keep you safe. I promise."

"Yeah," she said. "Like you promised me cherries." Turning,

she called loudly, "Bena, we're here!" Watching Nada lift her nose high and scent uphill, Em shivered.

At last, Bena roused enough to stick her head out of the rear window. She said in an reverential tone, "That peak is touching the sky."

Driscoll beamed as if he had invented the mountain for them. Then he finished securing the roof to the windshield.

"I wish you'd left the roof down," Em said, "We would see more, driving up."

He motioned to her puckering arms. "It's already getting colder."

She checked the high slopes for signs of habitation but it was impossible to see through the forest canopy. Then the ring of clouds sank to become a white collar, obscuring the peak. She opened her door for Nada, who settled beside her and stuck her nose out as Driscoll drove on. After a while the road rose more steeply, twisting into hair-raising curves. Then it narrowed into parallel wagon tracks, a line of unruly weeds in the center.

At last they came to where it leveled briefly before veering to the left. Driscoll stopped in front of a wooden signpost so weathered that the words edged upon it could no longer be deciphered. An arrow pointed to a narrow valley. In the distance a small town, buffered by green and golden rectangular fields, nestled against a backdrop of mountains. They formed the chain Driscoll had mentioned hours before. None of the peaks came anywhere near the lofty heights of the fiery hill, nor were they snow-capped.

Driscoll yawned, rubbing his eyes. "What do you think? Shall we head into town?" As if to answer his question, Nada braced her paws against the door frame, pointing her nose straight uphill. Driscoll examined the slope and discovered the faint signs of a path obviously no longer in use. "I think she wants us to drive up there. But what if the Doble gets blocked by a downed tree or some old rockslide, with nowhere to turn? It's dangerous to reverse a car on a steep grade, you see."

Em tried to recall details of her flying dream. "I don't recall any obstacles when Nada and I flew over it."

"Is that so," Driscoll said politely, scratching his beard. Then he asked Bena's opinion and Em realized he had dismissed her information outright. Truly, he made it hard for Em to like him for long, much as she tried. Whenever she succeeded with the effort he said something to ruin things again. "What do *you* think, Bena?" he

said. "Maybe we should ask someone in town where this trail goes."
As if Em's experience had been of no consequence whatsoever.

"To our shared dream, of course." Bena sounded eager. "Why
don't we just trust Nada's nose and Em's good sense?"

"Good point." He eased the car on to the overgrown tracks. "A
dog's sense of smell is hundreds of times better than ours."

At first it was easy going but soon he had to begin maneuvering
around the remnants of rock slides and other debris. Once she had to
help him drag off a huge dead branch, which they carefully laid
along the path's edge, afraid if they tossed it over the side it might hit
some innocent creature below. Nada was leaning out farther and
farther until Em looped an arm around the dog's hindquarters. That's
when she saw that a film of new hairs had begun to cover the bare
spots on her back and that the cracks in her pads had healed over
with pinkish, smooth skin. She put her cheek against the dog's side,
feeling it quiver with anticipation. "Your Brendan can't possibly love
you half as much as I do," she whispered. "No one can." Briefly,
Nada twisted her head around to lick Em's nose. Then she hung out
even farther. Em grabbed a handful of slippery fur, stifling a sob.

Immediately, Driscoll stopped the car. "Are you okay?"

"Why wouldn't I be?" she said, her voice coming out rougher
than she intended. At that very moment she disliked him and his
voice so much that she could not bring herself to look at him. If only
she had never gone to Clydestown. She and Nada would be living
happily with Bena right now, who, as it turned out, had been the one
with the best medicine, anyway.

"Why should you be?" he countered in an unbearably patient
tone. "Given how you feel about Nada."

"You don't have the slightest idea how I feel," she said, wishing
he would just leave her alone. "We've only just met."

"We'll proceed more slowly," he murmured gently. "After all,
there's no rush." He wasn't kidding. He drove on at such a low speed
that she could easily have walked alongside the car. But soon, all too
soon, they came around the last curve to where the path dead-ended
at a big pile of rocks. Nada gave a sharp volley of barks, clambered
out of the window, and hit the ground before Driscoll could bring the
car to a complete stop. "Wait for us!" he cried, but she was already
skirting the rocks and disappearing from sight.

No good-bye.

No thank you for bringing me home.

No I'll miss you.

"So, Driscoll," Em said in a shaky, blameful voice, brushing stray dog hairs off her lap. "Are you satisfied now? Your mission's accomplished. We might as well leave."

CHAPTER 10

EM GROPED IN THE SATCHEL FOR the fairy-tale book, opened it to shield her brimming eyes, and pretended to read while straining to hear the dwindling sounds of Nada's barking.

Bena climbed out and said mildly, "Come on, Em. We might as well go see how true your flying dream was."

"You go," Em muttered behind the big book. "I prefer to stay here. By myself." Only then would she feel free to acknowledge the despair flooding her insides. Without a word, Driscoll held out his hand to her. She ignored it, pointedly turned a page, and said, "Tell me all about it when you get back," hoping he would take the hint and leave without her. But he merely crossed his arms and spread his feet as if preparing himself for a long wait.

Bena unloaded the buckets. "Let's just take the berries, Driscoll, and leave the baskets for later." Her voice smothered that one fragile instant when Nada's barking became indistinguishable from the surrounding silence.

The print blurred. Em blinked back tears and strained to listen. All she could hear was an unseen bird trilling the same phrase over and over until she was thoroughly tired of it. Then, miraculously, the barking started again, rapidly picking up volume, moving closer. Soon Nada appeared at the side of the rock pile, counting her lost sheep before diving through the door to put her paws expectantly on the girl's bare knees.

Em lowered the book a few inches. "What is it you want?" Impatiently, Nada wrapped her canines around Em's wrist and tugged. Her bite was incredibly soft. "Oh, all right!" Em shut the book, letting the dog pull her out. "All you had to do was ask. Lead on!"

Together, they raced past Bena and Driscoll to the back side of the rock pile. The trail Em remembered from the flying dream took them through shoulder-high pines around a second wall of boulders, and across an adjacent patch of knee-high fir seedlings, their needles brushing her legs. And then a chaos of brambles grew across the path, blocking her progress. Nada crept under it and went on.

Afraid of losing sight of the dog, Em fought the belligerent vines, flailing first one stick, then two. Barbs hooked her skin and yanked strand after strand out of the braids Bena had so expertly woven. Finally, what was left of one caught on a vine and yanked her off balance. Wrenching her hair loose, she shouted over her shoulder, "Don't follow us! This trail's petering out!"

Then it was gone, leaving her blocked on all sides. She got to her knees and crept after the dog, thorns tearing the back of her blouse. Breaking free, she bumped into Nada's red rump. The dog was sitting on her haunches, gazing adoringly up the third heap of stones. Nature had arranged them to form convenient slab-steps. The man with the red bandana sat on top, his face toward the east, eyes closed. Tired of waiting to be noticed, Nada climbed the lichen-encrusted slabs to plant her nose on a slack, upturned palm.

Down below, Em sucked sweet-salty drops of bright blood from her lacerated arms. "Hello!" she yelled, sorrier than ever that she'd let Bena and Driscoll talk her into coming. "Is this your dog?"

The man opened his eyes, which were as fog gray as Bena had described them. A few white-blonde strands had worked themselves out of the headband to dance on the breeze. "Ah," he said lazily. "There you are." As if that wasn't entirely obvious. "Welcome to the fiery hill. Where are your friends?"

"Behind me a ways," she replied. "About the dog. How long has she been lost?"

He rubbed Nada's knobby head and got to his feet. "What makes you think she was lost?"

"Why else would she wind up half a day's drive from here? We wouldn't have known where to come if her owner's name hadn't been scratched in her collar."

"Owner?" He pronounced the word as if it were an insult. "No one *owns* Nada. She's as free to come and go as the rest of us are. And, by the way, I'm Alden. Or did I say that already?"

Boy, did he have trouble with his lines! And how awkward he looked when he descended the slabs, as if his legs had gone to sleep up there while they'd been crossed. She snapped her fingers smartly and Nada flowed past him to heel at her feet. It was most gratifying.

"Em?" Driscoll called from somewhere nearby.

"Here!" she shouted. "By these rocks!"

And then he and Bena came around the wrong side of the pile without a single scratch on them. "We found a good path just inside the woods," he told her, staring at Alden as if he had trouble believing his eyes.

"But of course. The brambles swallowed the old trail years ago," Alden said, only then noticing Em's tattered appearance. "You didn't—"

"I was only following Nada," she tried to explain, feeling stupid, nervously shifting from one foot to the other as the three of them stared at the picture she undoubtedly made—of a badly constructed scarecrow smeared with berry juice and blood, more brainless and ragged than any she'd seen in the fields.

"It's just a dog-sized short cut," Alden said. "None of us would ever . . . "

Em scowled him into silence.

Bena stepped between them and held out her hand to the man, introducing herself and Driscoll. "And you must be Alden," she said. "I remember that bandana of yours from the dream you sent us."

Ignoring the hand, Alden looked searchingly in the direction of the dead-ended road. "One of you is still missing. I was expecting four."

He had a nerve, expecting anything from them at all. "Well, then you were wrong, weren't you?" Em said coldly before turning to Driscoll. "Good news," she told him. "Nobody owns Nada. Which means she's free to go. And since she's already decided to stay with me we might as well drive down off the mountain before it gets dark." The sooner they left, the better she'd like it. She slapped her thigh, signaling Nada to heel, and started toward the trail Driscoll had mentioned. "We'll wait for you in the car."

"Em," Bena said, sounding impatient. "We've come too far for such a hasty retreat. It isn't seemly." She was still offering to shake with Alden, to no avail. "We're glad to meet you," she told him at last, capturing his clueless hand.

"I, uh, I'm Alden," he stuttered, limp-wristed. "But you already know that. I'm sorry. It's hard for me to focus back here when my mind has been elsewhere." He pulled his hand away as soon as she relaxed her hold.

"You were meditating?" she asked softly. "I can show you some tricks to help you refocus faster when you come back to yourself. I take it we're invited to tea?" She showed him her bucket. "We brought you the best berries that grow on the plains."

He looked in the bucket and wrinkled his nose with distaste. "Why? We have more berries up here than we can possibly eat."

Em though that remark was definitely uncalled for. "Bena went through a lot of trouble to pick those for you," she was quick to point out. "The least you could—oh, never mind. Take us to that Brendan of yours so I can tell him what I think about people who let their dog's collar grow into her skin."

They followed him single-file, first Em, then Driscoll, then Bena. Nada bopped around them all, joyously barking until the surrounding trees started to thin. Then she left them to run ahead and announce their arrival. From behind, Alden looked like a girl— blonde, slim-hipped, and oddly attractive. He walked on the balls of his moccasined feet. It made it seem as if he was floating. When he stopped at the edge of a big, sunny clearing Nada was already busy at the entrance to a long stone house, escorting its four occupants out into a shady part of the yard. They lined up on the grass as if waiting for a promised parade. There was a surprisingly lush garden off to one side, surrounded by a tall wire fence.

Alden nodded at a boy who was playfully tugging on Nada's ears. "That's Brendan." Upon hearing his name, the boy unbent, looking fully at Em. For no reason she could name she felt a cold blast of panic and stumbled backwards, bumping into Driscoll who gripped her shoulders to steady her. It was then that she finally realized how patient and kind he had been throughout the trip, even though she had baited him constantly. He had behaved like a true friend. The kind you could trust with your life. Filled with regret, she leaned against him and blurted, "I'm sorry I was so mean to you. Okay?"

"Okay," he replied.

Alden pointed at a chubby middle-aged woman with dark brown hair and a friendly, florid face. Her hands were dusted with flour. "That's our Hertha. As you can see, she is in the middle of baking our bread."

"Hello," Hertha said, attempting to wipe her hands clean on her apron.

"And this is Anckar." Alden nodded at a younger, wiry woman who was paint-speckled from her short cap of curls to her worn leather boots. "The girl hiding behind Hertha is Lupe, who is about your age, only more timid. She is afraid of strangers so you'll have to give her some time to get used to you."

Em caught a blur of black eyebrows and long hair so dark it gleamed blue, then Lupe ducked out of sight. Brendan was moving away from the three women, stepping out of the shade. The sun transformed his hair into a brown halo and made his skin shine like dark honey. Keeping his eyes only on Em, he came slowly toward her.

Em fumbled behind her and clutched at Driscoll's shirt. "I'm right here," he murmured, his mouth close to her ear. "Watching over you just as I said I would." Now Em could see that Brendan was walking with a limp, dragging his right foot. When he was about ten feet away he reached out to her as if expecting her to meet him halfway. She held back until Driscoll gave her a little push. She started to move forward, still clutching his shirt, making him keep pace. Then Bena called his name from somewhere behind them and Em let him go. With a final encouraging squeeze, he allowed her to proceed without him.

Six feet apart, Em and Brendan paused and looked each other over. A sudden wind came up, blowing through her bramble-shredded blouse and upsetting her hair. The air between her and the boy began to shimmer, turning liquid the way it did in Oren on an extra hot day. Reaching for her again, he closed the remaining distance between them and said, "I'm so glad you finally came." As if they were friends. It wasn't what she had expected him to say.

She could see a bee buzzing around his halo, and then another one. More of them were flying out of the garden and in from the woods. The sky overhead stretched and thinned so that Em could almost see what lay beyond its blue vault. Brendan's hand was still raised as if he were summoning her. Maybe he was, because she could feel herself moving toward him again even though she tried hard not to. Without her consent, her hand went out to meet his just as the small buzzing sounds in the background swelled to become an insistent drone. And then a shaft of lightning zagged straight down at them from above, transforming his halo of curls into a bright, dazzling helmet. An excess of light poured down his face, neck, along his arms, and over his hands, jumping from his finger tips to hers and spreading rapidly throughout her whole body.

It felt as if some powerful current was slamming into her, or maybe as if she was standing under a great thundering waterfall. She could feel her scalp starting to tingle. Then she smelled scorched hair. One instant she was as tall as the sky, the next she was the size of an ant. Her spine arced. She could hear Driscoll calling her name and tried to pull free but her hand was stuck fast to the boy's. Her knees buckled.

"Em!" Driscoll shouted, closing in. He was too late. She felt herself go limp all over, and then she was falling, her mind nowhere and everywhere at once.

CHAPTER 11

IT SHOULD HAVE BEEN EASY FOR DRISCOLL to keep his promise to Em. After all, there hadn't been much to watch out for except vague-eyed Alden, the three women in the yard, and the limping bare-chested boy showing off well-tended muscles the way boys often do at his age. There was no reason to expect trouble from him or from any of them. No reason for Driscoll to ignore Bena when she called to him from the edge of the clearing, eager to share something she had seen. And no reason *not* to let his attention wander for the few seconds it would take to see what it was, considering that everything seemed to be going so well at that point.

Bena was standing between two bunches of fern. "Look at the difference in size," she said, pointing first to the normal-sized bunch growing at the tree line and then at the other, only a few yards closer into the clearing. The second one was nearly three times as high as the first. "They're exactly the same kind of plant," she said. "Isn't that odd?"

"Odd," he agreed absently, trying to stay alert for unusual sounds. All he heard was the humming of bees.

"Do you think it's the soil?" She scooped up a handful, squeezed it, and released it to see how it fell. It landed just when the humming swelled into a deep kind of drone. And then came an ominous sizzling that made Driscoll's hair stand on end.

He whirled, calling Em's name. He saw the sky split apart by a lightning bolt. He saw Em standing where he had so carelessly left her, trying to pull away from the boy. He saw how the lightning was twisting her spine, lifting her up and then slamming her down. "Em!" he yelled again, sprinting to her in nightmare-slow motion. The boy collapsed before he could reach either of them. The next thing Driscoll knew he was kneeling by Em's side, reaching for her wrist to measure her pulse.

"Don't touch her!" Alden shouted.

But who was he to tell Driscoll what to do? He touched her. A split second later some unseen force threw him through the air, slamming him on to his back before three pairs of feet. A searing pain knifed through him and lodged in his chest, paralyzing him all the way down to his toes.

One pair of feet, wearing sandals, came a bit closer. He heard the middle-aged woman whom Alden had called Hertha suck in her breath and say, "Oh my stars!"

"Are they all dead?" the bare-footed Lupe whimpered from where she was cowering behind the woman's broad back. The scuffed, paint-speckled boots of Anckar now tapped impatiently against the ground. "Lupe, spare us another bout of hysterics," she said. "I'm sure you've cried your fill for today. Alden, what happened? What should we do?"

"Do?" Alden echoed, sounding bewildered. "Why, nothing, Anckar. Except stand back and wait."

Good advice, Driscoll had to admit. And then his eyes unfroze so he could blink again and let his gaze travel up to the three female faces anxiously peering down at him.

"Oh good. You're okay," Hertha said, bending closer. "Lupe, run and fetch him a cup of water." She produced a cordial smile and extended her hand. "Here, let me help you up."

He ignored her and concentrated on the nearly impossible task of bending an arm. Then Bena was at his side, crouching, putting her dirt-smudged hand lightly on his forehead. "Try and take a deep breath," she said. He did, gaining enough strength to bend the other arm, raising himself on his elbows.

Off to the side, Anckar muttered something about a kiln and hurried away. "Typical," Hertha grumbled. "The slightest trouble and off she goes on one excuse or another." Somewhat louder, she asked, "Where's Odasan? He'll know what to do. Lupe, fetch him out of the tipi."

"I saw him walk off into the woods right after lunch, with his bedroll and *gi*," Lupe said, still hiding behind her. "Or else he would be here now, helping Brendan." She forgot her fear long enough to glare at the unconscious Em. "What did that weird girl do to him?"

Abruptly, Hertha went across to where Brendan was lying to peer down at his insensible face, leaving Lupe to stand alone and unprotected. "I don't know," Hertha said, puzzled. "One second he was smiling at Em, then she touched him just lightly with her fingertips and he keeled over. I never saw anything like it. Alden, what happened?"

"Yes, please," Bena said, looking at Alden. "What's going on?"

But he seemed as confused as they were. "It wasn't supposed to go like this," he said petulantly. "Nada brought only these three and Em arrived in a contrary mood. It made her a bad receiver for the power pouring into her. Brendan's only problem was that he got in the way."

Ignoring the pain in his chest, Driscoll managed to get both knees under him. "You make absolutely no sense," he told Alden, creeping past Bena to get to Em. But the old woman easily warded him off with one hand while she passed the other first over the girl, then over Brendan, careful not to make direct contact with either. "They feel quite hot," she announced.

"Oh good," Hertha said. "Then all we have to do is wrap them in some wet towels to bring their temperatures down. Lupe, please bring us a few. And a couple of buckets of cold water." But Lupe stayed where she was, pulling the collar of her bulky brown sweater up to her chin, swaying this way and that, undecided.

Then Driscoll sat on his heels. "Hold it! If they were struck by some kind of lightning they might be electrically charged. Water will fry them. What we have to do is allow the excess power to drain out of them into the earth. But no matter what anyone says, as soon as Em comes to we're leaving. Turns out she was right all along—we should never have come."

No one was listening to him. "What kind of power?" Bena asked Alden, as if he knew more than the rest of them. "From where? It couldn't have been from above. There isn't a single thunderhead and the sky's clear as far as the eye can see."

Alden seemed surprised that she hadn't figured it out for herself yet. "Why, it's the power that lives in this clearing, of course," he said. "I'm sure you can feel it." He pointed to the garden. "It makes things grow. In there."

Bena considered the vegetable beds inside the fence and the fruit trees behind them. "I have to admit, everything in there is huge. Those blackberries along the back are as big as my thumb. No wonder you weren't interested in mine."

Hertha brightened and came to take her hand. "As it happens I have a blackberry cobbler browning in the oven right now. Why don't I brew us some tea to go with it while we're waiting for Em and Brendan to wake up?"

But Driscoll, still struggling to rise, said, "I wouldn't touch their food, Bena. No telling what they'll slip into it. You'll be safer staying out here with me."

Hertha gasped at the insult, swept into the house, and Lupe scurried along behind her.

Now there were just Bena and Driscoll and Alden. The old woman gave Driscoll a hard look. "That was uncalled for. They didn't do anything to deserve your nasty remark. If you need me I'll be inside. Visiting." She followed the others indoors.

That left Alden and Driscoll, who wasn't finished being hostile. He glared until Alden paled and threw up his hands, stammering, "You must have seen how angry Em was when she came. It made her resistant to the energy stream so that it knocked her right out of herself."

"So now you're telling me what happened was her own fault," Driscoll said coldly.

"Sort of," Alden hedged. "She wasn't knocked very far. Can't you feel her? She's still close—"

"Yeah," Driscoll said drily, "As close as our feet. But not for long. I'm afraid you'll have to lure a new bunch of unsuspecting fools to your mountain hideout. We're not interested. Understand?"

Alden blanched and fled after the others, leaving only one conscious being left for Driscoll to berate—Nada, who had the nerve to regard him with steadfast affection. He glared into her red, bottomless eyes. "Treacherous beast. It's an elaborate plot, I have to admit. A seemingly injured stray desperate for help. Just the thing that would draw in three flatland suckers. Who sicced you on us?" Nada bellied closer, baring her teeth in a grin. He flung out a hand to stop her. "Don't look so pleased with yourself. I won't be fooled twice. And I'll fight everyone here to get Em away."

Nada yawned, showing him all four of her immaculate canines. Then she settled herself at Em's feet as if she expected to be there for a while. In no time at all she was taking a nap, which showed just what sort of guard dog she was. Driscoll kept *his* eyes wide open and focused on Em's vacant face. After the sun dipped behind the summit, the mountain's deep afternoon shade crept over the ground. Bees wove in and out of the advancing dark line, their wings a bright blur. Pots were clanging and voices were murmuring from inside the wide open kitchen window. At one point they were all laughing, even Bena. In his opinion it was taking her attempt to be sociable too far.

Smoke drifted from the two chimneys along the eaves and swirled away with the breeze. The mouthwatering smell of baked cobbler wafted pitilessly toward him. How long had it been since he ate? He forced his attention back to Em's face, holding a finger under her nose. If she was still breathing he couldn't detect it. He whispered, "Em?" No response. "Please try to wake up now. We need to get going before it gets dark. I left my flashlight in the car." It was like talking to stone.

She was the breeze, brushing his cheeks. She was the one bee separating from the rest to fly a tight circle around his head. She was the white butterfly fluttering skyward like a small leaf to hover among treetops, watching him sit far below, blind to the beauty around him.

Driscoll hunched in the gathering dusk and knew exactly what had gone wrong: he had failed to keep the most important promise he'd ever made. By shifting his attention to Bena in that one crucial moment, he had taken it from Em when she needed it most.

CHAPTER 12

W HEN THE SHADOW OF THE MOUNTAIN HAD
advanced far enough to draw a line between Brendan's ashen brown
face and Em's pallor, Bena and Lupe emerged from the house,
carrying baskets. Bena waved at Driscoll from the garden gate.
"We're going to pick some veggies. Want anything special?"

His hostile stare made Lupe dart inside the fence. He wondered
why she went barefoot if she was cold enough to wear such a thick
sweater. He could hear her voice quaver as she led Bena from one
vegetable bed to another. Bena's tone was admiring and even
delighted. When they came out with their baskets overflowing Lupe
peered sideways at Driscoll and scampered into the house, but Bena
ignored his pronounce scowl and came to sit beside him, upending
her haul into the bowl of her lap. The deep-purple orbs she held out
to him looked like two prune plums in the fast-fading light.
"Blackberries," she said. "And look at this!" She passed a tomato
under his nose. It was the biggest he'd ever seen and smelled like
sweet-tart sunshine. Next she wielded a carrot as long and straight as
a sword, bearing little resemblance to the diseased roots he was used
to grating into his salad. The spinach leaf she held up for him shone
like an emerald, and the green beans she dangled were so perfectly

formed they might have been sculpted of wax. "People who can grow stuff like this can only be good," she said with conviction.

She was too easily fooled. "I won't be seduced by a lapful of produce," he said. "I admit everything is uncommonly large—but these eyes looking at your garden jewels are the same eyes that watched Em struck down the minute she walked into this clearing."

Bena calmly reloaded her basket. "We're making supper in there. Soup, bread, a salad." Gingerly, she balanced what looked to him like a shiny red melon on one of his knees. "Care for an apple? A pear? There are a couple of trees full of them by the back fence." Her eyes shone with an enthusiasm he hadn't known she was capable of. "Go ahead, take a look at the garden before it gets too dark. You'll never see anything remotely as good anywhere in our world. Go on. I'll stay here and watch over Em."

He remained seated. "They have nothing I want. Why don't you just go take your pretty baubles in to your new friends?"

She chuckled, unperturbed. "You are the most obstinate man." Pressing the berries into his hand, she closed his fingers around them. "Eat them before they burst." Then she rose, holding the basket at arm's length. "Hertha wove this one. It's nice and sturdy but not nearly as pretty as any of mine. I bet I can trade some of the ones I brought for a few of her incredible seeds, though I doubt they'll grow half as well in my stony soil."

At least she was intending to go back with him. He had begun to wonder. "Don't get too cozy in there," he warned, a little less gruff than before. "We have to get going while we can still see." She looked at the patch of dusky sky, at Em, and at him, keeping her thoughts to herself. Then she went back inside, closing the door behind her with a determined click.

Soon after, a white butterfly tumbled out of the clouds, fluorescent in the gathering dark. It fluttered on silent wings through the kitchen window moments before someone shut both panes from the inside. Small flames flickered to life behind a pale curtain. He imagined a glowing cook-stove, the air humid from various bubbling cauldrons, and a row of comfortably cushioned chairs around a long table, smiling faces lit by the sheen of kerosene lamps. Painfully, he shifted his weight from one hip to the other. The ground seemed to be getting harder with each passing minute.

WHEN HE had told Em it would get cold on the mountain, the

words hadn't meant much in the sweltering heat of the flatlands. He woke sometime in the night, feeling his temperature plunge as the earth beneath him drew off what was left of his body-heat. The two sleepers before him shone like matching lamps. How could he have dozed? How could he not, after all the driving he had done and had yet to do again? Half of the narrow bit of sky overhead was a dark velvet band dotted with stars, the other half a ribbon of clouds lit by an invisible moon. "Em," he whispered, "are you awake yet?"

She lay as still as finely wrought marble. With his bronze skin and his abundant curls mingling with night shadows, the boy was no less striking than she. He had intelligent features, a body well-built except for that foot. It looked ugly even in this softest of lights, as if it had been broken and badly reset. A cloven hoof? Horn nubs hiding in that woolly cap of hair? Were they together somewhere in their dreams? Driscoll winced. The only thing ugly around here was his own mind. How arrogant he had been just this morning, making her come and expecting her to give up the dog, when all along it was *him* who had been about to lose *her*.

The black lace of fir branches against luminous night sky was achingly lovely. He glanced at the dark house and saw that one window square was still lit. While he was looking a large rectangular space lightened briefly and was extinguished again as a slight shadow emerged from the door. It was Bena, wrapped in her cloak. She was holding a tray, which she sat on the ground before him.

"Hot soup," she said. "Warm bread. Cobbler and the promised tea—fennel, for your sour stomach. From their own herb plot. Are you cold yet? Lupe brought out a couple of blankets but was afraid to spread them over you in case you'd wake up and bite." She shook them out now, draping one over his legs, the other around his shoulders. He felt better at once.

"What about them?" He nodded at Em. "They're both in shorts. He's not even wearing a shirt."

She held her hand over the boy's naked chest. "Heat, rising," she reported. "Energy overload. Just as Alden said."

"Alden said," he mimicked, instantly ashamed of himself but unable to stop. "Why should we care what he says? Or what he wants, for that matter? What any of them want? Their plans have nothing to do with our own. Here's mine: the minute Em opens her eyes I'm getting us out of here. I've had a good rest. I'm ready to drive."

"And where will you take us, now that my yurt has become unsafe?"

"You can both sleep in the Doble. I'll park it in the woods near Clydestown and bring you food every few days. Once the posse sees how empty your yurt is they'll think you've abandoned it and lose interest. It is a long walk from Oren, after all. And then you and Em will be more secure there than anywhere else."

She brought her face close to his as if to make sure of his undivided attention. "What if she won't wake up until tomorrow?"

Feeling helpless, he said, "I have to be at the clinic early for the morning feed. It's part of my job."

"Alden made a fire in the living room hearth. We're going to tell stories. Come listen to our fascinating tales."

He laughed in spite of himself and looked longingly at the lit window. "I might lose my job if I stay."

"Could be."

"And then what would I do?"

"What, indeed," she said, looking up past the trees. "How bright the clouds are. Soon the harvest moon will break through them to light your path. If you must go tonight it will have to be without us."

He heard the determination in her tone and knew her mind was already made up.

"Here's what we'll do," she said firmly. "Em and I will stay for a week. Until your next day off. By then my little clearing will be safe again and we'll be ready to leave."

"A reasonable plan," he had to admit, although she obviously had not considered the many extra driving hours involved.

"Take my stuff out of the car before you drive off. I'll sort through it tomorrow. Meanwhile I'll ask Hertha to lend me one of her quilts for the night." She pulled the blanket tight under his chin, tucking in loose ends. "There's a reason we came, Driscoll. Beyond dreams and a lost dog. I want to find out what it is. Drive well. The week will be over before you know it." She thrust a parcel at him and gathered her cloak together. "Don't let your supper get cold."

He watched her shadow blend with that of the house, watched her slip through that brief rectangle of light. Soon the soup warmed his stiff bones. He began to thaw and then sweat. By the time he allowed himself to savor the first bite of Hertha's bread, infinitely more satisfying than the loaf he had bought from the Clydestown baker, he was smiling to himself. It was beautiful up here, especially when the clouds drifted away from the moon and it silvered the garden, the path, and the sleepers. "Happy dreams, Em," Driscoll whispered. "You'll have to tell me about them when I come back. I know Bena will take excellent care of you. Nada will too. Bena's right. This will all turn out fine." He refolded the blankets, plopped the berries he'd been saving into his mouth, and trusted the moon to guide him.

CHAPTER 13

LUPE SAT ON THE HEARTH STONES, FEEDING
sticks to the growing flames, their flickering light playing over the
sweater sleeves that covered the back of her hands. Hertha, sitting
nearby in Alden's chair, was hot enough to take off her vest. "Is
Driscoll all right?" she asked Bena when the old woman came to sit
at her feet on the braided floor rug.

"He appreciated the soup," Bena said, crossing her legs at the
ankles. "Where were we? I think you were about to launch your
tale."

"So I was." Hertha leaned into the cushions. "You grew up in
the last few good years. Your childhood was over before the troubles
began. I envy you that. What fine memories you must have. I was
only six when things started to go bad and too young to notice much
of what you probably took for granted. We were city people, or so
Mother used to say proudly although she and Dad had not left her
parents' farm until we'd celebrated my first birthday. 'I brought my
green thumb with me, see?' she'd laugh while she tended her plants.
She had transformed our apartment balcony into a lush garden, and
the yard below into a blossom paradise that stopped passersby and
had them standing in awe. I grew up pulling weeds for the sheer fun

of it. I had my own flowerbed by the time I was three. My bucket, shovel and rake were child-sized but real. I loved working beside her, copying everything she did, even the tunes she liked to whistle while she worked . . ."

Bena tilted her head and closed her eyes. "I see a riot of colors and shapes," she reported. "Black soil and the fine spray from a hose. It mists over petals and leaves, making a private rainbow that stretches from one end of a white picket fence to the other."

"Why, yes," Hertha said with a fond smile that instantly died when she glanced toward Anckar and saw her scowling at her sketchbook, where she had been rubbing shade into a drawing with her fingertip. Alden glanced uneasily at one of them and then the other.

"Go on, Hertha," he said, lying down flat on the rug. "We're listening."

"I was too young to notice the signs," she continued, looking inward now. "Too young to see what was happening outside our fence. For there must have been some warning signs . . ."

At the hearth, Lupe was shifting impatiently, feeding an arm-sized branch to flames that were painting her face orange and red. Hertha let her eyes rest with pleasure on the girl's finely chiseled nose, her strong chin, the hair reflecting only greens and blues. She heard Lupe yawn and mutter in a bored voice, "And then came the rains."

"And then came the rains," Hertha repeated, wondering if perhaps her friends were tired of the old story. Bena was a godsend in more ways than one. "In the night. While we slept. You've heard of the rains?"

"I was living in the woods by then," Bena said. "A lot of trees died."

"Trees and much more besides," Hertha agreed, glad of Bena's company, worried about Em, but not at all sorry that the unpleasant young Driscoll had refused to come in and join them. Hopefully, if or when he returned, he would have mellowed a bit. Everything was a shock to him tonight, of course, but next time he'd know what to expect.

LONG AGO AND far away, a very small Hertha stood on a high-up balcony, rubbing a night's worth of sleep out of her eyes. "Mommy? Mommy! The flowers fell down," she cried in dismay. Plants were sprawling *from their pretty boxes, tubs and pots, their stems liquefied, their petals shriveling as the little girl watched. And when she stuck her head through the iron railing—something she had promised her mother she'd never ever do again—she could see the whole downstairs garden destroyed, as if a giant had sat on it throughout the night. Her mother, rushing out of the sliding glass doors, knelt to pry Hertha's small fingers gently from the bars, then pulled her head clear.*

"Honey, you promised—" she started to say, but then, looking down, the alarm in her eyes rapidly changed to horror. "Bill, come out here, quick!"

Hertha's father emerged wearing striped pajama bottoms, a white towel draped around his neck. Half his face was shaved smooth, the other covered with fluffy cream. His intense blue eyes took in every detail. "Come inside. Wash your hands. Hertha's, too. Keep her upstairs." He ran downstairs just as he was, not even putting on his slippers. Hertha watched from the bay window as he poked at the ground. Straightening, he went to the picket fence and looked in all directions. When he returned to the apartment he stared right through her, making her fear she had become invisible. Then he fumbled with the dial of the clock radio they kept in the kitchen.

"Come on, Bill, I've got it right here. On the TV. They've preempted regular programming," Hertha's mother called from the living room. Hertha followed him to the couch and leaned against his knees as soon as he was sitting.

"State-wide," the man on the screen was saying. "Agricultural losses estimated to be in the billions . . ." There were pictures of flattened fields and of trees with shriveled leaves. ". . . deadly night rain," he went on. "Drinking water contamination . . ." Her mother's knee jerked, knocking a coffee mug off the table. She didn't seem to mind the stain spreading on the white rug. The screen was showing the inside of a supermarket, shelves lined with plastic water jugs, hands grabbing at them from all sides.

Decisively, her father wiped the fluff off his cheek, exposing a dark film of stubble at odds with the clean-shaven side. He hurriedly slipped on his clothes and snatched up his wallet and keys. "Call in sick for me," he said over his shoulder on his way out.

"MY FATHER came home from the supermarket rumpled and mad," the middle-aged Hertha recalled. "He had filled up a shopping cart with bottled water and when he wheeled it out to the car a couple of men started to grab the whole load. He grabbed it back but if the police hadn't shown up then he would have lost it all. I heard him tell Mother that those greedy men helped him see what he had to do next. After he locked the water in his car and made sure the police were staying to patrol the parking lot, he went back into the store with the cart and filled it up with camping food. Everyone else was only thinking as far as water but thanks to those men he understood just how bad it was liable to get. That's why he didn't unload the car until he was sure all the other tenants in our building were fast asleep. Then he brought our provisions up as quietly as he could while Mom guarded the front door. He didn't want our neighbors to envy what we had.

I couldn't get to sleep that night and hung on to Mom's skirt, listening to them talk. 'The shelves will empty fast,' he told her. 'And they'll stay empty. I'm just a little ahead of the mob, thinking things through. Once the power goes there won't be any energy for lights or refrigerators or stoves.' And then he did a strange thing. He let the air out of one of the car tires and brought up the spare and the jack. I saw him stash them in the back of the closet. He closed and locked all the windows, lowered every blind, and put the dead-bolt key in the lock from the inside.

The neighbors started to ring our doorbell a couple of days later, nice and polite, but soon they were hungry enough to pound. We tiptoed around the back rooms like a bunch of criminals. The TV stayed on with the volume so low that we could barely hear it ourselves. Mom saw the Browns carry suitcases to their car and drive off. The Feinsteins, from directly below, left soon after. But the Lindquists, downstairs to the right, they stayed. Until the warehouse riots. We saw the whole thing on TV."

"Warehouse riots?" Bena said. "That sounds grim. All because of the poisonous rain?"

"Dad called it the snowball effect," Hertha said. "It started with fear. People panicked, bought out the stores, beat up a couple of truckers driving in with fresh supplies, and helped themselves to whatever was in back of the trucks. The warehouses were heavily guarded by then. A national emergency had been declared. Everything was to be rationed. They were supposed to hand out food stamps, but it took too long to set it up.

I've never forgotten the warehouse riots. Hordes advancing, swinging clubs, rifle butts, sticks. Surging over the barricades. The guards were outnumbered and went down. When reinforcements finally arrived the mob had already broken in. People were fighting over boxes and carts. How much can you carry with just your bare hands? We saw the Lindquists in the crowd, behind a uniformed man who was being interviewed for the TV news. They pushed their way in with the rest of them.

It wasn't clear who shot first, the looters or the troops. Some of the looters had bottle bombs. A fire started inside. There was an awful explosion. Mr. Lindquist ran out with his clothes in flames. He fell down and didn't get up. His wife never came out at all—at least, she never returned to the apartment. A lot of people died in the warehouse fires but most died later when the riots swept through the streets.

That's when my father finally turned off the TV. 'Time for the basement,' he said. But first he got busy out in the yard. I watched him from the bay window, hiding behind pots of African violets and primroses as he smashed a few ground-floor windows, set a fire, let it char one of the outside walls facing the street, put the fire out, and tip over all the trashcans, spreading garbage around the yard and over the stoop. Then he came up to get me and I said good-bye to the plants in the bay window and to the rubber tree in the living room, the palm under the skylight, and the fern hanging over the bathtub. He had forbidden Mother to water them from the bottles he'd brought home. She and I cried as we ran our hands over the glossy leaves one last time. 'Are they going to die?' I asked her. When she didn't answer me I asked, 'Will we die too?'

My father took my hand, looked at me with his piercing eyes, and said with a resolute smile, 'Not if I can help it. I need you to be very quiet and brave. Think you can do that?'

I could only nod, because my throat had locked up."

A FLICKERING CANDLE. Dank, foul-smelling air. A rat, clinging to the side of the burlap sack that was swinging from the rafters, swept off with the broom only to be replaced by a bigger rat, and another. "You're not getting our crackers!" Hertha's mother whispered fiercely, her hair askew, her face smudged, cold hatred in her eyes. She gave a rasping cough and said, "Bill. I'm so tired. Bill."

He sprawled on the mattress, moaning, unable to rouse.

"I'll do it, Mommy," Hertha told her. "I'll take turns with the broom."

The rats were as big as alley cats, had long naked tails and sharp little teeth, jumped like kangaroos, and never gave up. Neither did Hertha as she stood on a chair with the broom poised while her mother sank into an uneasy sleep. Candle flames flickered. The room filled with advancing shadows, shifting shapes. "Get down," Hertha hissed, swinging. "Go away. It's ours. Ours." Her father staggered to his feet. "I'll do it," Hertha said. "You sleep. I can do it. I can." The rats were relentless. So was Hertha. But when her father roused enough to pry the broom from her stiff, pudgy fingers, she was asleep before he could pull the covers up to her chin.

"THE FIRST few days we heard shots and screaming," the adult Hertha recalled. "All far away. The voice on the transistor radio reported looting, desperate people ravaging houses, destroying cars, setting fires. Those with guns took from those who had none. The freeways were clogged. Bandits on bridges shot out windshields and ran down for the spoils. The city emptied. Dog packs roamed through abandoned neighborhoods.

The radio batteries gave out, then the food. When we were down to our last two jugs of water and the last box of crackers, my father unlocked the cellar door, opened it a crack, listened, and went out. He came back for the tire and jack a few minutes later. With his scraggly beard and hair he looked like a bandit himself. 'We'll leave around two in the morning,' he told us. 'Even hoodlums have to sleep sometimes.' Mom and he had already discussed where to go—the backwoods farm they had fled after high school. Now it was the haven they strove for, where surely Grandma and Grandpa were waiting with open arms. Wide fields. Plenty of good dirt. A fresh blue sky."

THEY CAME out of the cellar to a city that was an unrelieved black, the man carrying his frightened little girl, the woman close behind them with the remaining water and what was left of the crackers. The spare was on the car, ready to roll. As they started to drive their headlights cut through the dark, spot-lighting burnt-out cars that were parked any which way, smashed windshields, yawning car door, an arm sticking out here, a foot there, a pack of dogs busily gnawing on a limp hand from which the flesh fell easily.

"She doesn't have to see this. Hold her against you," the man said.

Hertha's mother pulled the blanket over the child on her lap, cocooning her, then absent-mindedly patting the little girl's back. "We'll run out of gas long before we get there," she murmured. "What then?"

"I'll fill the tank from the cans in the trunk. We'll find a working station. Or siphon from a disabled car. Plenty to choose from," he said.

The freeway appeared as deserted as the city streets had been except that here the abandoned cars lined both shoulders. Hertha got to climb to the rear and snuggle into a nest her father had prepared for her. "Good night, Princess," he said. "When you wake up we'll be where it's safe." As they neared the last overpass just before the city ended and the country began, there was a sudden crack in the windshield, flaring to the shape of a star, a hole at its center. The car veered to the left, then to the right.

"Bill!" Hertha's mother screamed. "Oh God, no. Bill!" Clutching at the wheel, she steadied it, tried to steer straight. The engine stalled. The car stopped. Thumb in mouth, Hertha struggled to climb to the front, wanting her mother's lap, but her mother gave her a hard push and turned on the inside light. Her father's head slumped sideways, his blood dripping all over her mother's blouse. Heels were drumming closer on the road. Hertha's mother turned off the light and cut the beams. Moaning, she heaved her husband's lifeless legs from beneath the steering wheel, climbed over him and squeezed herself into the driver's seat, her hands covered with blood. She restarted the engine, gunning the motor moments before the two shapes materializing at her side had a chance to grab at the door.

"Get down and stay down!" she yelled at Hertha, who was only too glad to submit. "Didn't Daddy tell you to go to sleep? Now do what you're told." Hertha did, as fast as she was able.

THEY DROVE into the farmyard in a different car so that the old man who was aiming a rifle at them from an upstairs window fired a warning shot in front of the tires. Hertha's mother sat bolt upright, both hands fastened to the steering wheel, her face white, her eyes as unfocused as those of a sleepwalker. "Grandma! Grandpa!" Hertha yelled out of her window. "It's us! It's only us!"

The old people rushed out to the yard. Hertha helped them pry her mother's ice-cold hands from the wheel and held one of them in her warm little pair as they guided her mother into the house and to her old room, which sat idle from one summer visit to the next. They put her in her girlhood bed and covered her with the familiar pink and green ruffled quilt, though they could not get her to close her eyes. "I just left him there. In our car. I have to go get him," she said each time one of them came into the room. She never got up again. Every day there was less life in those staring eyes, and then there was none.

It took them a long time to dig a hole for her in the hard ground. Hertha's grandpa wielded a pickax, her grandma fumbled with a spade, and

Hertha scooped with a small bucket. A desert stone marked the spot when they were done. The two old people looked at Hertha as if they'd never seen her before. "Now what?" her grandfather said, taking off his baseball cap just long enough to scratch at his bald spot.

"Now we eat," his wife said simply "Hertha gets Holly's room all to herself. And we teach her things. They grow up fast, as I recall."

"Too fast," he said. "By this time around I think she'll be the one left on the farm. I only hope we'll be here long enough to show her all that we know."

"MY GRANDMOTHER taught me about cooking," the grown Hertha remembered. "Plain food. There wasn't much of a variety of anything on their place. We had the orchard and a garden, but neither did well. We helped Grandpa build an indoor garden up in the sunroom, facing the back. In the outside garden, he kept using the lawful seeds, but for the upstairs veggie-beds we made from the best soil we could mix, he brought his stash out of hiding."

UNDER THE floorboards, hidden as carefully as bags of gold, were packets of forbidden seeds, the kind nature used to make. Her grandfather had squirreled this precious stock away, unwilling to use those rare seeds outside where they would surely get mixed up with the other kind. He kept them pure in the upstairs garden. The three of them lovingly tended the seedlings together, growing produce that tasted like real food—old timey tomatoes, salad greens, spinach, broccoli. That and Grandpa's grain horde, which would never grace the fields again, were the main parts of their diet, supplemented occasionally by the rabbits or snakes Grandpa's rifle stopped in their tracks.

Others had stolen the chickens, the livestock, and even their beloved elderly horses. Others had sneaked in the outside garden in the dead of night and ripped up not only the sickly crop but also the depleted soil it was trying to grow in. But no one knew about the upstairs garden, "the best kept secret in the world," as Grandpa so often said.

It was a tough, lonely life. Hertha learned to bring a gun when she gathered fuel for the rusty old wood stove out in the yard, where they cooked in the summer. In winter they used the one in the kitchen and kept all their firewood stacked along inside walls, out of reach of the thieves. They struggled to rebuild the outside garden mostly as a ruse so that the robbers wouldn't start suspecting about the treasures they harvested upstairs, away from prying eyes.

The seedlings were Hertha's babies, her siblings, her companions, her dolls. She told them how beautiful they would grow up to be and how perfect, and how very much they were welcome in the room that gathered the sun, with glass doors that slid open and shut and ceiling windows that admitted the sky. Unlike most of their neighbors, who kept to themselves, they still had a spring, gravity fed. "Just enough and not one drop more," her grandmother always said when she put a bucket under the kitchen spigot and watched it trickle in. As hard as they worked in the outdoors garden, every year it yielded less, the green fading little by little until it was gone, the same way the light in her mother's eyes had faded, as her grandparents faded while they waited for her to get big enough to fend for herself so that they could lie down and die.

"There's nothing left for us here," Grandpa explained. "This isn't the world we knew and loved. Save what seeds you can, add all you're able, and you'll survive until the world starts up again—hopefully before it's killed off all the good people who still walk upon it. We've done what we could. It'll be your turn next." When they died they weighed hardly more than the dried-out old relics of critters she found in the desert sometimes. She dug their graves within two weeks of each other, both times in the middle of the outside garden. It was the only place left where the ground would still yield to her shovel.

"AND SO I lived on, alone with my sunroom plant babies," Hertha told Bena. "I sang to them and talked to the bread I was kneading and to the trees that survived in the fields. When I got real stir crazy I'd walk the sagging fence lines and cobble rusting wire together as best I could. Years passed. I had wonderful dreams in brilliant colors, filled with friends who joked with me, danced with me. There were lots of books in the house but—you'll laugh—my favorites were Grandma's collection of cookbooks listing ingredients that were unheard of in our parts, with delectable pictures to show me what they ought to look like. I read the cookbooks like my grandpa used to read his Bible, lovingly fingering the pages, opening then at random, delighting in all that I saw.

It wasn't until I was in my forties that my night-time dreams started to include a certain man with long blonde hair, a bandana tied around it, his eyes the color of mist. They pulled like magnets, those eyes. He showed me pictures of the fiery hill and the clearing. He even showed me the incredible black soil lying fallow there, waiting for someone like me to work it. Every night I heard him whisper, "Come to me. Come climb the mountain. Come to me now." Maybe I never would have, but one day while I was out collecting firewood someone or something broke into the house, found the sunroom, brutally tore my friends out by the roots, strewed dirt every which way when they upended the beds and the tubs, and left me with what looked like mass slaughter.

I suppose I could have started again but the upstairs garden wasn't my secret anymore and soon the robbers would suspect about the precious seeds under the floorboards and pull them up too. So I did it myself, late that very night. I loaded them into the handcart along with my gun, added what was left of the grain and my favorite tools, covered everything with a pile of sticks, and walked to where my heart was pulling me. It took a long time; I traveled only by night. I wound up throwing the gun in a ditch because every time I looked at it I saw my father's dead face.

As soon as I arrived here Alden put me to work in his garden, which, you might already have noticed, has an abundance of truly miraculous soil. Everything I plant in it grows right before my eyes, greener and bigger than I could have imagined in my fanciest dreams. And everything tastes a hundred times better than the stuff we grew in the sunroom. Our clearing is the best thing this side of Eden, wherever *that* may be. And whatever we have can be yours too, Bena. Yours and Em's and even Driscoll's if he comes back. For as long as we stay here together."

CHAPTER 14

B̲ENA WAS LYING ON THE BRAIDED FLOOR
rug, so still that for one fleeting moment Hertha feared she was dead.
"Bena?" she cried, her voice shriller than she would have liked it to
sound. "Are you asleep? Did you miss the ending of my tale?"

The old woman opened her eyes. "Of course not. You said *if*
instead of *when*. It's *when* Driscoll comes back. And that will be next
week just as he said."

"Of course," Hertha agreed quickly. "I didn't mean to cast
doubt—"

"He's my friend. And he makes no promises he doesn't intend to
keep," Bena went on, just to make sure the message was clear. Then
she yawned. "That word you used. TV. It was a box with moving
pictures in it. Am I right?"

Hertha pushed her feet into her slippers. "Pictures and sounds."

"And the other word. Radio. I think I remember it too. Music
came out of it. And voices. Was it also a box?"

"Yes, but a smaller one. There were other kinds of these boxes,
all made of plastic and easy to smash. I think there are fake stars up
there even now, still talking to those smashed boxes, not knowing
they're gone. Isn't that right, Alden? Alden?" Hertha tapped her foot

down next to his head, startling him awake.

He sat up. "I was feeling around in my mind for Em. I think she's been in this room since you started telling your story."

Lupe crossed herself and scooted closer to the flames, but Anckar went to the window and pressed her nose to the glass. "Nope. Sorry to disappoint you but she's out there just as we left her, still asleep next to Brendan."

Alden dismissively flicked his wrist. "That's just her body. Her spirit broke free. It's out there and in here and everywhere. Listening. Learning. Collecting."

Bena smiled at the ceiling on the chance that an invisible part of Em was floating up there. "Collecting what?"

"Our lives," he said matter-of-factly.

She nodded. "You could be right. She's already learned mine." She clasped her hands behind her back and gave it a good stretch. The room was too stuffy; she was beginning to feel sluggish. If someone threw a quilt over her right now she just might roll on to her side and fall asleep in an instant

"And then mine. Obviously," Hertha said, sounding eager. "Who will go next? Alden, how about you? Tell us what made you come here in the first place."

"Me?" he said, cutting himself a piece of leftover cobbler. "Not much to tell. I grew up on a farm and led an excruciatingly dull life which would bore her and the rest of you to tears."

Hertha turned to Lupe. "Yours, then. Tell her about the nuns."

"My life is none of her business," the girl said, so incensed that she forgot to be shy.

"Never mind. No need to get prickly." Hertha cast around for another victim. Anckar was only one left and she was already scowling, but Hertha decided to ask her anyway. "You must have had an interesting life in the city. I wouldn't mind hearing more about it myself."

"You've been prying long enough, haven't you?" Anckar said. "I'm with Lupe. I'm not telling anybody anything, especially you."

It seemed to Bena that they were all a bit touchy about their pasts. Almost as if they thought they had something to hide.

"Let it go, Hertha," Alden said between bites. "Em will get the information she's after in some other way."

Bena smiled. "She'll dream your lives like she dreamed mine." She yawned, looking at Hertha. "Where do I sleep?"

Hertha seemed to have given the matter some thought. "The tipi's empty tonight. What with Brendan out in the yard and Odasan off in the woods . . ."

"No. I couldn't. What if he shows up in the middle of the night and finds me in his bed? I thought maybe the couch . . ."

"That's where Alden sleeps," Anckar said. "And my tent's too small for two people. So's Lupe's."

But Alden was in an expansive mood. "I'm willing to trade, just this once," he said, smiling at Bena. "You take the couch and I'll crawl into Brendan's sleep sack out back in the tipi. He's less likely to be as particular as our two girls."

Anckar was not amused. "Don't call me a girl. How would you like it if I called you a boy? Although, come to think of it, you sure act like one!" She tossed her sketchbook and charcoal sticks on a shelf and stomped out of the house.

"Wait," Lupe cried, scurrying after her. "Let me walk with you." In her haste, she left the door open, and Hertha called after her,

"Lupe, please shut the door before the moths start flying in." When there was no answer, she went to close it herself and stood leaning against the smooth wood, looking at Alden. "Is it my imagination or was Lupe more spooked than usual today?"

He shrugged. "She's always worse when Odasan's gone." He glanced at Bena and explained, "He's the only one who can make her feel secure."

"Usually, anyway," Hertha amended, collecting dirty cups and plates from the hearthstones and floor.

One brown moth had found its way into the room and was beginning to circle a kerosene lamp. Bena caught the agitated insect in her empty tea cup and released it out in the yard, watching it rise up and flutter away. Then she breathed in the crisp mountain-night air and went to check on the two sleepers. Brendan's skin gave off less heat than before but Em was still quite hot even though the harvest moon made her look like a cool alabaster sculpture. Nada, still at her feet, briefly raised her head, yawned, and curled herself into an even tighter ball. "I'm sleeping inside," Bena told the dog. "Bark if you need me." As she went back to the house, she wondered if Nada was the only one in the yard who could hear her.

Just as she started to go in, Alden came out, hugging a blanket. "I'm going to my thinking-rock for a while," he said. "It's roasting in there. Lupe stoked up the fire too high. You might want to open the door before you lie down. Just make sure you douse the light first."

"She's not used to the cold?"

"She grew up knowing nothing else," he said. "She considers sweating the ultimate luxury." He slung the blanket over his shoulder and melted into the night.

In the living room Bena found Hertha busy with sheets and a quilt. "Wait, let me help," she said, rushing to the couch.

"It's done," Hertha said cheerfully, shaking out the quilt and watching it drape itself over the entire length of the sofa. "I brought extra cushions in case you like to sleep with your head raised."

At the yurt, Bena had always rolled a blanket into a tube for that purpose. Nor was her usual pallet half as comfortable as Alden's couch.

Hertha stopped to rub at the mirror-smooth wood of one of the armrests. "Odasan and Brendan rebuilt all of our furniture. Lupe spent long hours sanding everything smooth. The day those three came to our clearing was a blessing for Alden and me. Our house was a wreck back then, and Alden—smart as he is—hasn't got one single carpentry skill. The only halfway usable room was the kitchen, but luckily Odasan is the kind of man who can do anything he sets his mind to."

"He sounds nice." Bena took the pillows Hertha was holding out to her. "He's Lupe's father?"

Hertha snorted. "Her father gave her away when she was a week old. To the sisters of Penitence. Poor thing."

"And who are they?"

"A bunch of crazy nuns who torture themselves for the Lord. They go to great lengths, Odasan said. He found Lupe in a ditch, where they had flung her like a sack of spoilt garbage. He said—"

Bena held up her hand. "Please don't tell me. It will give me bad dreams." She had lost any talent for idle gossip ages ago.

Hertha blinked at the rebuff and concentrated on tugging the quilt straight, her cheeks flushed. "Anckar's always complaining that I talk too much. Maybe she's right." She attempted a watery smile, nodding toward the hallway. "I sleep in the little room off the kitchen, if there's anything you need. We don't usually stay up this late. Obviously, breakfast will be delayed. But help yourself to anything you want from the pantry or the garden. Here." She held out a white nightshirt, waving it like a truce flag. "It's a bit large but it'll save your clothes from getting wrinkled."

"You think of everything," Bena marveled, though she liked to sleep in the nude. When she held the gown's collar up to her neck the ruffled hem pooled on the floor. "You've been so kind. Let's talk in the kitchen tomorrow, over some tea. Just the two of us."

Hertha's eyes glistened. Impulsively, she put her arms around Bena. "A womanly chat. That would be nice. You saw how off-putting Anckar can be. And Lupe, well, she's awfully young . . ."

Bena forced herself to hold still, fighting the panic close physical contact called up inside. After countless years of living alone, casual human touch from near-strangers was something she would have to get used to all over again. Gradually. "I hope you'll show me your entire collection of cooking gadgets, especially those you inherited from your grandma."

"You bet!" Hertha took one of the kerosene lamps with her. As soon as Bena was alone she blew out the remaining three lamps and the candles, changed in the dark, opened the front door, got under the quilt, and stared at the wooden ceiling, which was glowing with tints from the fire. The couch proved lumpy; apparently it was form-fitted to Alden's shape. Or was it just that she was unaccustomed to sleeping so high off the floor, surrounded by squared stone walls?

One of the walls in her yurt was nothing but a thick piece of canvass. She kept it rolled up and tied to the crossbeams for three seasons out of each year. It made the inside a part of the outdoors, the air fresh and full of the sounds of the forest: owls by night, songbirds by day, the breeze crooning through conifer boughs. She tied the tarp down in the winter, sacrificing light and air for stove heat. Hibernating in her murky den through the long nights, she sat close to the oilcloth window during precious daylight hours, twice removed from the sun, wove her baskets, stitched her quilts, and re-read her favorite books.

Compared to the round, open feel of her beloved yurt, this house was a trap, a rectangular box that wouldn't let her breathe properly. She tossed and turned on Alden's couch for half the night, kicking the covers into a ball and punching the pillows. At last she gave it up and rose to stand in the doorway, her eyes on the moon, which had traveled halfway across the sky. Gathering her bedding, she unrolled it next to Em and felt instantly better. She took one last look at the silvered girl and the bronzed boy, then pulled the quilt over her own face. "Good night," she murmured to anyone who was willing to listen, and was rewarded by Nada's answering sigh.

Sleep found Bena easily then, and just as easily left her again when an apple-green band appeared at the edge of the sky. The quilt was damp with dew. So was the borrowed nightgown. Quietly, she slipped into the house and put on her clothes. Then she walked briskly past the garden on to a faint trailhead leading up the opaque, wooded slope. She wrapped herself into her cape, welcoming its familiar embrace, and wove her way past massive trunks, veering up a steeply rising deer trail. It dipped in and out of a draw. The band at the horizon widened, turning turquoise and then pink.

As the moon paled she came to a high meadow and decided to sit on a downed log for her morning meditation. From there she had a good view of the dark kaleidoscope of clouds overhead, witnessing their gradual shifting through purple and red tones until they split apart to form a golden portal. A soft drizzle fell, hardly more than a mist, combining with the first ray of the still invisible sun. Together, drizzle and ray created a double rainbow that stretched across the wide sky to span the distant valley below, each end anchoring itself to a hillside. Through the rainbow's arches just below the cloud portal she spied a faraway chain of blue mountains. She let her eyes trace peak after peak.

When she looked back to the meadow she saw that she was no longer alone. A man stood beneath the rainbow, facing away, his hands raised to form a triangular window. His back tapered pleasingly from broad shoulders to lean hips. She wondered where he had come from so silently to stand motionless on the edge of the world. And then he began to dance, making sweeping gestures with his arms and legs, pivoting this way and that, crouching, kicking, and stretching his powerful body toward the blushing clouds. His hair was a luminous white, as was the suit he was wearing. The cotton belt, tied in a knot with long flapping ends, was a faded dark gray. His feet glistened with dew. At the end of his dance he leaped high off the ground, executed a double kick, and came down to stand bent over, chest heaving. Bena got up to leave. This was his meadow. She was trespassing.

Turning toward her, he said softly, "Don't go." His face was kind and strong, his slanted eyes an inscrutable black. "I am Odasan," he said, a smile crinkling the skin stretched over his prominent cheekbones. "Let us sit on your log together and watch the sun rise." Their gaze met and held, and in that instant the woods around Oren ceased to exist.

It was as simple as that.

No matter what she had promised Driscoll, she would not ride away from this man and this mountain on Saturday or ever again.

CHAPTER 15

ODASAN AND BENA ENTERED a kitchen smelling of roasted peppers and onions, toasting bread, and wood smoke. He insisted on holding her hand and she stood proudly at his side, feeling light and surefooted. Hertha, frying bread in two cast iron skillets, looked up from her task to focus directly on their joined hands. A shadow passed over her face but was replaced almost at once by a blossoming smile. "Oh," she said, her voice shaky but gaining in strength, "I see you two have met."

The others turned their heads to study the newly made couple. While Bena waited for some sign of approval, she heard dry sticks crackling and popping in the cook stove and some delectable concoction sizzling in a large pot on the glowing stovetop above. But what she saw was the growing alarm in Lupe's eyes, Anckar's disapprovingly raised brows, and Alden's utter befuddlement.

"We found each other up on the slopes," Bena said with a feeble attempt at a smile that none of her three censors returned. "And decided to watch the sunrise together. It was—breathtaking." She chose to omit the blissful hour that had come after. Perhaps the joy it had brought her still lingered in her eyes, or else why would Lupe's face close against her when she had been perfectly cordial the night before? There was no denying it, her gaze was frosty as it slid over Bena and thawed only slightly once it met Odasan' expectant look.

Lupe addressed him directly. "Aren't you guys a bit old for that sort of thing?" When he refused to react, she added, "I suppose this means you'll let her move into the tipi, since Brendan's in no condition to object."

Bena felt as if she had just been drenched in ice-water. But when she tried to yank her hand from Odasan's he refused to let go. Instead, he guided her to Lupe's side of the table and pulled out a chair. Obediently, Bena started to sit.

"Not there!" Lupe said sharply. "That's Brendan's chair."

Bena stopped in midair until Odasan pushed her down the rest of the way. "He won't be in for breakfast this morning, Lupe," he said mildly. "We just checked." He sat between them. "We are about to start a new seating arrangement. Brendan will sit on your left from now on. That way he won't have to talk to you over my head anymore." He put his hand on top of Bena's for all to see. "As for the tipi, it will be entirely his from now on. I've been thinking about building my own little house for some time. There's more than enough scrap lumber for what I have in mind. It needs to be used up before it rots. Is there some tea?"

Turning the bread in her skillets, Hertha gestured toward a big porcelain pot waiting on the counter and said, "Lupe, please pour."

Odasan favored each one of his friends with a dazzling smile. "Today I have watched the best sunrise of my life. Anckar, did you by any chance see the magnificent colors?"

She gave a laconic shrug from where she sat all alone on the other side of the table. "Of course. It's my job. Up here no two sunrises are alike." She thumped the notebook lying next to her plate. "I made some sketches from the lookout, double rainbow and all."

"Ah," he beamed. "Excellent. I wish to commission a painting of it, in full color, for my new house. I shall pay for it by stretching as any canvas frames as you think reasonable. And find you a new source of clay, since you mentioned last week your supply was running low."

"Suits me," Anckar said, leafing through her sketchbook. "Let me show you what I have in mind . . ." She started to slide it across just as Hertha arrived with the first platter of toast.

"Not now, Anckar," she said, decisively pushing the sketchbook away. She set the platter down on the middle of the table then went to give Bena a hug. This time, Bena did not feel smothered by it. In fact, she found it quite pleasant. "Do you realize that you and Odasan are our first pair?" Hertha said eagerly. "You might start a trend!"

"God forbid," Anckar muttered, rolling her eyes.

Ignoring her, Hertha urged Bena to eat, putting a slice of toast on the old woman's plate. "That there is hazelnut butter," she said, pointing, "and we have plenty of jelly." She slid three translucent glass jars toward Bena. Anckar snatched up the purple, Alden the blue. Hertha rescued the orange-colored jar for Bena. "Here, try this apricot jam, from our own tree. Lupe, fill Bena's cup first. She's our guest."

"Not anymore," the girl bristled.

"Please pour," Odasan said patiently, with a bit of an edge to his tone. Lupe obeyed while Bena spread nut butter over her toast and took a whiff of the jam. "Smells delicious," she said, recalling her mother's farm kitchen, fragrant on jam-making day.

"I canned the whole batch. By myself," Lupe volunteered, sounding proud in spite of herself.

"I helped pit the apricots, didn't I?" Anckar said grudgingly, holding her cup across to be filled. "So did Alden, as I recall."

"A double miracle," Hertha muttered, raising her cup so Lupe could pour for her too. But as Lupe reached over, the sweater sleeve pulled away from her wrist, exposing red puckered scars. In her hurry to yank the sleeve down again she spilled a trail of hot tea.

"Damn!" Anckar wiped her splashed sketchbook. "Clumsy girl. Watch what you're doing."

But Odasan was already blotting up the stain with his napkin. "No harm done, Anckar. Will it bother you if I sort through the lumber after breakfast?"

"Not in the least," she said tersely, slamming the pad on a chair. "As far as I'm concerned, the more you take the better. That grubby pile's been in my face far too long."

Meanwhile Alden had recovered from his astonishment. Leaning toward Hertha, he said in a discreet tone, "You were right. There's bound to be more couples soon."

Anckar's face darkened. She took a vicious bite out of her toast and said, "Including you two, I suppose. I'm surprised you haven't made your grand announcement before now. Personally, I've grown pretty tired of your cat-and-mouse games."

"What grand announcement? What games?" Alden sputtered, clearly confused.

"No need to get sarcastic, Anckar," Hertha snapped, moving the platter of toast out of her reach.

Just when Bena came to the conclusion that there was a lot to be said for living the life of a hermit in some dark, dreary woods, Odasan's foot found hers under the table and his slanted eyes twinkled at her. Immediately, the bickering around her faded to mere background noise as she listened to the blood singing in her ears. She never would have guessed that the lightest touch of another could make her feel so alive. "I can see they've stayed up past their bedtime again," he murmured into her ear. "It makes them sour as pickles." He piled her food on his plate, grabbed both of their cups, and whispered, "Come, I have something to show you." When they crossed to the door together they caused an immediate lull in the conversation.

"Hey, where are you two going?" Hertha asked. "We've barely begun. There are braised veggies and home-fries—"

"We're leaving it all to you," Odasan replied cheerfully.

"But we always eat together!"

"Not today. Too much squabbling in here," he said, already out in the hall. "I like a serene atmosphere with my meals."

Then Lupe shrilly delivered her parting shot. "I don't understand, Odasan," she called after him as he led Bena away. "If Alden is right we won't even be here this winter. Why build something you won't be here to enjoy?"

Out in the yard, Bena took a greedy breath of fresh morning air. "What did she mean, Odasan? Where will we go? I love this place. I don't want to leave."

"I was coming to that," he said. "First, let's examine the lumber."

She took the plate from him and followed him to the rear of the house. Firewood was stacked against the long wall from corner to corner, higher than she could reach. The pile of lumber on the far side hid a small green tent. Odasan pointed at it with one of the cups he was holding. "Anckar's. The little brick thing behind it is the kiln she and I built together." Another tent stood nearby, this one gray. "Lupe's," he said. Then he gestured at a third, much bigger than the other two and farther removed. It was supported by vertical poles and was shaped like a cone. "This is the tipi I shared with Brendan. In the winter we all sleep inside the house, the men in the living room and the women on the kitchen floor—except for Hertha, but her room's no bigger than a closet. Winters tend to be fierce at this altitude."

Bena wasn't sure she could get used to elbow-to-elbow living after a lifetime of solitude. "But Lupe said—"

He took her hand, nodding toward the garden. "Now I want to show you my favorite place so we can eat while the food is still reasonably warm." They settled on a small patch of lawn on the far side of the fence, shielded from the house by the orchard. The grass underneath them was well-tended. "I keep it trim," he said. "This is the only really private spot in the whole clearing. I've often thought of building a cabin right here. What do you say to two little rooms and a sleeping loft just big enough for one tiny couple?"

She laughed. "One room is what I've ever had. I wish I could show you my yurt. I pounded a stick in the ground, tied a vine to it, and scratched a wide circle into the dirt. The yurt grew around it like a cockeyed mushroom erupting after a hard rain. Is that what you had in mind?"

"I was thinking of something more . . . precise." He picked up a stick. "Let's plan out our kitchen. You first."

She took the stick and hesitated over a patch of near-black soil. "What are my choices? A square kitchen or a rectangular one?" She drew one straight line then laid the stick at his feet. "A box in a box, is that what you have in mind?" She crossed her arms. "You never did answer Lupe's question. And what's wrong with her wrists?"

"Ah," he said, weighing the stick. "I'll come to that after I tell you how the three of us came to this mountain and why Alden thinks we won't be here much longer. And when we're done with all of it we'll get back to discussing our new kitchen. Better yet, draw me a plan of your yurt. I am getting tired of rectangles and precise corners, myself. And a round house will be so much more interesting to build. My only aim, from now on, is this: to make you as happy as any man can make a woman."

Her soul swooped and rose so that for an instant it seemed that the ground was dropping away. "I couldn't be any happier than I am right now," she told him.

He regarded her closely. "Oh yes you can, Bena. This is just the beginning. Now I will tell you about Brendan and Lupe, my heart's children."

CHAPTER 16

LUPE TRIED TO STAND TALL ALTHOUGH SHE could feel her gown tremble along with her knees. She clutched at the high-backed chair on which the Mother had not invited her to sit. It was the only thing standing between them. The Mother's wilted cheeks were inflamed, her black habit puffed like the fur of a cat getting ready to pounce. "It has come to my attention that you have stopped using the whip," the old nun said in her most severe tone. "Show me your back!"

"No need." Lupe struggled to keep her voice resolute. "I've made no secret of it. I no longer believe that God commands us to tear ourselves to shreds. And I don't want to hurt anymore."

"God has seen fit to destroy our world, " the Mother reminded her. "We do this to save it. We have agreed to take on the sins of humankind and pay for their foolish mistakes. We are the lambs of sacrifice."

"Not me!" Lupe said, feeling the room tighten around her. She'd heard rumors of what happened to girls like her, rumors about what the old nun was capable of. But she had to go on. There was no other way out. "I won't use the whip or lie on my nail bed or cut myself ever again." She knew she was sealing her fate; her gown shivered from shoulder to seam. There was one final pause, a moment's reprieve. Then the Mother smiled, and Lupe knew she was lost.

"You won't?" the old nun said, suddenly calm. Then she took a fragile glass bell out of a drawer and rang it. Its pure sound lingered in the sparsely furnished room. Lupe's heart ceased pounding.

It started again when the door burst wide to admit the two burly nuns who had escorted her to the Mother's office. "Lupe has decided to leave us. Show her how it is done," the abbess said in a voice almost as delicate as the bell's.

It was useless to fight. Lupe's only resistance was to make herself limp so that the guards had to drag her out. They pushed her through a door she had not entered before, although sometimes she had heard the most wretched moans coming from within. While she tried to register the shackles and chains along its walls they fastened her arms to a post. Unlike prior victims, she made no sound as the horsewhip descended and only sighed briefly when it finally stopped. Once her hands were untied from the post the weight of her pain buckled her knees and she fell into a vast darkness out of the only world she had known.

She was glad it was over.

When she became conscious she was lying on a wagon. The face hovering over her belonged to a brown angel of mercy blessed with a dark halo of hair. "She's coming to, sensei," he said, dribbling water into her mouth. And then he offered her a radiant smile. "Hello! My name's Brendan, and I'm glad you're alive."

BRENDAN WAS the youngest in a clan of merciless hunters. His three brothers, like their father before them, kept honing their skills with rifles, arrows, and knives. Everything Brendan knew about killing he learned at their side: how to stalk deer, slaughter and skin them, how to tree bears and cougars with the help of the hounds, how to topple elusive mountain goats off their steep crags, a bullet for each.

One late evening he walked to the low end of town and saw Odasan dancing a few *katas*. Watching, he could feel invisible enemies vanquished in every direction. A man was big with a gun. Brendan wanted to be big without one. "Teach me," he said. "What will I need?"

"Absolute devotion," Odasan replied. "And a wide open mind."

Every morning thereafter, Brendan got up in the dark, went outdoors, and practiced a flurry of one thousand kicks, punches and blocks. When a hunt was planned he rose sooner. Every evening, without fail, he appeared on Odasan's doorstep to learn the next sequence of moves. One day, while he was practicing, he felt his entire brain light up and connect to his limbs in a new way so that they moved faster than the eye could see, than thought could allow. Although it only happened that once he knew it would happen again.

And then, on a hunt in the high hills, a rockslide pinned him, crushing his foot. He awoke in a hospital bed, hearing his brothers discuss amputation out in the hall. His hunting days were over. He recognized Odasan's voice, calmly counseling against surgery. "A crushed foot is easier to mend than a missing one," he told Brendan's brothers. What could they do but laugh at his foolish words and send him away, claiming only family visits were allowed? When Brendan refused the operation they laughed at him too, playfully punched his arm, and scheduled it for the following day.

Odasan came into the room after they had gone. "I'm leaving this place tonight," he told Brendan. "Lately my dreams show me a far-away mountain with a white top, a garden without weeds, and a man calling my name, inviting me in. You can come with me or not. There are other healers, you know. Elsewhere."

And so Odasan and Brendan, together, undertook the silent and agonizing task of moving his useless body out of the hospital window when they judged it was safe, to where a small donkey cart waited, cushioned with blankets and pillows. "Where's the donkey?" Brendan said. "I'm too heavy for you to pull by yourself."

"I couldn't find one this fast," Odasan replied "But watch me and see—nothing is too hard for a one-pointed mind."

The trip lasted for weeks because Odasan thought it best to avoid villages and towns. At last they came to where the road started to rise, and the land with it. Odasan stopped in the next village and managed to buy a worn-out old donkey to hitch to the cart. It was that evening, when the sinking sun painted the sky crimson, that they found a girl in the ditch that ran beside a high stone wall, near a metal gate locked from the inside. A small hand-lettered sign proclaimed: **ORDER OF PENITENCE**.

No one came when Odasan knocked. "She doesn't weigh more than a bird," he said, gathering the girl in his arms and carrying her to the cart. "How can we leave her? I'll push a bit harder. It was getting too easy anyway." With infinite patience he removed the blood-drenched rags caked to her wounds, wrapped her in a sheet, and put her beside Brendan so that the boy would be able to care for her. Then Odasan encouraged the donkey to move forward again. There was something about the wall and what was hidden behind it that made the beast want to apply himself to the task.

A week later, between the beast pulling and Odasan pushing the cart from behind, they made it to the last fork in the road. Without hesitation Odasan followed the lesser-used trail toward the mountain's white peak. Donkey and man strained step after step while Odasan kept his eyes focused somewhere above. Brendan trusted the unwavering determination in those black eyes. He had no trouble believing that Odasan would have made it to the top on sheer willpower alone, but they were overtaken by three strangers returning from market. Hertha, Anckar and Alden stopped bickering long enough to add their combined strength, such as it was, and helped bring Brendan and Lupe safely home.

The donkey ran off as soon as Alden unhitched him. No one ever saw him again. Hertha concocted a salve to apply to Lupe's wounds but she could do nothing for Brendan's foot. "Others will come and know what to do," Alden consoled him in his vague, distant way. Brendan demanded more clarity but Alden could not give it. He seldom could. Hertha said it was because he lived too much in his dreams where words did not matter. But Brendan insisted that these did and sat whittling, waiting, and watching for those who could make him whole again.

WHEN ODASAN's story was over Bena told him her own. Afterwards they put their heads together and scratched circles and lines into the dirt. "A bay window here, facing the garden, for our breakfast nook," she said, looking up to find three woebegone creatures standing before her like sheep cast from their flock.

"Hertha sent us out here to apologize," Lupe confessed. "And to ask if there is anything we can do to make up for our rudeness besides saying we're sorry—which we are."

"She threw us out of the kitchen," Alden said, sounding amazed. "And she promised we won't get another hot meal until you decide to forgive us."

"I think this time she means it," Anckar added. "So tell us—

what do you want us to do?"

Odasan sat resting his chin on steepled hands. "You first," he told Bena gravely.

"Well." She hesitated, waiting for an idea to present itself. "I did ask Driscoll to unload my things when he left. There should be a pile of stuff at the end of the road. Maybe you'd like to fetch it."

Odasan gave an approving smile. "They'd be delighted. Lupe and Anckar will carry it home on our stretcher and Alden will help me cut and peel some straight poles."

"Cut?" Alden asked with little enthusiasm. "Peel?"

"We'll need the bow saw, Alden. And both of the axes."

Alden gave a reluctant nod and wandered off to the rear of the house. The two women left too, but Lupe soon stopped and called back to Bena, "Oh, I almost forgot—Hertha said to tell you she'll be most pleased to show you every gadget we have in the kitchen whenever you're ready."

"Thank you, Lupe," Bena called back, taking pains to keep her voice gentle. "I appreciate the message."

Lupe rewarded her with a grateful smile.

As soon as the three supplicants were out of sight Odasan said, "Well done!"

"This couldn't have been easy for them."

"Not easy," he agree, stacking their dishes. "But necessary just the same. I hope you're ready to admire Hertha's gadgets right away. It will make her happy, and when she is happy she cooks outstanding meals for us. It's a pity she has no patience for my rice, though. It always turns out a little bit mushy or scorched."

Bena rose and picked up the dishes. "Rice?"

"The only food necessary to my on-going peaceful existence," he sighed. "Although it's increasingly hard to get. Unlike the potatoes Hertha keeps trying to interest me in."

"Tell me how you like your rice cooked and I'll do it from now on. If Hertha won't mind."

"Another dream come true," he beamed. "A bowl of perfectly steamed rice at the end of our day." He explained each simple step until they were both sure she understood every nuance of the delicate process. Then he kissed her on the cheek and, enraptured, watched her walk back to the house. Some people threw away treasure without knowing its worth. Others recognized value through any camouflage it might assume. That had always been his gift. His

111

much wished-for family was now complete.

Waiting for Alden, he measured the lawn, first with his eyes then with his steps, pacing off a circle to see if there would be enough grass left for him to dance his katas at sunrise and sunset. He would add a small deck too so he and Bena could sit, talk and sleep together outdoors in comfort and style.

Odasan knew that Alden had an aversion to tools. No doubt it would be a while before he could bring himself to collect and deliver all three. Not one to waste time, Odasan bent his knees to sink into a low horse stance and slapped the hard muscles of his anchoring thighs to remind them what they were capable of. Then he flowed into what rank beginners mistakenly assumed was one of the easiest katas, concentrating his whole being on each slow-motion move. Thus he missed hearing the murmur of two distant voices. He worked his way through the kata twice more, sinking deeper into the horse stance each time until he felt his thigh muscles quiver in protest.

It was then he became aware of the familiar shuffle-and-drag still capable of bringing grief to his heart. It was the sound Brendan made, walking. By the time the boy reached him, carrying the bow saw and the axes, Odasan had willed his face into a relaxed smile.

"There's a princess lying on the grass over there," Brendan said, nodding back at the yard.

"There was a prince lying beside her until some minutes ago," Odasan told him.

Brendan put down the tools. "Alden decided to help with the stretcher instead. You weren't really going to start building your cabin without me, were you? You and me, we're a team. Alden doesn't have the right sort of muscles for our kind of work."

"And doesn't want to acquire them," Odasan chuckled, taking both axes. "You look as if you've just returned from an expensive vacation."

"I feel like it too," Brendan said. "The funny thing is I don't remember a thing except—you know how you're always wanting me to meditate and I can't?—well, I think now I can."

Odasan gave him a brisk slap on the shoulder, keeping his hand there to lend unobtrusive support as he matched his steps to Brendan's. They went into the forest in search of the straightest poles they could find.

CHAPTER 17

SOMEONE WAS CALLING HER FROM BELOW. She plunged toward the caller and hovered. It was the boy Brendan, who had traveled with her part of the way before he got lost. Now he sat close by her earth-body, which lay in the dark yard showing no signs of life. "Em?" he whispered, as if afraid of being overheard. "Are you in there?"

"Of course not," she said. "I'm up here." But it was obvious that he couldn't hear her.

"How come I'm awake and you're not?" he asked. "Where did you go, without me? What do you know that I don't?" He looked at the space beside her he had so recently occupied as if wishing he were lying there still. "Will you come back and wake up so you can tell me all that you saw?" He bent to study every inch of her face. Odasan had assured him she was still breathing but he could see no trace of it, even this close. Then he felt another presence and looked up to see Lupe standing behind him, casting a shadow over Em's face.

"Who are you talking to?" she asked suspiciously.

He gave her a moment of disapproving silence before he said, "Don't you have some chore you need to get done?"

"Don't you?" she said with a pained look at him and the dog

114

lying at Em's feet. "I guess Nada is hers now. That dog hasn't moved since you both . . . fell." Without being invited, she sat at Em's other side, pulling at her skirt to cover her ankles. "What was it like when the lightning struck?"

A surge of conflicting feelings streamed through him so fast that he could not begin to sort them out, but he recognized among them a rush of joy and a touch of envy. "Nothing I can put words to," he said, wanting to be honest. "Except that there was more power in me than I could make room for, or Em could either, I guess. That's why it knocked us out. Only she managed to flow with it better than me."

Lupe shook her head. "Like, how?"

He tried to explain. "You know how an eagle glides, sailing the updrafts so easily with those wide wings? Em's that eagle. I was only a crow, flapping for a while in her wake."

"You were not!" Lupe cried. "I've seen your wings!" She leaned toward Em. "Can she hear us, do you think?"

"I don't know."

Lupe blew on Em's face. There was no reaction except that a curl slid over one of Em's eye-lids. Without thinking Lupe reached to brush it aside. The curl crackled, reared, and hissed at her finger.

"Lupe!" Brendan warned.

She moved her finger away and the curl settled over Em's lid again. She moved the finger closer and the curl rose like a snake. And then Em opened her eyes. They were terrible to behold. The irises were like two bright-yellow wheels, the pupils the hubs. The left pupil was the size of a pinprick, the right one had taken over most of the iris, out to the rim. Lupe gasped and scooted away but Brendan put his face so close to Em's that their noses were less than an inch apart. If they touched, would he go where she was, or would he simply disintegrate and disappear forever?

"Brendan, don't!" Lupe cried.

He peered at Em's eyes as if he wanted to dive in.

"She's so weird she's scary!" Lupe said.

"Weirder than you?" Brendan asked. "Weirder than me?"

"I'll be glad when that Driscoll comes back to fetch her," Lupe said. "We'll do just fine without her." Averting Em's staring eyes, she scratched a circle into the dirt. Or was it an eye? Around and around her finger went, finally stabbing the center. "Without Bena, too," she added darkly. "So everything can go back to how it was before they came."

Em 's lids came down as suddenly as they had gone up. Brendan straightened. "You don't know what you're talking about, Lupe. They wouldn't have come if they didn't belong here. Nada wouldn't have brought them. Besides, we're pretty much stuck without Em, aren't we? We didn't mean to stay here forever. I want us to move on."

She paled. "Well I don't. Why can't what we have here be enough for you? Everything's fine just as it is. As it *was*, before they showed up."

"If you really think that then you're fooling yourself," he said. "This place has become static." He inspected the house, the garden, the tarp he had helped Odasan stretch in front of the new building site so that Bena couldn't track the progress of their labors. "It was only supposed to be a way station. A collecting point. An apprenticeship program. She's going to take us to the next level. So Alden says. And Odasan too."

Lupe hunched her shoulders. "You all act like she's so special," she muttered, savagely scratching lines from the center of her dust circle to its rim. "But when I look at her I see nothing but a freak. I bet she'll prove to be utterly useless. A freak and a dud."

Brendan looked at her coldly. "Go scrub a floor," he said. "Or stitch on one of your pillows, why don't you? Nobody's making you sit here." She flinched as if he had slapped her but for once he was tired of tiptoeing around her easily bruised feelings. He stared at her, deciding he had nothing he wanted to add.

She waited as if she expected him to say he was sorry. But he wouldn't, not this time. "All right then," she finally said, blinking back tears, standing up, smoothing her skirt, and yanking the sweater sleeves down over her knuckles. "Be that way. See if I care."

"She's part of all this." He swept his hand over the clearing. "As much as you and me and the others. We're some kind of family. Can't you tell? Just look at what you drew."

She glanced at the dust circle and shrugged.

"It's the wheel," he said, counting each line raying from hub to rim. "The ten-spoked wheel. The reason she came. The reason we're all here."

Quickly, Lupe erased the drawing with her foot, sobbing, "We *were* a family, you mean. Before Bena took Odasan from us. And now Em's stealing you. With her crazy eyes and her skinny long legs." And then she ran off, leaving prince to princess.

He couldn't keep himself from calling after her, his voice soft and urgent at once, "Lupe! Nobody's stealing me! Nobody would want to!" But she was already rounding the corner. She'd cry herself to sleep in her tent, as usual, and come in to supper with a freshly scrubbed face and damp blood-shot eyes, smiling at him as if she'd forgiven him for God only knew what. She was like a sister to him but in all the time he'd known her he hadn't managed to figure her out yet. Was it his fault that he knew nothing about females? His mother had died before he learned how to crawl; he was raised by four gun-toting men.

SOMETHING was calling her down to the earth at the end of the day. It was the irresistible scene of her forever-friends sitting together to work side by side, all of them achingly lovely in soft lamplight in a homey, colorful room. One of the chairs at the table was meant for her. Soon she would claim it.

Lupe was bending over her linen square, adding one delicate stitch after another to a sharp-tipped triangular fir. A nearby lamp burnished her braids and showed the precise part she'd drawn with her comb at the end of her afternoon nap. Her cheeks were still shiny from the pre-dinner scrubbing she had given her face. Brendan, sitting on the hearthstones, glanced at her every now and then as he whittled his latest soupspoon, taking care to carve the ladle nice and deep. Anckar hunched at the outermost edge of their circle of light, her tongue sticking out as she squinted at the greenware plate she was painting with wildflowers. Odasan and Bena shared a kerosene lamp between them. He blew into the recorder he had just finished sanding, tonguing the high E.

"Strong and clear," Hertha said, sifted through a basket of dried flowers. "As usual, your work is too good for the back shelf of that store. Worth ten times the price Tilden has set. If his customers knew what bargains we're providing they'd be less picky." She looked at Bena, hard at work sanding another recorder. "This is the way we spend our evenings, Bena. I make the silly little sachets and dry flower arrangements that sell the best while Anckar's gorgeous hand-painted crockery hardly brings in more than plain dinnerware. And since Mira has decided we're garbage we have to deliver our goods after hours, to the backdoor. Like smugglers. Or criminals."

"Mira's the one who put that awful sign in the store window," Lupe said, cutting a short piece of green embroidery thread from a spool.

"Tilden could have made her take it out again," Anckar sniffed.

"But instead he's making us barter for broken sacks of grain and damaged merchandise no one else wants. He's cheating us left and right and we can't even complain."

Brendan brushed a small pile of wood chips into the hearth. "It's a good arrangement for him and he knows it, even though he likes to pretend that he's doing us a favor out of the goodness of his heart."

Hertha sighed. "The man's hen-pecked. But he runs the only grocery store in town. And Mira isn't the only female I know who throws tantrums." She looked meaningfully toward Anckar who luckily remained oblivious, her eyes on the plate, her tongue once more sticking out. "Mind," Hertha continued, smiling at Bena, "he doesn't admit to being a mere storekeeper. The white coat he insists on wearing has the word 'Pharmacist' stenciled on it. Everything seemed fine the first time we went to see him, though he claimed our good produce was hexed. So we put the excess by for the following winter and started to make craft items instead. The first winter Alden and I spent up here alone was the hardest. We had nothing then, and no one except each other."

"Not that again," Anckar muttered.

Hertha stopped smiling. "You weren't here at the start," she snapped. "By the second winter, Odasan and Brendan had taken the barn apart and used most of the lumber to fix up the house. But when I first arrived this place was a total wreck. Alden and I suffered through the worst storms and the deepest snowdrifts I could have imagined. Half the roof gone. Holes in the walls. Every window broken. As cold inside as outside. Not much to eat that first year except for what I had brought with me. Alden thought he could live on water and air. He nearly did, too, although he didn't mind flapjacks and beans one little bit."

"You can make sawdust taste good," Alden said mildly from his easy chair, head tilted back, arms spilling over the armrests.

"I might have left if I could have fought my way out through the drifts," Hertha said. "Except by then I had already seen what our soil could do and felt the power of the clearing."

Lupe squinted at the eye of her needle, trying to work her bit of silk thread through it. "Is it true that a coven of witches lived here before us? And that the town folks think we're their spawn? That's what Mira called me that one time I went to town with Odasan and Anckar."

"No one knows who they were," Hertha said. "Not where they

came from, or why they left in such a hurry. Maybe Mira just didn't like the color of your braids. I did ask you to wear a scarf, remember?"

"What difference would that have made? It couldn't have hidden my brown face, could it? Or Odasan slanty eyes, or Anckar's fickle temper. Try hiding that under a scarf!"

Anckar frowned down at her plate but said nothing. "Good point," Hertha continued. "Which is why I go by myself nowadays. With a black old-lady shawl on my head, in my dowdiest rags. Makes the people of Yates feel more secure."

Bena put down the recorder piece she had been sanding. "Town folks never had much use for me either. They chased me out of Oren like a dog. After that I sold my baskets in Clydestown for a while. Until my fame spread. You don't have to look different to frighten them, just think different. They smell it out. It scares them."

Hertha was stuffing blue petals into a small pouch. "I wish we could deal direct with the city. Our looks would matter less there. Funny that our Anckar was too odd even for them."

Startled, Bena glanced at Anckar and caught her rapidly escalating scowl. Whatever was wrong between the two women, she wished they could bring themselves to declare a truce. Then Alden said Em's name, addressing the ceiling. He made it sound like a hum. Bena looked up to see what he saw, missing the moment Anckar lost control and threw her pretty plate against the wall. They all ducked as the pieces rained down.

When Hertha had recovered her equilibrium, she said drily, "Too bad about that plate, Anckar. If you'd just sit a little closer to the light you'd see better. Make fewer mistakes."

Anckar jumped to her feet, shaking with rage. The paints she had arranged on an oilcloth spilled every which way. "Stop trying to *mother* me, fool!" she yelled. "The first one I had was bad enough. Maybe I'm not cut out to paint crummy plates for the townies, especially by the so-called light of this kerosene lamp. I'm sick of its stink, this stuffy room, and everyone in it. I need air!" She rushed out, slamming the door.

Em trailed in her wake like a cool draft and followed her into the green tent. She hovered, unseen, as Anckar threw herself on to her pallet to stare at the tent ceiling with trapped, desperate eyes. 'I'm an artist!' she sobbed furiously. "Famous!"

Em dipped to immerse herself in those haunted eyes and lost all sense of herself.

EM'S WHEEL

CHAPTER 18

ANCKAR WAS BORN IN A HOLE IN THE WALL. That was the way her mother referred to the village they had been forced to move to when the city died. Right away, Mrs. Field noticed there was something wrong with her baby's eyes. They saw too much. Mrs. Field found them shocking and avoided looking at Anckar whenever possible. Why couldn't she just be cute and adorable like other babies her age? With less piercing eyes? As much as Mrs. Field tried, she couldn't disguise the distaste she felt when she had to change the child or wash her face or feed her.

"I can't bear to touch my own daughter," she often whispered to her husband. "What am I to do?"

"Why, nothing, my dear," he would answer. "You're just a bad match. It happens."

His words were a comfort to her.

As Anckar needed her less Mrs. Field found it convenient to turn a deaf ear to the little girl's wails. It was amazing how many ways there were of not touching a growing child.

Anckar was confined to her crib on the day she first noticed that every little thing around her had eyes and was therefore alive. Even the wall paneling had faces in its swirls of wood fiber, some of them seen only once and never again, others becoming faithful companions. Shifting forms unfolded for her in every direction. No two lines were the same, nor were two days ever alike. Each morning had its own unique color, taste and smell, enticing her to look through the window at the sky beyond.

When she was ready for more she found a way to climb out of her crib and on to the sill to study passing clouds. Her mother soon learned to ignore the teetering child, for Anckar was better at climbing than Mrs. Field was at keeping her safe. Anckar kept her own self safe somehow, or perhaps she had a host of invisible angels spreading their cushioning wings all around her. Soon she taught herself to crawl down the stairs backward to stand on wobbly legs and rattle the doorknob until the door sprang open. Then she crept out into the yard and was instantly mesmerized, for everything in it moved and changed and spread out before her

Clouds sailed overhead, creating magnificent shapes with the aid of wind and light. Some of these shapes she recognized from picture books as thundering horses, great sailing ships, hounds giving chase. Weaving in and out of the clouds, gray geese flew in arrow formation, long necks stretched, yellow feet neatly tucked under.

Countless creatures crawled in the grass, among them ants and grasshoppers and gleaming metal-green beetles. Grass-flowers were like tiny white stars. The edge of the adjacent meadow was carpeted with buttercups. Puddles were bug lakes on which the breeze blew insect-high waves. There were creatures walking on water, which had a skin like milk, only invisible. Fat red worms made waves with their own bodies.

That spring Anckar was content to sit on the damp ground and watch. By summer she was up on her feet, toddling across the meadow all the way to the creek. She studied how its water flowed, what swam in it, and what sank to the bottom. She began collecting the most intricately colored rocks, the most fragile weed flowers, the heads of wild grasses.

In autumn she was drawn to a grove of trees on the far side of the meadow, where she gathered falling leaves. Her favorites were golden on one side and silver on the other. She picked hot-pink poison oak leaves without getting a rash, stuck them on the inside of her bedroom window, and sat enthralled as the evening sun transformed each leaf into a shard of stained glass.

It was a relief to see how contentedly the child played by herself. It kept Mrs. Field from the odious task of having to separate her from the ruffian village youngsters down the lane who picked their noses and scratched impetigo scabs off their crusty knees. If there was something decidedly odd about a toddler who was so easily mesmerized by every little thing around her, it had its compensations, for Anckar could be left to her own devices from dawn until dusk. Unless someone put a scrap of food in front of her every now and then she'd forget to eat and never know she was hungry. Mrs. Field discovered that once she started to put a whole day's worth of snacks on a tray in Anckar's room every morning, Anckar became self-sufficient at the age of two. Of course, one had to take care not to make the rations too eye-appealing or else the child would stare at them all day in delight and never think to take the first bite.

For her third birthday, Anckar's parents gave her a box of crayons and a coloring book. She soon discarded the book and colored her white walls instead—in most pleasing ways, Mrs. Field was the first to admit. Nonetheless, she took care to supply plenty of paper thereafter, starting with long butcher rolls pinned to the wall. They kept Anckar enthralled for weeks. But soon she used any surface that came her way to interpret the worlds she saw unfolding in every moment and every direction.

Anckar was seven the first time she spoke. "Paint," she said, carefully annunciating each letter. Then she continued, as if she had practiced for days, "I want real watercolors and oil paints and brushes. Please."

With Mr. Field's connections that was easily arranged. Generous art supplies arrived as Anckar's birthday gifts yearly thereafter. By and large, her mother had to admit, Anckar was easier to take care of than most kids her age, even if she never learned to be cute. But then her parents, terminally bored by country life, made the intelligent and far-reaching decision to move back to the city, which, to their delight, was undergoing resurrection and was drawing its former inhabitants the way bees are drawn to their hive. The Fields were at the head of the boarding queue before the first restored train could arrive on newly patched tracks,. They rode back to where they belonged and where Anckar did not.

In the city she lost the wide sky to a maze of brick buildings. No creek danced through the fields of gray concrete boxing her in. No silver and gold leaves shone. No green beetles sparkled like jewels on tall blades of grass. All the worlds she had known condensed into one world that slowed, stood still, and faded to shades of gray. For the first time she felt alone.

The Fields helped overhaul their old neighborhood. It earned them squatter's rights in a brownstone they fixed up for themselves. Anckar got the upstairs bedroom with the most windows, overlooking a cement courtyard. For weeks her parents went around with hammers in their hand and nails in their mouths. Those were exciting times, full of policy meetings and rules to be written. Despite the community gardens that sprang up in every unpaved nook food was a problem. The Fields built the first family sized algae tank and taught others how to make the green scum palatable.

Later, of course, the Harvey brothers took over, building giant commercial tanks and hiring people to work them. They donated the leavings of the manufacturing process to the gardens. Those leavings turned out to do wonders for depleted soil. With the Harveys' financial assistance, the Fields spent their days experimenting with hydroponics and their evenings planning and hosting community events. They were glad their strange daughter stayed out of the way.

By the time Anckar had grown into a charmless young woman, the city grid was firmly in place. The Harvey brothers were solidly established as the primary manufacturers of the many algae products they invented, from green snack bars to green smoothies to green Harvey loaves. In their greedy, capable hands, the hydroponics thrived. So did the algae-sludged gardens. Reclaimed parks, fertilized with algae waste, made the whole neighborhood smell like a fish tank.

Soon the Harveys opened their own bank. "A hand in every pie," Anckar's dad would murmur admiringly as he rattled the evening paper.

Other girls her age wore tool belts strapped to their hips, but no one expected that much from Anckar. In fact, by this time it was an unspoken neighborhood agreement to expect nothing from her at all. Like a feral cat she shunned daylight, emerging at dusk in search of the odd patch of grass. She would sit under one of the nursery sized park trees and listen to the tentative chirping of hidden crickets, the lonely cooing of underfed pigeons, the occasional insult yelled by a territorial squirrel. Often Anckar stayed in the park until first light, facing in the direction of her far-away childhood home.

When they had first come to the city her parents enrolled her in the new school but Anckar proved to be a constant source of embarrassment. Her teachers were forced to send home note after note. Anckar would not participate. She did not complete her assignments. She stared out of the window and did not respond when she was called upon. She was frequently teased and then suspended for throwing a well-aimed rock at the girl who ran off with her lunch pail. She was expelled after she took an angry bite out of the class bully's fat cheek. Then and there, her parents decided to keep her out of school altogether. They talked of home schooling but nothing came of the idea. Why bother as long as she was content in her room?

She seemed happiest when they went out and left the apartment to her. But one night they were giving a party downstairs and Sam Harvey mistook her bedroom for the spare powder room. He walked in without knocking and discovered her jungle of paintings, stacked every which way, with little space left for a cot and an easel. That night her life took a turn for the worse.

"Holy Christmas!" he said. "I've found Anckar's own secret garden. We've had this treasure in our midst and didn't know it. Young lady, you're the girl with the golden eye." He shuffled canvases and pulled out this one and that—the bigger the better was the motto he lived by. When he had gathered a great stack of them he opened his bulging wallet, asking, "How much for the lot?" She told him her paintings were not for sale and showed him the way to the bathroom. As soon as he was out of her room she locked her door, but Sam didn't mind. He knew just how to proceed. Before the evening was over he took her father aside, whispering words such as, ". . . great discovery," and, ". . . gold mine!" into Mr. Field's astonished ear.

They schemed to meet the next evening, waited for Anckar to take her usual after-dark stroll, and entered her room. Sam collected another sizeable stack and, to her parents' surprise, paid handsomely for them. In cash. "She owes us," Mrs. Field told her husband after Sam left. "For years and years of supplies. Don't you think? Besides, her room's so overcrowded she can't possibly miss what he took." To their further surprise Anckar sniffed out her losses at once and demanded the canvases back. It was unthinkable, of course, for Sam had done the Fields many favors and hopefully would do more. After that night Anckar was careful to keep her door locked whenever she went out, but it was too late.

At Sam Harvey's next penthouse party the guests were stunned by the luminous artwork gracing his walls. "It's like sitting in an old-fashioned meadow. Such detail! What colors!" they raved. "Who's the artist? We want some of her paintings too." To own a painting signed by Anckar became the new status symbol. She could not escape her fame. Strangers sidled up to her on the stoop at dusk, determined to at least shake her hand and offer their compliments. They were happy with any grunt she gave in response. Her first refusals only brought higher offers.

"It's like being there," a teary-eyed old man whispered when she relinquished the picture of a small turquoise beetle caught in a dew-pearled spider web.

"It makes me feel like a child again," said another, standing in front of the picture of a field of golden wheat swaying in the wind.

"She's been painting her memories," her father said. "Even the clouds she saw from the nursery window."

Anckar was invited to every party. Soon she became the main event. Everyone knew her face and her name. They told her she was the greatest artist the city had ever known and that she had an obligation to share the beauty only she knew how to create. So she made pictures of the tree seedlings in the park, silhouetted against a pristine sky and surrounded by rubble; of clouds racing by; of leaves and crickets and doves.

Everything she painted was in demand as long as it matched the décor. Her sparse words were treated as oracles until even she was impressed by her clever new phrases. The Harvey brothers took her under their combined wings, donating prime space for a gallery. Sam's wife set herself up as Anckar's agent. Orders poured in for more and bigger canvases—something to go with the couch and the curtains. Her still-lifes became the most popular: round, glistening apples, plump yellow pears, purple grapes.

Al Harvey, the youngest, experimented with algae wine and liquor. Nightlife flourished. "Drink your dinner in a shot glass," was his new slogan. "Your daily vitamins, the fun way . . . the healthful way . . . Al's way!"

His algae liquor was green, creamy, and potent. Anckar liked how the colors around her glowed brighter after the first glass. The second glass built a comfortable bridge between her and the rest of the world. She shared smiles with other revelers once she'd downed the third. The fourth loosened her tongue. By the time she had finished her first bottle she was convinced her parents had always loved her and wanted only what was in her best interest. She painted more still-lifes to go with the couches and drapes. She painted common garden flowers and vulgar red sunsets, favorite old dogs, and, most of all, the children of the rich who must always be rendered flawless no matter how they looked to the naked eye.

It was Al Harvey's little girl, Anastasia, who gave her the most trouble in that regard. He doted on the child, convinced she was the image of his petite wife, when, in actuality, she looked just like him and his brothers. Thus, he became Anckar's first critic. No one else would have dared. He refused the first baby portrait, and the second. "Her eyes aren't that close together. Her nose isn't that long," he complained when Anckar unveiled the third try. "This isn't good enough. I see you have no talent for doing portraits."

"I don't?" Anckar growled, hurling the canvas at the nearest window. It caused a most satisfying explosion of glass before it sailed out of sight. Unable to stop once she got started, she tossed every canvas within reach after the first. Then she pitched all her empty algae wine bottles on top of the heap, and in a final frenzy of rage heaved her entire stash of fulls over the sill. They broke spectacularly, making a slimy bile-green mess on her most valuable paintings. Her parents dragged what they could out of harm's way, frantically wiping at stains.

"This studio is now closed!" Anckar bellowed through the broken pane. "Don't send me any more of your ugly children. My brushes won't lie ever again!"

Down in the courtyard, her parents cringed and Al Harvey looked grimmer and grimmer. "Artists!" huffed Mrs. Field with a nervous titter, trying her best to make light of the scene.

But Al Harvey bristled anyway. "She's over the edge. Come to think of it, wasn't she always a bit strange? Out of touch with reality? A few months at New Haven might be the thing."

"It's your liquor," Mr. Field tried to explain. "It does something to her."

Al took that as a personal insult. "Healthiest drink ever made," he said. "Good medicine for *normal* folks. If it's bad for her system then there's something wrong with her system, if you know what I mean" He handed Mr. Field a card. "The doctor at New Haven happens to be a friend of mine. I'll drive him over tonight for a diagnostic look-see. Can't hurt, can it?" Al had just paid handsomely to have a corroded old car restored to its full glory. He had also negotiated a private supply of refined gasoline. It was nice to drive the only car in town. A definite head-turner.

Finding one last bottle, still sealed, Anckar drank it dry. It gave her the strength to slash the canvases that had been too big to toss. Then she fell on her bed, crying with fury and shame as the swirling room narrowed to become her prison. She vomited all over the sheet and slept.

A high clear melody pulled her out of a vivid dream and brought her fully awake. There had been a man in her dream, a man with fog-gray eyes and flaxen long hair. She recalled the pattern on the red bandana he wore, the tranquil forest around him, a rugged peak, and the winding road that would take her there. Before the vision could fade she switched on the light, grabbed a piece of charcoal, and drew his face on the walls, the closet, the inside of the door. When she tried to open it to get to the bathroom she discovered that this time it was locked from the *outside.* And then she heard stealthy footsteps on the stairs, in the hall, in front of her door.

Quickly, she tore off her vomit-soaked sheet, thrust it under the cot, and pulled the blanket over herself and the bare mattress. The key turned twice, slowly, She forced herself to close her eyes, breathe evenly, and listen.

"God!" Al Harvey said. "It reeks in here."

"It's your liquor," Mr. Field said, somewhat testy. "I told you, she can't tolerate strong drink!"

"Look, Doctor," Al went on coldly, "she destroyed the rest of these priceless paintings. Plain nuts, don't you agree?"

"Who is the man she drew on the walls?" a stranger's voice asked.

"It must be someone she met at our last party," Mrs. Field guessed. "She's never had any friends, male or female. When she's sober, that is. Because she's always locking herself in."

"She's getting worse," Mr. Field admitted reluctantly.

"Fame affects some people that way," the unfamiliar voice said. "Not everyone can handle success."

"She's never been like a regular girl," Mr. Field said. "But since she started drinking Al's liquor—"

"There's nothing wrong with my liquor. It's like drinking a meal, only more fun," All quoted from his advertising slogan. "Right, Doc?"

"So I hear," the voice said. "Although, at New Haven, there are some who have become addicted to it. I'd say, Mr. Field, that your daughter would most certainly benefit from a stay with us A few months of rest would give her the chance to rebuild her health and her life."

"But the expense . . ." Mr. Field said. "We can't afford—"

"Never you mind," Al interrupted smoothly. "I'll have my guy check over the pictures she slashed. Anything he can salvage, I can sell. She'll be treated like royalty. And she'll still be famous when she comes out. Is her sleep always this deep?"

There was a small pause. Then Mr. Field cleared his throat. "Uh—that bottle there, by the bed, you see. I'm pretty sure she—"

"Some people overeat," Al said loudly. "But you wouldn't say it's the fault of the food, would you?"

"She won't go quietly," Anckar's mother put in. "She gets violent when she feels threatened. We had to pull her out of school because of it."

"I'll send one of our horse ambulances first thing in the morning, and two men with a straight-jacket, if you think it's necessary," the doctor said.

"Oh, yes," Anckar's mother agreed. "That would be wise. We'll keep her locked in until then. But if she drank that whole bottle . . ."

"Marvelous!" Al boomed. "I knew we could count on you, Doc. Let me drive you home. Uh, Mrs. Field? If you could look around for any sharp objects? Scissors. Knives. Take them out with you before you lock her in."

"Good point," the doctor said. "Some girls, in desperation . . ."

"I'm talking about the *art*," Al explained. "To save the art. My guy can't work miracles, not yet. Shall we go?" Their footsteps diminished, though one pair stayed in the room, moving about. Things were lifted and set down. Drawers were opened and shut. Then there was the clink of something metallic, and Mrs. Field— Anckar had recognized the soft shuffling of her slippers—closed and relocked the door.

Anckar kicked off the blanket and sat, waiting for the apartment to grow quiet and the windows to go dark. When she was sure the streets were empty she switched on the light, packed only what she couldn't bear to leave behind, wrapped her duffle bag into her bedroll, and dropped the thick bundle on top of the bushes below. She took one last look at the man she had drawn, brushed shards and splinters off the sill, and reached for the metal-cold drainpipe. It held. She shinned to the ground, retrieved her luggage, chose the direction that felt best, and went to meet her desires.

How was she to know that Alden wasn't alone? That he had spent an entire winter with another woman who was standing by his side when Anckar arrived in the spring?

CHAPTER 19

THEY SAILED THE CLOUDS, SHAPING THEM with their thoughts. Alden formed a bird with huge wings that broke away in the wind and flew off on its own. Em tried to make a galloping horse.

"It's a dinosaur," Alden guessed wrongly. "The meat-eating kind."

Em thought a dark thought and her horse swelled to become a thunderhead. She arrowed through it, arms first, surprised at the cold moisture it held. Alden dropped a split-second later; they plummeted toward the ground, faster and faster, until at the last moment Em raised her arms and swooped up, forming a symmetrical crescent.

"That was fun," she said when Alden rose to meet her. "I like being lighter than air."

"Me too," he told her. "Sometimes a thought drifts up from below. A prayer for rain. Then I think of an ocean of fog, heavy, thick, cold, wet, and see clouds rush in from every direction, like stray cattle at a round-up. They push and shove until the sky sparks. But I like to make gentle rain best. The kind that has time to sink into the ground and do a farmer some good. The kind a tree can suck up. Ever notice how the leaves turn greener after a rain?"

"I didn't get much of a chance in dry Oren," Em said. "But at Bena's I did. Up here, I like to put on a spectacular show—great pitch-black cloud walls, brilliant lightning flashes, earthshaking cracks of thunder. And afterwards, double rainbows. They're stunning against a dark sky."

"How many shows have you put on, so far?"

"Only two," she confessed. "One over Oren. It rained buckets They need it there, you know."

"Yes, but—" Alden said. "It just runs off that way, don't you see? Taking the top soil with it."

"What top soil?" she scoffed. "There hasn't been any since before I was born."

"And the second double-rainbow?"

She smiled. "A gift for a friend."

He summoned a white cloud with gilded edges, soft as a bag of cotton balls, and swirled it into the shape of a luxurious couch. They settled next to each other.

"Shaping clouds isn't all I've been doing," Em said. "I've been watching lives, too. I just finished Anckar's. Did you know they're starting to use cars again in the city? The kind that pollute?"

"With gasoline engines?" he asked. "That's taking the world in the wrong direction. I've seen where it ends. Was Anckar's life . . . interesting?"

"Very," Em said. "But weird. And it didn't explain why you brought us together like this. What's our true purpose, on the fiery hill?"

"The questions you ask!"

She glanced sideways at him. "Or don't you know either?"

He thought about it for a while. "I know that on some level we've planned it all out together, Anckar included. She's one of us, same as you and me and the others."

"No." Em shook her head. "She's not just one of us. She's *the* one. The one in this whole world who's most like you. Whatever the reason was each of us came—*her* reason was you."

Flustered, he said, "Me? Hardly! She doesn't even like me. Scowled when she first walked into the clearing and hasn't let up since."

"Only because you've never really noticed her," Em said, fluffing mist into a plump cushion. "She's waiting for you to notice her. Except, she's the impatient sort, not like Lupe or Hertha. Anckar will get tired of waiting. One day you'll wake up and she'll be gone."

"She can't go. She's in the game."

"What game?"

"The project."

"What project?"

"Don't you have something to do?" he asked, a bit sharp.

"I was about to view your life," she said with satisfaction.

"Oh, that. Go ahead. Help yourself."

"Don't you mind?"

"Not at all," he said with a laugh. "Remind me to tell you why, afterwards."

"Tell me now."

"Now?" he said, rolling over and dropping off the cloud's gilded rim head first, into a splendid nosedive.

Leaning over the edge, she watched him plummet. Just when he was about to smash against the ground, he disappeared. "Show off!" she yelled. Then she called more clouds to her, shaped them into a great ship with unfurling sails, lay on its deck, and looked at a cluster of ravens flying by. "I'm going to read Alden's life," she informed them. They cawed. She closed her eyes and watched.

ALDEN WAS A DISAPPOINTMENT to his mother since the night he was born. From day one he refused to respond to her hugs and hung from her arms like a sack of potatoes. She cried when he grew big enough to push her away.

He was even more of a disappointment to his father who sensed a strangeness in his third son and made no secret of the fact that he wished the boy had never been born. Alden had colorless skin, colorless hair, and vacant pink eyes, "And his skull's not right either," his father complained. "Mark my word, there's something seriously wrong with this child."

As soon as the boy learned to walk he stumbled away from the farm while the village lay sleeping. He lurched across his father's stubby dark field to the stream and curled up in the reeds, watching the moon dance on water that bubbled and murmured all through the night. At sunrise he came out of the mist to seek his bed once more, sleeping the day away. When his mother made him go up the road to play with the village children he stood like a zombie, lids drooping, mouth hanging slack.

It wasn't long before the kids started calling him *you moron*. The adults preferred *our loony*. His two older brothers, Wain and Jon, who liked to knuckle his lopsided head every day, called him *fog-baby*. The name stuck, especially after it became common knowledge that he walked in his sleep.

His father wanted to install bars on his windows and a lock on his door but his mother considered it too cruel a punishment for someone who did no harm to himself or to others. In time, the villagers persuaded their kids to ignore him and let him come and go as he pleased, for every village must have its idiot and Alden most surely was theirs.

At the age of four, his head had become nicely rounded and covered with silvery curls. His eyes darkened from pink to a misty, transparent gray. But there was only one child who attempted to play with him. It was Nore. She came every now and then to draw him blinking into the sunlight because she admired the way it made his hair and eyes glow. Sometimes he let her lead him all the way to the end of the yard where they picked the flowers she liked to weave into garlands for his hair. Then she would clap her competent little hands and call him her angel.

"He's my angel too," Alden's mother whispered, watching them play one hot afternoon from the window over the kitchen sink.

His father, currying the mule in the shade of the barn, glared as the boy tilted his slack-jawed face up to the clouds, and muttered to the mule, "Like a turkey waiting to drown in the rain." He walked away in disgust but Alden's mother tarried behind the curtains and watched the two children run to the great oak. Nore pushed him patiently on the rope swing, helped him build a twig castle in the dirt, and threw her ball to his awkwardly cupped hands.

Because Alden's mother loved him she encouraged his devotion to Nore. When Nore's mom decided it was unseemly for her pretty daughter to spend so much time with the village fool, Alden's mother pleaded with her to let them be. One night she followed the boy to the reeds and stood in the shadows to watch him become entranced by water and moon. She saw him dance and then slide to the ground, his rapt eyes on the sky. Every now and then he laughed at a passing cloud. At daybreak, when he slouched back to his room, she sat waiting at the foot of his bed.

"Alden, where have you been?" she asked gently.

"Dream," he said, rubbing his eyes "School. Dream school."

"Where's that?"

He pointed vaguely up, crawled under his covers, sucked on his thumb, and fell fast asleep. His face looked so normal with his eyes shut that she was almost convinced he wasn't an idiot, after all—but what he was she could not name.

Had she known the right questions to ask, and had he been able to talk in full sentences, he might have told her about the school above the clouds. There, tender voices whispered to him of things he had forgotten at birth, and friends from before came to meet with him in their dream bodies to discuss the task of the ten-spoked wheel. If she could have seen how focused he was then, the things he knew to ask and to answer, the truths he already understood much better than she ever had, the taunts of the village children would have ceased to bother her at once. But she saw only one world and could not imagine another. The fact that he refused to join her wholly in it made her increasingly uneasy.

At the age of five his stumbling gait smoothed to a glide. He seemed to float a couple of inches above the ground on his nightly forays to the creek. For his birthday, his invisible guide gave him a new task. He was to take empty space and sculpt it to become whatever he liked. He could put in it anything he wanted, and people it with friends to share it with him. The guide's voice grew firm as he reminded Alden that he had come to the earth for this quest. It was time for him to begin focusing himself fully into his body.

"I don't want to," the boy whined. "My earth suit is slow and heavy, like a stone."

"Yet entering it was your choice long ago, and part of the plan," said his guide.

"That world is an angry place. No one there likes me," Alden said. "Please let me stay with you, where I'm so light I can fly."

"You won't be alone. We'll be watching," the voice said, beginning to fade. "What you ask will always be given. "You'll have your dreams and the tools and the help of the ten-spoked wheel . . ." Then both voice and vision were gone. He felt cut away. For the first time in his young life he had a sense of being utterly alone.

"Alden, get up!" his mother cried, shaking him awake and pulling him out of his shady hidey-hole into glaring sunlight. All around him scorched summer dirt lay cracked like an old hobo-face, with gray stubble of weeds sticking up every which way. "I want to go home," he said, reaching toward the sky. It was the first full sentence he'd ever spoken in front of his mom.

"But this *is* your home," she replied, cupping his chin to force him to meet her gaze. He clenched his jaws and squeezed his eyes shut, fighting her grip. She held on more tightly. "You're staying with me," she said. "I don't have time to go looking for you again. It's my baking day. You can help me knead our bread. When your brothers and your father come in from the field they'll expect a warm loaf." She sighed, dragging him toward the farm. "Your dad wants you to start school but I doubt you're ready for it this year."

He went limp. "School?"

"First grade," she said. "With the new teacher. Won't it be fun?" She relaxed her grip for one foolish instant. He yanked his hand free and ran like water down to the curve and then out of sight. Vexed with herself more than with him, she cried, "Alden, come back! Nore will be in your class. She'll sit beside you, I'm sure." No answer. Undoubtedly, he'd already slipped into another one of his secret places and would not come home until his stomach drove him. She'd make plum pie for dessert, set it to cool on the sill, and let the hot cinnamon smell draw him to the house. Alden loved his desserts.

In a grove of twisted cottonwood trees, he lay resting his head on a pillow of moss, enraptured by the way the invisible wind managed to stir the overhead branches and swirl clouds into singular shapes. He was amazed at a bluebird who jumped off a branch and, instead of falling to the ground like an over-ripe pear, spread feathery wings and flapped away on thin air. He raised his hands and wiggled each finger in turn, then all ten at once. Was his mind pulling their strings?

SOON HIS father noticed a change in the boy. Alden had finally closed his mouth and stopped drooling. "I've left him to you long enough," he told his wife. "What he needs now is a man's hand and some training." He meant well but he was not a gentle man and had no use for gentle ways. He had a farm to run and needed all the help he could get. The first thing he did was borrow his wife's sewing scissors to cut Alden's silver-blonde curls. They spun to the floor like fine angel hair. Alden cried at the unaccustomed feel of his cold naked ears. "No more tears," his father said sternly. "Big boys don't sit and cry—they do chores. Your first one will be to carry the kindling box to the woodshed and fill it with sticks for tomorrow's fire."

When his mother was alone with the dirty supper dishes, she gathered the cut hair into a neat pile, tied a blue ribbon around it, and put the keepsake into her memory box.

Later that night, when Alden was safely in bed, he called to mind the little he remembered of his guide's voice. He longed to hear it again but knew he would not. Wasn't there something about shaping space, the way the wind shaped water and clouds? His thoughts were like the wind, unseen yet strong. He never doubted that he could fill that space but no longer knew why he should.

"For what?" he whispered. "I'll do it for what?"

No answer came.

He awoke when a moonbeam poked through the uncurtained window. Rising, he went to the door; it was locked from the outside. He opened the window but could only slide it a hand's breadth. He stretched his hand through the crack toward the moon. A piece of the bright orb broke off and fell toward the earth, landing on a tree just outside. The moon fragment sprouted creamy white feathers, a round head, and black saucer eyes that regarded him steadfastly until he paid full attention. Then the giant owl folded its wings and blinked, lending the two tired fields behind it an surreal glow. Wheat sheaves were drooping in one and cornstalks were sagging in the other. Between them lay shadowy patches where things had already died.

The owl swiveled its great dish-face to Alden's left, flicked a wing, and the air stirred behind it. After it settled the sheaves on that side had become glinting lights. The air smelled of fire and tin. Wide bands of road stretched to the horizon. Dark machine shapes whizzed by, shredding the night with their beams. Growling, they shrank into the distance, leaving red trails of smudge.

Gone was the creek with its reed bank and gnarled trees. Gone was the village, the acreage around it. Instead the landscape crawled with machines of all shapes and sizes. Suddenly, something huge screamed over the farm roof, lights blinking under its belly. The sound of its passing shook the glass panes in Alden's window. On both sides of the dark road, a sea of small identical houses crowded together behind high brick walls. In the distance, loftier buildings were blocking the stars. Some of these buildings had tall chimneys that smoked. Some had red blinking lights way on top. There was a harsh, continuous whine where there used to be silence filled only by wind and whirring bug wings. Where was the wind when there were no more trees for it to move through? Where did the bugs go when there were no plants left to eat?

The owl hooted for Alden's attention. It swiveled its head to

Alden's right, raising the other wing over the cornfield. A sepia stripe of new land appeared on the horizon behind it. Then a wash of green spread upward, as blurred as a child's first attempt with watercolors. Thin swirls of paint ran together like half-formed ideas. Something sang from a spot of blue; something else hummed in a green circle. An unseen breeze stirred invisible leaves and brushed Alden's face with a fragrance as fresh as spring dawn.

The owl hooted again and extended his magnificent wings to their full widths, one against a background of smoke and soot, one against misty green. Centered behind the owl's head lay the remnants of his father's fields, waiting to be changed into one or the other. Alden was sure that if he could stretch his arm through his blocked window and stick a finger into the noisy world to his left it would come out squirting blood, as if he'd stuck it into an oversized grinder. If he then dipped that finger over his father's tired land, the blood would at best slow to a trickle. But if he could plunge it into the watercolor-green haze at his right, the same finger would come back to him whole.

"I want this," Alden said clearly, pointing to the right. The white owl beat its mighty wings as silently as only an owl can, swiftly rising toward the moon. When it was no more than a bright speck it veered toward the green.

In the morning Alden awoke to hear a key turn and opened his eyes to see his father stand at the foot of his bed, tossing Wain's patched, outgrown overalls on the covers. "Welcome to real life," he said, casting a satisfied eye at the window. "I see the screws I drove into the track held." He raised his hand for attention. "Today you'll find out that nights are for sleeping." He went to the door and waited until Alden sat up. "There's bread on the kitchen table. Eat fast and then go to the wheat field. I'll show you the proper way to handle a hoe."

On that day Alden learned that real life included blistered fingers and palms and a withering sun. His mother, coming to bring lunch and water, found him swaying on his feet with his eyes rolling up into his head. She lugged him back to the house in spite of his father's objections, bathed his sun-burned skin in vinegar water, and let him cry himself to sleep in his cool shady room. But the next day she tied her favorite gardening hat firmly under his chin and gave him up to his brothers, who led him back to the fields.

Real life was a room full of first-graders who did not want to sit beside him, including Nore. It was years of whippings for chores badly done. It was his father throwing Alden's childish drawings into the hearth. Alden's attempts at rhyming were snatched by his brothers and mockingly read aloud at the supper table to the amusement of all except him. Years hurried by. The day before Wain's wedding, Alden still wore his mother's old gardening hat, his palms still blistered, and the hoe was still a bad fit. Working alongside his brothers, he stopped to put his chin on top of the handle and gazed yearningly at the horizon.

"Get busy," Wain said.

"I'm thinking."

Jon laughed. "You, thinking? Now that's a first!"

"Thinking about what?" Wain said.

"About how the earth wants to rest, just like me. So it can heal."

Jon and Wain grinned at each other, then Jon smirked, "So now you're talking to the dirt as well as the moon."

"Shut up and leave him alone," Wain said benignly. "Go on, fog-baby, what else did our world tell you?"

Alden brightened at his brother's encouragement. "That it would still be green if we'd been kinder to it."

Jon spit on the ground in disgust. "Then tell it from me that it was the cities brought this long drought down on us all. It was them who spoilt the air and the water."

"Maybe," Alden said. "But it was the farmers who took from the earth year after year, without giving anything back, until it had nothing left to yield. When's the last time you've seen any real topsoil? That's the stuff supposed to hold in moisture."

Jon smacked his hoe into a furrow. "Whatever's on top *is* top soil, fool!"

"Shut up, Jon," Wain said again, smiling at Alden. "Tell us, what should we do while our world's . . . uh . . . resting?"

Trustingly, Alden returned the smile. "We could think up another one."

Wain grinned at Jon and said, "See how simple it is?"

"Oh, simple, all right," Jon hooted. And then he and Wain doubled over with uncontrollable fits of laughter.

"He's truly not of this world," Wain cried, wiping away tears of mirth. "Personally, I've always suspected he fell from the moon."

"Our own loony," Jon agreed. "Still the same idiot he was when he failed first grade."

Alden tossed down his hoe and stomped off, knowing his father would take him out to the barn that night for the usual belt buckle lesson. He no longer cared; he was that used to it. The only tough skin his body seemed capable of producing went to the part that needed it most.

The best thing about Wain's wedding was that Nore was invited to come. She had grown into a lovely young woman, good on a man's eyes. Although she greeted Alden fondly she soon looked over his shoulder at Jon. When Wain's bride tossed the bouquet, Nore caught it *and* Jon's roving eye. A year later they married. Alden refused to leave his room the whole day. After the dancing began on a platform out in the farmyard, his father grabbed two bottles of beer, hauled them upstairs, and thrust one at his youngest son. "You could have had Nore," he said gruffly. "If only you'd tried a bit harder and longer." Alden put his beer on the windowsill and peered around the curtain to where Nore and Jon were dancing together. "Listen here," his father said. "You're not a boy anymore and I'm not going to treat you like one. It takes *men* to run this farm. If you don't want to work there's no place for you here. You decide."

What was there to decide, that night? Alden was bound to the village. It was all he had ever known. Where else could he go? Maybe his father had been right all along and he was too lazy for his own good. He would try harder and longer to be the kind of man a farmer could respect.

ALDEN PUT aside every half-baked reverie he'd ever indulged in and forced himself to see only what was in front of his nose. He discarded his mother's old hat and burnt until one day his skin stopped peeling. He started to wear a rolled-up bandana to keep the sweat from stinging his eyes. Laboring alongside his two married brothers, he ceased to think and let his body ache as it would, hacking at the reluctant dirt until it produced sickly crops. They shared their corn with the worms that lived in its ears. A pest of birds pecked the worms along with the kernels. He let farm life wash over him, accepting each day as it came. He watched Nore bear Jon's first child, and then his second.

One morning he got up as usual, stepped into his overalls, tied the red kerchief around his head in front of the mirror, and discovered the first silver thread in his hair. He rubbed his eyes as if awakening from a bad dream. "I can't do this anymore," he whispered to his reflection. "I can't go on pretending to be someone I'm not." He flung himself on his bed, crossed his arms over his face, and sobbed in dislike of himself and what he was living. When the last tear dried his eyes were already focused on a small, insignificant stain on the ceiling, His breathing relaxed and grew even. Then, at long last, he heard his childhood-guide's tender voice again. "Your wait is over," it said. "The new space is ready for you. Find your way to it and make your visions come true."

He packed as much as he could comfortably carry and went out the back way, not saying good-bye. With his eyes fixed on the horizon, he took step after step until he found a good place to linger. There, he did exactly what felt right to him every day, no more and no less. Impulse by impulse, he felt his way forward on trust.

CHAPTER 20

ALDEN MATERIALIZED ON THE DECK of Em's ship, fluffed some fleece into the shape of a recliner, and settled on it with a contented sigh.

"I just saw your life," she said.

"Good," he replied, sounding bored. "I told you I wouldn't care."

"Why not? You said you'd tell me afterwards."

He laughed, peering at her from behind his pale lashes. "Because you won't remember it once you're back in your body."

"What?" She sat up. "You mean I won't remember any of this? Then why am I here?"

He wiggled his toes. "Where's here?"

"On this cloud ship, up in the sky." She gestured at the sails, the fleece, and the deck. He blinked, and everything was gone. There was nothing holding them up. She yelped, clutching at him. The cloud reappeared at once. "How did you do that? Why didn't we fall?"

"Because we don't really need it," he said. "It's only here to give you confidence, you see. We left our bodies below. Gravity means nothing to us now. Shaping clouds with your thoughts is one of the first things you learn in dream school. You've done fine with it but now it's time for you to move on."

She scooted to the railing to look down upon their world. "To where?"

"There." He pointed up at the sun, half hidden behind a vast cloudbank.

Em stared at the glaring light. "No way. I don't like heat. I'd burn."

He plopped back on to the cloud pillow and grinned. "How can you burn when you're not in a body? For you, the sun's a great energy vortex. Stare all you want. You won't go blind."

She touched one of her eyes, feeling her finger go right through it. "If I don't have eyes, how do I see?"

"The way you see in dreams. What do you feel, when you focus on the sun?"

She felt brightness without heat, an open gate. A gate to what? "You've been there?" she asked.

Alden shrugged. "Me? Hardly. You're in a different class."

She knelt, her face toward the sun, one hand on the rim of the cloud as if it could keep her from falling. "All right then. I'll tell you about it. Afterwards."

"There are no words to tell it with. What you find there you can't bring back—not consciously. Whatever you learn will settle so deep inside you won't even know that you know it. But it'll work on you just the same, beyond words and even images. When you need it it'll be there. Have you done Driscoll's life yet?"

She shook her head.

"Why not?"

"Maybe I'm tired of looking at lives."

"That couldn't be it," he said. "You don't get tired without a body. Don't need to sleep, either."

"It would be . . . prying. Besides, he took off and left me."

"He'll come back. With the tenth spoke. I'm sure." Alden leaned close. "Try to find out who it is. I can't get anything on it. I saw the rest of you so clearly. For some reason, *they* won't answer my questions anymore." He looked perplexed and lonely.

"Who's they?" she whispered, glancing behind her.

"Our teachers. The guides. You'll meet them soon."

"But you already said I won't remember anything. Most likely, meeting them will be no more real than the dreams that fade as soon as I wake. Come to think of it, I'm not even sure *you're* real."

Alden sat up and retied his bandana. "I'm more real up here than I am down there. Gravity doesn't agree with me. Makes me feel like an idiot. I think I'm allergic to it. Oh no!" He grabbed at the railing, his feet submerging in fluff. "I guess they want you to get on with it. But first, watch this." Sinking, he tore the cloud-rail loose. It unraveled to form a white arch that stretched to the ground.

What if everything she'd ever known was a dream? The kind she used to have when she was small; dreams within dreams, and within yet again—like those wooden dolls containing ever-smaller versions of themselves.

"If you want me to do Driscoll's life, I guess I will," she announced with some trepidation. She blinked and saw a carrot-haired toddler, his arms spread wide to a puppy dashing eagerly toward him. Another blink brought a graveyard of cars and a man in rags. He stood alone and defenseless inside a knot of men wielding metal pipes and clubs. Behind them, a small boy with auburn curls crouched in a rust-eaten wreck, hiding and peering through the dust-filmed windshield, hands clamped to his mouth, silently screaming. A third blink brought a close-up of the Driscoll she knew. His eyes were dark with fear. A rope tightened around his neck and an unseen voice sobbed his name in an oddly sulphurous twilight.

Em felt hot, then cold. "No!" she said. "Don't show me anything else. Why is it so dark?" In answer, the sky turned a brilliant blue, like a vast silken cloth, the sun at its center a painted-on star, beckoning her. She looked for a seam in the flawless expanse, sure if she could find it and pull there'd be another sky beneath it just as real, and another under it—layers upon layers of realities to dive into and get lost in.

The sun rippled and pulsed. She tilted toward it and thought herself there. And so she was.

LUPE WAS wearing a hand-sewn white linen blouse so pretty that Bena wouldn't let her get near the blackberry bushes. "It would be a shame to get a stain on that blouse. You help Hertha pull the green beans today and I'll handle the berries. We have enough of both to feed a legion. What are we going to do with this stuff?"

Hertha unbent, kneading the small of her back. "Ten people and one dog will eat a lot of canned green beans from one harvest to the next. Half the berries get canned too. I found a way of sealing them into jars that makes them taste fresh picked all winter. Lupe will turn a good part into jam. The rest ferments to become blackberry wine."

Lupe was kneeling in the shade, smoothing her hair back and smiling. "We like sweet snacks when we're snowed in. A slice of Hertha's good bread, smeared thick with jelly. An occasional cake with jam and nut butter between layers." She leaned forward to pluck a handful of pods, dipping her head into a sunbeam. It made her face glow like amber glass.

Struck by her beauty, Bena sat back on her heels.

"There's Anckar, pretending she can't see us," Hertha murmured, nodding to where the young woman was coming around the corner to go in the house. "I guess that means she's still in a lousy mood."

"She looks as if she's had a bad night," Bena said.

Hertha dropped an apronful of green beans into a bucket. "She doesn't sleep much. Sometimes she roams the dark slopes like a wildcat. She knows the mountain better than she knows the back of her own hands. Or so she says."

A minute later Anckar came out again wearing a pack. They watched her walk away on the upper trail until she disappeared into the forest. Hertha said, "She takes our leftovers and hikes until she's too exhausted to move. Then she's liable to lie down anywhere. When she's rested she climbs on. Eventually, when she runs out of food and energy, it's the hunger that finally drives her home to us. I used to send Odasan after her till he said it wasn't our business to interfere. Mine, he meant."

"What harm could come to her?" Bena asked, sounding amused.

"Plenty! There are dangerous spots up there. Boiling mud. Geysers. Steep fields of loose scree. A person could be swallowed whole, never to be seen again. Or break a foot. Why *shouldn't* I worry about her?"

Bena plucked a berry, as big as the one she'd given to Driscoll on the night he left, and held it at arm's length, admiring it. "She's a grown woman, not a child," she said. "Just accept her the way she is and let her be, is my advice." She popped the berry into her mouth.

Hertha chuckled. "I guess it's natural for you to take Odasan's side, now that—"

She was interrupted by a polite cough coming from outside the fence. It was Brendan, looking ill at ease. "Excuse me," he said. "Bena? Could I have a word with you, please?" He waited until she got to her feet. Then he moved out of earshot, around the side of the house.

"Are you finally taking a break?" Bena asked when she'd joined him. "I haven't heard any hammering for a while. What's happening behind that tarp?"

He grinned. "I swore I wouldn't tell. But we'll have the unveiling before you know it. There's something I've been meaning to ask you. About the herbs you're collecting." He tilted closer, lowering his voice even more. "Are you a healer?"

"Of sorts," she admitted. "I make my own salves and poultices. I used to tend sick beasts in the forest. They'd come from miles away."

Brendan peered around the corner to where Hertha and Lupe were still picking green beans. "Is there something you can give me for my foot? To make it stop hurting, at least?"

Bena had already studied it while he lay unconscious beside Em. "I wish I could, but it's beyond me. I'm sorry."

He gazed off into the distance, hesitated, then asked, "Driscoll? What exactly does *he* do?"

"He helps animals, same as me. But not forest creatures. Farm animals, mostly, and pets."

He held on to the wall. "It must be the tenth spoke, then. Do you have any idea who it is?"

She shook her head. "No more than you."

He let go and murmured, "But that's the only one left. If Alden's right, that is. Are you sure Driscoll's planning to come back?"

"As sure as I've ever been about anything."

He smiled at her then, looking relieved. "I promised Odasan some lunch. Anything I can get you from the kitchen?"

"Not as long as I'm picking berries," she said. "Half of them seem to be winding up in my mouth."

She watched him limp away, realizing that he was trying very hard to move with grace. He was not succeeding. When she started toward the garden she saw that Lupe had come out to intercept her, looking more resolute than she'd ever seen her.

"Bena, I have something to show you. In my tent. If you can spare another five minutes." She turned and waved to Hertha. "We'll be right back."

"Take your time," Hertha said, struggling to her feet and then stretching. "I can use a little break. I've been kneeling too long."

"After you." Bena let Lupe precede her, once more admiring the white peasant blouse, delicately embroidered at collar and cuffs.

In the tent, Lupe closed the flap and put her only chair against it.

Then she began to undo her buttons. She removed the blouse, hung it carefully over the back of the chair, and stepped out of her ankle-long skirt. "Look at me!" she said, turning slowly in the dusky, close space. From her neck down to her ankles, every inch of her skin was afflicted with jagged purple scars. Even her high breasts had not escaped the mutilation. "This is why I keep myself covered," she said in a quavering voice. "I even sleep in long-sleeved night-shirts just to make sure nothing shows. Because I know how repulsive I am. I heard you say you make salves. Can you make one for me?"

Bena backed against the chair and sat down. "A salve, for all that?" she choked out. "If the scars were still new, maybe. Yours are old wounds, long set, badly healed, but healed nonetheless. No herbs I know will make them go away."

Lupe's black almond-shaped eyes searched Bena's face. "Something to make them less noticeable? Just to soften them? Take the red out. Don't try to hide it—I can tell you're revolted. How can I expect anyone to love me like this?"

Impulsively, Bena rose to wrap her arms around the girl, feeling hard keloids under her fingers. "Not revolted, Lupe, just sad—and angry at what's been done to you."

"Most of what you see I did to myself," Lupe corrected harshly, drawing a ragged breath that brought on tears. "From the time I was big enough to hold my own whip." She bowed her head, allowing her glossy hair to flow forward.

"You were a child, Lupe," Bena said, coaxing it over the girl's shoulders again. "And these scars are only as deep as you let them be. Keep them on your body, at least. Don't let them take hold of your mind."

Lupe broke the embrace, yanked the blouse from the chair, and slipped it on again, angrily pulling it shut over her breasts. "Easy for you to say!" she cried, eyes flashing. "Your skin's flawless. You can take off your clothes for Odasan in broad daylight and not be ashamed. But even a blind man would know how repulsive I am. Brendan would puke if he saw—" She fumbled with a cantankerous button.

"He nursed you through the worst of it, from what Odasan said. He already knows every scar."

Lupe fastened the blouse up to her chin and stepped into her skirt. "That was then. It's different now. Listen—" She grabbed Bena's hands in supplication. "I'll drink anything, no matter how vile it tastes!"

Gently, Bena shook her head. "I have nothing here that would help. But . . ."

"Yeah?" Lupe said, breathless.

"If Driscoll brings the rest of my herbs there's one plant among them that works on deep-down wounds. We could give it a try. But it won't be a miracle cure."

Lupe smiled, her teeth as white as the blouse. "Maybe not. But if anyone can help me it's you. Even if it's only a little." She sounded reasonable enough, but her eyes were too trusting to suit Bena who suspected Lupe only heard what she wanted to hear.

CHAPTER 21

WHEN THEY RETURNED TO THE GARDEN
Odasan started to play his flute from the other side of the tarp. "A
serenade for three precious ladies," he said loudly between musical
phrases. "Until Brendan arrives with my snack."

Lupe started to pick more green beans but Hertha gestured for
her to just sit and listen. "He hardly ever plays for us," she whispered
to Bena. "This is your influence. I'm grateful."

It was the first time Bena had heard him play. Sitting under the
apple tree, she closed her eyes and allowed the pure sounds to
resonate through her until she felt a peculiar kind of warmth at her
back. Turning, she saw a tall shape standing at the open gate, a red
dog sitting beside it. "Em?" she said, rising. "Is that you?"

As if drawn by the music, the girl glided inside toward the
chipped stone statue that stood in the garden's exact center.
Repeating her name, Bena hurried toward her. "You've had such a
long sleep," she said, touching the girl's face. "How do you feel?"
She was relieved to find that Em's cheeks were much cooler than last
time she checked. But her eyes were entirely empty, unnaturally
bright, and unnervingly penetrating. "Em," the old woman said for
the third time, her voice sharp with concern, and was glad when the

girl broke her unsettling gaze to sit on the flower bed that ringed the statue. She grabbed onto pansies, weaving her hands through the stems, vacantly staring at thin air. The melody ceased.

"I'll fetch her some water," Lupe whispered and fled.

Hertha stayed, even daring to draw a step closer. "What's wrong with her eyes? Is she . . . blind?"

Odasan came around the tarp and walked in through the upper gate, bringing his flute. Signaling the women to remain silent, he sat some distance away and began a quiet, monotonous tune. Soon, Em relaxed her grip on the flowers, leaving most of them unscathed, and bowed her head.

"Hey!" Brendan yelled, rushing out of the house with a snack tray, which he deposited hastily at Odasan's feet before limping toward Em. "You're finally up!" he said. "Good! Now we can talk." But she had nothing to say. "Remember me?" he tried again, less certain. "I'm Brendan. We've . . . met." Still no response. "What's wrong with her?" he asked Bena. "Has she gone deaf?"

Then Alden strolled in, clearly unbothered. "Nothing's wrong. She's straddling two worlds, is all. It's making her unfocused in either. She's only beginning to return fully to ours, but most of her still hovers—" His hand made a sweeping motion across the whole sky. "—elsewhere."

At the sound of his voice she looked up at him, then let her gaze travel past his face to linger on the sun. Cupping her chin, he guided it down again. "In this place, we don't ever look fully at it, Em. Our physical eyes are too fragile for that." She kept her chin at the angle he'd placed it in. "Let's leave her alone for a while," he suggested. "She needs to get used to things. Everybody just go about your business for now. If she hasn't stirred by sundown you can come and fetch her, Brendan. But I'm sure she'll be fine."

"If you say so." Hertha picked up both buckets and nodded at the third. "You bring the berries, Bena. We picked enough for our next canning. We can keep an eye out for Em from the window."

It was a quiet afternoon, punctuated occasionally by the clatter of pot lids from the kitchen and the hoarse bite of metal rasps from somewhere behind the tarp. When the light finally dimmed Em was still sitting on the same spot. Brendan and Odasan helped her to her feet and escorted her indoors.

"It's shaping up to be one gem of a yurt," Brendan told Odasan on the way. "Though, if Alden is right—and I don't see how he could *not* be—you won't live in it long enough to enjoy it."

"But I'm already enjoying it," Odasan said. "Immensely. Just imagine the look on Bena's face when we show it to her."

They guided Em to Alden's chair. Obediently, she sat and stared at the nearest candle while the others ate in the kitchen. When Brendan came to light a fire in the hearth she shifted her gaze to the bigger flame. The others gathered around the dining room table, working on their crafts. Anckar's chair remained conspicuously empty. Gradually, Em's head sank to her chest; she slipped off the chair to rest her cheek on the dog's flank.

"It'll get cold in the night," Bena murmured, tucking a quilt around the girl. She was rewarded with the ghost of a smile.

"See that?" Brendan whispered to Lupe. "I bet Em will be fully herself in the morning."

"Whatever *that* is, it can't be normal," Lupe muttered.

"'Normal enough for me. Oh, the questions I've saved up to ask. I can hardly wait."

"Well, I can." She marched to the door. "I'm going to bed!"

"Hey, Lupe," he called after her. "Don't you want me to walk you to your—" She had already slammed the door before he could finish with, "—tent?"

IN THE morning Anckar appeared just as the first streak of gray light stole into the clearing. She had timed her raid for when she was sure even Odasan would still be asleep. Cautiously making her way inside, she crept through the living room, listening to the steady rhythm of Alden's breathing from the couch. Then she felt her way through the pitch-black hallway into the equally dark kitchen, where she found first the table, then the match box and a candle stub. From inside her little room, Hertha gave a melodious snore.

Candle raised high, Anckar went to the pantry, opened the breadbox, and helped herself to what was left of yesterday's loaf. She pocketed a fistful of prunes, blew out the stub, and stuffed it in with the prunes. Then she felt her way to the garden and tripped over a large foot. Barely able to stifle a scream, she grabbed at something that proved to be a shoulder, steadied herself, and peered into a shadowed face. It wasn't until Nada's cold nose poked at her that she guessed whose face it was. "Well, hello!" she whispered. "I see you're both up!"

Em's breathing seemed unnaturally slow. "Sleepwalking?"

Anckar guessed, backing away. She chose the ripest tomatoes by fragrance, felt her way to the trees to pick a few apples and pears, and headed for the trail. Just before she ducked into the dense woods, she looked down upon the garden, found the dark shape of Em, and murmured, "I was planning to camp out a couple more nights, but raw food just doesn't fill me the same way Hertha's good cooking does. Don't tell her I said that. I suppose now that you're up things will get interesting in all kinds of ways. So—count me in for a hot supper tonight."

AFTER breakfast Lupe volunteered to knead the daily bread dough.

"Keep at it till comes alive under your fingers," Hertha coached.

"Till it wants to bounce on to the floor," Lupe promised, straight-faced.

Hertha and Bena went to turn the soil in the green bean beds. "Hungry yet?" Bena asked Em, stopping to tidy the girl's hair. "We saved you some breakfast." She gave no sign she had heard. The two women went on to work side-by-side, turning under every tendril and stem before raking the soil.

"The earthworms will take care of the rest," Hertha said. "There are a million of them in this ground. By next spring everything in here will be castings." She sifted some dirt through her fingers. "This is my favorite part of the day. Out under the sun. I love playing with our soil. Did you know that some seeds lie dormant for more than a hundred years until something kindles the life waiting inside? Everything's alive, even stones. You think I'm a fool?"

"If you are, so am I," Bena replied. "Sometimes I look around me and see things shift into patterns of light. Worlds fit inside worlds without end."

Something about her words triggered Em to come fully awake. Stretching, she squinted at the sun, found herself sitting on a bed of squashed flowers, hastily scooted on to the path, and tried to coax crushed blossoms upright again. Neither of the women noticed. They'd moved on to the blackberry thicket and were examining the new shoots. "The garden was choked with brambles when I first came," Hertha said. "I used to call them the Army of Thorns."

"They walled in my little clearing, sheltering me inside." Gingerly, Bena snipped a finger-thick vine. "They protect small, defenseless creatures such as rabbits and grouse." She dropped the cut tip at her feet. "I've always loved them for that—but they do like to spread. The tips dip to the ground and form new roots, which rise again to become tips. Their slow-motion march is relentless."

Hertha chuckled. "The smallest fragment left in the soil soon grows into a new bush." She stabbed the ground with her shears. "We're always cutting them back but never do more than break even. Brendan wants to dig them out to the last root but Odasan won't let him. The berries are better than any I've tasted. If only they wouldn't fight getting picked!"

At last, Bena noticed that Em was on her knees, listening and looking their way. "You remember your birthday pancakes, Em?" she called across. "With Driscoll's big candle stuck in the middle of your stack?"

Em nodded and smiled.

Bena clipped another vine, grabbed it between the blades of her pruning shears, and added it to a growing pile. "The bramble sea you fought through on our way to this clearing has its uses, too, Em," she went on. "No casual hiker will cross it or suspect we live just a stone's throw uphill."

Brendan stuck his head around the tarp. "I've been dismissed. Odasan thinks I eavesdrop too much. As if I could keep my ears from hearing. Need any help battling thorns?" He came eagerly into the garden but slowed when he was halfway to Em, looking shy. When he reached her he crouched and addressed the dog, trying to gather his courage. "Well, Nada," he said, "I guess as of now your guard duty's over. At ease!" But she seemed reluctant to give up her vigil just yet and merely touched her nose to his hand. He scratched her back. "I can guess whose dog you've decided to be." Then he was ready for Em. "Odasan thinks you should take a little stroll to get your circulation going again. Want me to show you around?" She held out her hand to him and let him pull her to her feet. They slowly walked off together, Nada close at their heels.

"Come to the kitchen when you're done," Hertha yelled after them. "I'll heat up some soup." Then she asked in a whisper, "What do you think, Bena? Is she all right? You know her best."

Bena watched them until they disappeared from view. "She seems taller. Rounder, too. Maybe this soil can grow other things as big as it grows plants. She *was* lying on it for quite a long time."

Laughing, Hertha put down her pruning shears. "Now there's an idea for you if you regret being so short. I might even join you if I'll look like her when I get up again." She pushed a wooden wheelbarrow to the cuttings and poked at them with a garden fork.

"I used to wish I were taller," Bena admitted. "Until I met Odasan. He tells me I'm just the right size for him. I can't argue with that."

"You found the one, haven't you?" Hertha sounded wistful and pleased at the same time. "It must be nice."

Bena could only agree. "And I didn't even know I was looking for him until a few days ago!" She turned to face the tarp, raising her voice. "Is Brendan the only eavesdropper around here—or are your ears turning red?"

"Pardon?" Odasan said innocently from the other side. "Are you speaking to me? A little louder, please—I can't hear a thing. But whatever you do, stay away from the spot Em's been lying on!"

CHAPTER 22

Lupe WIPED KITCHEN FOG from the window and peered anxiously out at the clearing. "They've been gone a long time. Her soup's getting cold."

"Then we'll feed it to Nada." Hertha rapped her wooden spoon on the stockpot. "There's plenty more simmering in here. Now don't fret, girl. They're both a bit slow on their feet and I expect Brendan has a lot he wants to show Em."

Bena picked up a cucumber and reached for the knife but Lupe claimed it first, sitting down in front of a pile of onions. She rolled the first one around on the cutting board, then peeled it so fast that she had skinned the whole bulb before Bena could put a restraining hand on her forearm. "Didn't I hear Brendan volunteer for the job when he wheedled Hertha into making onion gravy?"

Reluctantly, Lupe put the knife down. "Maybe he forgot. Now that Em is awake and all."

Hertha speared a potato out of some boiling water. "His heart's in the right place, Bena. The trouble is, we haven't quite convinced him yet that his pants won't change into a skirt the minute he offers to help. The closest he's come to cooking so far was when he once asked me how deep he should carve his wooden ladles. I thought for sure we'd snared him this morning when I pointed out that cutting onions should be done by someone good at wielding a blade."

As Bena started to reply, Brendan and Em came in from the hall. He was holding her hand, sniffing appreciatively. Then he said, "It always smells good in here," and pulled out a chair for Em while Lupe looked on with pinched lips. Em sat. He pushed her bowl closer to her, dipping a finger in her soup to gauge its temperature. "Too tepid," he decided, putting the bowl on the floor for Nada, who had been fasting since the flatlanders brought her home. "Hertha, can we have some more? That hot broth will clear the cobwebs right out of Em's mind."

"Of course you can," Hertha said with a delighted chuckle. "Sit, Brendan. I'll bring it to you. Lupe, you might as well start on the onions."

But Lupe was no longer inclined. Sliding the knife toward Brendan, she said tartly, "Bena says it's your job."

"Not now," Hertha said. "Can't you see he's hungry?" She brought two new bowls, carefully placing them down on the table. He dipped a finger into his bowl and complained, "Now it's too hot."

"Good." Bena pushed the cutting board under his nose. "You can finish the job you volunteered for while it's cooling. Hertha can't make the onion gravy she promised you without the onions *you* promised to cut."

Not paying the slightest attention, he was breaking a bread slice into bite-sized pieces and dropping them into Em's broth. When he picked up her spoon, Lupe said drily, "Don't tell me you're going to hand-feed her, too. Hertha's waiting. Isn't there something you were meaning to do?"

He struck a palm to his forehead. "Water," he said, hurrying to the faucet to fill a glass. "Do you realize she hasn't had any since the day she came?" He held the glass to Em's lips. "You must be thirsty. I heard you were burning up for a while."

Bena took the onion Lupe had already peeled and held it under his nose. He grabbed it and rolled it to Lupe. "Sorry. Odasan told me to take care of Em. Ask Lupe to cut them. She always says yes."

With a long-suffering sigh the girl started to cut. Bena took the knife right out of her hand and replaced it with a small pair of snippers. "If you would be so kind. We need some dill from the garden. And parsley. And chives."

The girl rose and grabbed a small basket.

"Aw, Lupe," Brendan said. "You're the expert chopper around here. Em and I will be glad to get the herbs from the garden when we're done with our soup."

"Never you mind," Lupe said, going out. "You do your job and I'll do mine."

When she was gone, he said to no one in particular, "I'm sure the smell of raw onions is bad for Em's eyes."

"In that case we best forget about the onion gravy," Bena said. "I'll make a nice little salad dressing to put on our mashed potatoes instead. If we add an extra gob of cooking oil they should be fairly easy to swallow."

Brendan shuddered, said, "All right. I give up," and started to cut. For a man, he wasn't half bad at it. Bena supposed all those hours he put in whittling soup spoons must have done him some good. "I'll tell you what would really make the gravy special," he said after a minute's reflection. "Some of those mushrooms Anckar brought us last week."

Hertha moved the potatoes off the burner. "I doubt she'll repeat that impulse of generosity anytime soon. No telling when she'll be back. You know how she gets when she's in one of her tiffs."

Brendan slashed the blade through the air. "What goes up must come down. How long can she stay away from your cooking?"

Odasan appeared in the doorway, casually surveying the stovetop. Bena's face fell. "The rice," she yelped, hurrying to the pantry with a bowl, busying herself at the sink, rinsing the kernels. He relaxed on his chair. "I see you're starting to help out in the kitchen, Brendan," he said cheerfully. "I approve. A boy who loves to eat as much as you do should know how to cook." He proceeded to cut Bena's cucumber into paper-thin slices.

"*I'm* doing the salad," she said, measuring water into the rice pot. "You deserve a rest. You worked on the yurt all day."

"And I didn't?" Brendan scoffed.

The look Odasan gave him made the boy refocus on his task. Then the old man caught a tear sliding down Em's cheek. "Would you be so kind as to move operations to the far end of the table?" he asked Brendan, who did so at once. "Good. Now Em can stop crying and I won't have to start."

"What about *my* eyes?" Brendan muttered.

"The tears you shed will wash away all your impurities," Odasan said. "You tend to get too close to the rasp."

"Oh, good," Brendan grumbled, scoring another onion. "I've been worrying about impurities the whole day. But listen, *sensei*—now that Em's up and all, don't you think we should resume dream class tonight? We've already wasted three evenings."

"Time is never wasted, Brendan," Odasan said mildly. "There's always something useful to be done, such as cutting a mountain of onions."

"Seriously," Brendan said after a bout of fast dicing. "I vote for a session right after dinner."

Bena put Odasan's rice pot on a front burner and waited for the water to boil. "It's too soon. Em's not even fully awake yet."

"Sure she is. Aren't you, Em?" the boy said.

"She's not talking," Odasan pointed out. Em clutched at her throat as if she'd only just discovered the problem. He patted her hand. "No need to worry. Brendan talks enough for the both of you. Take your time, Em. Show him that silence really *is* golden."

The boy scraped his heap of diced onions into a bowl, suppressing a smile. "Such friends I have. Have you told Bena our news yet?"

Odasan gave a mock frown. "No, and don't try to beat me to it." He addressed Bena directly. "As Brendan just reminded me, I didn't walk in here merely to tease him. I came to announce that we're removing the tarps tomorrow afternoon. We have some final polishing to do in the morning—another reason for him to go to bed early tonight."

Bena covered the rice pot and pushed it to the rear of the stove. "You're finally ready to pull down those frayed tarps?"

Odasan laughed. "Unless you've fallen in love with them and want to keep them up forever."

She crossed her arms. "It's not the old tarps I'm in love with."

"I'm not in love with old tarps, either." He held her gaze until she blushed.

Brendan leaned toward Em. "Can you believe it? No sooner did my poor head hit the ground than Odasan moved out of the tipi we shared and on to more interesting company. The word is, Bena and Odasan took one look at each other and were goners."

"Precisely," Odasan beamed, sitting tall. "You do have a way with words!"

A rosy glow spread over Em's face.

Hertha came for the onions, looking pleased with Brendan's

work. Stirring them into a sizzling cast iron pot, she said, "Let's have a housewarming party tomorrow. We'll uncork a bottle of our blackberry wine. I'll bake a cake."

Now Alden came in from sitting on his rock pile, looking pleased. "Be sure to save a piece for Driscoll and the friend he's bringing. I have a feeling they'll be arriving by late afternoon."

"That can't be right," Bena said. "He told me he has to work at the animal hospital until Saturday. That's his day off." Em's color deepened. Bena came to put a hand on her shoulder. "Before he drove away from here I promised him we'd leave with him this weekend, Em. But for the first time in my life, I'm breaking a promise. You're free to do what feels best, of course—stay with us, where you're most welcome, or ride off with him. He hates this place. His only reason for coming back is to take you home."

"No!" Em cried, thick-tongued, emphatically shaking her head. "Not!"

Lupe brought in her basket of herbs and quietly chopped them without having to be told. At the stove, the onions hissed as Hertha added hot broth.

Alden sprawled on his chair. "I stick by my prediction. They'll be here tomorrow. Have I ever been wrong? Even once?" He surveyed the room for any challenge to his psychic abilities.

The only one who answered was Anckar, swaggering in from the hall. "Never!" she said, glancing at the table. "How long till supper? I'm starved."

Hertha pinched her mouth with displeasure. "It might have gone faster if you had been here to help."

"But I am helping." Anckar untied a cloth and spilled a heap of rare mushrooms on the counter. "I scoured the high-up woods for these, Hertha. They're already washed and dried. You got any earthly use for them, do you think?"

Hertha's expression mellowed. "We certainly do. Thanks to you, we've got the makings of some truly unforgettable gravy." With a kindly smile, she added, "Rest your feet, Anckar. You've done your bit. I think we'll leave the dirty dishes for Alden tonight."

CHAPTER 23

BENA WAS LEANING AGAINST HER new counter, relishing the sensation of smooth varnish under her palms. Looking out of the window, as yet without glass, she saw a disheveled Driscoll rushing into the yard from the direction of the lower trail. From his sweat-darkened hair and his ruddy cheeks Bena guessed he had run all the way from the end of the road. He stopped at the spot where Em had lain on the night he left, looking down as if he could see her there still. Then his gaze lifted to sweep over the house, the garden, and the yurt. Bena went out to her sunny deck and waved, and he jogged around the garden fence to her porch steps.

"I came back," he said simply.

"Just as you said you would." She opened her arms and he leapt up the steps for a hug. "You're just in time for the tail-end of our housewarming party." She drew him inside and showed him the remains of the cake, cutting him a generous piece.

He grinned. "The perfect reward after a long drive!"

"It's Hertha's creation. Carrot and zucchini. The cream between the layers is a clever concoction of hazelnuts and spiked jam."

He chewed with the rapt attention that was the usual reaction to one of Hertha's culinary inventions and did not speak until he'd taken his last bite. Then he studied the yurt's interior and said, "I could almost swear this place wasn't here last week."

"Not even as an idea," she chuckled, brewing fresh tea. "Everything you see is built to the size of its diminutive owners— except for these." She pulled two bar stools away from the counter, offered him one, and climbed gracefully on to the other.

He sat, bumping a knee. "These stools couldn't be Alden's work, could they?" He sounded so puzzled that she laughed with delight.

"*This* is Alden's work." She held up a vase containing a bouquet of white roses and poured their tea into two pretty cups painted with bright poppies. "These cups belong to a set Anckar gave me as a housewarming present. It includes both of these vases." She set down the one with the roses and shoved the second toward him, which was wide-mouthed and held an assortment of cooking spoons. "Brendan carves these for the store," she said proudly. "He and Em have become friends."

He didn't seem as happy with the news as she would have thought. And so she clasped her hands firmly on her lap, looked straight at him, and said, "I might as well tell you right away that I am reneging on everything I promised you last time we talked. As it happens, I have no intention of riding back with you today. Or ever."

He busied himself with the crumbs on his plate. "That's okay with me. I'm making some serious changes in my own life. As a matter of fact, I'm only here because I promised Em I would take her back home. The Doble and trailer are full of my things. Books, mostly. I've decided to move away from Clydestown and its endless drought."

"Where to?"

"Not sure." With a faint smile, he examined the workmanship of the counter, the cabinet door, the round pole walls. Then he said, "Does your decision to stay in this place have anything to do with the builder of this little marvel—which, I can't help but suspect, has been custom-made just for you?"

She laughed with delight. "His name is Odasan. *He's* custom-made for me too."

He nodded, then asked, "I take it Em is okay? Completely recovered? Ready to go? Where is she, anyway? It's too quiet around here."

She pointed uphill. "Brendan wanted to show her his special lookout. He claims she would see the whole valley from there—and the approach of the Doble—which, it would seem, might have been a slight exaggeration. As to whether or not she's ready to go . . . I told her she is entirely free to make up her own mind, without the least interference from us." She helped herself to a sliver of cake and looked sharply at him. "So, explain—how come you're giving up your job? It seemed the furthest thing from your mind last time we spoke. Did you have time to check on the yurt?"

He hesitated for a split-second, then said smoothly, "I'm afraid not. I had to worked double shifts all week. And as a reward for my dedication the vet fired me yesterday. But as it turns out, my few hours on these heights have spoiled me for the simmering plains anyway. Blame it on the clean mountain air and on the goodies Hertha packed for my return trip. Everything I ate in Clydestown afterwards tasted like sawdust, you see."

He went to the door, looking longingly upslope. All remained quiet. Jiggling some coins in his pocket, he said, "Or maybe whatever pulled you to this clearing is pulling me too. Now that you've been here a week, tell me—what exactly happened to Em when we first came? Who are these people and why do they want us here?—May I?" He cut himself another slice, bigger than the first. "I didn't have much of a lunch."

She pushed the platter at him. "Please don't let it get stale. But bring your plate outside." They sat on the porch stairs, her feet on the second step from the top, his reaching all the way to the ground at the bottom. She gestured to the orchard and garden. "It's lovely out here this time of day. When our new friends first came all this was choked with brambles. They cleared it and, in something Brendan calls 'dream class,' imagined what they wanted in its place. That's why everything's so huge: they think big."

Driscoll gave a polite little sniff. "Be that as it may, I've read that decayed volcanic soil makes great humus."

"So it does," she allowed. "But according to them, the garden's a sort of gateway to a new world they're making together. Alden calls it his green valley."

Driscoll raised a skeptical eyebrow.

Bena's voice became apologetic. "The rest of their theories are even more outlandish. For instance, Hertha thinks the earth is getting ready to birth a new version of herself because we have all but destroyed this one. The new version is calling to herself all those who venerate nature."

Driscoll speared a hefty chunk of cake. "Oh, well. At least the woman's a good cook. But I'm more interested in what your Odasan thinks. I'm inclined to trust a man who can use his bare hands to make something like this in a week."

"He couldn't have done it without Brendan. They're a team." She poked at a crease in her skirt, deep in thought, and then looked at him appraisingly. "Do you trust me?"

"Absolutely!" he said without reservation.

She leaned closer. "What if I were to tell you that I died when I was sixteen?"

He actually recoiled. "Huh?"

"A huge oak limb crashed down on my head. My parents were most annoyed with me for coming back to life—at the wake."

Driscoll's face fell as if he'd just lost his best friend. "Please tell me you're joking!"

Bena smiled at a bee investigating one of the painted poppies. When it landed on Driscoll's cake she shooed it away and watched it spiral toward the garden. "I still remember what it was like to be dead. I went through some kind of tunnel to a place very much like Alden's green valley. But an old woman appeared and sent me back to my body." She raised her chin. "And if I can come back from the dead, why can't there be other worlds, and why can't we make one? Odasan says when something exists as a thought it has reality somewhere. Thoughts create things, is how he put it."

"Why go to the trouble of making a whole new world? If they reclaimed the garden, can't they reclaim the wasteland our grandparents made?" Driscoll kneaded the back of his neck, frowning.

"Alden says most animals with fouled nests prefer to build new ones. It's easier to start afresh, you see." She played with her cup, swirling the tea. "Our friends dreamed this whole garden into place during one hard winter. It took me a lifetime to grow mine and it never compared. That must be obvious even to doubters like you."

He puckered his lips as if he'd sucked on a lime.

She was looking into her cup, her voice growing eager. "Here the plants grow out of their season, Driscoll. The whole place is an arrangement of micro-climates. The soil varies from sand to clay to rich humus, in well-designed patches as carefully put together as Odasan constructed this yurt."

Driscoll examined the deck, rose to run a hand over the curve of the pole wall, scrutinized a layer of mortar, and stretched to his full height to study the overlapping bark tiles on the roof. "So, what else does your Odasan say?"

The bee returned to crawl over a smidgen of frosting, blurred wings whirring with the excitement of its discovery.

They watched it in silence. Then Bena asked, "Do you really want to hear more?"

"I would love to."

"Then brace yourself." Her tone had become challenging. "He says everything everywhere exists all at once, and that people are forever reinventing the world they live in. Groups form of those who hold the same beliefs, positive and negative. They create from shared thoughts, whether they know it or not. He thinks all those in our particular cluster know one another from past lives or somewhere between, from where—or is it when?—we decided to come together again. Here and now."

"Ouch!" he said. And then, "Why would we do that?"

Softly, she answered, "To polish our souls."

He winced. "Souls?"

She flashed him a reckless smile. "You want the whole list? Here it is: to risk making mistakes and learn from them; to invent brand new games; to create beauty, together. He says we write the script as we go, but any one of us can mess up his part and ruin the whole play." He blocked his ears with a mock show of horror, making her laugh. "He also says all theories are right in the end, they just grab a different piece of the same thread. He says everything that *can* happen, does."

He looked sorry he'd asked. "You two sure did a lot of talking in just one week!"

"We spend our nights on the same pallet."

"Lucky you," he said, massaging his forehead. "Lucky him. As for me, I'm afraid I'm getting a headache."

She stroked his cheek. "I'm sorry for prattling on. You do look peaked. Why don't you lie down for a while? Catch a nap before—"

"Driscoll!" a voice yelled from somewhere above, its echo bouncing from slope to slope. And again, "Driscoll!" He stepped to the edge of the deck, shading his eyes and looking upslope.

"Ah," Bena said. "Em finally spotted the Doble."

All at once, they were no longer alone.

Hertha came dashing out of the big house. Lupe rounded a corner. A dog barked nearby. Odasan and Alden emerged from the woods with a stretcher piled with sticks. They dropped the load unceremoniously at the side of the yurt and hurried to the porch.

Odasan was extending his hand. "Welcome to our new home. We've been expecting you. Have you tried out the stool I made for you yet? Is it the right height?"

Hertha was rubbing her hands dry on her apron. "Lord, I must have had my back to the window the one moment you were passing by. Usually I'm the first one to see everyone and everything—after Nada, that is. Did you like my zucchini cake?"

"I never would have guessed it had vegetables in it," he said. "I'm thinking about a third slice. As I recall, you're Hertha, aren't you?"

"I am." She kept her distance, studying his face. "How long can you stay?"

He said, "I don't know yet," scanning the slope as if the answer lay somewhere above. Then Em dived out of the trees, her hair tangled with twigs, her cheeks flushed, and Driscoll involuntarily clutched at the deck railing. Deliberately relaxing his hands, he stood waiting, watching Em as she slowed down a bit more with each step until she stopped walking altogether and busied herself with a shoelace.

Lupe peered around Hertha to ask him, "Who did you bring?" Before he could take in the question, she'd run up the stairs and into the yurt to see for herself. She turned, disappointed. "There's no one in there. Where did you put him?"

"Who?"

"The tenth spoke, of course!"

While he was trying to fathom what she was talking about, Brendan came hobbling down the trail to stand at Em's side. Nada, who'd politely matched the boy's tortured pace, now made a dash for Driscoll. He knelt on the porch, letting her jab her nose at his cheek, lap at his beard, and lash him with her enthusiastic tail. When he looked up, Brendan and Em were on the move, walking toward him. Together. Driscoll rose, his eyes caught in Em's clear gaze. He tried to speak but couldn't make a sound.

Then Brendan rubbed at his own ears. "Man! Did you hear Em's ear-splitting yell? Just about exploded my eardrums."

"He came alone!" Lupe wailed.

"Alone?" Brendan repeated in a disbelieving tone.

Working a twig out of her hair, Em said, "Of course he came

alone. What did you think?"

"Don't you know anything?" Lupe said, descending the stairs. "Alden swore he'd be bringing the tenth spoke, and so far Alden's always been right."

But Alden didn't seem as sure of himself as he had been when he had made that pronouncement. Peering earnestly at Em's flushed face, he said, "Could I have been mistaken? My inner eye seems to have gone dark. Tell me, what do *you* see?"

"Nothing but bits and pieces, of this and of that . . ."

He came even closer, his face taut. "No tenth spoke?"

"No. Not like this." She stepped away from him, shaking her head. "Why are you asking me? I'm no good at this stuff." She went to the railing, looked up at Driscoll, and softly said, "Hi!"

"Hello, Em." His voice came out reedy and thin. He cleared his throat. "I came back for you as fast as I could. Is there someplace private where we can talk?"

They turned to Bena, who said, "Please, go inside. We've all got plenty to do. You might still want that nap once you're done talking, Driscoll. Feel free."

And then he and Em were the only people left at the yurt. Nada planted herself on the top step, guarding their privacy. Em led him inside to the bay seat. "This thing folds out into a bed," she said, rearranging cushions. "Until Odasan can build the sleeping loft."

He sat, poking at a window. "No glass."

"Not until the next shopping trip." Gingerly, she sat down beside him. It was a tight fit. "They only go to town once a month. They carry the heaviest stuff on the stretcher, one person to each pole end. It must be hard." She jumped up to freshen the fire in Odasan's small tin stove and set the kettle to boil before squeezing in beside him again. They were both wearing shorts. The intimate sensation of their thighs rubbing together made Driscoll squirm and put as much distance between them as he was able.

She pulled a cushion out from behind her back and put it on his knees for him to admire. It was embroidered with fall leaves of red and gold. "Isn't it pretty? Lupe made it. A housewarming gift. This little love-seat may be a tight squeeze for us, but it's just the right size for Bena and Odasan. Can't you just imagine them sitting here late in the evening, bathed in moonlight, holding hands?" Nervously, she divided her hair and proceeded to weave a loose braid just to give her fingers something to do.

"About last week," he said, lightly rubbing his knuckles over Lupe's cross-stitching. "I hope Bena explained that I never meant to leave you. It's just that I had to get home and everyone said you couldn't be moved."

"Nor can I be now."

He went on as if he hadn't heard her. "I promised to keep you safe and I didn't. I'm so sorry."

"I *am* safe," she said quietly. "So are you, for as long as you stay on this mountain."

Still caught up in his own thoughts, he continued, "They're looking for you, you know. The sheriff. Your mother. Nev. Going on a day trip with me was one thing. Disappearing for a whole week is something else. You *are* underage, you see."

The water was boiling. She brewed a new pot of tea, divided the leftover cake into two large slices and added some berries to each of their plates. "Eat up. If you're going to take a nap you might miss supper." She busied herself with a tray and deposited it at his feet. Squeezing in beside him again, she said, "A week is a long time. I'm not who I was."

"Neither am I. It's been one of the worst weeks of my life," he said, toying with his cake. "Things . . . happened. Things I didn't expect."

She balanced her plate on her lap. "Such as?"

"Such as Nev telling the sheriff that I abducted you. He told the same tale on the streets of Clydestown. I lost my job over it, so I left—just in time, I think. There's no way I can go back to the plains without you."

"Then you're not going back." She gulped a couple of berries, smiling guilelessly at him. "These are much better than Bena's, and hers were the best around Oren."

He nodded. "Her bushes are still full of them."

Em took a sip of tea and carefully put down the cup. "You went to her clearing."

"I did."

"What did you find?"

Driscoll upended the cushion as if the answer might be written on its other side, asking carefully, "What did you *think* I would find?"

"Whatever was left there *to* find, of course!"

He picked up another cushion, this one embroidered with three triangular spruces. "Does it matter now?"

She gave him a hard look. "It does to me. So tell me already!"

He glanced through the glassless bay windows as if to make sure no one was listening, and said in a hoarse whisper, "They trampled her garden. Tore everything out by the roots."

"What else?"

"Destroyed her little orchard. Ringed every tree."

"You mean they peeled strips off the bark? And the mushroom house?"

"Leveled."

"Did you tell Bena?"

Looking shocked, he pushed the pillows away. "Of course not!" He concentrated his full attention on sliding the tray back and forth with his feet without spilling a drop.

"But you told *me* everything?" she probed. "There's nothing else?"

"Such as?" he asked, not meeting her eyes.

"Sometimes I see things," she said drily.

"The doll?" he finally conceded in an outraged whisper. "Bena's effigy. They stuck it full of pins, shot a hole through what would be her heart, hung it by the neck from the apple tree, and scorched it along with the branch it hung from. I will never tell her about that."

"Never," she agreed. "I saw it in one of my dreams. Nev was in it, urging the villagers on. I hardly recognized his hate-twisted face. We've been like twins since we were old enough to crawl. When we got older we played endless games of bride-and-groom and prince-and-princess, he on the white charger, rescuing me from various villains. And now he rides a black horse and has turned into the sort he once rescued me from." Angrily, she swiped at her cheek.

"When he showed up on the morning I was waiting for you outside of Oren, there was something about his face that made my knuckles itch," he confessed, unconsciously making a fist.

"You wanted to hit him?"

"Just enough to dislodge that smirk of his. Terrible, huh? When he's only a boy." He dug his fist into Lupe's spruce pillow. "Bena was the best thing they ever had!"

Em put her dishes on the tray and uncurled his fingers. "They don't have her anymore. They never will again." When she'd finished straightening his hand, she held it lightly in hers. "You want to know the first time I felt really good about myself? It was when I was watching you climb out of your car at the animal hospital. The only man taller than me. I still feel good when I stand close beside you."

His feet jerked, upsetting the tray. Tea and berries splashed every which way. He groaned and helped her clean up the tea, meticulously rubbing the wood floor until he had restored its pristine luster.

Kneeling beside him, she said, "The thing about Nev is—he's only hurting you and Bena because he knows that will hurt me. And I have no idea why he wants to hurt me."

"Don't give him another thought." He tugged at the rag she was clenching. "If you're not going back he'll have to find someone else to pick on from now on."

Letting go of the cloth, she collected the berries they'd spilled. "Someone fat or crippled," she agreed. "Like Brendan." She crushed the berries, dropped them on the tray, stared at her stained fingers. "What a mess. I want you to understand something, Driscoll. I'm not a child anymore. So don't hide things from me."

"What things?"

"Last week you sent me out of the mushroom house before telling Bena they were coming for her."

"You would have thought it was your fault."

"I might have," she admitted. "But not for long. Bena's happier now than she's ever been. If that's my fault, I'm glad."

"There you go!" he said, sounding relieved. He went to the door. "It's almost unbearably quiet out there."

Em came to stand behind him. "The silence is full of music. Come and hear."

He followed her into the garden, where she motioned him to sit in the orchard.

"Listen," she said.

The air was alive with the buzzing of vibrating wings. Wasps swooped and hovered. A bumblebee droned over yellow blossoms. Butterflies fluttered like leaves, a blue one rising straight past the top of a conifer to blend with the sky. The breeze worked high branches like the strings of a harp. Birds sang in relays, some repeating the same few monotonous tones, others improvising up and down the scales. Beneath every sound was a deep, unifying hum, almost out of range. A swarm of bees?

"Can you hear the hum, too?" she mouthed. "I think it's the garden, growing. Raw energy."

When she leaned against his knee, the hum entered his body, his blood. Driscoll suppressed a sweet shudder, and although it was unbearably painful, pulled away from her flesh, inch after careful inch, determined to let the intimate moment pass while he was still able.

Em was right to say she was no longer a child. It was his job to wait until she realized she had turned into a woman.

CHAPTER 24

Em was sitting on a bench just outside of the kitchen window, the stone wall warm against her back. From there she could view the garden and most everything else in the clearing. Hertha had given her a sack of hazelnuts to shell. The sack sat to her right, the bowl for the hulled nuts on her left. Every now and then she pushed a lapful of debris into a bucket resting between her feet. Hertha had promised to help her make nut butter as soon as she was done. Meanwhile, she kept her fingers and her mouth busy while she worked, looked, and listened.

Poor Driscoll was still sprawling under the apple tree exactly where she had left him, taking a well-deserved nap. Brendan was only partially visible on the far side of the fence, working at the chopping block next to the yurt. Em enjoyed seeing him swinging his axe to split deadfall for Odasan's small stove. She admired the way the boy's muscles tightened and rolled with each stroke.

Lupe was working in the garden all by herself, spading the soil in a vegetable bed. Every now and then she would stop to rest, casting a surreptitious glance at Brendan's well-designed torso, unaware that Brendan returned each one of her glances as soon as she looked away.

Through the open kitchen window behind her, Em could hear Bena and Hertha's comfortable voices blending with the friendly sounds of pots clanging and knives chopping. In the mild afternoon sunshine, two blue jays, cursing from a tree, and a family of gossiping ravens, flying by, completed the pleasant sense-tapestry. Then the big black birds alighted on the jay-occupied tree and for a few seconds the insults and threats raining from branch to branch were so fierce that Driscoll stirred in his sleep. Then a black feather floated to the ground and the ravens lifted off in search of more hospitable surroundings.

Munching a sweet hazelnut, Em had to admit that the chore Hertha assigned her was as close to leisure as work could possibly get. Back in Oren idle sitting was judged a mortal sin. Em had only been allowed to indulge in it on Sunday afternoons when it became a once-weekly virtue. Even then her parents believed reading was inappropriate and frivolous.

As a result she had rarely opened a book without getting a tongue-lashing for it. Thus, she had done most of her reading at dusk, sitting upstairs on her sill to catch the dying light. Sometimes she would lean out at daybreak to devour the rest of a chapter before her mother called her downstairs. On the occasions she found it impossible to wait from evening till morning she made do with flickering candle stubs in the dead of the night.

". . . hardly ever does any chores," Hertha was complaining loudly inside the kitchen. For one guilty moment Em was sure she was talking about her. But then Hertha went on to say, "I think she considers herself too fine an artist to stoop to something as lowly as housework," and Em knew she meant Anckar.

"She does contribute by making that beautiful dinnerware you sell at the store," Bena pointed out. "Surely that's an acceptable substitute?"

"How can it be," Hertha cried, incredulous, "when the rest of us make things to sell at the store too? After *we* do our regular chores, mind you. Why should it be any different for her? It isn't the eating of meals she is shirking, just the preparation and cleanup. I, for one, find that distressing."

Straining to hear more of their gossip, Em didn't notice that Driscoll had awakened until she saw him leaning against the yurt, talking to Brendan. Then Odasan and Alden came out of the forest with new stretcher-load of sticks, which they upended at Brendan's feet. Soon the men were busily hacking the sticks into kindling, their congenial laughter drifting through the clearing. In the garden, Lupe stood resting her chin on the shovel handle, yearning toward them.

"Sometimes I wonder if she dislikes housework because she dislikes me," Hertha said next. But Em was no longer listening, for Driscoll had left the men to walk across toward her, waving to Lupe in passing and coming to sit on the other end of the bench. She could feel a board shift under his weight as he leaned over to pick a filbert out of the sack. Raising it to Em's cheek, he said, "It's the exact color of your eyes. Right now, anyway. I've noticed they change with the light."

He helped himself to some shelled nuts and ate one, asking, "Have you given any more thought to returning to Oren?"

"Not a one. We're staying."

"Then Alden will help me clear my stuff out of the Doble." He popped a second nut in his mouth, reached out to tuck a rebellious curl behind her ear, and got up to join Alden, who was carrying the rolled up stretcher. As Em watched them enter the forest at the lower trailhead, she grew aware that she was being scrutinized by a pair of unfriendly eyes. Lupe's. From the yurt came the pleasant sounds of Odasan and Brendan's back-and-forth bantering, but clearly, Lupe was no longer amused.

In the kitchen, Hertha said, "Bena, the tomatoes are ready for peeling. Careful, they're quite hot." Em liked that the two women were getting along so well. It was wonderful how social Bena had grown since last week. Em, too, felt more at home with their new friends than she ever had in Oren.

Now Brendan was at the orchard, plucking apples. Passing Lupe with a brotherly smile, he limped up to Em and handed her one. It was enormous. "I brought you the biggest one I could find," he said. "Though mine's got to be a close second." He bit into his, but before Em could taste hers, a hand dropped down from the window, whisked it away, and returned to demand Brendan's. "Don't spoil her appetite so close to dinner," Hertha said sternly. "We're having our last box of macaroni straws."

He gave up his apple without a fight. "With spicy sauce? All right!" Filling a bucket at the nearby spigot, he asked, "What are we celebrating—Bena's new yurt, Driscoll's arrival, or the resumption of dream class?"

"All three," she laughed, "and whatever else needs praising

before bedtime." Then Lupe came out of the garden with a loaded basket and Hertha said approvingly, "You're way ahead of me, Lupe! I was just going to ask you to pick some things for our salad!"

Lupe handed up the basket and watched Brendan carry his wash-water around the corner before she asked, "Did I hear you mention macaroni straws?"

"You have good ears," Hertha said.

"Can I set the dining room table with our fancy cloth and the good china?"

"A reasonable request. As long as I don't have to lift a finger to get it done. I'm sure Em will be glad—"

"I don't need her help. I've got Brendan," Lupe said. "Let Em make the salad. If her butt's not glued the bench, that is. She's spent an awfully long time hulling a handful of nuts, don't you think?"

Hertha choked out, "Lupe!"

Em just smiled. "I've made some fine salads for Bena and me. Shall I finish the nuts first?"

"Sure," Hertha said with a severe look at Lupe. "Take your time, Em. We're not in a hurry."

After Hertha had withdrawn from the window, Lupe took over Driscoll's spot on the bench. The planks barely registered her weight. She sneered, "I see you picked the easiest job."

"It's been fun," Em replied. "Until now."

Lupe scooted a bit closer, dropping her voice to say in a cutting tone, "It must be nice having men hover, bringing you apples and stuff. You remind me of a giant queen bee too sluggish to fend for herself."

"An interesting thought!" Unperturbed, Em kept shelling nuts.

"Taking Brendan off on a sight-seeing tour," Lupe said, continuing her catalogue of grievances. "When every step hurts his foot! Not that he'd ever complain, but surely you noticed how much he was limping when you came down from the lookout?"

"She's jealous!" Bena cried in the kitchen.

"Am not!" Lupe protested, hastily scooting back to her end of the bench.

"Anckar, jealous?" Hertha repeated indignantly, banging a pot against the edge of the sink. "Of me? You've got to be kidding. Was that the last of the tomatoes? Let's do the peppers next. Dice them extra fine. With the seeds. Brendan and Odasan like their sauce extra hot."

Over the sound of rapid chopping, Bena said, "Why don't you sit somewhere else at supper tonight? Leave the chair next to Alden's to Anckar. You might be surprised at the change in her mood."

Hertha gave a loud sniff. "But Alden and I have been sitting together since I first came. Besides, everyone knows that Alden and I are just friends. It's all we've ever been."

Outside the window, Em said softly, "Brendan and I are just friends, Lupe. I could be your friend too if you'd let me."

Lupe tugged viciously at her sweater sleeves. "I didn't want you to come."

"I didn't want me to come either. And I didn't have the slightest intention of staying," Em said. "But I do now. So you might as well get used to it. And to me."

The girls studied each other. Lupe looked away first. When she went back to her shovel, Em fought the urge to show her how well she could handle a spade, and reminded herself that she didn't come all those miles to pick up where she left off on the plains. Neither Alden nor Brendan had been able to explain what Nada had actually summoned her for, but she was sure it wasn't housework or gardening chores.

CHAPTER 25

WHEN DRISCOLL AND ALDEN RETURNED with the stretcher it was sagging with books. Em plucked up one that had the picture of a split-open rock on its cover. "We could start our own used book store with these," she told Driscoll.

He laughed. "We left an even bigger pile in the car. You can borrow as many as you want. Alden is letting me have the shelves behind the couch. If they don't all fit you can help me make a bookcase."

She put back the first book and picked up another, which had a picture of the top of a mountain blowing off steam. "You want me to help you put them away?"

"Good idea. That way you can browse through the whole collection for something you like. But wait till we've brought the rest. Then we can arrange them all by subject matter."

After he and Alden went into the house, Lupe called from the garden, "Books are a laggard's excuse for avoiding work." Em ignored her, but Lupe was not done yet. "Speaking of laggards," she went on. "Don't you think you've been goofing off long enough for today?"

Although Em wasn't sure why Lupe had taken such a dislike to her, she'd had plenty of experience handling insults. The trick was to keep her head down and mind her own business until Lupe got tired of hassling her. When the nut bowl was full she took the hulls to the compost pile, put the sack of whole filberts in the root cellar, and shelved the nut meat in the pantry. Then she sat down at the table to make the salad and watch the two women bustle around the kitchen.

Hertha was dipping a teaspoon into the sauce simmering on a back burner, conducting a taste test. After some thought she added a sprinkling of red pepper and put the lid back on the pot. Next, she poured a handful of salt into a steaming kettle, stirred, and began to drop in long, stiff macaroni straws. The only times Em had ever seen her sit down was in the evenings or during a meal, but even then she served others before serving herself. Bena was stoking the cook stove, rinsing pots and bowls in the sink, spooning biscuit dough on to a cookie sheet, and shoving it into the oven. Hertha gave her a wooden spoon with instructions to keep stirring the noodles. Then she came to the table and rummaged in Lupe's produce basket.

"Oh, good," she announced. "She remembered the basil." She pulled out a bunch of light green leaves and rapidly chopped them on a cutting board. "What would I do without our dependable Lupe? Sometimes I forget she's only a girl of sixteen." She glanced at Em. "Isn't that about your age, too? And Brendan's. How lucky you three are to have each other. When I was sixteen I'd been living alone in a dark old farmhouse for five years. The downstairs was always clammy. Every room I walked through gave off a forlorn echo."

"At least I had a happy childhood to remember in *my* solitude," Bena said from the stove, still stirring. "I didn't have brothers or sisters, but I had a best friend who did everything with me. Adra was always babbling, just like a brook. We'd talk for hours. I can still hear her contagious giggle."

"After how many years?" Hertha asked, chopping the basil a second time.

"I stopped counting long ago. By the time Em came along my voice had grown rusty, even though I made it a habit to prattle to myself every day just to hear someone talk."

Hertha laughed. "And I used to read cookbooks out loud for the same reason. Until Tomas came."

Em knew that name. But from where?

"My imaginary friend," Hertha explained. "He appeared to me in a dream one night and decided to stay. He told me what to plant when. I could see him most clearly in the sunroom, so I moved my mattress up there. He became the soul of my indoor garden."

"That Tomas," Em muttered to herself. "The master gardener."

Hertha turned pink and then pale. "What did you say?"

"Nothing. Please go on."

Hertha scraped the basil into a heap and diced it a third time, her knife moving so fast Em feared for her fingers. "Without him to keep me company I would surely have lost my mind during those lonely years," Hertha said. "Eventually, I grew up and became more and more skeptical. One day I couldn't picture him anymore. Soon his voice faded, too. But for as long as I let him he was more real to me than anything else in the world." Knife poised over the cutting board, she stared off into space.

At the stove, Bena stabbed up a slippery noodle, cut off its end, and announced, "They're done." She carried the kettle to the sink, tipped the noodles into a colander, and poured on cold water. "Speaking of imaginary playmates—I had my own from the time I first moved to the woods. Two toddlers solid enough to bounce on my knees but not so real that they would dirty up diapers or dishes. They, too, faded over the passing years. Maybe it was because I couldn't imagine them as adults—or me either. The truth is, I still feel like sixteen inside. There was no one around to show me how to get old, you see."

Hertha took the lid off the sauce, suffusing the kitchen with fragrant, garlicky steam, added the basil, and reseated the lid. "How you must have welcomed Em when she finally stumbled into your life!"

Bena smiled, recalling that day. "There was a big difference between a real flesh-and-blood little friend coming to drink tea and two make-believe toddlers who never managed to drain their cups."

Clumsily, Em sliced a white radish. "Did they have names?" Bena sat beside her with a grater and reached for a carrot. "They called themselves Ima and Vida and wouldn't answer to anything else."

"Ima and Vida," Em repeated, gazing into the salad bowl. And there they were, two laughing little faces, each on a piece of lettuce, beaming at her for a few seconds.

Then Odasan stood in the doorway. "Am I disturbing you, ladies? The living room is getting crowded with plates and flowers and books. It seems that no matter where I turn I'm in somebody's way." He gave a casual glance at the stove. "If you haven't started the rice yet I'll be glad to cook it myself."

"The rice!" Bena groaned, dropping a half-grated carrot to jump to her feet.

Hertha pressed her back down. "We're having macaroni straws in hot pepper sauce, Odasan. Why not give them a try?"

He found his measuring bowl, said pleasantly, "I'll have my sauce over rice, thank you," and went to the pantry.

"While you're in there, why don't you dust off a couple more bottles of blackberry wine?" Hertha called after him. To Bena, she murmured, "Let him fend for himself for a change. He's not working on the yurt anymore. I do wish he'd overcome his addiction to rice. It comes in big heavy sacks and is hard to get." She shook her head. "You should see him when he runs out of the stuff. It's the only thing guaranteed to wipe that sunny smile off his face."

BRENDAN and Lupe had covered the dining table with a maroon linen cloth and set it with Anckar's fine butterfly dishes. The center was decorated with lit beeswax candles and roses. Their heady scent permeated the living room as Hertha carried in the noodle dish. Em followed with the salad, Odasan with his wooden bowl filled with rice and topped with red sauce, and Bena brought wine and biscuits. Once everyone present was seated, Hertha took her customary place next to Alden, started dishing out, and nodded at the empty chair beside Bena's, saying,

"Anckar's lost track. Again. Typical!"

Busily setting down tumblers, Lupe paused to ask, "Do you want me to go get her?"

"Never mind. She'll come when she's hungry enough." Hertha served herself last. "Em, if you would pass around the salad . . ."

Then the door flew open, upsetting the candle flames, and Anckar stomped in. She was carrying a large rectangle covered with a raggedy sheet, which she propped carelessly against the nearest wall. From there she proceeded to her chair without speaking, adding the pungent odor of turpentine to the aroma of tomato sauce, beeswax, and roses. Her clothes were more spattered than usual; the back of her hands were freckled with oils.

"What uncanny timing!" Hertha said, her voice thick with sarcasm, handing Anckar the plate she'd just filled for herself. "The only thing left for lucky you to do is pick up your fork." She rose to pour wine into the tumblers, making a point of pouring Anckar's last.

But as she tipped the bottle, a paint-smeared hand blocked the top of the glass.

Anckar said sharply, "If you don't mind, I would like water."

"Don't be silly!" Hertha cried. "This is a special occasion. Everyone's drinking wine tonight."

Anckar snatched up her glass. "Stop trying to boss me around," she said irritably, stalking to the kitchen. "I'm not *like* everyone else!"

"She got that right!" Hertha muttered to herself. Bena tapped the empty chair next to hers. With a shrug, Hertha filled another plate for herself and plucked herself down on it, fondly surveying the tabletop. "Didn't Brendan and Lupe do a beautiful job?" Recklessly clicking her tumbler to Bena's, she cried, "Here's to changes!" The others raised their glasses and repeated the toast. Everyone but Odasan drank. And when the others starting eating and exclaiming over the dish, he bowed his head and morosely picked at his food with a chopstick.

The behavior was so unusual that Hertha immediately worried something might be wrong with his sauce. When she asked him if he had any complaints, he forced himself to take a bite. "No. None. None at all. But when I went to the pantry for my rice I discovered that I'm almost out. What I thought was a spare bag turned out to hold rye kernels. I'm afraid you'll have to go to the store tomorrow."

"Rye porridge is good too, Odasan. It tastes nice and nutty."

"I don't want nutty," he said firmly. "I want *rice*. And glass panes for our bay windows. And I finished three flutes."

Hertha took a long sip of her wine. "Well, I can't go tomorrow. We're canning. Applesauce and apple-butter."

He looked incredulous. "Surely the apples will keep for a couple of days!"

"If Hertha can spare me I'll be glad to hike to town and do the shopping," Bena said.

Hertha sighed. "And I'd love to let you. But I'm afraid Tilden will only barter with me. After dark. So that the good people of Yates won't see what undesirable types he's doing business with."

Meanwhile Anckar had brought in her water and gone to her chair, where she stopped, amazed to see Hertha on it.

"I hope you don't mind sitting with Alden tonight, Anckar," Hertha said brightly. "Bena and I have things to discuss."

Anckar stood dumbstruck, but then Alden motioned her to his

side. "No," she said, settling in Hertha's old place. "No, I don't. Mind. At all." She drank her water and said with a laugh, "Last time *I* went to the store, one of the good old guys spit on my boots and asked if I was a boy."

Hertha shuddered. "I remember. You spat right back at him."

Lupe gave a vigorous nod. "It was after that day that Mira put the sign in the window. Hertha, I'll be glad to help you carry the groceries home on the stretcher, but only if I can wait for you at the first field."

Driscoll rubbed a napkin over his beard. "What is all this about hiking to town with the stretcher? I'm here with the Doble. I was going to drive to town anyway, for a good look. What is it called?"

Hertha said, "Yates," making it sound like a dirge.

It made him laugh. "Write me a list, Hertha. I'll go in the morning."

There was a long pause while everyone busied themselves with their food. Then Lupe said, "*No Freaks allowed*, Mira's sign says. That means all of us."

Driscoll shrugged impatiently "She couldn't possibly mean me. We haven't even met yet."

For some reason, Brendan thought that remark was funny. "If you don't mind my saying so, you look more like a freak to people like her than any of us. Especially if you show up in your car."

Driscoll gave a dismissive wave. "She'll get used to it. And to me. The people in Clydestown did." He looked at Em. "How about you? Can I interest you in a ride?"

"Sorry," she said, trying to find a plausible excuse real fast. "I'm climbing the mountain tomorrow. To get my blood pumping again. I've been lying and sitting around for a week now. If I don't use my muscles soon they'll waste away."

Anckar speared up a forkful of salad. "You're climbing the mountain to where?"

"I don't know. Straight up, I guess. As far as I can. Don't look so worried. I'm a good hiker. Always have been."

Anckar exchanged a meaningful look with Alden. "You can't go alone," he told Em. "You need a guide for the rough spots. In some places the soil is so thin that you can see steam rising out of it. At night, whole patches of ground glow fire-red."

Driscoll's eyes shone. "Volcanic vents? I've read about them. I've always wanted to see some."

"They're dangerous," Anckar said flatly. "I tell you what, Em— I'll go with you. We'll picnic by the lake."

At her side, Alden was turning thoughtful, playing with his noodles. "You'll love the lake, Em. I was only there once but I still recall that fantastic green. It was so clear it seems you can see to the bottom, though Anckar says it's incredibly deep." He looked at Anckar with unaccustomed resolve. "If you don't mind, I'd like to come too."

"But you hate to sweat," she reminded him. "Last time you came you swore you'd never climb the mountain again."

"A man *can* change his mind," he said loftily. "At least now I know what to expect."

Driscoll fidgeted, his expression fluctuating between serious and joyful. At last he sighed and said, "I promised myself I'd climb the mountain first chance I got. And this is it, Odasan. I'm afraid you'll have to wait for your rice one extra day. I'm going with them."

"There may be as much as one good cup left in the bag," Odasan conceded with a humorless smile. "Broken kernels, mostly, and chaff. It'll have to do."

Anckar slid her chair closer to Alden and tilted in his direction until they were practically rubbing shoulders. "If you're serious about coming," she said with great animation, "here's what we'll need." She ticked off a list on her fingers. On the other side of the table Hertha choked on her wine.

Impulsively, Em asked, "Hertha, when's the last time you took a day off? Come with us. All of you. What could be better than a family picnic on the shores of a mountain lake?"

"I can't spare the time!" she quickly replied.

Brendan noisily slurped sauce through one of his macaroni straws and said, "Sorry. The lookout's my limit. Besides, I'll be chopping wood most of the day."

"And I promised to help with the apples," Lupe put in.

Em turned to Bena. "You and Odasan?"

"If I'm not going to the store I'll be helping Hertha, just as we planned. And then Odasan and I are searching for a very rare wound-healing plant. He thinks he saw it grow near where we first met."

Lupe flashed her a grateful smile.

"Oh, that reminds me!" Anckar jumped to her feet and pulled the sheet off the package she'd brought with her. "Custom ordered, custom made," she said, exposing a large painting. It depicted the double rainbow sunrise she'd promised Odasan, complete with golden cloud portal, distant mountain chains, misty horizon, and the valley below. But that was not all. She'd added a moss-covered log lying off to the side. The two figures sitting on it were holding hands. One had waist-long black hair threaded with silver, the other a thatch of white.

"Ah!" Odasan said, brightening. "You remembered the log. This is wonderful!"

"Gorgeous," Hertha breathed. "Anckar, is *this* what you've been doing all day? You deserve nothing less than one of my famous picnic sandwiches. And when you get home in the evening I'll have your favorite dessert waiting—hot apple pie."

After some effort, Anckar managed to give her adversary the ghost of a smile. It was her first real try at amiability—and it was contagious.

"All right, Driscoll," Em cried, "I'll ride into town with you the day after tomorrow. I want a look at Yates too." She regretted the offer as soon as it was out of her mouth. If Mira consider one giant freaky she'd hardly be delighted with two.

CHAPTER 26

MOST OF DRISCOLL'S BOOKS TURNED OUT to be boring. Maybe they'd make adequate winter reading once she was stuck in the house with not much to do except cook, eat, and work on some kind of craft. But until then Em could get along very well without knowing what lay inside a stone and inside a mountain. "You sure have a lot of books about cars," she complained, sitting on the floor in back of the couch, unable to keep her disappointment from showing.

"I inherited most of them from my father. They're invaluable." He caressed the one she held on her lap. "What kind of books do *you* like?"

She let her eyes travel over the various stacks. "Ghost stories and tales of adventure with the word 'suddenly' in them."

He looked amused. "I don't have any of those. But you don't have to *read* about adventures anymore—you're *in* one. And sooner or later the word *suddenly* will jump into your own life—maybe more often than you'll find comfortable!" He pulled a slim volume from one of the stacks. "Here. My father had a whole room full of these. He only rescued this one—the rest burnt along with the room."

The book was thin, with a slick cover. *National Geographic*, she read, and opened it to find a world she knew nothing about. "Where's this?"

"Africa." He passed along another book, this one heavy and big. "And this is a world atlas. See if you can find the continent of Africa in it."

She abandoned all pretense of helping him organize the pile and surrendered herself to the pages before her, peering at the small print by weak lamp light. The atlas contained the greatest adventure story of them all, about stars and constellations, black holes, something called supernova, and roundish balls the book claimed were other worlds.

"We didn't learn any of this at school," she said with a growing sense of wonder. "How come?"

"That's because we've re-entered the dark ages. These days most people consider outer space pure fiction." He knelt, leafed through the atlas, and tapped on one of the pages. "Here's where we live, but it doesn't look much like this anymore. See all those roads? The mega-cities? Gone. Our world has shrunk from encompassing thousands of miles to the walking distance between Oren and Clydestown. The only thing they teach at school these days, besides the alphabet and simple math, is that the earth is flat and surrounded by a sea of darkness."

Em stared at the picture of a round blue and green, cloud-speckled earth. It was true—she *was* uncomfortable with the idea of separating herself from what she'd always known. Was that why the mountain had seemed such a threat to her when they approached it last week?

"Curiosity is dead," Driscoll said, slamming an armload of books onto the bottom shelf with unnecessary vigor.

Across the room, Brendan and Lupe sat side by side on the hearthstones. He was whittling and she was squinting at her embroidery frame. Bena and Odasan were at the cleared table, their heads together, focusing on his treasured martial arts opus. Every now and then he closed his eyes and swept his hands through the air, sometimes with the fingers straight, sometimes clenched into very tight fists. Then Bena would lean away from him and, with an indulgent smile, watch him execute miniature thrusts, blocks, and punches.

Hertha was sitting in Alden's chair, her feet on a stool, staring distractedly at her toes. Every now and then she wiggled them and emitted a heart-felt sigh. At last Bena came to sit on the stool. "I think our dinner went well," she said. "By the end of the meal Anckar looked quite comfortable with the new seating arrangement."

Em, still on the floor, was browsing through the slightly singed *National Geographic*, looking at the pictures of animals she'd thought lived only in myths. When the two women decided to sit on the couch together, her ears couldn't help tracking their murmured conversation. "Can you believe it?" she heard Hertha say. "Anckar actually told me to put up my feet for a while. Then she volunteered to wash the dishes, and Alden—praise be—offered to dry them. When they both despise that particular chore! Now I have nothing to do. I don't know how to do nothing!"

"Then maybe it's time you learned." Bena gave her an encouraging pat. "Just like Alden and Anckar are learning that doing the dishes can be a lot more fun than they realized."

Having nothing to do had never bothered Em—or so her mother had frequently claimed, probably with good reason. Come to think of it, her mother and Hertha had something in common. They both loved to talk about how overwhelmed they were but were not satisfied unless they had something to overwhelm them. Em bent over the atlas to study the picture Driscoll had shown her. It was captioned *North America* and consisted of countless squiggles and lines. "What do they mean?" she asked him.

He leaned close enough so that his beard almost tickled her cheek. "It's called a map," he explained. "The blue lines are rivers. The red ones are the old roads—highways and freeways, they were called. These brown things, they're mountains. Green is for the plains because they used to be full of growing things. And all that blue wash, that's oceans. The circles are cities. And these fat strokes, they mark the different states. There used to be fifty, I think."

What good did it do anyone to study something that was no longer there? She'd rather practice math and keep watch for her favorite word.

"Odd," Hertha murmured from the couch. "We are five women but only four men, and everybody's getting ready to pair off except me. The others don't notice it yet but I can see it coming. Now that I'm out of the way, Alden and Anckar—well, that's just a matter of time. You and Odasan have already done it. And anyone watching Brendan and Lupe, or Driscoll and Em . . . Bena, you know what I think?" Hertha lowered her voice to a whisper, so that Em could barely hear the rest of her words. "The missing tenth spoke must be a man. Meant for me! Coming any day now, don't you think, Bena?"

There was such yearning in her voice, and such hope, that Em said just loud enough for them to hear, "No one's coming up here to be with you, Hertha. No one at all. I swear it." Then she realized how awful it sounded and clapped her hands to her mouth, but what was said could not be recalled. "I'm sorry," she stammered. "But it's true just the same."

Hertha gave a sharp exhale and Bena glanced down at Em with a hint of exasperation and an almost imperceptible headshake. Em felt her face heat with chagrin. Tact had never been her strong point.

"No one at all . . ." Hertha repeated listlessly, eyes glistening.

The woman had everything else wrong too. There was nothing between Em and Driscoll. Sometimes she didn't even like him very much. And Brendan and Lupe were more like brother and sister than not. Surely there was more to life than waiting to be half of a couple! Em considered the map. Its squiggles and lines were the colored strands of a web made of promises as broken as the land it depicted. She shut the atlas and slid it onto the bottom shelf next to the books about old-timey cars. Driscoll should label that shelf, "Things that are gone and will never be again." Not one of the tomes had anything to do with her, here and now.

From the kitchen came the clinking of glass, gay voices, shared laughter. Hertha winced after each peal. At last Brendan put his whittling aside to pick up a darkly shining guitar. While he tuned it Lupe moved from the hearthstones to sit at his feet. She drew up her knees, smoothed the skirt over her ankles, and watched him tune the strings.

"Oh, good," Driscoll said. "We're having a sing-along. I have something that might come in handy." He thrust a songbook at Em. She dropped it as if it were a dead fish. She never sang.

Brendan played something mellow and vaguely familiar. A lullaby? Driscoll cocked his head to listen. "Five minutes of that and we'll all be asleep," he muttered and rummaged through his heap of belongings. "Alden?" he called out, earning a dirty look from the musician, who seemed to have expected a more rapt audience. "Alden?" Driscoll called again. "Have you seen my fiddle?"

Alden poked his head into the room. "I shoved it under the couch so no one would step on it."

A few seconds later Driscoll was caressing an old violin. Putting it against his shoulder, he coaxed forth the first gust of bright sound.

Brendan looked quite annoyed. "Hey," he said. "Don't screech that thing now!"

Grinning wickedly, Driscoll produced a loud caterwaul and then a musical shout of pure joy. His long, flexible fingers holding the bow seemed as sure of each note as if he'd practiced the tune for a lifetime. The exuberant melody canceled the sleepy end-of-the-day feeling Brendan had aimed for on his mellow guitar.

"You're ruining the mood!" Brendan protested.

"No—I'm saving it!" Driscoll replied, playing faster.

Lupe was tapping her toes, Hertha clapped along, Bena jumped up, swishing her skirts, Odasan closed his books, smiling, and Alden glided in from the kitchen trailing a dishtowel.

"I know this tune," he said. "People dance to it at weddings." He skipped around the table in his moccasined feet, turning complete circles at each corner. Lupe danced in his wake, shoeless and light on her toes. He took her hand, bowed, and whirled her in and out of tight turns. She held out her other hand to Bena, who motioned to Hertha, who motioned to Anckar, coming in from the kitchen. They formed one big circle, turning and stomping and clapping along with the tune until even Brendan's good foot twitched to its rhythm and his sullen expression gave way to a grin.

Driscoll shut his eyes, yielding to the jubilant sounds of his fiddle, but Em shrank away from them all, content to watch the fun from a distance. She knew exactly what would happen if she tried to dance. She'd trip over everyone's feet including her own. Then they would laugh at her awkwardness. Even Driscoll. She envied the ease with which Lupe and Hertha hooked elbows and twirled. To make her feel even worse, Nada abandoned her for the first time since they met, joining in the fun and adding an occasional bark to the fiddle's shrill tune.

Em was glad when Brendan held up his hand and said loudly, "Enough. Driscoll, we need to move on. Let me just do a quiet number on the guitar to soften things out before we get started."

"Get started with what? A sing-along? Here, we can use this." Driscoll tossed him the songbook.

After a perfunctory glance, Brendan dropped it onto the hearthstones. "I don't read music." He launched into the opening chords of "Sacred Hillsides," and Anckar, laying a hand over her heart, began to hum along. The others sang the refrain. Em managed a couple of strained notes before she decided to do them the favor of mouthing the rest of the words. Her voice had cracked permanently in third grade while she was singing a solo, which her classmates mocked mercilessly for weeks afterwards.

Then Brendan strummed his last chord, put the guitar aside, and announced, "Dream class!"

CHAPTER 27

THEY SAT ON THE ROUND BRAIDED RUG, the six old-timers casually crossing their ankles and closing their eyes, the newcomers copying the posture. When something soft and furry brushed past her knees Em knew it was Nada, settling at her feet for an extended nap. The fire crackled in the hearth. A candle hissed. Alden began to speak, each word clear and deliberate.

"At our last sitting we worked on our new garden," he said. "Attracting more earthworms and enriching the soil. Where do we go now? Who wants to be first?"

Anckar said, "I do!"

"Good," Alden told her. "Show our friends how it's done."

"Okay then." She rubbed her thighs and rotated her shoulders, trying to relax. "Watching Odasan and Brendan build the yurt made me think about where I want to live. Now don't interrupt." She took a deep breath. Her face softened. "My house sits high above the new valley. It's made of peeled logs and is surrounded by a stone terrace. I like to sit on the outside bench in the evenings, watching luminous sunsets. I grow geraniums in my window boxes and have my own little orchard. There's an apricot tree. Pears. Apples. And plums. A stone's throw uphill from the house stand three spruces. The one in the middle is tallest. There's a big boulder beside them, flat on top.

It's covered with moss. That's where I sit on warm afternoons. From there I can hear the brook bubble in and out of the swimming hole. My studio is in a lean-to at the rear of the house."

Em's legs tingled. Soon she could no longer bear to sit still and quietly straightened her legs until her toes encountered luxurious fur. She squinted at the dog who had completely recovered from her mysterious ailments. With pleasure, she rubbed her soles over Nada's back, grateful for Bena's healing salve.

". . . and my shop has skylights, for shadow-free light," Anckar was saying. All at once, Em felt herself tilting. The vague picture she'd formed in her mind became sharply detailed. She smelled wet clay and saw a long, dusty table, nearby utility shelves crammed with supplies, a potter's wheel in the far corner. Painted canvases leaned against one wall, blank frames against the other. Charcoal sketches were thumbtacked to the log siding. On a sturdy easel, a half-finished oil painting glowed in the overhead light.

Anckar said "Yes! Like that!" and went quiet. Her chin sank to her chest. Eventually, she continued in a dreamy voice. "It's all getting clearer—the log walls, the big windows in the kitchen, the great view from the little breakfast nook, the hand-painted fruit bowl on the table full of apples and pears." She paused as if to admire her vision, and concluded with, "There's a loft upstairs, just big enough for a bed, a couple of dressers, and a two-sided wardrobe."

Em's rump was getting sore. She shifted her weight from one hip to the other, walked her toes over Nada's flank, and saw a colorful patchwork quilt and uncurtained windows thrown wide. On the lush meadow below a misty figure was picking flowers.

"Is your bed big enough to sleep two?" Lupe asked mischievously.

"Lupe!" Hertha huffed.

Brendan cleared his throat. "You know the rule. *Don't interrupt.*"

"No, wait," Alden said slowly. "Lupe has a point. You can't change the shape of a log house after it's built. So, Anckar . . . is it?"

"Is it what?"

"Big enough for two."

She chuckled. "Didn't I just mention a couple of dressers? Of *course* the bed can sleep two—not that it has to, you understand. But the quilt is king-sized and cozy."

Alden said, "Lots of pillows on top and a rug at each side. I can smell the pinesap beading on the logs. I see clouds sail over the roof."

With her eyes shut, Em once more looked out at the misty figure on the meadow below. It was wearing a red bandana.

"Your little brook flows steeply downhill," said the Alden who was sitting beside her on the floor rug. "It connects with other brooks to form the creek that runs to the valley floor, where it streams into a wide lake. There's a small island in the middle, thick with birds."

"Ah! A bird sanctuary," Driscoll said with interest. "And look, see that glint on the far hillside? It's glass, reflecting the sun." And then, to Em's surprise, he asked eagerly, "Are you done, Anckar? Can I go next?"

"Fine with me," she said. "Just remember to keep everything positive."

"I'm catching on. Mine's a massive round house," he began. "The double entry doors are carved from oak and so tall that I never have to worry about ducking again. A stone fireplace. A stone chimney. Well-cushioned couches and loungers in convenient locations." With his bare hand, he brushed an imaginary picture on thin air. "Our kitchen. It has a glass wall facing east. We've painted the opposite wall a bright red."

"Red!" Hertha repeated, appalled.

"Beet red. The whole room turns hot pink every morning. It's like sitting inside a sunrise."

"Good touch," Anckar told him.

"Long, smooth counters. Easy to wipe," Driscoll went on, "and just the right height for us so we don't have to scrunch over when we're cooking."

"'That's a negative," Brendan said. "The part about ducking was, too."

"Let it go," Alden decided. "He's got the idea."

"Okay," Driscoll continued, obviously enjoying himself. "There's an enormous table for dinner parties and such. Odasan and Brendan built it right on the spot. It's so heavy it'll never be moved."

Em poked her big toe at the root of Nada's tail. A wet tongue licked her heel. She winked at the dog. Nada blinked back.

Once more closing her eyes, Em saw tall-backed oaken chairs with needlepoint upholstery. There was a cat on the banister outside, its striped yellow fur highlighted by the early-morning sun. It was washing one of its paws.

"The deck's got lots of cat trees and dog beds for my four-legged friends," Driscoll explained. "It wraps around the whole house. Great for entertaining. I see musical evenings. Special dinners. Potlucks. Our friends have the run of the downstairs, but the upstairs is private domain. Our bed is so long we can comfortably rest our heads and feet on the mattress at the same time—with room to spare! A ladder leads to the observation tower. It has an incredible 360-degrees view." He gave a perplexed little laugh. "I can even see the tower's glass ceiling. It opens and shuts. There are mats on the floor for star-gazing."

Brendan cleared his throat. "He thinks big. I'll give him that."

"He *is* big," Lupe said. "But tell us, Driscoll, what's with the 'we'?"

Em had been wondering the same thing, though she'd never have asked.

"A slip of the tongue?" he offered. "Although I *am* planning to get married one day."

"I'll dance at your wedding," Lupe promised. "But before you get hitched, will you invite me up to your observation tower? To show me your favorite stars?"

Hertha said, "Lupe, that'll do!"

The girl tittered. "Hey, Driscoll! In your house built to fit giants, is there a place in it for visiting elves to sit—or do we need ladders to climb up on your chairs?"

He gave a good-natured shrug. "There are stepstools in every downstairs room."

"I'm relieved," Lupe said. "But will we be able to climb those giant-sized stairs?"

"Please try to be serious," Hertha said. "You've obviously had too much blackberry wine."

"And too much fiddling!" Brendan muttered.

Lupe giggled. "Don't stop me now. I'm about to check out that 360-degrees view—and see how *she* likes it when the shoe's on the other foot."

"My shoes would never fit you, so don't even try," Em said.

"Too true," Lupe told her. "And you could never squeeze into mine, even if you hacked off your toes *and* your heels."

"Are you sure you even *have* shoes?" Em retorted. "I've been here over a week and I haven't seen you wear any yet."

"Now look what you've done," Brendan told Driscoll. "I told

you the fiddle would set the wrong tone."

"But I *like* the tone of his fiddle," Lupe protested. "Driscoll, I hope you play for us every night. And I love your round house. It's only right that a giant should live in a giant-sized house."

Brendan glowered. "Who's next?"

"No, wait!" Driscoll sounded intrigued. "I'm not done yet."

"Yes you are," Brendan said. "Let somebody else have a turn."

"In a minute," Alden told him. "I expect Driscoll's house is ideal for dances and parties. I see banjos and mandolins. I hear Odasan playing his flute. The table is crowded with great food and home-brewed wine and beer. People are dancing."

"I brought my guitar," Brendan said, mollified. "We're making up songs."

Em rubbed at her throat. "And I'm singing them with my new voice." Why *not* think big? A good singing voice was something she'd always wished for. "It's as pure as a meadow-lark's and can go just as high."

Lupe gave a derisive laugh. "You croaked like a frog a few minutes ago."

"I couldn't have!" Em said hotly. "I was only moving my lips."

"My mistake," Lupe said. "Driscoll, are you done? Okay—I'm going next. This is what I see: Brendan's foot is entirely whole. He runs like the wind. We have two horses. Mine's the color of sorrel, with a flowing black mane and a bushy black tail." A smoldering log burst into flame, tinting every face pink. Even Bena's glowed like a child's.

"Mine's the color of blue smoke," Brendan told them. "His name is Kiran. There's none faster than him."

Em saw a rolling pasture below Driscoll's house. She saw two horses cavorting, their tails and heads high. She heard their hooves drumming. The air smelled like cool lake-water and newly cut hay.

Hertha held up her hand for attention. "Now me!" She straightened her back and began. "I see a man," she said in a resolute voice, "stately and tall. The crowd parts for him wherever he goes. His name is Tomas. He's the master gardener, just like Em said. He knows all there is to know about every plant. Some claim that as soon as he looks at a seed it starts sprouting. Our valley is thriving under his care. At dawn, he walks through the mist, his hair dripping with dew. He studies the heads of grain, the ears of corn, the compost pile in our new garden. He keeps track of the moon's waxing and waning. He makes the sun shine and the clouds rain, sometimes both at once. And as he walks over the land he's looking for me!"

Nada pushed her nose hard against Em's arch, and then Em saw Tomas directly below her, his head tilting to scan the sky, his eyes dark and compelling. He was so close she could have reached down and touched his intense face. *From above*? Somebody gasped. Em grew aware that Nada was looking at her. On the far side of the circle, Hertha gave a startled cry and covered her eyes.

"For a second, there . . ." Brendan's voice shook. "See what I mean, Lupe? Things are speeding up now that Em's here. We never had a dream class like this before." Em couldn't decide if he was excited or frightened. He asked, "Em, what did you do?"

"Me?" she said. "Nothing. I was just listening to you all." She tried to wedge her toes between Nada's back and the floor, but the dog yawned and sat up.

Alden was following a different thought. "Hertha, do you know what you've done?" he said in an awed tone. "You put a stranger into our dream valley. We're not alone anymore."

"You started it," she replied. "With parties and music and potlucks. Who did you think would eat all that stuff?"

"Do we *want* people there, waiting for us?" He shook his head. "I'll have to think about that."

"Don't think him away!" she pleaded.

He rose abruptly. "I expect we've done enough for tonight. You can all add to our creations as you drift off to sleep or first thing in the morning. Just remember to focus only on what you want. Ignore everything else."

"What will you do about Tomas?" Hertha asked.

He flopped face-down on to the couch. "I haven't the slightest idea."

Odasan gave Bena a hand up and put an arm around her. "Ready for bed? He's right, you know. Our dream house is already built. All we have to do now is to envision where we want to put it. We can do it between us, right on our mat." He swept up his book and led her to the door.

Bena stopped on the threshold to smile back at Em. "I told you there was a reason we came. You're taking us on a fantastic ride. Tonight was only the beginning."

Wincing, Brendan rubbed at his legs. "Let's have another dream class tomorrow night. To keep the momentum going."

"After our hike? I doubt it," Alden said.

"I'll consider that a maybe," Brendan told him. Then he asked Lupe, "Can you ride? What did you name your mare?"

She shrugged. "I've never even climbed on a horse, but what does it matter? If I can imagine myself riding her it will happen soon enough. And I'm calling her Sorrel."

"Good choice!" Tenderly, he pulled the sleeves of her sweater down over her wrists the way she liked and said, "If you want help with the apples tomorrow, I'll be glad to slice them up for the pies, now that I've practiced on onions."

Alden unrolled his bed sack. "We're done," he said, sweeping the couch cushions onto the floor. "Go to sleep if you can. If not, dream anyway. Good night."

"We could think our little yurt next to the lake. Or on a forested slope," Odasan told Bena as they wandered out into the yard. Lupe, running out behind them, reached for the stars and turned in an exuberant circle. "He runs like the wind," she sighed when Brendan took her hand to escort her to her tent. "And she's the color of sorrel."

In the living room, Alden wiggled under his covers, murmuring, "A bed big enough for two. A feather-light quilt . . ."

Driscoll, who had no place to sleep, folded himself onto the chair by the fireplace and stared at the dying flames. The round house took shape in the coals, so clearly defined that he could have stepped from one hearth to the other. Before he could rouse himself to attempt the feat a pleasant ease overcame him. His head sank sideways and the only thing he stepped into was a dream.

Lying on her pallet out in the yard, Em pulled the blanket up over her head and put a finger lightly over her throat, quietly experimenting with scales. Nothing, yet. But she had no doubt it would come. "This has been the best day of my life," she told Nada. "I wonder what last week's dread was all about." She smiled sleepily at the moon, which gleamed like a large silver coin. "I wish things could always stay this good." When the metallic light darkened to the color of a tarnished old penny, she knew it would not.

CHAPTER 28

EM SHIVERED AWAKE JUST AS THE GRAY end of night gave way to a new beginning. Her clothes were sweat-dampened under the blanket and the socks she'd kicked off in her sleep lay on the grass, soaked with dew. She snatched them up as she rose, clutched the blanket around her, and fled to the yurt, relieved to find a banked fire in the tin stove. Odasan and Bena's bedding was tidied away; they had already left for what they liked to call their meditation meadow.

Em threw some twigs on the coals and watched them come alive. Soon a cozy stick fire crackled and popped and the kettle she'd put on the burner started to boil. She hung her socks up to dry, brewed tea, and took her cup out to the deck. Settling on the top stair, she cocooned herself in the blanket and took tiny sips, appreciating the heat they provided. Nada burrowed under the improvised tent to lie at Em's feet. Automatically, she put a hand on the dog and surveyed the sky. Gathering clouds were tinged by the as yet invisible sun, becoming a shifting mosaic of pinks, lilacs and reds. Ground fog, swirling around the yurt like white smoke, rose from the garden to waft over the clearing and shroud the surrounding trees, leaving only the crowns visible, then nothing at all. The porch became a raft adrift in a strange sea. It could have been anywhere in or out of Em's universe.

A twig snapped, then a gray shape solidified out of the mist. It was Alden, carelessly dragging the blanket he'd draped over one shoulder. "I *thought* I heard friendly sounds from this direction," he said, climbing the steps. "Are you drinking something hot?"

"Inside," she said, moving her legs just enough so he could squeeze by.

He brought a steaming cup back out, sat beside her, and slurped his tea. "That's better. The amount of heat generated by a cup of this stuff is truly amazing. Poor Driscoll's all bent out of shape from sleeping in my chair. He would have been wiser to bed down on the floor."

"It wasn't much fun for me out here either," Em said. "We need more permanent sleeping arrangements. Maybe Anckar will let me share her tent. And Driscoll could move into the tipi, although he and Brendan don't seem to have quite hit it off yet."

Alden looked surprised. "I thought you'd set up a tent together."

"Driscoll and me?" She blushed. "I've only known him for a week!"

He shook his head. "You know better than that."

Part of her did, part of her didn't. "I don't *know* what I know," she said. "Sometimes I get flashes of insight. I'm blind the rest of the time. Who gets to tell me where to sleep when? What are the rules on sleeping arrangements?"

He stared into his cup and said, "There aren't any. You decide for yourself. If you always go toward what feels right in the moment you won't need any one else's old rules. You make up your own as you go, about Driscoll and everything else. Those flashes you're talking about are part of what you've learned this past week. They're inside you now, like seeds waiting to sprout."

"What if I can't tell the difference between what I feel and what I think I should feel?"

He pointed his cup at her chest. "Weigh it in there. You'll be sure."

"Is that what *you* do?"

He gave a wry laugh. "I don't practice what I preach. Now that I've turned out to be wrong about the tenth spoke, I haven't got the slightest idea about what to do next. My mind's in a fog, just like this clearing."

"You're putting too much faith in me," she said.

"Or not enough," he replied. "I agree with Brendan that you are the key to our future. It's you who'll be leading us from now on."

She shivered. "I'm making no claims. I'm not a natural leader. In this soup I couldn't even lead you to the garden gate without getting lost."

"How can you be lost when you know you are here?"

She spread a hand. "Where is here?"

He chuckled softly. "Wherever *you* are, of course."

She was beginning to like this conversation. It wasn't the kind she could have had with logical-minded Driscoll. "What if our world dissolves every night and we shape it from scratch with our thoughts the moment we wake up in the morning?"

Alden laughed again. "If you replace the word 'thought' with 'expectations', it sounds just about right."

"You don't think it was a dumb thing to say?"

"Not at all. How else would anything change? Listen—I hear Anckar hacking away. She always coughs just before she wakes up. She'll soon have us organized and on the trail. I've already forgotten the list she mentioned last night. Wasn't there something about apples?"

"Water flasks," Em remembered. "Dried fruit. Let's go inside and pack. I'll toast some bread for a quick breakfast. Will the fog stick around all day?"

"It'll burn off as soon as the sun comes over the rise," he predicted, standing up. "It always does this time of year." He wrapped the blanket around his shoulders. "I'll guide you to the kitchen. I haven't lost my way to it yet, not even in blizzards. And chances are, Hertha's already got everything prepared, including our breakfast."

"You take a lot for granted."

"I know Hertha," he said. "If she likes to cook for us, is it right to deny her?"

She laughed and tapped on his chest. "Weigh it in there."

AMPLY WARMED, fed and provided, they set off an hour later just as the fog started to lift. But first Anckar made Hertha promise to keep Nada indoors for the day. "I'll have enough worry just trying to keep the two-footed ones safe," she said. "Besides, the sharp rocks up there would cut up her pads all over again."

After they went outside Driscoll stopped to gaze toward the

shrouded summit. "Say, Anckar—can we go all the way to the top?"

"You'd need special equipment for that. The lake's high enough for you tender-footed beginners. Let's get going while the air's still cool. Climbing gets unpleasant with the sun beating down."

They trooped across the yard to the trailhead. Alden cut in front of Driscoll to claim second place and said, "Anckar has hiked this path so often she could get to the ridge in pitch-black."

She quickened her pace. "I often do!" Indeed, she seemed made for the task. Small and compact, lithe as a cat, she was a full head shorter than Alden but managed to outdistance them all as the slope grew rapidly steeper.

"Short legs must be better for climbing," Driscoll said when they'd fallen hopelessly behind. "Em, if we want to catch up you better stop admiring every little wildflower we see."

"Can you blame her?" Alden asked. "You don't find any like these on the plains." He was already starting to sweat. "Just wait till we get to the lake meadow, Em. It's got swaths of them. God, I forgot how endlessly steep this part is."

Gradually, the timber around them took on a crisper, hardier look. The forest floor was thick with old needles and pinecones. But the higher they climbed, the poorer the soil grew, until at last pines and firs became stunted, with wind-twisted limbs. Anckar was waiting for them where the last of these gnarled shapes clung to a knoll. "Now it gets tricky. Be sure you follow my steps exactly!" Somewhere ahead something bubbled, smelling rotten-egg foul. A shrill whistle came from Em's left, and then a jet of water exploded out of the ground. She jumped, nearly twisting her ankle.

"Boiling hot," Alden panted.

Limp, spindly ferns clustered between stones framing the trail, which wound through a shallow soil basin. From it, steam hissed and whistled and moaned. "It looks like we've come to the entrance to hell. Sounds like it too," Driscoll said.

"And you'll get to the brimstone part real fast if you step off this path," Anckar warned. "In a few spots the ground's so thin-skinned, I've had it collapse under my feet. I almost got dunked in a pool of bubbling mud once."

Em stopped abruptly, causing Driscoll to bump her from behind. "What if the four of us are too heavy, walking so close together? Maybe we should cross one at a time."

Anckar gave her an approving look. "Good idea. That way, in

case the ground caves, we'll only lose one of us."

Em took a step backward. "Are you *trying* to scare me? What makes it so hot?"

"There's fire under our feet," Anckar said with satisfaction. "It'll stay underground for as long as the mountain is sleeping. I'll go first, then Alden, then you."

"*Sleeping*?" Driscoll chortled under his breath, but Em was in no mood to share his amusement as she waited for Alden to gain solid ground. Then she followed his footsteps around unnerving holes in which black soup blistered and heaved. "How can this ugly place be so close to our beautiful garden?" she asked Driscoll when he'd caught up.

It was Anckar who replied. "It's not ugly after the sun sets. At night, this slope shimmers and glows with earth magic."

Em shuddered. "You walk through this maze in the dark? You'd never get me up here after sundown. But I'm grateful you volunteered as my guide. If you hadn't, most likely Hertha would have one less mouth to feed at supper tonight."

Alden laughed and took a long drink from his flask. "Don't thank her yet. Wait until we get past the scree. It's desolate enough under any light—and no less dangerous than this."

"And yet," Anckar said, "I've seen it reflect every tint sundown has to offer. One day, when I get good enough, I hope to paint the colors I've seen."

Alden was right; the scree was a vast field of treacherously shifting stones with no visible trail across. Stepping carefully from one loose rock to the next, Em recalled that Brendan's foot was crushed on a similar slope.

"The poor fool was running after a goat," Anckar said, "and started an avalanche. They happen here too—after a storm, or a heavy snowfall, or for no reason at all. That's why *we're* treading lightly. See those boulders up there? If you aim straight for them you'll be fine." She forged ahead, not disturbing a single rock.

Halfway to their goal Driscoll sat down to take off his boots. "I'm getting blisters," he said, smoothing his socks before retying the laces. Then he took a long drink of his water. "I'll be all right after we rest."

"Did I hear the word 'rest'?" Alden groaned. "It has a wonderful ring to it. Anckar, what do you say?"

"I say not yet. I know you too well. Once you sit down nothing and nobody can make you get up again. You'll doze and miss all the fun."

"That was last time. Because no one warned me how hard it was going to be."

"This time you know. Does it change anything?"

"Not much," he confessed, massaging his calves. "My legs are turning to putty as we speak."

"Mine are quivering like jelly." Driscoll heaved himself upright again. "Why aren't yours, Anckar? There must be some trick to this climbing business you haven't told us about." He tipped his flask back for another long swallow.

"You're right," Anckar admitted. "There *is* a trick. It's to keep to a steady rhythm and measure each breath. All this stopping and going, the tiresome chitchat—it's sheer waste. Maybe if you'd use your car less and your legs more, the climb would be easier for you, Driscoll. As for you, Alden—you obviously sit on your thinking rock too much. You could both learn something from Em."

Em had not expected the praise. Perhaps her long hikes to Bena's woods and to Clydestown were finally paying off. So was a childhood spent stooping over furrows under the unblinking eye of a pitiless sun.

"We men have no choice but to admire you women," Driscoll grinned, unbuttoning his shirt. "What do you say, Anckar—let's you and me hike to town tomorrow to fetch a month's worth of supplies. We'll carry it home on the stretcher. Okay?"

Anckar laughed in spite of herself. "I suppose cars can be useful occasionally, though I've never met one I liked. I've seen too many wrecks littering city streets." She forged ahead smartly, a proud Em in her wake. The men lagged farther and farther behind, but whenever Em glanced over her shoulder she found Driscoll's gaze trained upon her. It made her so self-conscious that she forgot how to breathe and move naturally. What did he see when he looked at her? What *was* there to see?

Finally, Alden collapsed to his knees, gasping, "Anckar, what's the rush? We have all day. Is there any reason why we can't just enjoy this climb? If you keep running ahead like this, you'll wind up picnicking at the lake all by yourself. In case you forgot, the sandwiches are in my pack."

Anckar stopped. "Going fast is an old habit of mine. I tend to speed up the higher I get. It's the mountain, pulling at me." She turned to sit at his side, taking a sip from her canteen. "I've stormed up here so often that I can't feel the difference between level land and a rise anymore."

"I can!" Alden said. "With every part of my weak-muscled body." He raised his flask to his lips and then shook it. "Empty." She gave him hers. He drank greedily and lay on his back after carefully putting aside a few of the sharpest rocks.

Driscoll pulled off his boots and socks, gingerly touching the weeping red sores on his toes and his heels. "Some of Bena's wound salve would come in handy right now."

"Dab on some spit," Anckar instructed. "Until you can give them a good soak in the lake." She nodded uphill. "You two go ahead. Alden and I will catch up as soon as he's able. You can't go wrong from here—once you get through the pass, take the left fork of the trail. It'll take you straight up to the ridge. You'll see the lake from there."

Driscoll and Em climbed to where the two slopes formed a deep gulley. A high wall of stones plugged most of the cut, leaving the narrowest gap in the middle. Poised on top of the wall, a lone boulder stood on end as if ready to roll.

"You think it's steady?" Em asked.

"Rock-steady," Driscoll said with a twinkle. "It's probably been balanced like that for centuries."

"Maybe." Em studied the boulder with suspicion. "But just because it hasn't moved doesn't mean it won't." She was startled to hear Anckar's voice in her ear. "I only take a few sips while I'm climbing," she heard her say. "That's why I never sweat."

Em turned, sure that Anckar had caught up, but there was no one behind them. When she squinted downhill she could see her sitting with Alden far below.

"I've read that sounds can do strange things on a mountain," Driscoll said. "A voice can travel up and down canyons just like the breeze." They went through the gap in the rock wall and soon came to where the trail forked. The part veering off to the right crossed a desert of dark, welded stone. Stray weeds clung to the occasional crack, unsure if they wanted to live or die.

Following Anckar's directions, Driscoll and Em soon stood on the high point overlooking a sheltered valley. It was framed by a stand of majestic trees that swooped to the edge of a lush meadow. The grass encircled a calm lake whose waters shone like an emerald held up to the light. On a couple of islets, brush had already turned golden and autumn-red. Along the shore, white-barked young saplings shivered in a slight draft. The meadow grass was a patchwork of multi-hued wildflowers.

Awed, Em took Driscoll's hand. "There's our heaven," she said, and they started down. A violet-washed mountain chain undulated along the far-off horizon. Another chain, still farther away, was airbrushed against the sky with delicate strokes of pale lilac. Overhead, stately cloud ships lay docked just below the bright sun. "Worth every blister and drop of sweat," Driscoll said when they came to the lake.

Em dipped in a hand. It rapidly turned a raw pink. "Liquid snow!" She rubbed the hand dry on her shorts as she looked past the ridge from which they had come, hoping for a glimpse of the elusive summit. But it remained shrouded. "Anckar says she's seldom seen it without those hovering clouds. And under the snow cap we noticed from the plains the top is covered by a solid sheet of ice."

His upward gaze was full of yearning. "One day I'll stand on that top, with Anckar or without her," he said, "even if I have to hammer nails into the soles of my boots to get there."

Em did not share his ambition. For her, the lake was plenty high enough. "Do you think the water will warm a bit in the afternoon? Enough so we can go wading?"

"Why wait? Didn't Anckar order me to soak my feet?" He pulled off his footgear and rolled his pants up to his knees. "This will cool me right down." He sloshed in and yelped when the chill waters rose to his thighs. Then he fished for a pretty stone and tossed it straight up. It came down even faster than it had risen and sank to the bottom, stirring up silt. Together, they watched it resettle where he'd found it. "I've had all the pain I can tolerate. I give up," he cried, wading back to the shore, his legs mottled. He did a few jumping jacks to restore his circulation. "I had no idea water could get this cold!"

They traced the shoreline, stepping over downed, rotting logs on which small lizards soaked up the sun. A pair of damselflies, brilliantly blue, hovered above miniscule waves and buzzed their propeller wings over a cream-colored water lily. A small snake, copper brown with a red collar, lay stretched across a flat boulder, too lethargic to flee at the approach of human feet. Then Em noticed a white, glittering stone formation stretch down the hillside on the far shore, a green waterfall silently spilling over its rim. She pointed to it with delight. "It has its own sandy beach. A cove. Let's go and explore it." She guessed the secluded bay, backed by sheltering rock, would store heat more easily than the meadow grass, which was still pearled with dew in shaded spots.

Again they held hands, walking toward the other end of the lake. Halfway there they came to a screen of brush shielding a little hollow, perhaps a dried-up old pond, now covered with moss. Em peeked in. "It's like a bed with a green canopy. Funny, I almost feel as if I've been here before."

He crouched beside her to look, his head so close that when he turned toward her, their lips almost—

"Hello there!" Anckar yelled from the meadow. "Hey, you two! Come and eat!"

Driscoll straightened and said under his breath, "Tarnation! That Alden revives awfully fast!"

CHAPTER 29

THE SANDWICHES HERTHA HAD MADE FOR them were so thick she'd had to nail them together with toothpicks. Em's concoction fell apart as soon as she took the first bite; a tomato slice slipped out one end and an onion ring out of the other.

"Hold it this way," Anckar instructed, sealing both hands around her own sandwich. "Don't tilt the bread."

Soon Em got the hang of it too. "It looks as if Hertha put half of the garden in these," she said. "What's that squashy thing? It's good."

Alden informed her that she was eating one of Hertha's most popular creations, an eggplant sandwich. "Nobody makes them like she does. We've all tried, haven't we, Anckar?"

Anckar's face darkened for an instant. Then she admitted reluctantly, "She's a food artist. Life on the hill wouldn't be half as nice without her good cooking."

"Without her, period," Alden corrected, staring at her until she agreed.

They ate in reverent silence. Then Driscoll gathered the four canteens. "Any objections to my filling these with lake water? Is it safe to drink?"

"There's none better," Anckar said. "It comes straight from the top."

Em went with him into the shallows. "Just think how many fields this lake would turn green around Oren," she said, seeing her father and mother surrounded by tall plants, the hay loft filled, grain to sell . . . "It would change everything for the farmers."

But Driscoll would not agree. "It's too late for that, Em. All the top soil is gone." He held two of the canteens under the surface and watched the bubbles rise. "But it's a good thought." He sighed. "This is a bad time to be a plains farmer. In fact, their time may be past. Such regions have withered before and forced entire population to migrate elsewhere. At least, so I've read."

She pushed the other two canteens under and asked, "Where would they go?" He only shook his head. Then she looked over his shoulder and caught a glimpse of the symmetrical, snow-covered peak. "Oh, look!" she said, but already the ring of clouds spiraled back into place so that Driscoll, turning, caught only the faintest blur of what he'd been longing to see.

"One day . . ." he said.

"What do you expect to find on the summit? It can't be a view. It *is* above the clouds."

"A big crater, maybe. Some signs of old volcanic activity."

"You mean, like boiling mud and steaming spouts and fire under the soil? The entrance to hell?" She grinned at him, dodged when he threatened to douse her with lake water, and added, "Besides, Anckar says the peak's hours away. And she made some kind of pact with the mountain. Apparently, the snow line is sacred. If we cross it he'll bring his full wrath down on us. So she said."

"*His* wrath?" he scoffed. "*He*? Does she think he's alive? God, now she's got me doing it, too. It's only a pile of old rocks no matter how imposing it looks."

She plugged her flasks, tossed them onto the sand, and then bent to drink lake water out of cupped hands. "Delicious, but still freezing cold!" She rubbed her hands dry. "To Anckar, everything's alive, even a stone—or maybe *especially* a stone."

He muttered, "There's something . . . uncivilized about her, don't you think? Something wild."

"That's because she honestly doesn't care about anybody's opinion but her own. It's what I happen to admire most about her." When they returned to the picnic site, both Alden and Anckar were lying on their stomachs, peering at the insect population under the grass and talking in whispers.

". . . you to my sacred grove . . ." Anckar murmured, breaking off when she realized they were no longer alone.

"What sacred grove?" Em asked. "Can I come, too?"

Anckar and Alden exchanged secretive glances. Then Alden said gently, "Why don't you go back to exploring the shoreline with Driscoll? It has plants and creatures not to be found anywhere else. You may not come this way again."

"Any particular spot we need to avoid?" Driscoll asked with just a hint of sarcasm.

Looking somewhat puzzled, Anckar scanned the beach. "Why, no," she said. "Not this time of year. The water freezes by November and won't melt until June. It was a good idea to come now. That's why I was so quick to agree, Em. Just don't pick any flowers. They'd die before we get home."

Once more, Driscoll and Em headed for the far shore. The lizards scurried away at their approach, but the little snake still napped on its sun-warmed boulder. A short distance away, two identical fawns cavorted in knee high flowers, their own little white blossoms bobbing as they jumped for sheer joy. When a doe cautiously stuck her head around the trunk of a tree they ran to her and followed her into the forest.

Driscoll began to collect pebbles and skimmed them one by one over the water while Em praised the best throws. Afterwards, he put a companionable arm around her, drawing her so close that she could hear his heartbeat. With a self-conscious giggle, she broke free and skipped ahead to the white beach. By the time he caught up she'd already discovered that the green waterfall was actually a mass of spilling plant ropes, grown tightly together, with small, delicate leaves.

They settled at the edge of the rock-shelf, dangled their feet over the lake, and counted the silvery fish flashing by under the surface. The sand they sat on was just as warm and soft as it had looked from the meadow. "Poor Alden," Driscoll said, lying on his back. "I bet that sacred grove of Anckar's is shaded and cold. I prefer this, especially with you."

Em resumed counting fish. He nodded off, his mouth relaxed into a half-smile, his blisters drying in the sun. Let him rest; she'd just as soon explore on her own. The white rock formation seemed to continue all the way to the lake bottom. She could see it gradually dimming under the surface. A gray blur flitted in her peripheral vision. It was a dove, flying behind the plant curtain. When it flew out again a minute later, unharmed, Em got up to investigate.

The long plant-ropes covered a hole in the rocks. She squeezed through it and found herself inside a good-sized cave. The leaves at the entrance provided filtered light. The sandy floor continued for a few yards, where it was stopped by a round and seemingly bottomless pool hardly wider than she could stretch her legs. Everything lying beyond it was heavily covered in moss. She jumped across to where a long, low shelf jutted against one side of the cave wall.

Centered against the back of the cave, on some kind of dais, stood an object that looked like a cross between a couch and a coffin. She touched it and thought it was only an oddly shaped boulder, but when she lay down upon it she discovered that the curves of her body fit into a mold that seemed to be tailor-made for them. There was even a small rise under her head not unlike a neck-pillow. She adjusted her spine to the best angle and slowly, the ceiling grew lighter until she could see the outline of a wheel etched into it. A beast with four legs and a tail was stretched at the hub, and a number of two-pronged things resembling tuning forks radiated from the hub to the wheel's rim.

And then the stone beneath her began to throb. It was a soothing sensation. She closed her eyes, feeling the couch grow balmy. The throb changed to a drone below her threshold of hearing. It hummed through her bone marrow and flooded her body. Without fear or thought, she basked in the sheer pleasure of being.

In some dark glimmer of dream, she saw two upturned faces. One belonged to a vaguely familiar lank-haired and bare-chested man, the other to a woman so old that her skin was a network of cracks surrounded by lengthy tendrils of lichen-pale hair. Sunken eyes bored into Em's. The dark hole of her mouth gaped as she droned, "Emmm ooof the tennn-spoaked wheeeel. Heeear mmmeee aaand liiissstennn . . ." Em's consciousness dipped, floated, and sank.

It surfaced unhappily some time later to a nagging voice and hands that pulled and pinched until they managed to break the sweet spell she was under. Who dared drag her away from the Source before her knowing was complete?

It was Driscoll, urgently calling her name, entreating her to wake up. For a moment she hated his voice and him. He had pulled her out of the comfortable mold to a sitting position and was shaking her like a puppet. She put her feet on the floor of the dais and felt it vibrate under the soles of her shoes. "Mmmm," she mumbled. "Don't!"

"What were you doing?" he asked, jerking her down and holding her tight. "Why couldn't you hear me?"

Her head lolled against his shoulder. "I guess I fell asleep in here, just like you did out there."

"You were gone when I woke up. I called and called without getting an answer. Part of me thought maybe you'd drowned." Already, the ceiling had dimmed. He ran his hand up the wall in back of the dais. "Some kind of etching. A head? Surrounded by light rays?" He scraped aside layers of moss in an attempt to decipher more. Then he knelt, raking additional moss from the molded stone bench. "Hand-hewn. Archaic. That bench over there too. And the pool blinked." He guided her toward the cave entrance. "Like a huge eye," he said. "I jumped across and it blinked. I swear it." With a perplexed smile, he shook his head. "Maybe I've had too much sun, but this cave gives me the creeps. Let's get you back into daylight." He paused at the pool, looking down. "Funny—it's different now. I must have imagined the blink while my eyes were adjusting to the gloom." He jumped across and held out his hand to her as if she hadn't already accomplished the feat once without his aid.

Deliberately ignoring his offer, she peered at the water and saw a vertical shaft drop away. Something shimmered on a narrow ledge close to the surface. She reached for it, brought up a pebble the exact shade of the lake, and rubbed it dry on her blouse. It was shaped like a heart. Without thinking, she slipped it into a pocket and leaped across into Driscoll's waiting arms. And then, just inside the luminous leaf curtain, he drew her close and fleetingly touched his lips to hers.

She didn't bother to giggle this time but pushed him aside, squeezed out of the cave and ran past his boots and his socks, back the way they had come, covering her mouth as if to wipe the kiss off or to preserve it. When he finally caught up, his boots properly laced and tied, she'd already slowed to a sedate walk.

He fell into step beside her. "I'm sorry," he said. "I don't know what came over me. I promised myself I wouldn't kiss you until you're ready. Do you want me to keep waiting?"

"Maybe," she said in a small voice.

They didn't speak again until they came to the picnic place. Anckar and Alden's packs were still there, but they were not. Em cut an apple, gave Driscoll half, and shared out some hazelnuts. She ventured a smile when they were done eating. "So far, everything about this hike has been a surprise. I can hardly wait to see what's next."

It wasn't long before Anckar and Alden came out of the forest, hand in hand. "So," Anckar said, her face aglow. "Are you two prepared to move on?"

Driscoll looked hopefully toward the summit. "Thataway?"

But Anckar was pointing to the ridge. "To the other path. I'll show you my private castle. You think you have another hike in you, Alden? Or would you rather just sit where the trail forks and wait for us there?"

"Lead on," he said, shouldering his pack and clipping the canteen to his belt. "I'm walking on air."

CHAPTER 30

SOON THEY WERE CLIMBING a slope that resembled a war zone. "This black stuff was once liquid fire," Driscoll informed them, studying a fist-sized, shiny black stone. "A glowing red river. I have pictures of it."

In her mind, Em had a glimpse of magnificent slopes covered with tall trees. She saw a group of log cabins, heard a woman's laughter. Then a fiery stream cut a wide swath through it all, burning and burying everything in its wake.

"The ashes got coated with lava that soon froze and fused into rock." Anckar said.

Driscoll put the black stone in his pack. "I wonder how many creatures lie buried under our feet."

"The whole earth is a graveyard, covering those who lived before us," Anckar told him. "Let them be." She pointed uphill. "See that odd little rise? That's where we're headed. It's my favorite place on the mountain."

Driscoll looked disappointed. "You hike up this far just for that? I expected something more spectacular." When they got to the rise it turned out to be more imposing than it had looked from below. He was still not satisfied. "You call that a 'castle'? It's only a cliff. A bald cliff."

Anckar flashed him a mischievous smile. "I'm betting you'll change your mind once you get to the top."

"You've climbed this?" he asked, a trace of respect in his voice.

"I didn't fly up!" There was a challenge in her eyes. "But maybe it'll be harder for you. You're probably too heavy to lift your own weight."

"You think so? Watch this!" Driscoll dropped his gear and hoisted himself up the cliff a few feet. "If you can do it, so can I."

She stayed where she was, arms crossed, and watched him struggle from one precarious hold to the next. "You look like a spider. The kind with long, skinny legs."

"Right now I wish I were," he wheezed, straining for a just-out-of-reach crack to claw into. "I've seen them run up slicker walls than this, and even crawl upside down across ceilings." His boots slipped. He dug four fingers into the crack and groaned with the effort.

Anckar's smile grew entirely feline. "Are you sure you can make it? Don't be afraid to give up. There's no shame in it." He didn't bother to reply but grunted himself higher by sheer willpower alone, twisting this way and that, miraculously finding just one more place to clutch on to until, utterly spent, he heaved himself over the rim to collapse, panting. "Very nice," she called up to him. "But *our* way's easier. We'll meet you on the north side."

There, the hill rose at a much more leisurely angle, offering an abundance of holds. Even Alden, the least athletic among them, managed to scale it with only minor laments. Soon the three of them were sitting beside Driscoll, who had lowered his head to his knees, drawing ragged breaths. "No fair," he complained when he could speak. "You conned me."

"You asked for it," Anckar said. "How could I resist?" She offered him a drink from her bottle and pointed to the hollow, bowl-shaped inside-core of the hill. "Welcome to my house-with-no-roof. Follow me." She scooted over the edge and slid down the hollow on her rear end.

Centuries of wind-blown dust had cushioned the castle's floor. For a good part of each year it was probably waterlogged. The weed and fern seedlings deposited by birds and wind had sprouted and died for countless seasons to add layers of undisturbed soil. While she waited for Em and the two men to join her, Anckar pulled a couple of tightly rolled blankets out of a crevice. "I've got every convenience," she said, spreading them side by side over the ground.

Then she unearthed a pillow and lay down with her head on one half of it, offering the other half to Alden. "I like to watch the clouds drift past. Especially in the evening."

"Do you ever sleep here?" Alden asked, settling beside her.

"Only sometimes. It gets cold." As if to prove it, the wind started to moan, cutting itself on the bowl's rim. Then it sped skyward, corralling white wisps into a semblance of sheep, which it proceeded to drive across a bell-curve of satiny blue. "This one looks a bit like a cat," she said, pointing. "And here's the dog chasing it."

Alden played with her short curls. "Thanks for showing us your special house."

She gave him a wide, affectionate smile. "You're family. Who else would I show it to? Besides, you're all such lousy climbers, I doubt you'll ever make it this far again."

"Unless I'm fleeing some biblical flood this'll do me," Alden admitted.

Em put her cheek on Driscoll's chest and felt a rumble of laughter. "You know what?" she whispered when he had quieted. "This isn't a castle. It's a fortress. The safest place in the world."

In answer, his finger traced the shape of her ear. She held still, wanting the moment to last.

THE NEXT morning neither Alden nor Driscoll could be tempted with breakfast. They sprawled on the living room floor as if felled by the same axe, their feet blistered, complaining about sore legs and stiff backs. "I'm sorry, Odasan," Driscoll told the old man. "I've got to postpone the town trip one more day. Right now I can't raise my foot high enough to get in the car."

In the afternoon Em hiked to the lookout to sit and think. The pulsating stone dais and the drone that had vibrated through her bones—what did they mean? And why did she feel that the drone was still somewhere inside her, ripening like some kind of fruit? Leaning against a tree, she toned the remembered sound, trying different pitches until she found one that made her bones tingle. She practiced it until it was time for supper.

It was a subdued meal, for Odasan's last bowl of rice was not up to standards. He sat picking out chaff and swallowing what was left with no sign of enjoyment. Once he caught Driscoll's eye, gave a sorrowful sigh, and asked, "Tomorrow?" Driscoll answered with the same word. After dinner Odasan consoled himself with his martial arts book, sharing his circle of light with Driscoll, who was happily leafing through a well-worn poetry volume, stopping frequently to savor a favorite passage and to mouth entire stanzas as if trying to learn them by heart.

Lupe put a lamp on the hearthstones so she could see the stitches she was making on the floral design in her embroidery hoop. She was sitting in what seemed to be her favorite place, next to Brendan's feet, raising her eyes frequently to watch him pluck chords on his guitar.

"Oh, here—I almost forgot." Em held out the green pebble to him. "I found it for you on the beach. Your own bit of lake." She dropped it in his hand and they examined it together. The stone's color seemed to have intensified while it was in her pocket.

He tightened his fingers around it. "This is the closest I'll ever come to being up there." He slid it into his shirt and patted the little lump it made. "It'll be my good-luck piece." In thanks, he dedicated an old ballad to her and strummed it with a worshipful air. On impulse, Em decided to accompany the melody with a hum. When it held steady she risked using her treacherous voice. Pretending she was alone at the lookout, she put one finger on her vibrating chest, another against her throat, and allowed her voice to flow as it would. Odasan glanced up from his pictures and Driscoll from his verse, both listening with undivided attention. And then Em felt some kind of power surge through her, amplifying the voice past its limited range. She was singing!

Still singing, she went to sit on the rug, holding one hand out to Driscoll, the other to Alden, who'd been watching with deep interest from his padded chair. The men came to her without hesitation. Then Nada crawled out from under the table, sat in the middle of the rug, and gave a commanding bark. Laughing, the others gathered around the dog and completed the circle.

The voice continued to flow out of Em from some unfathomable place deep within, making her bones throb until they felt as if they were dissolving. And then, abruptly, they were elsewhere—inside some inky black space both narrow and long, drifting toward a faraway light. Em gasped. The voice broke and they were yanked back to a hard landing on top of the rug.

"That was the tunnel!" Bena cried. "I recognized it."

Brendan touched his lucky stone. "Where was it? Where did we go?"

Driscoll rubbed his eyes as if to banish an unwelcome illusion. "Nowhere," he replied drily. "Unless I'm mistaken we're all still right here."

Em decided to ignore his sarcasm. "Whatever we did, let's do it again. Exactly the same way. Right now." She recaptured his hand and tightened her hold on Alden's. "I think I know what went wrong. I was trying to use the voice but I have to let *it* use *me*."

"Sure. Why not," Driscoll said. "Just as long as everyone here understands this is only a parlor game."

Brendan scowled at him. "This may be a shock to you, Driscoll, but we don't exactly need your permission. Although we could use your cooperation. If you don't mind."

Driscoll's smile was coolly polite. "Not in the least. Go right ahead. Em, we're all yours."

Again, nine pairs of hands completed the circle. Em offered a low, clear hum. Almost at once, the voice rose out of her to intone a compelling melody in some primeval tongue. Moving effortlessly through Em's vocal cords, the voice climbed from octave to octave until it found a pitch so pure that the lamp chimneys trembled. And then Em had a mental glimpse of the wheel she'd seen etched in the cave ceiling. Taking the cue, she lay on her back, the soles of her feet against the dog. "Copy me," she said between breaths. As soon as they did they became part of a living wheel. It spun ever faster until at last it grew transparent and lifted effortlessly to the ceiling and through the roof. Then it whirled over the dark clearing into a far darker domain, reeling through an endless expanse that had never known light.

At last the wheel burst through glowing red layers of clouds and hovered over a pasture tinged by a setting sun. Below them, two women were picking flowers. One looked up as if she had heard someone call and then began to run toward them, shouting and waving. The wheel hurtled up and away. In an instant, the nine human spokes were back on the living room floor in their separate bodies.

Alden raised himself on to an elbow. "We were actually there!" he said, stunned. "In my valley! But who were those women, and why weren't they frightened? I would have been if I'd seen a human wheel spinning through the air."

"She didn't even look surprised," Em agreed. "As if she'd been expecting us." Was she still running on that flower-sprinkled pasture, staring at the hole they had left in her sky?

Driscoll gaped as if he'd never seen Em before. "How did you do that? What did you do?"

"I have no idea," she admitted. "But whatever it was, let's try it again. Three is my lucky number."

Odasan said lightly, "What's the rush?" Yet he looked oddly pleased, as if she'd just passed some kind of test. "Twice in one night's plenty, especially after your hike. How do you feel?"

She thought about it. "Scorched. Like I've traveled from one end of the heavens to the other on a lightning bolt. Will it get easier, do you think?"

"If you expect it to," Odasan said. "You look a bit tired. Why don't you rest? You've had a long day."

Since he mentioned it, she did feel quite spent. She let him massage her tight shoulders, his knowing fingers unknotting the muscles that needed it most. "Thanks for always being so kind," she murmured drowsily, wrapping her arm around the dog and sinking toward sleep.

"She's out like a light," Odasan said from far off. "Let her stay on the rug. Cover her well."

Lupe quipped, "What else can we do? She's too big to carry."

That wasn't quite true. Driscoll could, if he wanted to. If she asked. But she was too tired to ask.

CHAPTER 31

"I'M KIND OF SLOW ABOUT SOME THINGS," Hertha said to Driscoll the next morning as she reached into the cupboard for the cash jar. "It's what you'd expect from a woman who lived alone most of her life. But I'm beginning to suspect Tilden wants more from me than the crafts I deliver once every month." She upended the jar on the table, deftly blocking errant coins from rolling away. "I've been pretending I'm too dumb to pick up on his hints." She began to stack the smallest coins into silver columns.

Em paused while drying a plate. "What kind of hints?"

Driscoll flushed and told her, "Why don't you get ready to go?" He might just as well have said, "Hertha, not in front of the child!" As if Em were six instead of sixteen.

"What's to get ready?" she replied. "Odasan brought the stretcher over at breakfast and Hertha's wrapped some leftovers for us to eat on our way home."

"Then why don't you go outside and find Nada? She'll want to ride with us."

Em went to the window and called Nada's name. Driscoll chose that moment to ask Hertha delicately, "You want me to set the man straight?"

She gave her head an emphatic shake. "Goodness, no! One wrong word and we'll sit in the dark every night without candles and kerosene for the lamps, eating nothing but canned green beans. In fact, I don't even want him to know you and I are connected. That's why I'm giving you real money instead of our crafts. With cash, you might do better than the usual torn sacks of grain and weevily flour. Here's the list you asked for." She pulled it out of her apron. "Get as much as you can cram into the car—the biggest size of everything, doubled. I've put the most important stuff first. I'll make Tilden wait for the crafts till next month, on the principle that less supply leads to increased demand."

Driscoll scanned the sheet, then the growing columns of coins. "How would it look if we plopped a bag full of small change on the store counter? Tilden would have to sort it all over again. He might not have your degree of patience for it." He showed her a thick stack of bills in his wallet. "I closed out my savings account before I left Clydestown. Keep your coins for an emergency." He helped her scrape them back into the jar. "And don't worry about Tilden. I'm used to dealing with difficult people. Dr. White always referred the most irate clients to me. He said I have a knack."

Hertha's lips twitched. "Then you're just the right man for the job. Of course, Tilden's an angel compared to his wife. Let's hope you're lucky and Mira won't be around when you get to town. She keeps all the books and fits her work-time in between household chores. If you can manage to arrive at the store around eleven she'll be at home in her kitchen chopping up vegetables for Tilden's soup." She heaved the jar into the cupboard and gave him the lunch basket. "That Doble of yours is a blessing. So are you."

They went out to the yard, where she watched Driscoll and Em carry the stretcher to the lower end of the clearing. Em whistled for Nada who immediately came running out of the woods. "We're letting you have the back seat all to yourself," Em told her. "Try to look fierce. You'll be guarding the Doble while we're shopping."

Hertha waved, shouting, "If you run into trouble, at least try to get Odasan's rice!"

Driscoll yelled back, "I wouldn't dare come back without it!"

WHILE THE Doble meandered down the serpentine trail Em played distractedly with Nada's ears. All too soon they arrived at the crossroads and the weather-bleached sign with the arrow pointing toward the hamlet of Yates. Where the last trees gave way to the outermost field, he stopped the car for a close look at the shopping list. "It'll go faster if we split it," he said, tearing it neatly in half. Tickling her under the chin with her part of it, he said, "Cheer up. They'll love us. These small-town stores are all alike. Most everybody buys on credit. Tilden will welcome our cash."

She stuffed her list away without so much as a glance and looked back the way they had come. "How long do you think it would take me to walk home from here?"

"Back to Oren?"

"Don't be funny!"

"It's nothing for you to consider since you have me and I have the Doble." He moved the steam lever slightly, taking the car over a gradual rise. From there they could see the whole valley spread out before them. Rectangular acres of green, brown and gold surrounded a distant island of red-roofed and whitewashed houses. "Pretty," he said. "I wonder if by any chance they need a vet."

"Why?"

"Because sooner or later we'll need more cash and I'm no good at whittling spoons and embroidering pillows."

She had to laugh. "I thought helping Odasan make his flutes wouldn't be half bad. And if everything goes according to Alden's plan we'll be in his new valley before winter."

"Perhaps," he said, keeping his tone neutral. "But this place seems okay, too. See those channels running through the fields? They carry water. The soil's exhausted, just like everywhere else in this world. Granted, Alden's green valley is much more fertile—but at least this dirt is real."

She couldn't believe her ears. "Meaning his dirt is not? How can you doubt it after last night?"

He patted her arm to help soften his words. "About last night— I'm afraid the whole thing was some sort of mass illusion. Fact is, we didn't go anywhere, Em. We just thought we did."

She was stunned. How could he deny the experience they had all shared? "What about the strange voice coming out of my mouth? That ancient song?"

He had his explanation all ready. "It's called 'speaking in tongues.' Certain types of old-time religions used to encourage that kind of thing."

It was a low blow. "Tell me," she said, shrugging off his well-meaning hand. "Do you think all eight of us—excluding you—are equally slow-witted, or do you think I'm worse than the rest?" Nada gave an uneasy whine and stabbed her nose at Em's ear. "Lie down!" she said. "And mind your own business!" Scowling at Driscoll, she went on, "Considering the way you feel about our new friends, why did you bother showing up at all?"

"Ah," he said, smoothing his beard. "I didn't know what they were up to at first. I was only trying to keep my promise to you."

Incensed, she cried, "It was you who insisted on dragging me to the fiery hill in the first place. Talking about shared dreams, as I recall."

He gave a cool shrug. "I admit I was curious. That's a different state of mind than yours and Bena's. You're both somewhat naïve due to the isolated lives you have led."

"What's *naïve*?"

"Gullible."

"And that?"

"It means 'easy to fool.'"

In a hurry to return the slight, she said, "If some are easy to fool, others are just plain fools," and shifted away from him.

He began to deliver a cutting retort, then switched to a chuckle. "I can't help being logical, Em. If you think you can prove me wrong, please do—later. Right now we're on a mission, remember? So let's call a truce and get on with it." He studied the scene before them. "Look at those cows." He nodded at a herd lying companionably in the sunshine, chewing cud. "They make the ones around Clydestown look puny, don't you think?"

Across the road from the cattle two horses stood cheek to cheek, their tails pointing in opposite directions. They shied when the Doble rolled by. The brown mare gave a shrill whinny and ran away from the fence, but the white one galloped alongside it, head and tail high, keeping pace with the car until she was stopped by cross-fencing. Nada insisted on leaning out to bark at the horse. The air was pungent with sun-warmed manure. From the faraway church steeple a bell chimed four high notes. Another struck a long series of low, measured tones.

"Eleven. On the dot," Em counted. They passed an acre planted with potatoes. At the far end, some women were digging them out of the furrows and tossing them into heaps. In the next field, a team of reapers, their backs to the road, were swinging long-handled scythes, cutting down barley. Not one of the them noticed the Doble passing silently behind them, making no noise except for the slight sound of the tires swishing over the surface of the clay road.

Halfway to town, Driscoll and Em came upon an unusual tree. It grew at the edge of a field and was the only one of its kind. The trunk was divided into three massive offshoots. One giant branch arced over the roadway. As the Doble passed under it, Driscoll said with a nod, "I give you the golden archway to Yates." The tree had no bark. Instead, it was covered with a smooth, tight-fitting skin of red-gold.

"Let's get out and touch it," Em said.

"We'll do it on our way home."

Did he really say 'home' as if he belonged on the fiery hill with her and the rest of them? Em hid a relieved grin. The first house they came to had a wrap-around fence penning a gaggle of dirty-white geese. Unlike the field workers, the geese noticed the Doble in plenty of time to charge at the pickets with their necks menacingly thrust forward, honking and snapping their bills. Nada barked back, trading insult for insult.

Driscoll silenced her with one word and brought the car to a stop. "According to Odasan this is the glass shop. He gave me the window measurements, but I'm not walking in through that gate. Have you ever been nipped by geese? They're meaner than any watch dog."

He considered a long driveway leading to the rear of the house. "I bet the workshop's back there. Let me run in and give them the order. If we're lucky they'll have the glass cut and ready by the time we're done with our shopping." He got out and strode along the outside of the fence. The geese kept pace in the yard, hissing at him.

He returned to the car looking pleased. "Half an hour, the man said." He climbed in and released the hand brake. "Don't let me forget to pick the glass up on our way out of town."

Driving on, they came to a cobblestoned roadbed. "Main Street," he said. "We're almost there."

Anxiously, Em finger-combed her tangled hair. They passed a bakery displaying baskets of rolls and crusty loaves in its window. The air smelled of fresh-baked bread. Farther on, at the town square, a huddle of farmwomen were stationed at stalls heaped with the overflow of their harvests.

Driscoll slowed the car for a good look. "That's a lot of veggies. I'm impressed," he said. "Really, this is a prosperous little town, considering how isolated it is. Oh-oh. They don't look particularly pleased to see us." He gave a cheerful wave, calling, "Good morning!" The women's faces went blank.

As they passed the stands Em saw that the green beans on offer were curled and covered with blotches. The chard was a sickly yellow, and the tomatoes a watery pink. Driscoll muttered, "They looked better from a distance. I thought, with the irrigation and all—but I suppose we could get used to it if we had to."

"Luckily, we don't have to," said Em.

"Not right now, that's true," he corrected. "With a garden like ours, we're hopelessly spoiled. But you never know . . ."

'Ours,' he'd said. She gave him an innocent smile. "What? Don't you think our garden is—what was your word—a *mass illusion*?"

"Not a chance," he replied with unshakable conviction. "I can *see* our bright-red tomatoes. I can smell them. I can eat them. Therefore, they're real. If you had been able to pick one single blossom, or even a blade of grass, from the pasture we *seemed* to be hovering over last night, we'd have something to talk about. And the first thing I'd say is, 'I'm sorry.'" He regarded Em with exasperating patience.

She understood how easy it would be to let him discourage her, how fast new dreams could be squelched. But not this time, and not by him. "Well," she said. "I'm going to proceed with the energy wheel. With you or without you."

He looked flustered. Then he gave an elaborate shrug. "If we can agree to call it an experiment in consciousness, I'm in. I told you—I'll go wherever you go. Even if our interpretations of events differ."

They were nearing the end of Main Street. The last house was the biggest. It was painted yellow, its shutters and front door a dark green. The two long benches along the front wall were painted green too. They were occupied by men dozing in the late-morning shade. Driscoll slowed the Doble to read a bold sign fastened over the entrance. YATES PHARMACY AND GENERAL STORE. As the men elbowed each other awake, he murmured, "We're here," passing out smiles and steering the car around the building to park in the dusty rear lot.

Em shrank down in her seat. "They were swigging beer. At

eleven in the morning. And staring at me." She dropped her part of the list on Driscoll's lap. "There's no way I'm walking past them. You'll have to go in by yourself. I'm helping Nada watch over the car."

Calmly, he pulled the emergency brake and opened his door. "Every store has its pack of old drunks."

She gripped the sides of her seat as if he might try to drag her away. "I've got a bad feeling about this bunch. They don't look friendly."

"Most small towns are suspicious of strangers. They don't get much practice. We have to give the people of Yates a chance to get to know us. And, frankly, I'm counting on you. We have to work fast to avoid Mira, remember?"

Em's eyes burned. "I can't walk past those guys. I just can't," she whispered. "I'd stumble and stutter. I'd make a total fool of myself—and of you."

Driscoll sat back and watched her. Then he pulled a tiny parcel out from under his seat. "From what I've read, people used to be much taller than they are now," he said calmly. "But the more they depleted the soil, the more they shrank. There are more runts with each new generation, especially since the poisonous rains."

"So?"

"So we're the ones who are actually normal."

"Tell that to them if you think it'll make us more popular."

He offered her a patient, benevolent smile. "Our cash will do that."

She drew her knees to her chest and hugged them tight. "It's your cash. You go," she said angrily. "I'm tired of being everybody's idea of a joke. For some reason people seem to find oversized men much more forgivable than oversized women."

He considered the little box he was holding. "Close your eyes."

"Why?"

"So you can hear me better."

"I can hear you just fine."

His smile deepened with affection. "The first time I saw you, you were walking into Clydestown's used book store with your spine ram-rod straight and your head high. You looked as if you were wearing a crown."

It had only been her attempt to overcome the suffocating feelings of inadequacy that always lamed her in public places. Some people mistook it for arrogance.

He opened the box and pushed aside rustling white tissue paper. "I saw this in the jeweler's window the day I left Clydestown. It reminded me of you. I was saving it for a special occasion. I guess this is it. Here." He lifted out a small pendant and swung it between them. "The exact color of your eyes." It was a drop of amber. Held to the light, it shone honey-yellow. He wove the delicate golden chain it was hanging from through Em's flyaway curls and centered the pendant over her forehead. "Your crown. To remind you that you are my princess."

That got her out of the car. She was still glowing when they rounded the corner. Then the bloated, self-satisfied faces of the drunks who were watching her approach drained the eagerness out of her step. Her knees locked. Somebody sniggered.

"Keep moving. You're doing great," Driscoll whispered, linking his arm through hers to provide extra support.

The old man sitting nearest popped his striped suspenders and gave a loud burp. "Looky here, Jones," he said, nudging his immediate neighbor with the neck of a bottle. "The scarecrows are taking a break from the fields. My, my, what a sight. No wonder them crows flapped away screaming."

Jones smirked, exposing a double gap between tobacco-stained teeth. "Shows all *you* know, Fraser. Only one's a scarecrow. The other's a stick-legged crane."

Fraser slapped his thighs and wheezed out a laugh, which the rest of the geezers echoed. By then the damage was done. Glancing at her reflection in the store window, Em could only agree. From her naked bird legs to the frizz on her head, she was a deplorable sight.

"An oversized, underfed crane," Jones grinned, raising his own bottle in a mock salute. Then he tapped on the display window. "Hey, what's the matter, strangers? Can't read?"

That's when Em noticed an obscene, hand-lettered sign affixed to the inside of the glass. NO FREAKS ALLOWED. With three exclamation points. Her gasp was drowned by a volley of manly jeers. Driscoll guided her to the shop door, triggered a piercing chime when he opened it, and helped her inside. He ducked and she didn't. Colliding painfully with the doorframe, she refused to react until she had managed to pull the door shut behind her. Then she sucked in a lungful of air and rubbed at a bump rapidly growing at her hairline.

"Are you all right?" he whispered in the dim, quiet room.

"I've been better," she said through clenched teeth. He straightened the chain in her hair and re-centered the pendant. She took a steadying breath, smelling sour pickles, perfumed soap and penny candy while Driscoll went to a row of rusty carts and brought back two.

"First one done gets a black licorice rope," he said, pushing his cart down one of the aisles.

Em's heart fluttered like a trapped bird. If she had known where the rear exit was she would have made her escape without hesitation. Since she did not, she considered the shopping expedition a better choice than walking out the front past the guffawing drunks, and so she uncrinkled her list, kicked at a misaligned wheel, and pushed her cart to the baking aisle. *Honey. Cooking oil. Sugar.* She lowered two jumbo sizes of each into the cart and was reaching for the yeast when she noticed a pretty display on the top shelf. It consisted of a complete set of Anckar's cheerful, hand-painted dishes (lilac wood-stars mingling with tiny buttercups) and a wide-mouthed clay vase filled with Brendan's fine wooden spoons (everything from a huge bowl-sized soup ladle to a miniscule, long-handled blending spoon with a hole through its flat center). She touched each piece like an old friend. "Baking powder," she read, reaching for a couple of tins and smiling as she remembered how Hertha had pulled a pan of golden-brown biscuits out of the oven for breakfast that morning.

"Matches," she said, moving on. "Macaroni straws. Spaghetti." She wandered from aisle to aisle, keeping an eye out for Odasan's rice. Straying too near the pharmacy, she saw the counter lined with great jars full of penny candy and licorice ropes. Behind the register were floor-to-ceiling shelves, painted white and lined with blue and amber bottles of various sizes. She touched the pendant to make sure it was still on her forehead.

Then she heard a man's deep-chested cough from behind the long row of pharmacy shelves. Tilden? Heart thumping, she fled down the next aisle. From there she could see the remedy section at the other end of the store. Driscoll was standing at the middle, a dropper bottle in one hand and a tin of pills in the other, holding them up to the light to study their labels, his near-empty cart forgotten beside him. She tiptoed closer, intending to clamp a hand to his shoulder and make him jump. But somebody else got to him first.

"Well, hello there," a sultry voice crooned while Em was still moving toward him. "Can I help you find something, stranger?" One inhale later it purred, "My, you're a tall one. I like tall men. What's your name? Mine's Celie."

Em hid behind a display of pickles, rearranged several jars, and peered through the slot she had created to where a girl was materializing beside Driscoll. She was half his size, all S-curves and painted lids, which she lost no time batting at him. Her straight blonde hair flowed down past her hips and looked as if it had never been cut. Uneasy, Driscoll tilted away from her, clutching the remedies to his chest. The girl closed the space between them, expertly swaying her hips. Then another cough came from the pharmacy section, this one louder and closer to the counter. Tilden was on the move.

"That's my dad, spying on me again," she murmured. "But he goes home for lunch right at twelve every day. Leaves me to tend the store by myself for a whole hour. You find that . . . interesting?"

"Uh—yes, Miss . . ." Driscoll stammered as the upper curve of her S strained against valiant blouse buttons.

"Celie," she said, tickling a feather duster over his beard.

There wasn't one part on the girl that could be called stunted. For most of Em's life, she'd have given all she owned to look exactly like Celie, but she was quite sure there was not a single second in Celie's when she would *not* have minded looking like Em. From the sleek, gold-spun hair to the dainty feet embraced by elegant powder-blue slippers, Celie was the real princess, and every part of Em was as crude as her make-believe crown.

CHAPTER 32

Em COULD HEAR DRISCOLL'S CART rattling along the next aisle as he sought to make up for lost time. When he appeared in her lane she had just found a display of Hertha's sachets. "Look how pretty they are." She inhaled the sweet scent of roses. "Didn't she do a good job?"

"They're not on your list," he said. "I was hoping you would be farther along."

"You should talk, considering how much time you wasted in the remedy section."

"What about Odasan's rice?"

"I haven't been able to find it yet."

"Well, then ask somebody," he said. "I saw a girl around here a minute ago . . . There!" He pointed to the pickle display, where Celie was busy pushing the jars together. "While you're at it, ask her to show you to the dairy goods."

"Why don't *you* ask her!" Em hissed. "Maybe you can get her to groom your beard some more with her feathers."

He had the grace to look embarrassed. "That wasn't my fault," he said, reversing his cart. "Never mind. I'm going straight to the source." He parked by the register, calling, "Hello there!" Em inched apart two cartons of oatmeal for a discreet view of the coming transaction. If Driscoll was about to demonstrate his people skills she wanted to be close enough to see how it was done.

"Coming!" a resonant voice boomed from the back room, and then Tilden stepped up to press his belly against his side of the counter. He had fleshy pink cheeks, a bald spot fringed by lackluster brown hair, the white frock of a medical man, and a practiced storekeeper's smile. A label on his frock spelled, PHARMACIST.

Driscoll said in his friendliest tone, "Nice store you've got here. An impressive variety."

"Why, thank you, stranger." Tilden tried to sound welcoming but couldn't quite cover an underlying taint of hostility. "I've got the best connections. Know all the good traders." He brought out a rag and started dusting the register from top to bottom. "Treat them like kings when they come through town. Home-cooked meals. The spare bedroom. Fishing. Since we've started ditching the run-off, they've been buying our produce by the bushel. It's in the water, you know."

"What is?"

"Why, the secret of our great produce!"

Great produce? No wonder the marketing women had been angry with him for not looking properly impressed.

"And the soil?" Driscoll asked.

Tilden shrugged. "We keep trying. Is that your car in the lot?"

Driscoll relaxed into a slouch. "Yep. It's a Doble."

Tilden looked around the store and then leaned over the counter. "I'm a car buff, myself. Got boxes full of old car magazines and pictures under my bed. There hasn't been a live one parked on that lot since my daddy ran the store. How much are you asking?"

Driscoll recoiled. "It's not for sale!"

"Everything under the sun has its price," Tilden said with jaded smile. "Name yours."

"It's an heirloom. My sole inheritance. Priceless."

"No gasoline around here," Tilden said. "Where will you fill it?"

"It runs mostly on water."

Tilden wagged a finger at him. "Go on, now. The engine would rust."

Driscoll eased his elbows onto the counter. "It's a steamer. The only one left of its kind." He embarked on his well-practiced explanation of the car's history and virtues, and finished proudly with, "My dad modified it so you can fuel it with anything handy— coal, kerosene, even dry sticks you pick up alongside the road!"

Tilden looked duly impressed. Then he put his elbows on the counter too. Staring over Driscoll's shoulder as if he could see the car through the wall, he said, "If it were mine I'd hook a wagon behind it and trade direct with the city."

Driscoll shifted uneasily. "It's not that simple. My dad trained me to take care of any problems that might come up but I bet you don't even have a mechanic in Yates. No tools, no tires, no spare parts."

Tilden put his face close to Driscoll's. "You fixing to settle here?"

"Maybe. I'm a veterinarian."

"An animal doctor? We don't need another one of those." Tilden's face grew determined. "Got a great deal for you, though—a nice little house on the edge of town, over by the church. White picket fence all around it. Worth more than any car. And I'll hire you on as my driver and mechanic." He nodded at the half-filled cart. "Free groceries—within reason."

Driscoll did not seem at all tempted. "I appreciate the offer, but I promised my dad to keep it in the family. Sorry." He took hold of his cart. "I better get on with my shopping. I need some milk, and butter, and eggs."

Tilden squeezed out a meager smile. "Fixing to bake a cake? I'll send Celie over to the dairy. How much of each do you want?"

Driscoll thought for a moment. "Ten dozen eggs? Five pounds of butter, and a couple of gallons of milk."

In Em's opinion, what they really needed was a cow and some chickens, but there wasn't enough grass on the mountain for the one and too many natural predators for the other.

"Some cake," Tilden said, taking a close look at him before hailing Celie. She came practicing her slinkiest walk and pushed her chest toward her reluctant target. Driscoll stepped back, looking flustered.

"Quit that!" Tilden said as she batted her eyes. "Button yourself up decent, girl, and stand straight. You heard the man, I suppose?" He turned to Driscoll. "The farm will want cash."

Celie tossed the feather duster on the counter, took the crisp bill Driscoll held out to her, folded it small, and stuffed it down the front of her blouse. Then she sauntered off with a coy giggle, tossing gold-spun waves over her shoulders. Speechless, both men watched her sway her hips around the end of the aisle.

Em gave up her post to intercept Celie at the shop door. "Excuse me," she said, keeping her voice low. "Can you tell me where you keep your rice?"

Celie stared with amazement at Em's clumpy, over-sized shoes. "In the grain room. Through there." She pointed to a dark hallway, a gleam in her eyes. "Careful, though—we've got a disgusting old rat hiding in the corner. Best go in on your tiptoes and run out as soon as you're done."

"Thanks," Em said, starting toward her cart.

Celie lingered. "You look just like him, you know. Are you twins?"

"Of course not!" The girl must be blind not to notice the difference.

"His homely 'little' sister, then," Celie guessed, chortling at her own wit. "You have to admit, the height looks better on him." She put one of her dainty feet next to Em's, tapped the floor smartly with the heel of her slipper, and swaggered outside.

"About Celie . . ." Tilden began as soon as the sound of the chimes died away.

"Yes?" Driscoll asked warily.

"My little girl's having a tough time these days, trying to grow up and not sure how. Last night she wanted to cut off her hair. The wife wouldn't let her, so Celie stomped to her room and slammed the door so hard that the jamb split, top to bottom." He shook his head with an expression of parental pride mixed with awe. "Last week I found her hiding under some tarps in back of a trader's wagon just as he was about to pull out. She wants to go to the city so bad she's willing to do all kinds of foolishness to get there. I'm aiming to keep her safe with us for as long as I'm able. Your car's bound to give her ideas. Pay her no mind. Understand?" There was no mistaking the warning note in his voice.

"She . . . I . . . you've got it all wrong!" Driscoll stammered.

Em left him to fend for himself using the enviable social knack he'd boasted to Hertha about, and maneuvered the misaligned wheels of her cart through the dark hall into the grain room. She could see the shadowy forms of wooden barrels standing before shelves that were crowded with sacks. There were lots of snug spaces for a rat to hide in. Praying she wouldn't step on it in the dim light, she went to the window and pulled up the blinds.

With the help of bright sunshine she counted four kegs. Their labels were stenciled right into the wood—wheat, rye, barley, and oats. On the lid of each rested a scooper. The shelves behind them were crammed with filled and sealed burlap sacks of diverse sizes, ready for customers too uppity to shovel their own. She found the rice among them. There was only the one sack, big and dusty, looking as if someone had trampled on it more than once.

She hefted it with a groan and dropped it heavily into the cart, which started to roll, clattering against one of the barrels. There was a high-pitched squeak. She jumped, anticipating a panicked rat running up her naked legs—but the noise came from a rusty-hinged door she had not noticed before. It opened wide and a thin, angular woman marched into the room, clutching a stack of papers. She had plucked her natural brows and drawn on fake arches. They started too close over her nose, soared like startled birds, and drooped to sad ends at her temples. Underneath the brows, the cold eyes of a predator flicked over Em's outlandish shoes, up her naked legs, past worn shorts and a much-wrinkled blouse to her wild tangle of hair.

"Can I help you?" she asked. It sounded like an accusation.

"I've got it, thanks," Em said quickly, trying to push the unwieldy cart to the door in the hopes of avoiding a potential confrontation.

The woman got there first, blocking the way out. "You new in town?"

Instinctively, Em's eyes rose in the direction of home.

"I thought so!" The woman slapped her papers onto the nearest keg and grabbed the cart's front end. "You're from the witch camp, aren't you? They sent someone different to try and confuse me. Didn't you see my sign in the window? We don't do business with freaks anymore. Our merchandise is meant for decent town folk."

"I . . . I don't know what you mean," Em spluttered. "We . . . we're cash customers."

The woman nodded toward the parking lot. "You came in that thing out there?"

Em glanced at the Doble. Nada was hanging out of a rear window, baring her teeth at a couple of the town drunks who were attempting to take a close look at the car.

"That demon dog gave you away. Used to come down with the hag who carries that box crammed with trinkets. Tell her to save herself a long trip. Next time she knocks on the back door it won't be Tilden who answers. Now git!" She let go of the cart and heaved at the rice sack within. The wheels rolled until the cart was stopped by the doorjamb. "Don't you dare push it any farther, you heathen," the woman said with a terrible scowl.

The only thing Em could think to do was to hang on to the other end of the sack, wailing, "Driscoll! Come here!" It slipped away from both of them, landing back in the cart with a dull thump just as he appeared in the doorway, Tilden close at his heels.

"What's up?" Driscoll asked jovially, as if it weren't obvious to anyone with even one eye.

"She won't give me the rice!"

"It's already spoken for," the woman said. "Tell them, Tilden."

The shopkeeper went to stand by his wife. "Quite right. It was pre-ordered. There's a name on the bag, see?" He tapped on a red H scribbled on the stitched paper label.

Driscoll's eyes warned Em to keep quiet. Casually leaning against the cart handle, he said, "It's obviously been sitting for a while. Are you sure you won't sell it to us? We pay hard cash." He pulled out his wallet. "Order a nice new bag for your other customer. We'll take this scuffed one off your hands."

"I expect she'll be along any day now," Tilden said, carelessly putting his hand on the H. "No one else around here cares for the stuff. I tried it myself once. It tastes downright vile, especially if it gets scorched. Give me potatoes instead, any time. They're local and you can fix them a different way every night. This here rice—there's only one way to cook it and it comes out so dry that it's liable to choke you. I don't recommend it."

The woman's eyes glittered. "No use trying to hide that red letter from me, Tilden! I know what the H stands for—your after-hours visitor. The hag."

He raised his hands placatingly. "Now, Mira!"

"Don't 'Mira' me!" She planted one foot on either side of the cart. "Without our store they would have had to move on long ago, don't you see? We could have starved them out when they first showed, if it wasn't for you!" She glowered at Em and Driscoll. "The whole bunch of you are a blight. Too much hair. Clothes that smell like soot. Not enough baths, I shouldn't wonder."

Em blushed at the insult, but Driscoll offered Mira a good-natured smile. "We've been traveling," he said, serene and reasonable. "I'm the Clydestown vet, come up from the plains. I'm thinking of settling in your beautiful valley."

"Don't bother," Mira snapped. "We don't fancy drifters. Especially if they come in one of them devilish cars."

"Now, Mira," Tilden tried again, mildly. "I'm fixing to buy it from him."

"Is that before or after I arrange to have it pushed over the cliff?"

Nervously, Em tugged at her hair, whereupon Mira scuttled off a couple of steps in a great show of horror. "Just look at her scratching! I bet there's lice in that overgrown wool! Makes my skin crawl to be in the same room with her. Tilden, they need some of your varmint mix. Get enough for the whole tribe." With surprising force, she yanked the cart out of Driscoll's relaxed hands. "Lice powder's the only thing you can buy from us, mister. You two miserable liars aren't fit to be anywhere near decent people like us, and I'll thank you to leave my store before I send for the sheriff. Celie! Come here, Celie!"

Tilden sagged, adding several inches to his girth. "I guess this isn't a good day for us to do business, stranger," he muttered uncertainly. "Some other time . . ."

"Over my dead body!" Mira shrieked. "I said git!"

At last Driscoll's famous people skills deserted him. "Why, you old harpy," he said, his voice rising to match her tone. "We're not desperate enough to waste our good cash on you. We'll find better towns, better shops, *and* better service! Come on, Em!" He marched her through the store while Tilden danced in their wake like an oversized gnat. "No need to insult the wife," he whined anxiously. "I'm sure between us level-headed men we can work something out later. About the Doble—"

But Driscoll was already tearing at the shop door, dragging Em behind him. They both remembered to duck. As soon as they were outside he gave the door a furious shove. She caught it to keep the glass panes from shattering and closed it more softly with an apologetic smile at Mira for which she hated herself immediately after.

In the back lot, Nada stood in the driver's seat, keeping a half dozen geezers at bay with her menacing growl. Fraser tossed his bottle at her, barely missing her head. The glass broke on the car's metal frame, raining shards. Driscoll lunged, but Em clutched at his arm, slowing him down. She told Nada to get in the rear and stuffed Driscoll behind the steering wheel with a strength she hadn't known she possessed. "Start it up!" she commanded. "Let's go!"

As soon as she got in the passenger seat the Doble whooshed out of the drive and along Main Street as fast as the uneven cobblestones allowed, speeding past the hostile marketing women and the belligerent geese on to the rutted field road. The car whizzed by the golden-skinned tree and the reapers tying cut grain into sheaves. It passed small boys crouching around a smoldering potato-leaf fire, then the bellowing cows, the spooked horses, toward the safety of the dark-green forest.

Driscoll stopped at the crossroads, clutching the steering wheel. "Sorry about the potholes," he said. "Another run like that and I'll start losing parts." Behind them, the church bell tolled twice. "Half an hour in the chamber of horrors." He covered his face. "Varmint mix! I can't believe I let her goad me like that."

"Who can blame you? She's worse than my mother."

Driscoll showed her his empty hands. "No rice. No window glass."

Em poked around in her hair. "And I lost my little gold chain!"

"That does it." He started a turn.

"What are you doing?" she asked in alarm.

"We're going back for our stuff. They can't just kick us out. We're part of the public. We've got rights."

Appalled, she opened the passenger door and stuck out a foot. "*You* go back! Nada and I will hike home from here!"

"No. Stay where you are," he said, pushing on the brake. "I told you, you don't have to walk as long as you've got me and I have the Doble. I'll drive you up. We'll think of another plan later. Mark my words—Yates hasn't seen the last of us yet."

Reluctantly, she settled back on to her seat, shut the door, and hoped that he was wrong and it had.

CHAPTER 33

THEY FOUND HERTHA AMONG THE ROSES, gathering petals for her sachets. Pulling his beard, Driscoll confessed to the failed shopping trip.

"It isn't your fault," she said calmly, as if she'd expected as much.

He stripped an overblown maroon rose for her and said contritely, "I'm willing to drive to the next town. Just point me in the right direction. I'll be back with the rice before supper."

She snipped off what was left of the flower and added it to a pile at her feet. "Most likely you won't find a single kernel within driving distance. Odasan brought a few sacks with him in that old donkey-cart of his, and when he ran out, Tilden had already discovered the value of our flutes. One of the traders sells them direct to the cities. Both he and Tilden have always considered it a cozy arrangement—until now. Our flutes have a fine reputation among more civilized people but they're worth next to nothing in these backwoods. I gave Tilden a flute for each bag of rice he could find, no questions asked. I guess he never bothered to tell Mira about our deal."

"And now?" Driscoll asked, stroking a fingertip over a velvety petal.

She stepped closer, murmuring, "I didn't tell you the whole truth this morning. The fact is, last month he spelled it all out. Said he wouldn't deal with me anymore unless I raised my skirt as part of the bargain. I refused, and he said I'd change my mind once we started to run out of things. I guess he's still waiting."

Driscoll's face flushed to rival his beard. After a surreptitious glance at Em he turned his attention to squeezing the rose petal into a tiny black ball. Rubbing it over his palm, he said, "I take it you haven't mentioned the proposition to any of our friends, Hertha? Let's keep it that way for now. Maybe we can think of some kind of solution to our little problem by tomorrow. I guess I'd better go tell Odasan I came back empty-handed." He tossed away the scented little ball, sniffed at his hand, gave Em an apologetic smile, and headed toward the yurt to break the bad news.

Em was glad she didn't have to watch the old man's reaction. "The people of Yates are an unfriendly bunch," she told Hertha. "And that Mira is just plain nasty. I won't go there again, even if I have to start reading by the light of a wood fire and eat canned green beans for a year."

Hertha chuckled. "I doubt you'd last very long, but you can see why I get so pushy about preserving our food. These pears will be next." She went to pull two off the tree, passed one to Em, and leaned forward with her first bite to keep the juice from spilling on her apron. Then she settled herself comfortably in the shade under the tree and patted the grass at her side. "Come sit and I'll tell you a story." After the next bite, she began.

"It was this way," she said. "In Tilden's version, anyway. In the days before the poisonous rains, some strangers arrived in a beat-up old truck and decided to settle. Up here." She scribed a wide circle with her dripping pear, including the garden and house. "They found the place in ruins, just as we did, and decided to fix it up. They had enough cash between them to buy materials for the renovation and for some sheds they built—badly, according to Odasan."

She blotted juice off her fingers, using the hem of her apron. "Yates loved their business at first, even though they dressed funny and never put scissors to hair or beard. Behind their backs, the townspeople called them 'the horde on the fiery hill,' and laughed at their outlandish ways. All except one. That was Mavis, the prettiest girl in town, married just long enough to feel trapped in a life she hadn't imagined. Her baby wailed day and night, always wanting more than Mavis thought she could give."

She finished her pear and used the apron to wipe her sticky chin. Rubbing her hands on a patch of grass, she said, "Mavis was curious about the horde. Especially about the guy with the truck who drove down once a week for supplies. It seemed every time he came to the store Mavis had some urgent shopping to do. Soon the town folks were buzzing. When the gossip reached her husband Kirk he thought it best to lock Mavis in the cellar whenever the truck rolled around. One day he missed, and Mavis was gone. His neighbors swore they saw her climb into the truck just outside of town.

"Kirk waited for a week or so, tending the fussy infant until his sister took pity on him and moved in with them. Then he collected some of his buddies and they drove up the mountain together. They found the clearing and the garden and house all empty, even though the truck was still there. Kirk was sure he recognized Mavis's shawl spread over the back of a chair.

"The men raided the cupboards for brandy and wine, and after they drank it they decided to burn the place down. But every fire they lit blew out. So they made do with smashing the garden and windows, slashed what furniture they could, and wrestled the doors off their hinges before returning to town.

"While they slept off the booze, the horde struck back—or so the men claimed when they awoke to the devastation of the poisonous rains. That next morning they saw that everything in the fields had died along with the animals pastured there. They were sure it was the horde's doing. That they'd put some kind of curse on the town, a curse that soon spread from Yates to everyplace else. At least that's how Tilden tells it." She sighed, shook her head, and leaned back against the tree trunk.

"Kirk was busy trying to keep himself and his little one alive, but a year later he hiked uphill for signs of his wife. Of course, by then the good people of Yates had pushed every vehicle they could find off a steep cliff, creating a car graveyard in the canyon below. Come to think of it, maybe I should tell Driscoll about it. There might be all kinds of things down there he could put to good use. But anyway, Kirk came up here and found everything just the way he and his buddies had left it, except that Mavis's shawl was gone, and the garden was once again bursting with good things to eat. He stuffed himself, filled a mildewed bed sheet with produce, carried his harvest home, and told everyone to get their own.

"A bunch of townspeople came up that day, helping themselves to what was left. For good measure, they pushed the old broken-down truck over the nearest edge. What's left of it got hung up on some trees on the way down. I've seen it myself." She pointed in the direction of the road. "Down below that sharp turn."

She looked around the garden, her face bleak. "Those who ate the stuff they took out of here got real sick. Naturally they were sure the witches had put a hex on this place. No one set foot on the old trail afterwards, except for Kirk. Once a year, in spring, he carried his daughter as far as the first boulder and called Mavis's name, swearing he could hear a faint answering cry from somewhere above.

"That daughter was Mira. She never got over her mother's betrayal. In Mira's mind we're part of that horde, and she insists on reminding everyone in Yates that evil once again lurks on the mountain. Her own daughter, Celie, looks more like Mavis every year. Acts like her, too, Tilden says. He showed me pictures of both, and I couldn't tell them apart. Every time Mira sees one of us she fears the worst for her Celie."

"Now it's all starting to make some kind of sense," Em said, wiping her hands clean on the grass too. "It's a wonder Tilden agreed to do business with you at all."

Hertha laughed. "*He* knows we have nothing to do with any of it. And maybe he thought his story was warning enough. Besides, he likes a good trade, as long as he comes out on top. At first, not knowing what we know now, we brought him our produce to sell, but he crossed himself and refused to touch any of it. And *he's* the most progressive man in the valley! They'd elect him mayor if he would let them, but he loves the pharmacy and his store beyond reason—them, and his Celie."

"Not Mira?"

Hertha grimaced. "Who could love Mira?"

"Why didn't you tell the others about Tilden's . . . suggestion?"

Hertha shrugged. "I really *was* hoping he'd give it up once he realized I'm prepared to stop bringing him the flutes."

Em looked at the house with fresh eyes. "When Alden first got here, what did he find?"

"A leaking roof. Rotting floorboards. Wood rat nests in every room. A garden gone to seed under one vast blackberry hedge."

"Why did he come?"

"He said it was a place of power waiting to be used." Hertha got to her feet and continued her rose-picking. "As for me, I appreciated what was left—a well-hidden root cellar built into the slope, thick stone walls and sturdy oaken beams strong enough to withstand heavy snowfalls, a gravity-fed spring, a plumbed-in sink, and miraculous soil. I kept myself busy and let Alden deal with his dreams."

When Hertha went inside to cook, Em settled back under the orchard's green canopy and groped with her mind but could find nothing evil anyplace near.

AT SUPPER that night Odasan stared at his plate with distaste. "Potatoes remind me of boiled turnips," he said, rising from the table to bring an oddly shaped bottle out of the pantry. "If I can't eat my rice, I'll drink it." He uncapped a ceramic shot glass and filled it with great care. Then, taking meticulous sips, he chewed and treasured each drop.

Once the kitchen was tidied they all went into the living room where Hertha pulled back the curtains and blew out the lamps. "We might as well save on fuel. Between moonlight and the wood fire, we'll see anything that needs to be seen."

Brendan sat on the hearthstones, backlit by wavering tongues of flame, and strummed his guitar. Em practiced her hum. Her throat tightened in anxious anticipation, but at last the ancient voice once more rose from inside her and rang through the room. This time everyone knew just what to do. They formed a circle and sat on the rug, joining hands. As before, Em sat between Alden and Driscoll, her feet resting against Nada's flank.

The wheel shuddered alive, gathered speed, and spun up through the roof. For an instant it hovered over the dark clearing. Then it accelerated smoothly through some cramped, lightless space. They emerged into a sky bathed in delicate lilacs, the sun a sinking red flare.

The wheel found a stream and traced it uphill to the spring it had been. There they discovered Anckar's imagined cabin, complete with the three spruces, the boulder, the bench standing against the house wall, the sketchpad lying open upon it. The wheel looped slowly around to the back. It passed the workshop and kiln, then it curved, dipped, and skimmed over mountain forest toward the lush valley floor where the leaves had already turned autumn-bright. In the distance, the lake surface reflected the evening sky.

Em navigated the wheel over a sprinkling of roofs, crossed the shimmering water and steered upslope on the far shore toward a tall round house. Its glass front was tinged pink. The wrap-around porch had already melted into the night shadows, but some measure of light remained on the wide pasture below where two horses pranced, their tails high. One horse was the color of sorrel, the other the color of smoke. Between pasture and lake stretched a vast, well-fenced garden.

The young woman who'd run after the wheel the previous day was just stepping out of its gate, shouldering a hoe. She saw them, dropped the hoe, and came running. Waving at them with both hands, she shouted something Em could not quite make out. It sounded like "Ai-ya!" or "Eea!" The reason she couldn't hear it properly was that a couple of much nearer sounds competed for her attention—of breaking glass, and of Nada, growling.

All at once, the wheel snapped back to the plank floor, which was eerily lit by glowing coals and the moon. A shadow stepped away from the broken window. Nada leaped in pursuit, diving straight through the remaining glass. While the shards were still falling, Driscoll yanked the door open. A moonbeam streamed in. Nada's barking grew distant. Somewhere downhill a child howled in protest and pain. Driscoll plunged through the moonbeam and disappeared into the night.

With trembling fingers, Hertha relit the four lamps. The match singed her thumb at the last wick and she sucked on the burned skin. A moth fluttered into the room and silently spiraled around the glass chimneys.

"Did you see our horses?" Lupe whispered to Brendan, but he was focusing his full attention on the open door and on Driscoll, who had returned and was dragging a slight figure behind him. Nada squeezed past their combined jumble of legs, a torn piece of fabric fluttering from her bared teeth like a banner. Driscoll pushed his captive toward the lamps and shut the door, barring it with the full width of his body.

The skinny boy-captive scowled, pulled the shirttails from the waistband of his pants, and gingerly tugged the ample material over his rear.

"Nev!" Em cried, astonished. "What are *you* doing here?"

"I was looking for you," he said, defiantly clenching his fists. "Thunder and I came to save you."

"From what?"

He pointed an accusing finger at Driscoll. "From him and the rest of his gang."

Em wanted to laugh and weep at the same time but pulled a chair away from the table instead and said, "Sit. You look like you could use a good meal."

His feet stayed glued to the floor. "So they can slip something in my food?"

Em's urge to laugh grew stronger. "You don't make any sense, and no wonder—you must have been riding that poor horse past his point of exhaustion. Past your own, too. And for nothing, as it turns out, because I don't intend to ever go back, with you or without you."

His scowl deepened. "You're in with a bad lot, Em. Real bad. If you haven't noticed it yet, it's only because they're keeping you drugged so you can't think for yourself."

And now she could no longer hold the laughter inside.

He flinched as if she had struck him, then glared at Bena and said, "She's the one who brought you here, isn't she? She and the red-haired devil. In Yates, they call this place the witch camp. Don't you know that witches are famous for sacrificing young girls in exchange for a good harvest? Why else would she have you sit in a spell-circle in the dark?"

Odasan put a protective arm around Bena, who gently brushed it aside. Getting to her feet, she offered Nev her most gracious smile along with a courteous hand.

He brandished double-crossed fingers at her. "Stand back, Satan worshipper!"

Behind Nev's back, Driscoll ground his teeth and rasped, "Get it straight, Nev—*you* are not the accuser here. You're the trespasser, sneaking around like a thief, breaking windows."

Nev spun around, crying, "Only one! And that was an accident. You can't scare me. I've got this!" He pulled a small wooden cross from his trousers, held it up high, and bellowed, "Get Thee behind me, Satan!"

Driscoll curled his lips to show him his canines. "I'm already behind you," he said. "Now what, little boy?"

Nev shook the cross at him with one hand while claiming Em with the other. "Let her go. Let us both go. Now! Or else I'll ride straight back to Yates for the sheriff. Kidnapping is a hanging offense."

Somebody gave a brief, hysterical giggle. Lupe clapped a hand over her mouth. Then Hertha cautiously made her way toward Nev, holding her palms out to him the way some people do when they are trying to calm a frightened dog who is unsure whether or not he should bite. "Let's settle down," she said in a soothing singsong. "Em's right. You look exhausted. Why didn't you knock? We'd have been glad to invite you in. I think we're *all* ready for apple pie and tea."

"What's your plan?" Nev sneered. "To slip me the same drug you're giving to Em or to murder me outright so I can't go to the law?"

Hertha gulped and looked helplessly at Bena. So did Nev, although his mouth hardened almost at once. "In Oren, we know what to do with witches like you! The people below will learn it soon enough, once I tell them how it's done." He pointed a trembling finger at Driscoll. "And you'll be next. You sicced that foul dog on me. I'll remember that—and so will the dog."

Something in Em exploded. She shoved Nev to the door. "Why on earth did you have to come? Nobody asked you to. Now get out. Driscoll, stand aside!"

"With pleasure," he said, his voice fierce as he pushed the door wide open. "Go on, boy, scram!"

Nev looked at Em. She looked away.

"You don't mean it," he said. "I rode Thunder all this way just for you." When she didn't respond, he went on, "I'll be in Yates, waiting for you to come to your senses. I promised your mom I'd find you and bring you home." Slowly, he backed out of the door, aiming the cross at every face except hers. Nada chose that unfortunate moment to trot up to Em and proudly present her with Nev's pant-seat. Again, someone giggled. Again, Lupe covered her mouth.

Nev tugged at his shirttails and said, "You'll be sorry, all right!" but it was unclear at whom he was directing the threat.

Ignoring it and the cross, Driscoll clamped his big hands on Nev's scrawny shoulders. "I believe I'll escort you straight to the road, little mischief-maker. I want a good look at that horse to see what all that hard riding has done to him."

As soon as they were gone Em knelt and wrapped her arms around Nada, accepting the dog's spoils. "I wish you hadn't torn his pants," she said. "In Oren, they kill dogs for less."

CHAPTER 34

"AN UNPLEASANT CHILD!" Hertha said, sweeping up the broken glass. "What on earth was he talking about, Em?"

Brendan, feeding sticks to the fire, agreed. "He didn't make any sense."

Lupe tittered, "He came to rescue his fair maiden, of course. For a minute I thought he was going to drag her away by the hair."

"Not likely," Brendan snorted. "Since he's only half her size. But say, I had no idea Driscoll could get so angry. I swear, for a minute there his beard was actually standing on end."

"It bristled like a boar brush," Lupe said.

Alden slackened into his chair. "It reminded me of the day he brought you to us, Em. He was plenty mad then too, especially when he realized he'd have to leave without you. Come to think of it, he and Nev are on the same side, even if they don't know it."

"And what side is that?" Brendan asked.

"Why—Em's, of course."

"So what? We're all on Em's side. Aren't we, Lupe?" Brendan teased, watching Lupe's expression grow frigid.

Then Odasan and Bena brought heavily loaded snack trays in from the kitchen. "The poor foolish boy doesn't know what he's missing," she said, cutting the pie while Lupe lined up dessert plates and Odasan quietly poured tea.

"I think I found every shard," Hertha announced from the floor by the window. "But just to be safe, please don't walk around barefoot until the sun shines on any slivers I might have missed. Odasan, do we have enough glass left to replace what Em's little friend broke?"

"Driscoll ordered some from the glazier in town. I'll write down the measurements for the broken-out pane. For tonight, just draw the curtains shut tight to keep out the moths." He sounded the slightest bit less patient than usual.

Lupe put a generous slice on each plate and Em passed them around the table before she sat down to her own. After savoring her first bite, she said, "Nev's not my friend. It was his fault I had to leave Oren." She explained how she and Nada had first met, and the part Nev played in it.

"It's no wonder she dotes on you." Brendan fed the dog his pie crust. "I see there's no use being jealous of the bond you've formed between you."

Then Driscoll walked in, his eyes blazing, his color high. "I escorted him out to the road. He'd had the audacity to tie Thunder to the Doble's front bumper. It made me mad all over again." He sprawled in the chair next to Em's and picked up his fork. "That horse doesn't look good, Em. Nev's been pushing him too hard, not giving him enough time to browse and drink his fill every day. If it hadn't been for Thunder I'd have packed the boy into the car and driven him back to Oren right then and there. But neither of them would thrive without the other, I suspect."

"He does love his horse," Em said. "More than anything else."

Driscoll swallowed half of his pie without any visible signs of chewing. "I wouldn't be so sure of that. Not after his heroic rescue attempt."

Em was getting thoroughly tired of this particular conversation. "The part about my mother's sudden concern has got to be an outright lie. The only reason he came was because he was bored and looking for some kind of adventure, and the only reason he wants me to go back with him is so that his dad won't kill him for taking off in the first place and ditching his chores."

Brendan rapped the table for attention. "Enough about *him*. Did you all see Anckar's log cabin and the round house? They were exactly how we envisioned them, eh?" He turned to Driscoll. "What do you think about dream class *now*, Mr. Skeptic?"

Driscoll gave an embarrassed grin. "It was . . ." he began, searching for just the right word, "it truly was—"

Em clapped his shoulder, completing the sentence for him. "A form of mass hysteria. Right?"

"Did I really say that?"

"At around eleven this morning, as I recall."

"How conceited of me! About the round house, Brendan—if we hadn't been so rudely interrupted I believe we would have had a tour of the wrap-around porch, cat trees and all. I don't know how real it is, but boy, would I have loved a close look."

With an indulgent smile, Bena scraped the last of the pie on his plate and then began to stack the dirty dishes. "I was hoping for a close look at the observation tower's glass ceiling," she said. Then her hands went still, and she looked directly at Odasan. "The girl with the hoe? I think she was calling my name."

IN THE morning Driscoll waited until the others left the table before he told Em, "I've worked out Plan Two. It's fool-proof."

"Good for you," she said lightly, putting an extra dollop of jam on her toast. "I've been thinking. The traders wouldn't come all this way just for Tilden. I'm sure there must be at least a couple more little towns along the road we followed up from the plains. I bet if you left now you could be back before dinner. Get all the rice you can hunt up."

"I'm not so sure we could find as much as a kernel. Sounds to me Odasan's rice is a special order, strictly in exchange for the flutes. You heard Tilden. This is potato country. I think there's only one sack to be had, and that is in Yates. That's why we're going back there. Today."

She stared, aghast. "You've got to be kidding. Not after Nev told us he'll be waiting there for me. With half a day's head-start, there's no telling how many lies he's spread about us by now."

"Don't laugh—"After a quick glance at Bena, who was busy washing the dishes, he continued in a lower tone, "but after I saw him with Thunder, I felt kind of sorry for them both. So I gave him a handful of money and made him promise to ride back to Oren—in short stages."

Em was surprised. "He took money from *you*?"

Driscoll shook his head. "Not at first. In fact, he threw it in the bushes. But I bet you anything it was just for show. He probably picked it up right after I left. Most likely he's well on his way by now. It must have been obvious even to him that you're not going back to Oren. He said it was getting real cold at night—so I gave him one of my blankets too."

Bena put down the dishrag and came to give him a hug, dripping suds all over his shirt. Then she resumed the wash-up, offering Em such an affectionate smile that the girl was compelled to unhook a dishtowel and began drying the dishes. "If you're really serious about going back to town you'll have to do it without me," she told Driscoll. "I'm sure Celie will be delighted."

"She's minding the store by herself between twelve and one. She'll be easy on us."

"Easy on *you*," Em corrected, briskly wiping a plate. "And eager to give you whatever you want—as long as you show up alone."

"That's precisely why I need you to come with me," Driscoll told her. "To encourage . . . restraint. Besides, we'll have to shop fast in case one of the old geezers gets word to Mira about our transaction. I've reworked Hertha's list." He unfolded a new scrap of paper. "Now that we know where everything is I'll go after the heavier items and you grab the matches and such. We'll buy a map too so we can locate a friendlier market town for our next shopping expedition. And don't forget your necklace. It must have slipped out of your hair during the fracas in the grain-room. You wouldn't want Celie to find it, would you?"

"Why not?" Em slammed the plate on to the counter. "It'll look much better on her!"

Bena wrung out the dishrag and dried her hands. "Never mind, Driscoll. If Em can't bring herself to go with you I will. Women my age are invisible to girls like this Celie."

But how invisible would the little witchy woman be, entering Tilden's store beside the tallest man of the flatlands? "Have you forgotten how upset you get when you have to come out of the trees? Remember how you felt when we left the forest at Oren!" She pressed the dishtowel into her old friend's hands. "You finish drying. I'll go." She turned to Driscoll. "Tell me the rest of Plan Two."

WHEN THE church bells chimed noon the Doble was parked at the outermost field. Giving Em an appraising look, Driscoll said, "It'll be all right, you know. We'll assume Mira and Tilden need ten minutes to clear out and ten to come back. That leaves us with forty minutes in which to drive in, shop, pay, and stop at the glass shop on our way out of town. Are you ready?"

She nodded, not trusting herself to speak. He whistled for Nada, who had jumped out for some exploring. Obediently, she returned and they drove on. The cows were lying close together, complacently chewing their cud, and the horses were grazing calmly on the far side of their pasture. "In my mind," Em said, "there's no shape as pleasing as the graceful curves of a horse."

"In *my* mind, there's one other," Driscoll countered, looking straight ahead.

Once, the high valley must have been stunning in its beauty. It still looked better than the drought-stricken plains but the grass on the pastures and fields was thin and the soil looked anemic. And yet, Em found the landscape appealing. After spending a week on wooded slopes where flat spots were at a premium she felt the urge to run across an expanse of level ground.

Driscoll slowed as they approached the golden tree. "I promised you yesterday—"

"Not now," she interrupted. "I'm way too nervous and we don't have enough time. Let's just get this whole trip over with as fast as we can."

He picked up speed, glanced at her sideways, and said, "We're not doing anything wrong, you know. Going back to the store is no crime. Didn't Tilden imply we could work something out with him?"

She nodded, half admiring his courage, half deploring his foolhardiness. "What if Mira shows up while we're there?"

"She won't," he said firmly.

On the field of partially harvested barley, reapers sat in a circle, eating out of their lunch pails. In the next field, pickers crouched by a campfire and poked roasted spuds out of the coals. Even the watch-geese that belonged to the glazier had gone off to dine, leaving the front yard empty. When Driscoll ran to the glass shop to order the additional pane, its door was locked and a hand-scrawled sign over the knob informed him the shop would re-open at one.

Main Street was deserted. So was the front of the store except for Jones and Fraser. The old man had loosened his suspenders and lay stretched out on one of the benches. On the other lay Jones, his eyes covered with a handkerchief against the glaring sun. Neither of them stirred when the Doble approached, quietly rolled around the side of the building, and stopped in the rear lot. Driscoll turned it off and set the emergency brake. "So far so good," he told Em in a low voice.

The midday heat oozed the kind of light-drenched languor Em remembered from lazy Sunday afternoons in Oren. She gave the dog a reassuring pat. "You stay," she whispered. "We'll be right back." To her dismay, the dog's shoulder was petrified with fear, her eyes fixed on some nameless dread. *Don't go,* they seemed to plead. *Don't leave me out here all alone.* Em shivered. "Something's wrong. Look at Nada. I'm not getting out of this car."

"Oh, come now!" Driscoll was beginning to sound impatient. "She'll be fine. And I'm counting on you." He stalked around to the passenger side and held out his hand but Em did not take it. "She's spooked," she said, heeding her instincts. "And so am I. Just buy what you can throw into one basket and then let's get out of here. We'll work on Plan Three later. Trust me—Plan Two is flawed."

Her eyes bright with gratitude, Nada scrambled to the front seat and pressed herself against Em's hip.

"She'll be fine," Driscoll repeated. "I need you more than she does."

"No, you don't." Em held the trembling dog tight. It was only after Driscoll's footsteps receded that the girl whispered, "I'm sorry."

Flushed with irritation and heat, Driscoll made his way to the front of the store. Fraser's arm was hanging over the side of the bench. His shoe soles were worn through in several spots, exposing his socks. Jones's mouth gaped. Neither man moved as Driscoll stepped between them and opened the shop door so slowly that the chimes stayed silent even as he closed it behind him. Now that he was familiar with the layout it was a simple matter to push the best-oiled cart to the pharmacy counter. He was expecting to see Celie but she was not there. Fine. He would rouse her when we was done filling the cart.

Striding purposefully through the dark hall to the grain room, he pulled the curtains aside and searched the floor for the telltale sparkle of Em's lost necklace, but saw only dust balls and spilled grain. He found the rice, hefted it on one shoulder, lifted an equally large sack of wheat to the other, and deposited both in the cart as silently as he could.

Retracing yesterday's steps, he easily reclaimed most of the items he and Em had selected. He deliberately avoided the remedy section, knowing his resistance to browsing its shelves would always be low. While he was loading two gallon-sized jugs of honey, Celie stumbled up to the pharmacy counter from the back room. Her cheeks were creased from a lie-down, her eyes sleep-drenched. They instantly focused on Driscoll "Aha! I thought you might show up today," she said, sounding smug. "Decided to try again, huh? I see you left your ghastly friend in the car this time." She studied the cart. "You've been busy. I recognize most of what you've got in there. My mom made me reshelf every item after you guys abandoned your groceries. I took your butter and eggs down to the cellar but we had to sell the milk. It would have gone sour."

"True," Driscoll said. "I'm almost done. By the time you bring our stuff up from the cellar I'll be ready to pay."

"Not so fast!" She pushed through the low swinging doors next to the counter and advanced, working her hips. Then she tilted her face up to his. The light from the window revealed what hadn't he hadn't noticed before—her eyes were inflamed. She'd been crying. "Are you really just passing through on your way to the city, like you said yesterday?" she asked.

"City?" he hedged. "I never said 'city.' Which reminds me—do you carry maps? I'm not familiar with the local roads yet."

"Do we carry what?"

"You know . . . drawings of the surrounding area. So we can see what lies on the other side of the mountain."

She took a brush out from under the counter, smoothed her nap-tousled hair, and tossed it decisively over her shoulders. "Why would we need those? No one around here ever goes anywhere. Every now and then somebody's grown child leaves, but none ever come back. I won't, either." She came around the counter and pressed herself against him. Then, without warning, she snatched his hand and plunged it into the front of her blouse.

Shocked, he tried to pull free, but she clung to his arm. "My mom locked me in my room last night 'cause of you," she said, half flirting. "As if I couldn't just have climbed out the window anytime I felt like it." Her tone grew more urgent. "Take me to the city with you and I'll let you do whatever you want with me."

She was too young to make such an offer. He was too young to take it. Her skin was hot; his hand seemed to be drowning in it. With a polite, non-committal smile he managed to reclaim every one of his mutinous fingers and wrapped them firmly around the shopping cart handle. "I'm not even sure where the nearest city *is* from here," he said, sounding hoarse. "That's why I asked for a map. Maybe Tilden keeps a stack in a drawer somewhere. Don't you occasionally get strangers passing through, needing directions?"

She looked at him with pity. "Are you daft? You and the scarecrow are the only strangers I've seen all year." She teased open the top button of her blouse, exposing more than could possibly be good for her. And there, encircling her short, stocky neck was Em's golden chain, the amber pendant nestling in the well-cushioned V of her breasts. The stone did not match Celie's eyes. They were a pale blue.

"My mom's always jabbering about keeping me safe, till all I want to do is just run and run," she said, tugging on the chain as if it were trying to choke her. "Sometimes the traders tell tales over dinner about how the city people don't have to cook. How they drink their meals out of throw-away cups. They have this green soup growing in huge fish tanks, see—and pills that have everything in them that used to grow in a garden. They take one with their soup every day. No dishes to wash! No weeding, either!" She pulling the cart flush against the counter. "Go on, then," she said, pressing a key on the register. "Get the rest of your stuff while I ring up what you've got in here. I'll bring up the eggs and the butter after you're done. You'll want them on top of your box, anyway. We'll be halfway down this sorry mountain before my dad comes in. I'll write him a nice little note and stick it inside the cash drawer so he won't worry."

All at once, Plan Two lost its appeal. Impotently dangling his hands, Driscoll said, "I can't just take you away from your folks like that."

"Why not?" she shrilled. "You took *her* from hers, didn't you? Without asking."

"Are you referring to Em?" Celie hadn't known that little detail yesterday. It could only mean that someone had mentioned it to her since then. "That's not how it was," he tried to explain. "Our original plan was to go on a day trip. And besides, *her* mom didn't want her anymore but your mom wants you."

"You leave my mother out of it," she said, her voice frosty.

"You've got it all wrong, Celie. The only reason Em and I drove all the way up here was to return a lost dog. Go ask her if you don't believe me. I see you found her necklace. She'll be so pleased."

Celie's stubby fingers followed the chain down to the amber drop. She buttoned the blouse over it. "This little thing? My father gave it to me last night because Mom made me cry. Are you calling him a thief?"

"Of course not!" he stammered. "I'm just glad it turned up, is all. Here." He laid his shiniest silver dollar before her. "Your finder's fee. With our thanks."

She barely gave it a glance. "I'll hand the necklace over as soon as we arrive in the city. I know you've got plenty of room for me in that car of yours. Why, I'll even sit in back with the dog!"

In his discomfort, he said, "I'm sorry. We're not ready to move on yet."

A shutter dropped inside her eyes. "So Mom was right about you after all!" Each word a dagger of ice. She swept the coin off the counter so hard that it bounced on the floor a couple of times before speedily rolling down the center aisle. With equal speed, she yanked the cart through the swinging door to her side, hissing, "You're mixed up with that filthy bunch on the mountain! And the girl's drugged, just like Nev said. You better leave while you still can. I'm not selling you *nothing*!" With a furious sob, she tried to pry his hands off the cart handle. He hung on by sheer instinct, already knowing he'd lost.

CHAPTER 35

THE CHIMES ANNOUNCED A CUSTOMER even though the space inside the shop door seemed to remain empty. Then a small boy appeared in the remedy section.

"Is that you again, Garner?" Celie yelled.

The boy froze.

She glared at him and let go of the cart. "Didn't you hear my mom yesterday? You can't come in here anymore if you don't buy anything. You hung around those shelves for a whole hour, getting in everyone's way."

Garner made himself smaller. "But Celie, my cat's sick. I think she'll die if I don't find some medicine for her so she can breathe."

Angrily, Celie straightened her blouse. "Take her to the vet, then."

"I tried that already. He says I don't have enough money for an *examation* and besides he's too busy to look at every sick kitten that comes along. He says if she dies I can just get another one because there's so many out there. Only, I don't want another one, Celie. Don't you have something for her nose, like what people take for the flu? I brought all my money this time, see?"

He showed her a handful of coins.

She ignored it. "We don't carry medicines for cats. Just leave, why don't you—and you too, mister. My father doesn't want me talking to you." But Driscoll had already shifted his entire focus to the boy. In vain, Celie rattled the cart to reclaim his attention. "Put everything back where it belongs before you go," she demanded. "I'm not cleaning up after you again."

"Uh-huh," he said in an abstracted tone, already striving toward the child. "You need help with your cat?" he asked gently when they were face to face. The boy looked at the floor and rapidly nodded his head. Driscoll hunkered down until they were the same height. "Listen, Garner—I'm a vet too. With cat medicines."

Garner wiped a sleeve over his cheeks. "She's just a little bitty thing. I found her in a sack full of drowned kittens, down by the ditch. She was the only one still moving. She asked me to save her. I'm still trying."

"Good for you," Driscoll said.

"Only, she doesn't want to eat anymore. She's right across the street. That's where I live." Garner fumbled with the doorknob, spilling half of his savings. Driscoll helped him pick up stray coins and opened the door.

"Wait! Hold it!" Celie kicked at the cart. "What about this? What about me?"

"No, thanks," Driscoll said absently. "Your price is too high."

At first she looked puzzled. Then she shrieked, "The nerve of some people!" and shoved the cart down the aisle with all her might. He swung the door shut. It muffled the sounds of a collision.

Outside, things seemed calm enough. Fraser and Jones hadn't moved a muscle, although now they were snoring in relays. The rear lot was quiet except for the Doble. In it, Em was engrossed in the fairy-tale book, automatically stroking the sleeping dog. While Driscoll grabbed his black bag he explained about Garner who stood hugging the store's corner, anxiously watching in every direction.

Em closed the book. "And the groceries? I thought you were determined not to let anything get in your way."

Driscoll looked at her soberly. "Turns out you were right all along. We'll do better elsewhere. Will you come with me to Garner's house? This won't take long if you help."

She couldn't refuse him a second time. "Will we be done before one o'clock?"

"I'm counting on it. See, Nada settled right down. She'll be fine for a few minutes, won't you, girl?"

The dog struggled into a sitting position, the tip of her tail wagging doubtfully. "Bark if you need us," Em said, getting out, determinedly ignoring the tremor that passed through the dog and the paw stretching pleadingly toward her. In a firm voice she said, "Stay in the car. You'll be okay." She could feel the dog's despairing gaze scorch her back even after they were out of her sight, could feel the dog's mind touch her own so that she hardly knew where she was going until she found herself inside an unkempt garden, knee-high in weeds.

"My mom won't let me keep my kitty in the house," Garner was explaining to Driscoll. "She's in the shed, over there." He led the way to a squat, unsightly wooden structure. A rake and a hoe hung from bent nails on the outside wall. A spade leaned against the warped door. When Garner moved it aside the door slowly creaked open.

Em gagged on the stench drifting out. A shaft of light shone upon rusting tool heads and chipped clay pots crowding the packed dirt floor inside. Among them lay the limp bit of fur that was Garner's kitten.

Driscoll propped the door wide and then knelt for a close look. "We'll need a bucket of warmish water and soap, Garner. And a bunch of clean rags. Quick."

"Yessir." The boy sounded relieved to have someone taking over.

Em knelt at Driscoll's side, covering her nose. The kitten was soaked in her own filth, nostrils and eyes plugged by thick, greenish mucus but stubbornly sucking in air through a mouth long since gone dry. "What's wrong with her?" Em asked.

"What isn't, you mean." He wet a square of gauze from a bottle and worked on loosening the scabs clogging the miniature nostrils. "He was right. She's fading fast."

"But you'll save her." It wasn't a question.

"Garner will." Driscoll groped for his thermometer and inserted it beneath a limp and uncomplaining tail. Garner reappeared, loaded with gear. He set everything in front of Driscoll and watched him hold the thermometer up to the light. The vet's face lost every vestige of a smile. "Hmmm," he muttered to himself. "Drastic measures." He readied a syringe, jabbed its sharp needle into loose neck fold, gave an additional shot into each flank, and started to clean the kitten's face and ears—leaving the other end to Em's ministrations.

She dipped a rag into soapy water and began with the tail. Eventually, her fingers made contact with Driscoll's at the cat's mid-section. Brushing his knuckles with hers sent an electric tingle up the full length of her arm. They both paused, their unguarded eyes locking. Then they went on with their shared task. When every inch of fur was finally clean and towel-dried, Driscoll swaddled the damp kitten in a torn, voluminous shirt. "Now we need a small box, Garner," he said, "to keep her off the dirt floor. I bet it gets mighty cold during the night."

The boy nodded, leaving again.

"It'll be better for her if we take her with us," Em whispered once he was out of earshot. "We can bring her back as soon as she's okay."

Driscoll shook his head. "It wouldn't be better for Garner. He needs to feel he can do this for her." He raised the bundle up to his cheek, closing his eyes. The kitten's head lolled against his cheek. His face took on a look so tender that Em barely recognized it. Those large capable fiddler's hands, cradling that fragile spark of life, seemed to promise a happy ending. She almost wished the hands would cradle her too. Bewildered by an onslaught of raw emotions, she busied herself with fluffing the leftover rags on the bottom of the box Garner brought.

Driscoll lowered his tiny patient tenderly onto the soft nest. "How long has she been sick, Garner?"

"It started a couple of days ago. She threw up and stuff came out the other end, smelling awful. I didn't know what to do."

Driscoll beckoned the boy closer. "I'll show you. Keep her nose clear, feed her, and give her these pills." He counted out a heap of pink ones and a smaller number of yellow tablets, poured them into separate envelopes, and wrote the instructions on them in big, plain print. "A yellow one every morning and night. A pink one right after, with an extra pink one at noon. Got that?"

"Two yellow, three pink," Garner repeated.

"Right!" Driscoll gave him an encouraging smile. "Here's a neat trick for you." He steadied the kitten's head with one hand, pried the mouth open with two fingers of the other one, and rapidly slid a pill in as far as it would go. The little cat swallowed. "If you don't push it far enough she'll spit it out. Keep her fur clean. The box, too. Sweep out this shed while you're at it. Why, I've known cats to get sick just from being around filth like this! Most important, you've got to keep feeding her, but only a few drops at a time."

He produced a medicine dropper and explained about egg yolk, cream and persistence, then had Garner practice by dribbling a drop of water on the cat's bloodless lips. A pale tongue licked it away. "See, she's extra thirsty because of the fever and all the fluids she lost. Keep giving her a couple of drops of the egg mix every few minutes for the rest of the day, and then a dropper's worth every two hours during the night." He looked square into the boy's eyes. "Her life depends on it. Can you do it?"

"I'll sneak out of my bedroom window and sleep here with her," Garner promised.

"When she gets stronger you can put the mix in a saucer for her to lap up, next to a bowl of clean water. We'll be back in a couple of days. Okay?"

Garner nodded, casting a uneasy look toward his house. Driscoll helped Em to her feet. They both swished their hands through the soapy water and wiped them dry. Garner accompanied them to a narrow side gate half hidden in the shaggy hedge-fence. "I'm not allowed to talk to you freaks," he whispered, nervously glancing behind him.

"We're not freaks—we're friends!" the young vet whispered back. He and Em stepped into the street. Behind them, Garner clicked the gate shut.

A gang of men stood in front of the store, watching Driscoll and Em cross over.

Something had changed for the worse.

Fraser, suspenders restored to his sloping shoulders, called to someone through the gapped shop door. Tilden came out, wearing his spotless white pharmacist's frock and holding a bottle of wine by its neck. Planting his feet wide, he said,

"Mister? You wait a minute, right there. We have to talk."

Em's hand found Driscoll's and clung.

"Celie told me all about your unwelcome visit. Didn't Mira make it plain yesterday that you're not to set foot in our store?" Tilden dangled the necklace by its gold chain and threw it. It skidded to land against one of Driscoll's shoes. The silver dollar he'd offered Celie sailed after it. "Pick 'em up!" Tilden ordered.

Em hastened to retrieve both items.

"Celie tells me you tried to force your attentions on her.

Touching her. Trying to lure her to the car with those cheap trinkets of yours."

"Your daughter is lying," Driscoll said evenly.

"My girl doesn't lie, mister. I don't know what goes on up on the mountain and so far I've seen no reason to care. That could change if I ever catch you anywhere near her again. Understand?"

"Tell 'em, Tilden," Fraser slurred. "Scum o' the earth."

Driscoll's biceps turned to steel under Em's hand as she steered him toward the corner. She forced her voice to sound steady. "We were just leaving, see?"

Fraser twanged his suspenders a couple of times to get Tilden's attention. The pharmacist surrendered the bottle, wheeled, and marched back inside his store.

Em dragged Driscoll to the lot. "You're breaking my arm," he muttered through clenched teeth. "Will you let go already?"

"Not until you're in the car," she told him. But when they reached it they found a new problem. Nada was gone. Em called her name softly, hoping the dog was merely exploring the far side of the shrubs. Driscoll whistled. There was no response. They sat in the Doble, not sure what to do next.

The drunks drifted into the lot and surrounded the car. Pot-bellied Jones offered an amiable gap-toothed grin. "Fancy machine."

"Thank you," Driscoll replied absently, scrutinizing what he could see of the field adjoining the lot.

"Devil's work!" Fraser cried, raising his bottle of wine. "Ought to be smashed!"

"Only the gasoline ones," Driscoll amended. "This one runs clean."

"If that ain't the biggest lie!" Fraser retorted, his voice rising. "Pervert!" He aimed the bottle at the windshield but Jones wrestled it out of his grasp.

"Hey, don't waste good wine, you old fool," he chuckled. "You promised to share."

Since he was the only one smiling, Em addressed her question to him. "Have you seen our dog?"

His smile widened. "Ran off into the bushes, chasing after a cat or a rabbit, I shouldn't wonder." He chuckled again. "Made an awful racket, didn't he, boys? It gave me the creeps, especially toward the end. I'm surprised you didn't hear it over at Garner's place. I expect it's them overgrown hedges of theirs. They swallowed the sound."

Em and Driscoll exchanged worried looks while the men passed a snigger around.

"Smite the evil among us," Fraser muttered.

Jones continued to smile. "Don't mind old Bob here. He likes to talk big. But listen up, little lady. . ."—another snigger followed the first— "There's no use looking for the pooch around here. He's long gone. Knows the way home, don't he? That's where I'd look if I was you."

Driscoll started the car.

DRIVING down the bumpy cobblestoned street, he said, "I never should have talked you into coming today!"

"Then Garner's kitten would surely have died."

"If only I'd let you stay in the car with Nada she'd be safe with us now instead of God only knows where." He hesitated in front of the glass shop and then drove on, turning onto the dirt road.

She clutched at the dashboard. "If I hadn't made you go into the store by yourself Celie couldn't have lied about you. Besides, Jones is right—Nada does know her way home."

He narrowly avoided a gaping pothole. "Do you really think she'd just leave us in town to run off like that?"

"Never!"

"Jones knew something he wasn't telling. He had the foulest smile." He rubbed at his arm. "I would have knocked it right off his face if you hadn't been there."

"You could never hurt anybody," Em said with conviction.

Driscoll's mouth softened. "Got me all figured out, have you?"

"I have."

The children in the potato field ran toward the passing Doble, pointing and waving. One of them shouted something and the women kneeling at the end of the furrows turned and gaped. Em scanned the drying barley sheaves in the next field. No Nada. "Go faster!" she said. He accelerated until Em's head bounced to the ceiling. She clung to her seat.

He slowed down. "Too many potholes. Know what? I left all of my tools in the trailer. Smart, huh? If we puncture a tire we're walking." To their right, the placid cows were already bored by the spectacle of a rare Doble passing for the fourth time in two days. The two mares, grazing, didn't even bother to look. The Doble crawled on at a slug's pace, and no matter how many times Em craned her neck from side to side, there was no red dog running for home. It wasn't until they came to where the steep mountain trail dead-ended at the first pile of boulders that she saw something sprawled next to Driscoll's utility trailer.

"Nada!" She dove out before the car could stop, ran and then crouched, unable to take in the blood-covered muzzle and teeth, the two legs oddly twisted, the back torn by deep gashes, the belly scraped, swollen, oozing pink. "Nada?" she whispered, gently touching the familiar shoulder, now limp but thankfully still warm.

Grim-faced, Driscoll dropped down beside her, groping in his bag. "See the hoof marks churning the ground? This is Nev's work."

"It can't be," she said. "He wouldn't do anything this cruel."

Driscoll shook the stethoscope out of its pouch. "Farm boys learn early to whip sacks filled with newborn kittens against a barn wall. It's a short step from that to this." He put on the earpieces, eased the disc over Nada's bludgeoned chest, and listened.

CHAPTER 36

HOW SOON AFTER EM TURNED HER BACK on
the pleading dog had Nada been surrounded by hostile strangers?
How long had she growled at those she could see while one she
could not sneaked up behind her with a stick or a bat? "Please tell
me it's not as bad as it looks," Em said with a sob.

Driscoll lowered the stethoscope. "It's bad."

She dug her nails into her forearms, trying to numb one kind of
pain with another. "You'll save her," she told him, and then realized
she was repeating the words she had spoken at Garner's shed.

Driscoll looked at her for long seconds without comment.

"I'll do anything," she sobbed. "What do you need?"

He nodded at the stretcher, conveniently propped against the
side of the trailer, waiting for groceries an impossible journey away.
"Put it behind her."

She quickly complied. Together, they slid the dog on the canvas
and eased it through the woods and the clearing into the house,
where they lowered it and Nada onto the living room floor. Then Em
shouted, "Hello? Hertha? Bena? Anybody?" Her voice echoed from
the walls.

"Sound the alarm," he said, already pulling things out of his bag.
"We'll need all the help we can get—especially Bena's."

She dashed to the kitchen to fetch two of Hertha's least valuable pots, took them outside and clashed them together. They made a racket horrible enough to flush Hertha out of the garden like a spooked hare, her flesh jiggling and her long skirt fluttering behind her.

"What?" she cried, her face pinched. "What's wrong?"

Em nodded toward the door, watched Hertha steel herself and step inside. Then she heard her sharp gasp. The sound brought fresh tears to Em's eyes. She blinked them away, crashing her makeshift cymbals with renewed determination. There was nothing to weep about—yet. Wouldn't be, if she had anything to say about it.

Anckar ran around the corner, half a day's worth of paint speckles on her arms, still clutching a turpentine-soaked rag. Bena and the others came from a nearby plant-gathering expedition. Em couldn't stop banging the pots until Brendan captured her arms. "We're here!" he said. "What's the problem?"

Hertha chose that moment to come out the door with a bucket of water and a brush, dragging the blood-streaked stretcher behind her. "Em," she said, tears streaming over her plump cheeks, "put down those pots. They are as old as my grandparents and as dear, and I'm hoping to keep them dent-free a while longer."

Bena glanced from Hertha's face to the stretcher, counted heads, and hastened inside. "Nada's been hurt," Em explained to the others. "Beaten."

Hertha dabbed at her eyes. "She's dying."

"She is not!" Em cried. "She can't be!"

Anckar, Brendan and Lupe looked at each other soberly and went in the house, but Odasan stayed behind. He took the pots away from Em and cradled her face to get her full attention. "Listen to me. No matter how bad things look, you still have a choice. You can either accept what is or change the outcome. It's up to you."

Hertha made a rude noise. "Don't give the girl false hope. Things die when it's their time. Choosing has nothing to do with it. Sit with her, Em. Say your good-byes." She dipped the brush in the bucket and began a bout of furious scrubbing, letting her tears fall where they would.

Em went in to see Nada lying on Hertha's best quilt. The frayed sheet meant to protect it was already blood-smeared. Her broken legs were splinted and wrapped. Driscoll and Bena knelt side by side, dabbing wet rags over her fur. Driscoll's came away bright red.

"More hot water," he said without looking up.

Lupe went off with the dirty bucket and returned with a clean one. "What made those terrible gashes?" she asked in a quavering voice. "Was it a whip?"

"Hooves." Driscoll rinsed his rag, turning the water pink. "A club. Boots. In the end she was thrown from a horse—against a boulder, is my best guess."

Brendan blanched and slung an arm around Lupe to comfort them both. "The little weasel took his revenge."

Em sat close to Nada's head, smoothing the dog's floppy ears. "I'm sure it was someone from Yates," she said. "That town's full of mean people." The kind who would punish a harmless dog merely for living with the freaks on the fiery hill.

Brendan eased himself to the floor beside her and asked, "What are her chances?" Driscoll shook his head without speaking. "I see," Brendan moved his crippled foot into a more comfortable position. "Is it all right if we keep sitting here?"

"As long as somebody keeps bringing hot water." Driscoll spread suturing material on to a folded towel that lay between his and Bena's knees and gave the old woman a small pair of pliers. The two healers worked swiftly, flushing out cuts, pulling torn skin together, stitching and tying knots. Halfway through, Bena sent Odasan to the yurt for some herbs. He prepared them in the kitchen according to her instruction and brought in a bowl filled with green paste.

After the worst cuts were sewn Driscoll listened to Nada's heart again, looking discouraged. "I've done all I can," he told Bena, "but it's not nearly enough. I hope that bowl holds a miracle cure."

"So do I!" She stirred the mixture and smeared it on all of the dog's cuts. Then she stared at her paste-covered fingers and bowed her head. "I can feel her life ebbing. She's broken *inside*, and I have nothing for that."

Hertha murmured agreement.

Em studied her friends, finding in each face but one a profound sense of defeat and acceptance. Only Odasan had the strength to meet her gaze without flinching. He gave her an almost imperceptible nod and cocked his head as if waiting for her next move. She nodded back and cried, "We're not giving up! Not while Nada's still breathing. I'm surprised at you, Bena. You ought to know better."

Confused, Bena asked, "What do you mean?"

"A long time ago you told me about a rabbit," Em said, on impulse. "The one you held on your lap."

Bena's mouth relaxed as she remembered. "He had the fluffiest coat. Somehow, he'd broken his spine and the only parts he could still move were his whiskers and eyes. I discovered him lying on the path. He looked up at me so expectantly that I felt compelled to gather him up in my arms and breathe into his velvety fur. After a while he wiggled free, jumped to the ground, and hopped away. I never could explain it to myself."

"Do it again—with Nada."

"But I didn't *do* anything!"

"Wait!" Driscoll said eagerly. "What about that wounded doe I tracked to your place? I saw you wrap your arms around *her* after you treated her leg. She walked away without limping."

Bena shook her head. "I hugged every beast who let me apply this stuff. It can do wonders. But not always. Not now."

Odasan gave an encouraging smile. "Why not give it a try? One little hug—what could it hurt?"

Bena looked at Em. "I'm *not* making a promise I can't keep!"

"Nobody's asking you to." Em scooted away to give Bena plenty of space. Driscoll cleared his stuff off the floor and sat with the others. They watched Bena envelop the dog in her arms, cheek to cheek. The room grew so quiet that Em could hear a wind coming up, stirring evergreen branches. A bird called. Another answered.

"Anything else you can think of that we should do, Em?" Odasan asked. "What comes to mind?"

She couldn't think of a thing. Except maybe . . . "The circle," she said. "We ought to sit in a circle around Nada and hold hands."

Anckar grimaced at the suggestion but Alden cajoled her into moving onto the rug beside him. When they were all sitting with their hands joined, Em asked Driscoll, "How did we build your round house and Anckar's log cabin?"

"I don't really know. What are you getting at?"

"We did it with words," she said. "Words like these: You and I are eating dinner at your fine oak table, sitting on chairs that are just the right size. Nada is lying at our feet under the table, patiently waiting to clean our plates. You peel off your socks and run your bare toes through her curly pelt. She's moaning with pleasure. She likes a thorough massage."

"Good for her back and good for my feet," Driscoll said, catching on.

Brendan gave a tremulous smile. "All right, now me. When Lupe and I go riding Nada runs with the horses. She's light on her feet."

"But what she likes best," Hertha added, "is to lie on the wraparound porch of the round house on her special quilt. I collect the heels of old bread, let it get rock hard and then bring it to her for a good chew. It makes a mess but she always licks up every last crumb."

"In the evening," Em added, "when the sundown tints the lake, Driscoll plays his fiddle and Nada settles against my feet. And then she gives that low, contented sigh of hers . . ."

"The melody Driscoll's playing. I know it from somewhere," Brendan said.

"It's a ballad," Lupe chimed in. "A love song, I think."

In the quiet that followed, Em heard the seductive call of a violin. She risked humming along until there was a tickle in her chest and she felt something inside her start to expand. The others attempted to match the pitch of her hum, producing an eerie overtone that stirred the air above them into a misty vortex. From it, a column of light descended to enfold the unconscious dog. The circle they had formed soaked up the light and the hum and started to vibrate with a new kind of energy. At last Nada gave a long sigh, arced her spine, and relaxed.

Bena sat up.

"Her heart?" Driscoll asked.

She put her ear to the dog's chest. "Steady."

Driscoll rechecked Nada's gums. "Pink," he announced.

No one moved. "A steady heart beat? Pink gums?" Em finally repeated, as if the words were foreign to her. Suddenly she was in Driscoll's arms and he was twirling her around, laughing. Then she reached down to give her old friend a hug. "Thank you, Bena! I knew you could do it!"

Bena warded off both her and her enthusiasm. "It wasn't me. I just held still and let some kind of warmth move through me. Personally, I think Driscoll deserves most of the credit. He worked harder and faster than anyone I've ever seen."

And then Driscoll said something Em never thought she'd hear coming out of his mouth. "Oh, who cares who did what or why it worked? There's life beyond logic and reason. Let's not waste this moment trying to figure it out!" He plucked Bena off the floor as if she were a child, held her high and steady, and twirled her around while the others clapped and cheered. When he put her on her feet he kept his arms around her until he was satisfied she could stand by herself.

As Bena waited for the room to stop spinning, Brendan caught her eye. He had stopped smiling. "I've heard about this kind of thing," he said. "It's called 'laying on hands.' Cripples have been known to toss away their crutches afterwards and the blind start to see. If you would hug me the way you hugged Nada you might fix what the doctors couldn't. You might heal my foot."

Startled, she said, "But it's *already* healed. Crooked, I know—but surely past mending."

"Then why does it still hurt every time I move it?"

Bena turned to Odasan for moral support. "Will you please tell your son that what he's asking is far beyond my skills as a miracle worker?"

But he sided against her. "Why not humor the boy?" he asked lightly. "If he thinks it will help maybe it will."

Without waiting for her acquiescence, Brendan sat at her feet. "I'm ready. What do you want me to do?"

"I have no idea—lie down, I suppose."

He did, his eyes on Em. "Will you all hum for me too?"

Glad to oblige, the friends re-formed the circle. This time there was no waiting. The power came the moment they linked hands. In Em's mind she saw Brendan outrun a deer, saw him leap across a wide gulley, saw him laughing and dancing, dressed in purple and gold. Dancing with whom? She allowed an imaginary Lupe to appear at his side. Like lovers everywhere, they were holding hands and walking toward the sunset together.

It seemed a good script. If Brendan still thought of himself as Lupe's brother, that could change any day. And since this was Em's own private vision and she had the power to make Lupe do anything she wanted in it, she imagined her turning her head and smiling, all resentment wiped from her eyes.

The real Brendan, within Bena's embrace, began to report his every sensation. "Your hands are growing amazingly warm. Especially the one on my foot. Now it feels actually hot. And the heat's starting to rise up—"

"Hush," Odasan told him. "Be still. Just . . . be."

Brendan obeyed, as he usually did when Odasan offered the slightest suggestion. The vortex reformed above the boy; light and hum merged to enfold him. His skin shone from the inside. He shuddered, wept, and went limp.

After a while Bena wiped the tears from his cheeks. "I think we're done."

"What happens next?" he asked in a drowsy child's voice.

"Nothing much, I should think." She considered the dog. "Stay where you are and rest next to Nada."

"Okay. I'll sleep in here tonight." He yawned. "If everything goes well, let's have a party tomorrow for Nada and me. Lupe, could you bring me my bedroll?"

But his faithful assistant had concerns of her own. Thumping her chest, she wailed, "Me, Bena! What about me?"

Understanding dawned in Brendan's eyes. And Em received a clear image of a naked, bloody young girl lying in an old wooden cart, every inch of her skin battered and flayed, an equally young boy blotting the seeping blood.

Slowly, Bena rose, rubbing her knees. "Come then. But if you don't mind, we'll do your healing on our feet." She opened her arms for the third time. Lupe walked into the embrace. Side by side, they looked as if they could have been kin. Both were slim and graceful, with black hair spilling to their waists, though Bena's was silver-laced and she was shorter.

"Em?" Lupe said. "The circle, please?"

Em was willing to oblige her but Anckar gave an impatient sigh and Alden gazed with longing at his comfortable armchair. Even Hertha couldn't resist stealing a glance toward the kitchen as if she remembered some half-finished chore she needed to return to.

Odasan drew himself up to his full height. "If you don't mind," he said with impeccable courtesy, nonetheless making the words sound like a threat. Immediately, the friends resumed their formation, Brendan included. Before they could finish linking their hands Bena's fingers were already tracing the first keloid hiding under Lupe's embroidered white blouse.

Humming the air alive once more, Em had no trouble picturing every scar melting under Bena's touch, leaving Lupe's brown skin soft and rose-petal smooth. In her mind, Em saw the girl walk toward the sunset again, wearing nothing but a crown of white blossoms and her long hair. At her side, broad-shouldered Brendan wore even less. This time when Lupe looked over her shoulder Em chose to smile first.

IN THE middle of the night Alden began a round of loud snoring. Em woke on the floor, in the near dark, to see Driscoll's outline bending over Nada, his stethoscope reflecting red coals.

"Still stable," he whispered when he noticed Em's gaze upon him.

"Mmmm . . ." she said, shutting her eyes and pulling the covers up higher. She heard him heap wood onto the grate. Then he lifted the far side of the big quilt they seemed to be sharing to cautiously slide into the pleasant cocoon beneath. As the first bone-dry twigs caught fire, popping and bursting into flame, Em moved her right foot, touching Nada's flank. It was the way they'd slept together from the day they first met.

Once she was certain Driscoll had dozed off she inched her other foot toward him until skin touched bare skin. The crackling flames, Alden's multi-toned snores, even Lupe and Brendan's measured, rhythmic breathing blended into a fragile symphony meant just for her ears. The air was fragrant with wood smoke and Driscoll's good soap.

A gentle wind was caressing Em's face the next time she opened her eyes. Driscoll had moved in his sleep until his nose was within an inch of her cheek. And yet it wasn't his breath that had awakened her but some small, unusual sound. Then she heard it again—half whimper, half moan. Nada's pallet was empty. A trail of chewed bandages and sticks wound its way to the door. There the dog stood, swaying on all four of her feet. Her eyes were alert and patient as she looked pointedly from Em to the doorknob.

Em shook Driscoll awake. He stared uncomprehendingly at Nada and then ran a hand through his tousled hair, chuckling. "It's a good thing no one told her how long it's *supposed* to take bones to properly heal!" Across the floor, Lupe gave a disapproving sigh inside her bag. Her hair, gleaming blue, fell away from her face as she turned from the first hint of daylight.

Driscoll and Em took Nada outside and followed her to the discreet screen of brush behind which she always chose to perform her daily toilette. He pulled Em close. "A few days of rest and she'll be better than new." He scanned the sky where colorless clouds floated, waiting for dawn tints. "It's going to be an outstanding day. What do you say we climb up to the lake, just you and me? I think it's time for us to be alone together."

She thought he'd never had a better idea.

CHAPTER 37

SHE WROTE A SHORT NOTE TO HERTHA about their hiking plans, stressing that Nada was to stay indoors. Then they escorted the dog to her pallet in front of the hearth. As they tiptoed to the front door, Lupe murmured something unintelligible but slept on. So did the others, allowing Driscoll and Em to make a clean getaway onto the trailhead. Before the first gilded ray touched the mist shrouding the easterly slopes they were deep within the uphill forest, pausing occasionally to admire an oddly shaped tree or iridescent mushroom.

"What I love most about walking beside you," Em said on one of the rare occasions they could comfortably hike abreast, "is that we're close to the same height. When I'm next to anyone else I'm always trying to scrunch to their size."

He patted the trunk of an ancient pine. "And yet we are mere dwarves compared to these giants. And they're like ants compared to the mountain." But eventually the trees shrank, growing twisted, and the two hikers crept past geysers and mud pots, crossing the shallow basin of treacherously thin ground Anckar had warned them about. The faintest of trails took them to the precarious scree. After a long, sweaty climb, they collapsed by the stone walls of the pass. There they ate their boiled yams, washing them down with water from their canteens.

Then they continued to the ridge, where they sat munching on sandwiches and admired the vibrant hues below them. A flawless expanse of sky reflected on the green lake, tinting it turquoise. Purple and lilac mountain chains receded to the horizon. Swirls of flaming leaves mingled with patches of short purple flowers.

"I've never seen a more beautiful sight," Em said. "The white bluffs across the lake make a great contrast. I'm glad we came."

"As much as I like our clearing, I do miss a view," Driscoll told her. "I've traveled near and far and have seen a lot of great scenery. This one goes straight to the heart. How would you like to live in the cave behind the green waterfall and eat fish every day? Of course the lake has less friendly aspects. In winter everything around it will be covered in deep snow and crusted with ice. But it would make a great summer retreat." He stretched and pointed at the sun. "Almost noon. Where has the time gone?"

Em laughed. "Anckar would say we're slow as snails. And she'd be right. But what's the rush as long as we get home before dark? We've got at least a couple of hours to play and explore. Today even I'm hot enough for a dip."

They descended on a carpet of tiny white blossoms, each like a miniature star. Fifty feet from the shore Em dropped her gear and sprinted straight for the frigid lake, letting momentum carry her past her fear of the plunge. Then she was in, shoes and all, stirring up silt. Screaming with shock and delight, she immersed both herself and her clothes, which were in desperate need of a wash.

Driscoll, more prudent, peeled off everything except for his briefs. "The idea of spending the rest of the afternoon sopping wet doesn't thrill me at all," he said.

"Does this?" she asked, slapping a sheet of iced water straight at his belly. He gasped and retaliated by diving at her feet and sweeping them off the lake floor. She went under and came up sputtering. His head rose at her side. She dunked it mercilessly, barely giving him time to inhale. Then she waded to the safety of shore, her teeth chattering. He followed to sit at her feet. "Where did you learn to swim?" she asked. "There was never enough water in Oren to practice."

He shrugged. "I told you, I get around. Before I homed in on Clydestown I spent some time at the ocean. I ought to take you there one day. There's water as far as the eye can see, though you can't drink a drop, nor irrigate parched fields with it."

"Full of salt," she said. "I do read, you know! Oops—my button's about to pop!" The top button on her shorts was dangling from a single thread. Rakishly raising a brow, she pulled it off and stowed it in a secure pocket. "If I'd known on the day I put on these shorts that it was going to be my last day in Oren I would have worn something sturdier. And longer." With a mischievous grin, she undid the rest of the buttons, stepped out of her dripping clothes, tossed them on the nearest bush to dry, and kicked her shoes high in the air. Then she ran off in her underwear, shouting, "Catch me if you can!"

He managed to topple her at the hidden grove. Together, they tumbled through yielding branches to roll into the mossy indent below. She landed on him, chest to chest, nose to nose. Following her immediate impulse, she put her lips to his. With a small part of her mind, she heard a bird warble. Then the sound and the world dropped away and she rose on the breeze, feeling sensations she hadn't known she was capable of.

Later, they lay cheek to cheek until Driscoll offered his well-muscled arm as a pillow. "You do know that I made the round house for the both of us?"

"I know it," she said with a yawn.

"And that we'll always be together from now on, no matter what?"

She leaned into him, shutting her eyes. "No matter what," she confirmed.

He yawned, too. "I got very little sleep last night, especially once your toes started playing with mine."

"Oh," she said, blushing.

"I held still for hours to see what you'd do next."

"Nothing else occurred to me—until now."

His chuckle ended with another yawn. "I promised I'd wait until you were ready. And I did." His muscles went slack, and he slept.

She chose the opportunity to examine every pore of his skin and every hair in his beard as if she'd never seen him before and never would see him again. She ran an adoring finger over his straight, handsome nose and traced tiny laugh lines at the corners of his eyes. Even his lashes were red. The longer she looked at him, the more his face softened; the bearded-young-man mask covered something so tender and pure that she was dismayed.

He could be hurt. But not by her. Then by whom? She claimed him with an arm and hooked a leg around his. Thus anchored, she sank into slumber.

THE AUTUMN sky was fickle on the heights. One friendly white cloud, looking like something a child might draw with her first crayons, was joined by another, and another. They swept ever closer, growing dense and dark until an oppressive mass hung low over the lake. Sweat beads formed on the brows of the two sleepers and slid unheeded down their cheeks. Then Driscoll rolled on to his side, facing away from Em. Having lost her anchor, she drifted through several blurred dreams until she heard a quarrelsome voice.

It belonged to a heavy-set man who stood wheezing on Garner's ivy-choked front porch, talking about loyalties and outsiders treating town pets, a job that had been rightfully his for longer than he cared to remember. The woman inside the sagging screen door shifted her feet and called Garner's name, her voice shrill with vexation.

Now Em's dreaming-self moved to the farthest corner of the overgrown garden, where Garner was crawling through tall weeds, holding a glass jar aloft. Behind a cluster of unkempt bushes, he swept a pile of leaves off a rusty oven grate and lifted it to expose a newly dug hole, one side lined with a down jacket, the other crowded with a small box of sand, a bowl of water, and a saucer. When he poured the contents of the jar into it, a tiny pink nose twitched from one of the coat sleeves. Then his kitten slipped out and launched herself at the yellow liquid, her round head trembling with strain as she lapped. Garner scratched behind the triangular ears, triggering chirps of delight.

"It won't be much longer, I promise," he whispered. "Just till she calms down some, is all." While the kitten was fully occupied with her meal he replaced the grate and the leaves, marked the spot with a heavy stone, and crept to the side gate. Behind the screen door his mother's voice swelled with anger. Ducking, Garner pushed at the latch, quietly opened the gate, then slammed it shut again, yelling, "Coming, Mom!" He checked his clothes, picked a stray twig out of his hair, a blade of grass from one knee, and sped to the house.

Drifting over the hedged fence and across the cobblestoned street, Em grew aware of two low voices nearby, one as familiar as her own. She let them draw her downward and found herself floating just under the ceiling of the noon-quiet store. In the faint, curtained light, she recognized the grain bins directly below her, the contested sack of rice restored to the corner shelf behind them. In the dimmest part of the room stood two figures, their heads touching. One was Celie's, her blonde hair disheveled, her blouse half-unbuttoned. The other head belonged to a brown-haired boy whose hand was inside the blouse—Nev.

Celie pressed it in farther. "Please," she said in her much-practiced whine. "I can't stand it here anymore. My parents treat me like a slave. They even started locking me in my room after dark, supposedly for my own good. As if there was something exciting to do in Yates during the night. Will you take me with you when you ride out of town? You won't be sorry." She rubbed herself against him until his knees wobbled. He buried his face in her hair and moaned as she pulled away. "Not until after we're gone from here, Nev," she said. "When?"

He studied her with a mixture of fascination and barely hidden distaste. "Tomorrow, around midnight. And be quiet about it. If your dad finds out—"

"He won't. I'm not even leaving him a note now that he's gone entirely over to Mom's side. It'll teach him a lesson." Celie slipped out of his embrace. "Tap on my window. It's the one with a doll on the sill. I'll be waiting." She bumped him teasingly with a well-rounded hip and went into the hall, buttoning the blouse up to her chin.

Alone in the grain room, Nev stuffed his shirttails into patched trousers, smoothed down his hair, and leaned against the wall, soundlessly laughing. "Idiots," he whispered. "Especially her."

And then came the worst dream of all. In it, Em squirmed on rough ground, her hands tied behind her. Through some warm, sticky veil, she saw Driscoll surrounded by men holding rifles and clubs. Two led him away and he twisted around to meet her eyes one last time. The black silhouette of a large tree was outlined against a pre-dawn sky, a rope coiling from its hardiest branch. Someone screamed Driscoll's name.

There was a fierce crack of thunder. Em's mossy bed shook. She sat up, her heart racing. Wet leaves clung to her face. Beside her, Driscoll lay on his side, knees to chin, trapped in his own nightmare. They were still at the lake but everything else had changed. She shook him awake and he clutched at his throat.

"Em?" he cried hoarsely. "Where did you go?"

She held him close and rocked him like a baby, only then realizing there wasn't a thread of fabric between them. His skin was as cold as hers. "There, there," she crooned. "It was only a bad dream. A storm's breaking. Any second it'll start to pour. Our leafy roof will leak."

At last, his eyes focused. "Is it dark already? How long did we sleep?"

"Hours. The sun's disappeared but I believe it's still afternoon."

They crawled out of the hollow just as a bolt of lightning seared the sky overhead. It was followed by booming thunder. Clouds dipped and burst.

"We could run to the cave," Driscoll yelled through the din, "and wait it out there. But by then it might be too dark to see and we'll have to stay till morning."

"No!" she yelled back, pulling strands of wet hair out of her face. "I promised Nada we'd be home tonight."

"We better run for it then. We'll want to get past the mudpots while we can still see!"

"Or we're stew," she laughed with relief.

As they collected their waterlogged clothes a brilliant flash illuminated wind-driven waves lashing the shore. They stepped into squelching shoes, shouldered their gear, and fled up the meadow. The air hissed with rain. Wind screamed through whipping branches. The higher they climbed the more the wind pushed against them, as if determined to force them back down to the lake. After fighting their way to the ridge they turned to wait for the next fire bolt. When it came they captured one final black and white glimpse of their special valley, the boiling lake a cover of foam over a fathomless pit.

All at once the storm changed direction, pushing them along the ridge toward the pass. Right after they started descending the scree, the air softened. Driscoll stopped to hug Em tight. "There hasn't been a dull moment since we've come to this mountain. Maybe we'd better start getting used to it."

They passed the steaming mudpots as the last glimmer of light waned. Soon after, Em lost her right shoe, and no matter how long they groped on the ground, they couldn't find it again. She took off the other and limped on her bare feet the rest of the way. At the upper edge of the clearing they feasted their eyes on the solid black shape of the house and its familiar clean angles.

The rain had gentled. They struggled to make themselves look reasonably decent but gave it up as an impossible task. There was a faint glow from the front of the house. When they rounded the corner it seemed to Em as if someone had lit every candle left in the pantry and filled the sills with them to provide a spectacular welcome. There would be friendly faces around the table, and hot soup, and a roaring wood fire.

Driscoll drew her to him for one last, private caress as they stood outside the door. "First thing is to get you into dry clothes. I have some spares that should fit you—but no shoes." He reached for the knob and hesitated. "I hope you know that this is the best day of my life," he said quietly. "Nothing can ever change that."

When they walked in his face shone brighter than all the flickering candles. The living room was warm and dry. The table was covered with Hertha's best cloth and crowded with platters and bowls filled with party food. There was gay laughter from the kitchen. Then Nada rose from her quilt by the hearth and came trotting toward them, eagerly wagging her tail.

They were home.

CHAPTER 38

EM HID HER NEAR-NAKEDNESS IN THE shadowy alcove behind the couch and wrapped herself in Driscoll's bath towel. What had been so right at the lake seemed unnatural inside the house they shared with so many others. He rummaged in his valise and tossed some wrinkled corduroy trousers to her, stretched at the knees. "They always were a bit short on me," he said, adding a worn, extra-long flannel shirt. Kneeling, he fumbled under the couch and pulled out a scuffed pair of boots. "These are the shoes that gave me blisters on our last hike." He placed them by her chafed feet and added two pairs of socks. "Put these on first. If the boots are still too big, stuff the front end with rags and pull the laces extra tight."

She shivered and dripped on his pile of offerings, unwilling to let go of the towel until he had moved off to change into his own set of dry clothes. He sat on the edge of the couch tuning his fiddle until Em finished tying her laces. "Feeling better now?" he asked. She nodded. "Ready for company? Brace yourself!" He put the fiddle to his shoulder, set the bow on the strings, and brought forth a shout of pure joy that bounced off the walls. It was the opening phrase of a tune so happy and loud it almost managed to distract Em from some nagging questions of self-doubt. Would the others look at her and see that she had changed and what had changed her? Would Bena think she and Driscoll had done something wrong?

Hertha rushed in from the kitchen, brandishing a worn wooden spoon. "Oh good. You're back safe and whole. Anckar had us all worried, claiming storms are deadly up there." She'd taken unusual care with her appearance. Her hair was braided and wound around her head like a tiara. Silver hoops dangled from her ears. A green frock, new to Em, glimmered from under the usual apron. Best of all, she'd outlined her lips with berry juice, or perhaps beet. "Oh, Em!" she cried. "You're leaking. Here, bend over." She picked the towel off the floor and rubbed Em's hair with it. Then she hung their sodden clothes over the hearth screen.

Driscoll aimed his bow at the table. "Why the fabulous spread? It looks to me as if you've cleaned out the pantry. Is that wise?"

"I didn't think so either, at first," she began. "But I was outvoted at breakfast when—"

Alden came in from the hall to finish the sentence for her. "When we decided a great celebration was in order. Look, I found Hertha's stash of Christmas sweets." He brought them a plate heaped with candy canes and chocolate truffles.

"I guess this is as good a time as any," Hertha said, passing them out. "Why leave anything for the worms?"

Alden, too, was dressed in his finest, as if intending to take Hertha to church any minute. "It all started this morning when we saw Nada standing on all fours," he tried to explain, unwrapping the first truffle and offering it to Nada.

Driscoll snatched it away before the dog could react. "Few people know this, but chocolate is poison to dogs," he said, throwing Nada a piece of bread from the table, which she devoured with obvious pleasure. He lifted the fiddle up to his chin. "Where is everybody? I was kind of counting on Brendan to make a fuss over my music again."

"Him and Lupe have been busy in her tent all day," Hertha informed him, laughing. "He wanted her to teach him to sew."

"Not true," Brendan protested from the front door. "I already knew how." What was that on his head? A golden cap! And he was wearing purple pantaloons and a maroon vest embroidered with silver stars. There was nothing under the vest except bare, dusky skin. "I just jogged all the way to the Doble and back, limbering up for my *kata*," he said, leaning non-chalantly against the doorjamb.

"Your what?" Driscoll asked.

"You'll see." Brendan came to snatch up a candy cane and bit off its hook.

"Are we in time for the performance?" Odasan said, coming in from the yard dressed in a black ceremonial *gi* and hugging his beloved martial arts book.

Beside him Bena was dazzling in a tunic that matched her violet eyes. "The rain stopped as soon as I put on my cloak." She draped it over a chair and ran her hands over Nada's back. "It gets better and better." Looking from Driscoll to Em, she asked, "Was the lake everything you hoped for, today?"

There was no doubt in Em's mind that Bena knew the answer to her own question.

"It was . . . wet," Em said, glad that the poorly lit alcove hid the heat she felt rising to her cheeks.

"No more small talk." Brendan sounded more impatient than usual. "I want everyone to sit on the couch. I need lots of room." Once they had obeyed he steepled his hands and bowed low before them. "Since my accident I've danced this kata only in my mind. But thanks to you three flatlanders I can actually do it again for real. With both of my feet. Here goes." He launched into a choreographed flurry of powerful kicks and punches. Scowling, yelling, and vanquishing unseen opponents coming at him from all sides, he pivoted his heels splendidly on the plank floor, finished with a double kick, and stood heaving. "Not bad, huh?"

Odasan inclined his head. "Could be worse."

Brendan beamed as if he had just received the highest of all possible praises. "It will get even better now that I can practice again!" Em applauded along with the others. He grinned, giving a deep bow of appreciation. "I was only the first act. Here comes the second." He gave a piercing whistle.

Lupe slithered into the room, covered with a slinky fringed shawl. As she sashayed once around the table, she let it slide lower inch by slow inch until she reached her own chair. With a flourish, she pulled the wrap off and flung it over the backrest. She was wearing her favorite white peasant blouse, re-tailored for maximum exposure—no sleeves, no collar, no tails. The exquisite brown skin stretching over her ribcage and belly was anointed with something glossy emitting a strong scent of roses. The hip-hugging skirt, which was the exact tone of her skin, left little to the imagination, embracing her with no fabric to spare. It was slit on both sides to show a good deal of firm, flawless thigh. She strutted around the table a second time and then she bowed, her breasts triumphantly filling the top of the low-cut blouse.

"Lupe!" Hertha cried, snatching the shawl off the chair. "What's gotten into you!" She wrapped it around the girl like a bib, tying two ends at the back of the blouse. "Go change. You're not coming with us looking like that. What were you thinking?"

"That I have a lot of catching up to do," Lupe retorted, shrugging the shawl off. She attempted a curtsy and smiled at Em, Driscoll and Bena. "For the first time in my life I feel beautiful. Thanks to you three."

"You have always been beautiful to me," said Odasan. "And always will be. Tonight you are a vision I'll carry inside me forever. Both you and Brendan have made me feel proud."

Em went to finger the shawl. "What delicate fabric. Where did you get the material?"

"From Hertha's quilt stash," Lupe replied. "She made us sew endless squares in the winter." She draped it around Em's shoulders. "Go on, borrow it for a while. I'm plenty warm without it." She rubbed her forearm and then held it out for Em's inspection. "Why would I cover something this smooth?"

Nada gave a sharp bark and gazed at the table. Brendan laughed. "Hungry, huh? You'll have to wait while Driscoll plays us a jig. Lupe and I feel like dancing."

Driscoll lifted his bow. "I never thought you'd ask!"

"I never thought I could dance a jig," Brendan replied with a grin.

The fiddle launched into something fast and exultant that soon had Brendan and Lupe stomping with vigor while the rest of them clapped along. Then Driscoll put the instrument in its case and carefully stashed it under the couch. "Can we eat now?" he asked. "Em and I worked up a huge appetite. I don't see Anckar. Do you want me to fetch her?"

"Best leave her alone. She's moping," Hertha said with a hint of the old, habitual satisfaction. "She went into one of her moods as soon as she found out you were hiking up the mountain without asking her first."

"It's not her mountain," he said as they all went to their chairs.

"True, but you'll never convince her of that." Hertha pushed a small glass bowl at him. "This goes with the artichokes. Try them."

Driscoll put half of a garlic-roasted artichoke onto his plate and slid his teeth along the inside of a leaf. "It's good!"

"It's even better with the dip." She pushed the bowl some more and watched him scoop some of the sauce with the next leaf. When she saw that he savored the taste, she gave a contented smile and said, "Anckar's mood didn't improve when Alden announced that she could only bring one thing on our journey. You should have seen her storm out of here. We haven't seen her since." She sighed, rubbing the wooden spoon she'd laid beside her plate. "Mind, I'm not much better at choosing than she is. I've been pawing through all my lovely gadgets and cookbooks, but as it turns out, this wooden spoon is the one thing I can't bear leaving behind." She smiled affectionately at Brendan. "It's the first one you made me, remember? I've used it every day since. I swear it keeps my batters from going lumpy and makes my cakes rise extra high." She slipped it into an apron pocket. "It's been a busy day. Bena helped me transplant the rest of our fall starts. I just hope they can survive without us."

Lupe put down her fork, looking troubled. "You want to know what'll happen to your plants after we're gone?" She slashed her hand dramatically through the air. "The brambles will rise like a green flood and drown the whole clearing. In a few years the vines will push in the windows and invade the inside of this house. In ten, no one will know we've ever lived here."

"And yet," Alden said, gazing dreamily at the ceiling, "we've always understood this clearing was only meant to be our temporary home. Our gathering place, where we practiced making things thrive."

"You've got to admit we've passed every test," Hertha said. "I would have hated leaving this garden if I hadn't seen the new one in Alden's valley with my own eyes. It's waiting for us. Time to go. The sooner the better."

Driscoll cocked his brows at Em. "Am I too faint with hunger to think clearly or are we both missing a few pages of a story everyone else has already read? Will someone please explain?"

Then the front door burst open and Anckar glowered at them from the threshold. "You're eating without me? Why didn't somebody call?"

"Because you're in a foul mood and we know better," Hertha said, calmly cutting a squash pie into wedges.

"Wrong, as usual," Anckar snapped. "I was only preoccupied. With this." She carried her large art pad to the mantle. Pushing candles and vases aside, she propped it against the wall. "Remember I said I'd paint my favorite place once I get good enough?" she asked Alden. "I'm not good enough to do this in oil yet, but I think I've made a fine start with watercolors. It's already dry, which means I can roll up the picture and take it along." She pulled out a loose sheet and held it up. Em recognized the moonscape, the castle, and the clouds ringing the summit, all rendered in shades of purple and lilac, the whole scene awash with luminous evening light. Scowling at Em, Anckar said, "I would have loved to go with you to visit my castle one last time. Why did you sneak off without me?"

Em, who was savoring her first bite of creamy pie, only managed a guilty grunt. So Driscoll elected to answer for her. "We didn't go up that high," he said firmly. "We just picnicked at the lake, is all."

"Not *just*!" Anckar growled. "And judging by Em's red face, not *all*."

Em's bite lost every nuance of flavor. Before she could swallow the sawdust left in her mouth, Driscoll drawled, "Anckar, why don't you start minding your own business?"

"The mountain *is* my business!"

"But we're not!" He directed an amiable smile at the painter and extended it to include every face at the table. For a moment, nobody spoke. Then Alden cleared his throat.

"Quite right. Anckar, the sunset you painted is splendid. But no need to worry—we're not ever going to bother the top of your mountain again." He pulled out her chair. "Come and enjoy your last earthly meal so we can get ready." She sat without saying another word.

"What are we getting ready for?" Driscoll asked.

Em washed her bite down with some wine. "I think they've decided we're leaving this world for good tonight," she said, surprised at her own dismay. "Don't ask me how they could possibly have reached that conclusion."

"Oh come now," Brendan said, twirling his glass. "How can you doubt it after last night? There are three miracles in this room because of Bena and you. That pitch you had everyone hum—it went right through me. I could feel every cell in my body dissolve and reassemble. I actually felt myself melt." He slapped the table, overcome with mirth. "With you at the helm we can do anything and go anywhere. At breakfast we decided we're ready for the big jump tonight. That's why Hertha cleaned out the pantry and let us raid her quilt stash. There's nothing to save *for* anymore. This is our last night in this sorry world." He raised his glass. "Third time good luck!"

"Third time good luck!" Hertha repeated, lifting her own. Then Anckar followed suit with her tumbler of water and an instant later seven glasses were aloft. They were waiting for Em to join them. With a weak smile, she added hers to the mix.

Driscoll stared into his wine. When he noticed they were all looking at him, he shrugged and said, "Yesterday I would have laughed at your plan. Now I think Em can pretty much do anything she sets her mind to. And, as I've pointed out to her more than once, wherever she chooses to go, I'm going, too!" He raised his glass alongside the rest.

Em wasn't sure she liked his new attitude or the blind faith of the others. What if she failed them all?

CHAPTER 39

NOT EVEN THE SOFT CANDLE LIGHT COULD hide the shadows under Bena's eyes.

"Are you all right?" Em murmured discreetly, thinking that perhaps performing three miracles in a row had drained her old friend.

Bena attempted a smile. "It's just that everything is happening too fast. I agree with Lupe. I don't want to leave either. Everything is perfect here. Why risk losing it now?"

Odasan broke off the conversation he was having with Brendan to say, "Because it will be even more perfect there."

"Anything that is already perfect can't *get* any better," she pointed out.

"Everything in the universe expands, even perfection . . ." He put his mouth to her ear and whispered, " . . . and love."

She stroked his cheek. "Yes. Perfect love, still growing. That's what we have."

"And we'll keep it wherever we go," he assured her. "Though I hope it's not just love between the two of *us* that is growing, but between everyone here."

"Even the love that isn't lost between Hertha and Anckar?"

"Especially that," he chuckled.

"Let's drink to it!" She clinked her glass to his.

Wine flowed like water that night. The good food disappeared rapidly too. When not one of them could be enticed to eat one more bite Brendan settled himself on the hearthstones and tuned his guitar. "I hope it's okay with you if we mellow out a bit," he said to Driscoll. "I thought some slow dancing ought to be next on the program."

"I can't think of a single thing I'd like better right now," Driscoll replied, helping them roll up the rug. And then he took Em by the hand.

She held back. "Not me. I have no talent for it."

"It's easy," he said. "Just close your eyes, trust your feet, and trust me."

It seemed good advice. As soon as Brendan launched into the first languid ballad, Driscoll put his arms gently around her. That's when she knew she would gladly follow him anywhere. Shutting her eyes, she allowed him to lead her from one easy turn to another. Soon she realized from the faint sounds of shuffling nearby that they were no longer alone on the dance floor. Blinking once, she saw Anckar lean against Alden, all lines of annoyance erased from her forehead. Blinking again, she saw Bena aglow in Odasan's arms. The varnished guitar on Brendan's lap glowed, too, reflecting coals on one side and candles on the other. Lupe, who was kneeling at his feet—no doubt because it was impossible for her to sit comfortably in her tight skirt—gazed up at him with mute adoration.

Only one person was left out of the fun. It was Hertha, still at the table, swishing the dregs around and around in her glass, her eyes glistening. How unfair that she who took care of them all from morning till night should be so neglected. Em resolved there and then that Hertha must come to live with them in the round house. They'd give her the best spare room. She could teach them to cook and to properly garden and would always have a home with them. But what about the others? Would they disperse once they no longer needed each other? A pulse of profound regret washed through Em. Deep in her heart she had to agree with Bena and Lupe. With so much to lose, was it worth the trouble to try and move on?

"That's enough dancing for me," she whispered to Driscoll. "Go ask Hertha. I can see her feet twitching from here." He tightened his embrace, then released her. They walked to the table together. Em asked Hertha, "That delicious squash pie—did you make up the recipe or is it something out of your grandmother's cookbook?"

The heartfelt compliment perked Hertha right up. "It was a tradition with us," she said brightly. "It tastes good hot or cold." Then Driscoll extended his hand to her, and she said, "Me?" as if he couldn't possibly have meant to ask her to dance.

"Most definitely you," he said, pulling her to her feet. She took off the apron, smoothed her hair, and let him lead her away. As soon as they had shuffled into their first turn, Em took the guitar from Brendan, shooing him and Lupe onto the dance space. Em hadn't held a guitar since she and Nev were both little and his father had given him a child-sized one for Christmas one year. Neither of them had had the patience to sit still and practice, which was why she now had to content herself with a random, rhythmical strumming, augmenting it by slapping the wood with her palms.

It was lovely to see a wave of pure joy spreading over Lupe's face. Even better was watching her gather the courage to gaze fully into Brendan's eyes. Tenderly, he returned the look, his hands straying to the smooth skin on her shoulders and arms. Em allowed them five minutes of uninterrupted bliss. Then she put the guitar aside and said, "I'm mellow enough. How about the rest of you?"

Driscoll and Brendan repositioned the rug. Everyone settled upon it. As usual, Nada claimed her place inside the hub. Lupe attempted to lower herself to the floor in small stages, inadvertently bringing first her rear, then her well-filled blouse to Brendan's undivided attention as he gallantly helped her sit without splitting a seam. Odasan tucked his book inside the *gi's* jacket; Brendan adjusted the guitar strap to fit tight across his shoulders, carefully centering the instrument so it would not be in anyone's way; Driscoll cradled the fiddle on his lap, and Bena, who had chosen to bring her beloved cloak, fastened it under her chin; Hertha wedged the wooden spoon into the belt of her frock; Anckar stuffed her rolled-up painting inside the front of her shirt, and Alden merely centered his favorite bandana, since his special armchair was too unwieldy to take.

To Em, their preparations seemed slightly insane. *She* chose to leave empty-handed. In a final bout of unease, Alden leaned toward her and whispered, "About the tenth spoke . . ."

"Not coming," she said, utterly certain.

"Poor Driscoll," Brendan teased. "It's a pity you can't bring the Doble. It'll sit on its tires until they go flat. And the metal will flake into rust."

Driscoll looked stricken, but then he touched his fiddle and said resolutely, "Everything I really need is right here in this room." He clasped Em's hand, muttering, "Still trying to get my goat, isn't he?"

Beaming at Em, Brendan said, "I've noticed that each time we form the wheel we do it faster. I bet tonight it will take next to no time at all."

He was right. As soon as they joined hands and began toning their distinctive hum, that astounding voice rose from within her and the wheel erupted into a vast arching sky in broad daylight. The fertile fields below were crisscrossed by the very streams they themselves had imagined into being. They spun over the spacious garden they had seen the last time, its soil black and moist. Every plant growing out of it had the satiated air they'd come to expect from the garden they were leaving behind.

The wheel homed in on the meadow below the round house, where a group of people stood waiting on the dense grass. Some held covered dishes; others gaily waved their kerchiefs at the approaching wheel. Em hovered above the upturned, welcoming faces, wondering what they saw from their vantage point. The wheel appeared far from solid even to her—when she looked at Hertha she could see the sky beyond; her face was no more than a collection of vibrating points of light, fading in and out of Em's visual range.

But then the young woman who'd hailed Bena on the last flight waved what looked like a pillow case, shouting, "Bena, it's us—Ima and Vida! Welcome home!"

Stunned, Bena let go of Odasan's hand. "Ima?" she repeated incredulously. "Ima and Vida?" The wheel wobbled and tipped, careening toward the crowd, which broke apart just as a sickening jolt catapulted the spokes up and away. Something was pulling them in the wrong direction. There was a sucking sound; the guitar Brendan had so lovingly centered disappeared; Driscoll's fiddle dissolved into a void shaped like a bittersweet memory; Bena's cloak became a white flag before blinking out, and Odasan's book left a rectangular gap in his *gi*. Their anxiety over the fate of their beloved objects unbalanced the wheel further. It spun out of control.

The crowd below shrank to insect size. With great deliberation, Em fine-tuned her focus and thought the wheel down to the meadow until the crowd was only a moment away. It parted for one man, tall, lean, and tanned. While Em struggled to land he studied their ghostly images until he found Hertha.

"Tomas!" she breathed in abrupt recognition.

He merely looked at her.

A wizened crone stepped up beside him, draped in a cape of fine cerulean silk. Her long silver strands danced on the breeze. The face they framed was ringed like a tree, with sparse, exquisite bones. She too was tall, and suffused by both grace and power. There was no doubt in Em's mind that she was the ancient one who had greeted Bena after she died, sending her back to her earthly life.

The crone said in ringing tones, "I count nine spokes in a ten-spoked wheel that is unbalanced by old attitudes and possessions. You'll never land without the tenth spoke, dear ones. Go back for it while you still can. The portal between our worlds is closing but you can cross it once more if you hurry. Next time leave everything behind, especially your worn-out beliefs." She swept an arm up and away. The silken cloak billowed. The wheel rose like a kite on the wind.

Tomas's gaze followed Hertha until the distance widening between them severed the spell. "Tomas," she keened, her voice breaking.

All at once Em realized that the people below were as much part of her family as those whose hands she was holding—even if she never saw them again. Then brightness and color were replaced by ear-popping silence. A nauseatingly rapid descent disconnected the spokes from each other. The pain of that separation was fiercer than any Em had ever known. And no wonder. They had landed on the splintered remains of the guitar and the fiddle. The martial arts book lay charred at Odasan's feet.

Anckar pulled the painting out of her shirt. It crumbled to ashes along with their dreams. "This is your fault!" she shouted at Em. "You told Alden there would be no tenth spoke. The fool believed you. *We* believed you. You let us all down. I should have known that you'd consider the little games you were playing with Driscoll on my mountain more important to you than our trust. You can both pack your bags and drive back to wherever! We don't want you here anymore!"

"Please calm down. You are too harsh!" Bena stammered, sounding frail.

Anckar turned on her next. "And you're nothing but an old fraud," she spat. "You've led us around by the nose long enough. Go with them. Odasan's better off without you. So are we all." She leaped up and slammed out of the house. Close-by, somebody wailed. It was a white-faced Hertha, trying to straighten the snapped handle of her wooden spoon. She let it slip through her fingers, raised her hands to her face, and wept.

CHAPTER 40

HERTHA STUMBLED TO HER FEET AND WENT to the hall, quietly shutting the door behind her. "That door has never been closed," Brendan muttered, rubbing his leg, not looking at anyone.

"Alden?" Em said in a small voice. "I heard what the crone said, but I swear—"

Alden chose to ignore her, throwing himself onto the couch and staring up at the ceiling. Em looked around the living room with burning eyes. It no longer seemed as attractive as it had when she and Driscoll came home from their hike. In fact, it was beginning to look downright shabby, its many faults thinly disguised by tapestries and pictures, its walls out of true. A number of floorboards were buckled by some long-ago disaster. The furniture which Odasan had done his valiant best to salvage and repair was still gouged in some places and charred in others. Under varnish and wax, on wall hangings and paintings, the colors seemed washed out and faded, the way a house fades after its owners are gone.

Driscoll sought to make up for Anckar and Alden's angry reaction by gently pressing his thigh against Em's. An hour ago she would gladly have pressed back. "We could return to Clydestown," he whispered. "Get married on the way. They can't do anything to us then. There's a little house up for sale just down the alley from the clinic. It has a big yard for Nada."

She shook her head.

"Or we could rent something in Yates, wait till the townspeople get used to us," he tried again. "I'm sure they will once we start our own practice. I take it pets are beneath the notice of the regular vet."

"Forget it. I would rather die first," she whispered.

"We could even—"

"No!" she shouted, pulling away.

Across the rug, Brendan got up, clutching at his leg. "I *tried* to tell you all that there was no time to lose but no one would listen. Did you hear that part about a closing portal? I was right, Odasan, and for once you were wrong." He went to the front door, dragging his foot. "I'm going to bed. If those people are still in that horse pasture maybe I can find my way to them in a dream. Until morning at least."

Lupe watched his limp grow more pronounced with each step. Then she examined her arms, snatched the shawl off Em's shoulders, flung it over herself as best she could, and ran past Brendan out into the night. It was raining again.

Driscoll scooted after Em. "Did you see her skin pucker?" he murmured. "Did you see him drag his foot?"

Em had nothing to say.

Bena looked at them out of sunken red eyes. "The laying-on of hands wasn't my idea. They made me do it. I promised them nothing. I never claimed it would last." Some light inside of her seemed to have gone out. She doubled over with pain, lusterless gray-threaded hair obscuring her features. A stray tear fell onto the back of her paper-dry hand. Clutching at Odasan's *gi*, she pulled herself up, not quite managing to straighten her spine.

"Brendan is right," she said, sounding reedy and faint. "Dreams are all we're likely to get from now on. If we're lucky. Ima and Vida. So close I could almost have touched them." She looked at Em one more time. "You recognized the sorceress? It's the second time she's turned me away." Ignoring Odasan's offer of support she shambled out on her own, leaving behind a musty scent, a dead space.

Odasan continued to sit, lost in thought. Then he scooped his charred book off the rug and tried to smooth a creased page before rising to follow his mate.

"Everything's coming apart," Em said as soon as he'd gone. "Anckar's right. It *is* all my fault."

"It is not," Driscoll said, getting to his feet. "You have no reason to blame yourself. They stopped believing, is all."

"You're way ahead of them then," she replied, unable to keep an accusing edge out of her voice. "Since you never believed in any of it in the first place."

He attempted a smile. "I believe in you. And I promised to follow you anywhere."

So he did. But such promises were easily broken. With the slightest excuse. She decided to give him one. "You can't follow me if I don't want you to."

"No, not then," he said, unbearably patient.

She stared at him with growing dislike. "Tell me why you're so cheerful when no one else is."

He gave a low laugh. "Tell you? I'll do better than that. I'll *show* you!"

On the couch, Alden turned to the wall, shifting into a fetal position. "I need some quiet. Please blow out the lamps and leave."

Driscoll ignored him. "Watch this, Em." He put a wedge of squash pie on a plate, picked up one of the lamps, and went to the kitchen. "Nada, you want to eat?" he called back through the hall. "Come and get it!"

Nada dashed after him. Em's pace was more measured; the dog had already licked the plate clean when she arrived.

"What did you see?" Driscoll asked.

"She gobbled it up. Obviously."

He grinned. "But what did she do in the living room when I called her?"

"Nothing. She perked her ears and ran in here for the pie."

"Precisely," he said, sounding pleased. "She ran. She didn't limp or drag herself along on her belly, even though last night—only last night, Em, think!—she had two broken legs and was dying. Until Bena touched her—the same way she touched Brendan and Lupe. Nada still runs yet Brendan is limping again and Lupe feels obliged to hide under a shawl. What does that tell you?"

"That I might wake up in the morning to find Nada stone cold?"

"Guess again!"

"I'm too tired to guess."

"Then let's go to sleep. Everything will look better by sunlight, you'll see."

"What I see is that no one cared enough about me to organize a bed. It's too cold and wet to sleep outdoors tonight."

He stepped into the hall. "Come into the living room with me. We'll spread a quilt and sleep right next to the fire just as we did last night."

"I can't. Alden hates me now—with good reason. *You* spread a quilt by the hearth. I'll curl up in here, under the table, alongside the dog."

Looking dubious, he said, "Isn't that just a bit . . . extreme? Why not just invite Nada to come sleep—"

She shut the door on his face and on the lamp. In the dark, she felt her way to the cedar chest that doubled as a spare seat. She knew it contained extra bedding. Crawling under the table with it, she curved around Nada for comfort. It wasn't so bad except for the occasional half-stifled sobs coming from Hertha's cramped room. When they finally stopped they were replaced by the noise of a dripping faucet. Em was too weary to get up and tighten the handle. She couldn't imagine being confined inside these walls for a whole winter. Counting Bena and Odasan, whose yurt still lacked window glass, seven people would have to stretch out on the floors of the house every night. At least Alden had the couch and Hertha her own chamber, even if it was hardly bigger than a closet.

Em knew she'd go mad before Christmas. She was used to having a big room of her own. Should she go back to it and to Oren? Never! Should she remain here and make the best of what was left? There was nothing left worth staying for, not when they blamed her for everything that had gone wrong with their dreams.

Nada crept to Em's head and devotedly licked at her ear. When Em objected mildly, the dog put her full weight across the girl's ribs and systematically washed her whole face. Em giggled in spite of herself. "So you think I'm being childish, do you?" She pushed the velvety muzzle away. "Let's follow Driscoll's sage advice and sleep on it. Maybe something good will happen to us in the morning."

But even this simplest of plans did not work out. In the middle of the night, without warning, came a mighty rumbling from every direction. The floor heaved. The table creaked and rattled above her. She scrambled out from between two of its dancing legs to bump into the plump flannel-clad form of Hertha. The woman cried out in fright.

"It's me," Em said quickly. "And Nada." They ran into the yard to where a blurred shadow stood clutching his head. It was Alden, moaning, "Something heavy fell on me on the couch."

From the yurt, Driscoll voice called, "Bena, are you in there? You okay?"

One might have assumed he'd want to ask his sweetheart that question first—after rescuing her from whatever peril had befallen her. But obviously, in the end, Bena was more important to him than she was. Not that she cared. The magic that had been so briefly between them was gone. Still and all, it wasn't as if the old woman needed his help, not when she had a capable old man watching out for her.

Then something deep in the hillside woke, growling. Rocks cracked, trees creaked and trembled. The earth roiled under their feet. They clung together for lack of more stable support. At the end of the attack came a high-pitched hiss from somewhere above. It was followed by a blood-curdling scream from the rear of the house.

Em ran to help. It was Lupe who was screeching like a demented teakettle. Her tent had collapsed on top of her and the zipper in her door-flap was stuck. As soon as Em managed to undo it halfway, Lupe squirmed through, climbed over her, and, still screaming, ran to the front. Em picked herself off the ground. "Brendan?" she called, noticing that his tipi had also caved in.

"Is it safe to come out?" he asked from under the tarps.

"The house is still standing." Em bent, untangling tarp and up-ended poles. Then Anckar bulleted out of nowhere and grazed her in passing, pushing her off-balance again. As Em teetered, Nada dove at her from behind, knocked her down, and pressed against her, pinning her to the ground. Brendan crept out of his tarps and helped her up again. Then the three of them returned to the yard.

Lupe was darting around and around, emitting spine-chilling screams while her white granny nightgown sailed out behind her. Unnerved, Hertha caught it by the hem and reeled the girl in. Lupe spun and climbed Hertha as if she were a pole, digging her nails into the woman's well-rounded shoulders. "Judgment Day has come," she whimpered. "Now I'll be punished for everything I've ever done wrong." It had been a popular theme among the Sisters of Penitence.

"You've done nothing wrong," Odasan assured her, helping Driscoll pry her fingers out of Hertha's flesh one by one.

"This isn't the end of the world, Lupe," Driscoll said. "Just a mild earthquake." He studied the dark clearing with the detached interest of a scientist. "I've always wanted to be in one. It's almost over, I think, except for the aftershocks."

"You call this mild?" Hertha said weakly.

"Yes. Mild," he repeated. "Compared to some of the others I was reading about. Earthquakes are just . . ." He paused as if searching for the least frightening and complex explanation of the event. And while he struggled to put it into words Anckar shouted out her own unique interpretation.

"You've upset the mountain today. Poked around where you shouldn't have poked. Crossed his sacred line. And now he's shaking us all off like so many bothersome flies." With her hair and pajamas askew, shaking an evil finger at him, she looked like an escaped lunatic.

Incredulous, Driscoll asked, "Say what?" And then he actually laughed. "I *told* you we only went as far as the lake. Even if there *is* some mythical line farther up, we never went anywhere near it."

"Oh yeah?" Anckar jeered. "You did *something* up there you shouldn't have done while the mountain was watching."

"Enough of your spewing," Odasan said firmly, pushing her accusing finger aside. "We are still a family here. We must stick together in times of need."

Anckar swallowed the rest of her venom.

Heartened by Odasan's support, Em cried, "I'll get us to Alden's green valley yet, you'll see!"

"Not without the tenth spoke," Alden said, sounding bitter. "If it hadn't been for you I'd have kept searching. And now it's too late."

"Too late!" Bena lamented, collapsing on the bench that stood outside the kitchen wall. "Too late for me. Something is pulling me under. My life is done."

"Don't say that!" Em sobbed, shocked to hear the acquiescence in her friend's tremulous voice. "I need you to be strong for me, the way you used to be in our forest. You were always so wise."

"Wise?" Bena cackled. "Me? When I'm going blind and deaf? Don't count on me, Em. Not anymore. I'm sorry you ever did."

The girl couldn't bear to see her old friend giving up when she needed her most. It amounted to treason. "No sorrier than me!" Em snapped, suddenly furious. "You've become as spineless as Lupe and Brendan and the rest of this bunch. I'm finally seeing you all for what you are—a sorry collection of fools without focus or nerve!"

"Em!" Driscoll admonished in his adult voice. "Leave Bena be."

She whirled on him, no longer caring whom her words cut. "You're always putting her first! And you're as feeble as they are!" She hurled the remains of her speech at the others. "You don't want me here anymore? Well, I don't want you either! Better no family than one this scraggly and shameful! I'm done with you all and with the wheel and with this mountain. You'll never see me again!"

Pivoting away from eight equally stunned, moon-pale faces, she ran into the night. Somewhere behind her there was a short scuffle, a yelp, then Driscoll's quiet voice, saying,

"Nada, this time you stay!"

Good. She didn't need the dog, or him, or any of them. What she needed was to run and run and run—away from everything they had known and been together.

CHAPTER 41

PANTS SAGGING, BORROWED SHIRT-TAILS flapping behind her, she crashed through the woods skirting boulders, the trailer, the car, and fled down the spiraling ruts. The mysterious hissing was still coming from somewhere up high. Her soles slapped against uneven ground, slipping, dislodging small stones. Her lungs sucked air. She could hear the breeze whistling past her, along with an occasional sob she was unable to squelch.

Then, losing track of time and distance, she heard nothing except the blood roaring in her ears. The nightscape revolved around her. Her heart drummed. Her chest fought for rhythm, her knees and ankles for balance, until she felt smooth bark against one hand while the other clutched at a side ache. The cool, polished bark could only belong to the 'golden archway of Yates.' Leaning against its massive base, she slumped, sat between bulging tree roots, and welcomed the wet grass, which was a balm for her overheated skin.

Her heart drummed faster, louder, merging with the sound of hooves beating on the dirt path. She wiped sweat from her eyes and saw the bulk of a black horse heading her way.

Thunder.

The black-cloaked rider in the saddle had to be Nev. Em slithered behind the tree and pressed herself against the ground, hoping the trunk and the overgrown weeds would keep her invisible in the faint light. When Thunder drew even she raised her eyes to the rider and discovered what had been hidden before. There were two, one clinging to the back of the first, pale hair and scarf streaming. Coming from Yates! In deepest night! She watched them gallop to the fork and then veer on to the road winding toward the plains.

She could make no more sense of them than of anything that had happened that night. Long after shapes and hoof beats dwindled, she stayed with the tree, hugging as much of the trunk as she could get her arms around. She imagined herself lying in Driscoll's arms under the big fluffy quilt by the hearth and could no longer recall why she had refused the tempting offer. Eventually her grip loosened and she slipped to the ground, her clothes soaking up the rain that coated the weeds. Being wet no longer felt pleasant, for she was growing increasingly cold but was too tired to do anything about it. Before long she heard herself moan and realized her mind had gone numb and her bones were becoming ice. She understood she must get up and move on. In what direction?

Turning, she looked longingly up the inky slopes toward home, and higher to where the summit was hidden by the same clouds that screened the moon. She wished she could relive the last few hours and take back every reckless word that had brought her to this. But home was too far away; what she needed was shelter now.

Blinking back tears, she saw the mountain break into halves, the dividing line coming for her, gashing under her feet, splitting the earth between them. To the left of the crack were the sparse fields of Yates, murky in a sulphurous light not unlike that of an oil lamp with a bad wick. In the small town behind them a lonely church bell mourned the late hour. One.

To the right of the crack was richer loam, fat heads of grain, cushioning grasses, bubbling brooks, a half slice of moon in a lucid and clear late evening sky. Friendly house lights twinkled ahead, offering snatches of faraway music and laughter. She stared down at Driscoll's scuffed boots and saw them slide on shifting ground, sinking one moment, floating the next. Try as she might, she could not raise the left boot across what she now guessed was a gap between worlds. Watching it grow ever wider, she thought it would swallow her whole. What would it be like to tumble into that primeval abyss unseen and unmourned, forever and endlessly falling? She crouched to scrape at the ground and felt rough dirt where her eyes showed her fat grasses, and wet plants where her mind perceived only dizzying space. If she could will her left foot across the pit she would be where she truly belonged. But the foot was welded to the old, outworn world that was refusing to let go.

"I don't want to stay here," she said. "I want to go over there." She reached and strained and willed until she could no longer tell left from right and up from down, and felt her body tear itself apart for lack of focus. In order to be anywhere at all, it seemed she had to give up one world for the other.

"Okay," she conceded. "Right now, I am here. Only here."

Seamlessly, the gap came together. The new world disappeared. The old solidified to reclaim all of her senses. Ahead was regrettable Yates, unwelcoming, unfriendly Yates. She knew only one place in town where she might curl up and hide until morning. A couple of hours of rest under a roof, no matter how humble—to gather her strength, to get warm—and then she would walk—no, run—back to where she belonged, where they would surely forgive her and take her in all over again.

SHE'D FORGOTTEN about the dirt floor and the mess. Rather than stumble into a space she could not see, she sat where the kitten had lain, just inside the shed door. She tried not to remember what the kitten had lain *in*. Crossing her arms, she clutched at her shoulders through the borrowed shirt. To be wrapped in Driscoll's clothes, sodden or not, was almost as good as a hug. She folded her knees to her chest and listened to her chattering teeth. Then there were hesitant steps just outside. Hinges creaked. A light blinded her. She rubbed at her eyes, feeling trapped.

"I knew it was you," Garner's voice whispered. "My mom sleeps on the other side of the house and she snores, but I heard the gate latch click shut. Why are you here?"

"I ran away."

He nodded, setting the lamp on an overturned bucket. "I've thought about it myself," he said. "Lots of times. Only, where would I go?" His tone was as pure as Nev's had been at that age.

"My problem exactly," she confessed. "It's starting to get cold at night, have you noticed?"

His eyes searched her face. "Why did you run? Were they mean to you up there?"

"Never. I got mad, is all. Now I'm just tired. You mind if I rest here until daybreak? I'll be gone when your mom gets out of bed."

"Before," he said. "You have to leave before daybreak. That's when the farmers get up." He wrung his hands as if silently pleading without knowing why.

"All right," she promised. "I will. How's the kitten?"

"Better. I did everything your friend told me to do."

She leaned closer. "You're hiding her from your mom?"

He backed away. "How did you know? Is it true that you're all witches up there? Brewing an evil soup?"

"Who said that?" she asked, already guessing but wanting to be sure.

He shrugged, his voice deliberately vague. "I hear things. People talk as if I'm not even there."

"They won't once you grow bigger."

"As big as you? What's it like?"

"They notice you more," she said.

He nodded, thinking. Then he looked fully at her, steeling himself. "My mom asked the vet to put my kitty out of her misery. So I told them I already buried her. It isn't even an out-and-out lie."

"No," she agreed. "Not entirely. Tell me, is she still in that hole under the grate with a stone on top? I had a dream about it."

He stared, speechless.

"What'll you do once she gets well?" Em asked. "She'll want to come out and play."

He nodded. "I'll trap me a mouse and set it loose in the kitchen. The only thing that'll make my mom scared. Then I'll say I found me a new little cat who loves to catch mice. She won't know the difference." A tear slid over his cheek. "That *will* be a full-out lie, won't it?"

She sighed in commiseration. "If that's the only way to save your cat's life, what choice do you have? It doesn't mean you ever have to do it again. You and me are the same that way. We both like the truth." She rose to stand on mud-encrusted pant cuffs, awkwardly patting his thin shoulder blades.

"You look funny," he said, stepping out of her reach. "Not like before."

"It's these clothes. They're Driscoll's. Got a piece of rope?"

He froze solid, his eyes going blank.

"For these pants. They keep slipping down." She grinned, pulling at the lax waistband.

"Tell him to stay away," he said, his voice rising. "Tell him I said thanks for helping my kitty but to stay clean away from here!"

"Okay, okay." She hoped his mother was a heavy sleeper. "I will."

He rummaged in a crowded cupboard and dangled a short piece of rope in front of her. It was covered with sticky webs. She wiped them on a sleeve and threaded one rope end through the belt loops. He stood watching, his face lit by the lantern. It looked like an angel's—round eyes, fine features, small, pouty lips. Even Nev's sorry bunch of new friends had looked like that once, and their voices had been clear as bells too. What made them change? What turned a fluffy, light-footed lamb into a plodding sheep? In a couple of years he'd look like his mother. Poor kid.

She was going to ask for a blanket next but could see he'd reached the limits of his compassion. Nev had gotten to him some-how with his smooth lies. Witches and spells. She rolled up the stiff trouser cuffs. "You best get back to your room now. Good luck with your kitten."

He grabbed the lamp and went to the door. "Who made the ground shake if you're not witches?"

"Nobody. It just happened," she said, thinking of sacred lines and cave pools that blinked.

"If there are fire pits up there how come you all don't fall in and burn?"

"It's not like that where we live," she said. "It's beautiful there."

He went out, carefully closing the shed door. She sat with her back to the wall, waiting for morning.

AT LONG last, a rooster crowed. She startled awake, cramped and shivering. The night was almost at an end. She left Garner's yard even more quietly than she'd entered it, making sure the gate latch closed soundlessly behind her. Crossing the street to walk past the blind eyes of the store, she saw her murky reflection. Each hair stood on end. She could imagine the rest—mud plastered, wrinkled clothes a couple of sizes too big, the sleeves torn by brambles on her heedless descent. Old Fraser was right; she was scary enough to put a whole treeful of crows to flight.

For an instant she thought she saw black shapes recede inside the glass and felt a sharp pang of fear. She hadn't felt one that strong since she was four, when she'd imagined huge moths in her room, fluttering in the dark, until she learned to squeeze her lids tight as soon as her mother blew out the light.

The boot leather had hardened; it squeaked treacherously with every step she took. She untied the boots and carried one in each hand. The clouds overhead had a strange yellow tint, as if they were heavy with snow. A dog barked at her passing, starting a chain reaction that preceded her all the way to the end of the street. Lights came on in some of the upstairs windows. Another rooster crowed somewhere behind her and was answered by a bellowing cow. White swirling fog rose in the fields ahead, breaking apart to drift and then sagging again. She went by the last yard and heard the furious honking of the ornery watch-geese. They stormed to the fence; she veered across the road until the mist swallowed her and made her invisible to them and to Yates.

Once she was safely on the dirt road that divided the fields, she slipped on the boots, tying the laces with double knots. Above the blanket of fog, the hillsides were splashes of soot draped in long rusty veils. She wondered how much time it would take her to hike home and felt sorry for herself. Then she remembered that before the advent of the Doble, Hertha had come this way every month, laden with barter goods like a mule—and had returned to the slopes staggering under a different burden. Including Odasan's rice. No, that couldn't be right—didn't someone say that the others waited for her in the sheltering dark at the edge of the fields to help with the load?

Noises seemed louder inside the fog: plodding hooves, a snort from one of the fields. A whisper, nearby? Stealthy footsteps? Fluttering moths? She reminded herself to keep looking straight ahead. Finally she came to the big tree and veered to touch the smooth-skinned trunk, the way she'd touch a good friend while saying good-bye. That's when she saw two awful round eyes stabbing through the fog. Without thinking she dove to the back of the tree, but as soon as she landed in the weeds she knew it could only be Driscoll coming for her in the Doble. Gathering what little courage she had left, she stepped into the road, waving, and was bathed in bright beams. The Doble stopped so close to her that she could feel the car's heat.

"Em! I've been looking for hours!" Driscoll leaned out of his window. "What were you doing in Yates, of all places? You're so obstinate that I took it for granted you'd decided to march over the plains back to Oren."

Before she could reply he was out of the car, sharing the spotlight, his arms wrapping around her. She rested her cheek on his shoulder. How could she have spent even one minute being jealous of Bena? He had a heart big enough to love them both.

"I missed you," he said.

"I missed you too. I shouldn't have run. It was childish. I still haven't figured out how to maneuver the ten-spoked wheel but I'd rather be stuck on the mountain than off it. Let's get out of here, quick."

As soon as she slid in beside him she told him to cut the lights. When he drove on in the dark, looking for a good place to make a U-turn, her stomach lurched. She cried, "No! Turn here. Now."

Too late.

Before he had a chance to reverse a startled cry came from the mist-shrouded fields. It was followed by a shrill, continuous scream.

Driscoll clutched at the steering wheel. "A horse!"

"We've got to get out of here!" She looked longingly up the ascending road toward safety.

"A hurt horse!" Driscoll said in a strained voice, switching on the beams. "I can't maneuver without lights. The Doble's not a small vehicle." He hadn't gone more than a car's length when a slight figure broke through the fog and hurtled toward them, frantically waving. It was Nev, mud-spattered, unraveled. "This trouble we don't need," Driscoll murmured, twisting the wheel. But Nev stretched his arms wide to block the road.

"Wait!" he cried. "I got thrown! Thunder tripped and fell down a ditch. I was taking a shortcut across the fields, see—"

"In this fog?" Driscoll growled.

"It was a stupid mistake. I was in a hurry. Or so I thought." The boy came closer, bracing his hands on the hood. "We have a quarrel, I know, but Thunder's done nothing to you. Em, please make him help. He's an animal doctor, he can't let my horse suffer—"

Gritting his teeth against his own monstrous refusal, Driscoll inched the car forward, forcing the boy out of his way. The horse screamed again and Nev clung to Driscoll's door, shouting, "You can do anything to me you want, only please save my Thunder!"

The vet's heart was not tough enough to ignore the boy's final appeal. He set the handbrake but left the engine on to remind Nev as well as himself that he was pressed for time. Then he fished for his flashlight, grabbed the black bag of his trade, and followed Nev into the mist to a newly dug pit, close to a couple of narrow canals. Perhaps the plan was to connect them and use the pit as a watering hole for livestock. It was a pity they had neglected to put safety barriers around it.

Thunder thrashed on the bottom, black on black, eyes wildly rolling, foam at his lips. Driscoll snapped on the light, playing it over the horse's legs. He swore. "Bad break. No point in waiting. Em, hurry, get the gun under my seat. He'll never leave this pit, alive or dead."

"No!" Nev whimpered.

Sobbing, Em ran to the car and came back holding the gun as if it might explode in her hand. Nev stepped in her path. "Don't give it to him. He has to save Thunder, not kill him."

She stopped, undecided.

"Bring it here. Hurry," Driscoll said from the edge of the pit, bending over the horse's terrified head. Nev hauled out to hit Em but she sidestepped and ran past him.

"Are you sure?" she asked Driscoll, suspending the gun over his outstretched palm.

"I wish I weren't," he said, pale but determined. The horse was still screaming.

"You can't!" Nev yelled, ramming Em. She dropped the gun. Driscoll caught it. Nev dove at him and pelted him with his fists. "You're a *vet*! With a bag full of *medicines*! Can't you give him something for the pain? Knock him out? Then set his leg the way I saw you set the dog's?"

Driscoll struggled to keep his balance and the gun. "It's not the same!" he yelled back.

Nev clutched Driscoll's beard. "You have magic on the hill!" he shouted. "That dog was as good as dead, no better than Thunder is now. You can hate *me* all you want, but don't hate *him*. Nothing's his fault."

With a sweep of his arm, Driscoll brushed the boy off. "I don't hate Thunder, Nev. I don't even hate you. But I didn't heal Nada. I'm not sure who or what did. See, I can pick up a dog and carry her. I can't pick up your horse. There's no way he'll ever walk again." Driscoll pushed out the drum, making sure the gun was loaded.

One day Em would ask him why he had a fully armed weapon under his seat. No need—she remembered the helpless boy-child hiding behind a wreck and watching his dad go down under clubs.

"It's not true!" Nev cried. "You're doing this just to punish me. What if I apologize to all the freaks and promise to never do anything bad ever again?" He steepled his hands, sobbing. "Please. Get them down here. Let them sit around Thunder in their magic circle. Let the old witch put her arms around him. I saw you through the window. I'm begging you!"

Driscoll lowered the gun. "I wish I could help you, Nev, but the magic is gone. Bena's sick and the rest of us are falling apart. Besides, I think the healing you saw had more to do with the place than anything else. Something about the garden. None of it's going to help your horse. Listen to him—he's asking to die. Every moment we wait is a sin."

He aimed the gun and took off the safety. Nev threw himself on his arm. The shot went wild. Driscoll swore, pushing the boy aside, but Nev clung, biting and kicking. With a regretful sigh, Driscoll put the gun down behind him and directed a punch at Nev's chin. The boy flew through the air, landed a man's length away, and lay still.

Driscoll picked up the gun. "I'm sorry, Em," he said, looking guilty, ashamed, beaten. "You shouldn't have seen any of this. Wait for me at the car. Cover your ears."

She watched him slide down to the horse, watched Thunder watching him, ceasing all struggle, waiting. When the shot rang out she found herself halfway across the field, hands clamped to her ears. She heard it anyway, along with the terrible echo rolling across the whole valley. Another shot followed a few seconds later. Then Nev screamed as if the bullets had struck at the core of his being. His lament of rage, loss and grief made Em understand for the first time just how important Thunder had been to the boy.

Cursing at the top of his voice, howling with pain, he came charging out of the shredding mist, racing past her to head for the road, disappearing into another pocket of fog. She wanted to go after him, hold him until some of the agony faded. He'd once been her friend and she realized she cared for him still.

But Driscoll needed her more. She went to where he was bending over the horse's motionless chest. "I'm sorry," he whispered, stroking the glistening neck. "I'm so sorry."

"I know," she said, holding her hand out to him from the rim. "Nev's bound to understand once he calms down. There was nothing else you could have done." She helped him climb out and made him sit down beside her.

He held himself apart. "I want to save them, not destroy them," he said, looking away. "I want to be a true healer, like Bena."

"You are." She stroked his rigid shoulder, feeling his muscles contract. "The kitten's much better, Driscoll. Eating and drinking. This wasn't your fault. Nev killed Thunder when he rode him so hard. All through the night. He loved him, though. Let's call it an accident. You only did what you had to."

He would not be consoled but wept into her hair and mumbled about his useless hands, his useless life. When he was done she helped him to his feet. "Let's go home," she told him. "I'll find us something to eat and then you can lie down on the couch."

"I'm not hungry. Just tired. Will you sit with me while I sleep?"

"We'll lie down together," she said.

"And will you hold me? I need you to hold me."

"For as long as you want," she promised.

But when they got to the car it was ringed by hard-eyed men with sticks, clubs, and a rifle. Nev stood among them, his face twisted with hate.

The first ray of sunshine slashed through the mist, painting Em's favorite tree a rich red-gold, its opulent small oval leaves bright green against a blue rent in the clouds. It was morning.

CHAPTER 42

EM KNEW THIS SCENE. SHE'D DREAMT IT. It did not turn out well.

"There he is, Hal," Tilden said. "That's him."

A beefy man stepped out of rank, his look as severe as her father's. He trained his rifle on Driscoll. "Put your stuff down," he ordered. "Easy."

Driscoll dropped his gun and the black bag. Em added the flashlight. She counted nine hostile men, roused from their sleep too soon. And Nev.

"That the girl you were talking about?" Tilden asked him, nodding at Em.

"He carried her off from Oren," Nev said. "I came to fetch her back to her parents."

"But that's the freak that was in the store the other day. She wasn't trying to get away from him then, far as I could see. Didn't say a word about being kidnapped either."

"Drugged," Nev lied smoothly. "Drugged out of her mind. They have a garden full of that kind of stuff, and a witch handy with potions. He shot my horse."

Driscoll bowed his head, his shoulders sagging.

"His horse fell and broke a leg," Em explained. "Driscoll's a vet.

319

He couldn't just let the horse suffer. You must have heard Thunder scream. Tell them, Driscoll!"

But he had nothing to add.

"Forget the horse," Tilden said. "It's my daughter this is about. Like I told you, Hal—after the tremor I had a hard time falling asleep. I thought I heard something around midnight, and when I looked out my window, I saw the tip of her white shawl whip away around the house corner. By the time I'd slipped on my pants she was nowhere in sight. Her window was wide open, a short note left on the sill. Scribbled, like—I could hardly recognize it as her hand. Usually she writes like an angel. Best penmanship award in every grade, Hal, just like I said."

Hal, still leaning the rifle butt against a meaty shoulder, waved the barrel irritably from side to side. "I know all that. I know! What was it she wrote again that made you drag us out of bed? When we'd just settled in from the quake? You never did show me the letter."

"Locked up at home," Tilden said. "For evidence, any time you want it. About how the redbeard invited her to some kind of bash up on the mountain. About how he promised to drive her to the city right after, for a look-see. Her one weak point. Always dreaming about life in the city. Their pills and parties and moving machines. You know how the traders come through here and stop at my house. She could never get enough of their tales. Always hoping one day somebody would drive up in a real car and invite her to hop in. The one thing she couldn't resist."

Em took Driscoll's slack hand. "The last time I saw her she was sitting on Thunder's back behind Nev," she told them. "They seemed in a big hurry. In the middle of the night."

Nev gasped his outrage. "That's the most barefaced lie I ever heard out of her mouth. She's in his power, that much is plain." His eyes skipped to the Doble before they fastened on Tilden with all the sincerity he could muster. "She'll say anything to save him now. But there's one way to get to the truth real fast. Search the car. If Celie was in it she might have left some clue."

Em could tell from his gloating tone that he'd made sure something would be found.

Hal jerked a thumb. Old Fraser, cold sober and unhappier for it, opened the passenger door, and Tilden bent to the task.

Seconds later, he shouted, "Oh my God! That's her shawl under the seat. Full of her blood!" He held up the evidence.

A stir went through the men, a shared look. Without a word, one of them bumped Em aside. As she stumbled, they surrounded Driscoll, cutting her off. Fighting for balance, she caught the stench of her own fear. Weak-kneed, she pleaded, "Say something, Driscoll. Tell them they're wrong!" She could see his face tower over their heads. All the color had drained out of it, highlighting every freckle. He was still looking down.

Through a gap between two of the men Em saw Tilden carry the rust-spotted shawl into their circle and lay it at Driscoll's feet. "Here's your proof," he told Hal. Then the men drew their shoulders together, forming a tight ring, isolating Driscoll in its center.

Hal waggled the rifle barrel. Without further warning a stick struck the back of Driscoll's legs. Mute, he collapsed onto his knees. The men wielded their clubs. Each blow made a dull thud as it hit home. At last Driscoll fell face down onto the ground, groaning. Half the men held him there while the others tried to wind twine around his wrists.

"Driscoll, fight!" Em yelled, balling her hands. "Get up! Do it for me!"

And then men flew in every direction as the stunned giant struggled to rise. He was bleeding from one ear.

"Don't let him get away," Tilden wailed. "He killed my Celie!"

"Lasso him," Nev shouted from his safe place outside the ring. "Tie him up like a hog!"

Throughout the commotion the Doble continued to quietly purr in the background, waiting. "Run for the car!" Em coached. Then something cold and hard rammed the back of her head.

"I'll blow you apart if you so much as take one single step," a rough voice growled from behind her. "With your own gun. How's that for justice? Now be a good girl and kneel in the dirt. On your hands. Make it snappy."

She obeyed. Driscoll stopped fighting.

"Hey, leave her out of it," Nev protested. "She didn't do anything. She's a victim, like Celie. The same age, just in an oversized body."

"You shut up," Tilden said. "I've just about had enough out of you. This is man's work. Hal, what do you say? The hanging tree?"

Hal narrowed his eyes, thinking. Then he spit on the ground. "It's not like they're real folks," he said, "up on the hill. Bert, you got that rope handy?"

The tallest, reediest of them uncoiled a length of it at the foot of the tree, tossed one end over the massive branch Driscoll had found so welcoming just a few days before, and proceeded to fashion a sturdy noose. The horizon blushed in the distance. The clouds above it lit up like a lampshade. From where he towered over his captors, Driscoll's tousled hair took on the color of sunrise; his beard was aflame.

"Stop it!" Em shouted, trying to get to her feet. "You can't kill him. He's done nothing wrong!" The gun crashed down on her skull with a vengeance. She swayed. Something warm trickled over her forehead. The light dimmed.

"I *told* you to stay down on your knees," the man behind Em said. "I wouldn't try that again if I was you."

At last Driscoll spoke. "I won't fight anymore—if you leave her alone. You want my hands? Take them."

Em knelt, her eyes seeking his as the man behind her jerked her hands back and shackled her wrists. Driscoll was gazing inward now, first in horror, then resignation. Did he remember his nightmare up at the lake? It had followed him off the mountain to claim him. One man tied his hands and two more led him to the dangling noose. He twisted to look at her over his shoulder. To make sure she was all right? To say good-bye? Then he plodded on like a sheep marked for slaughter, accepting its doom.

Tilden retrieved the shawl and stroked its fine silk. "I'm almost afraid to find the rest of her," he said. "But there's one thing I know for sure—we've got to wipe them all out tonight. The whole tribe. Level the place proper, like we should have last time they rooted. So there won't be a next."

"I'm with you, Tilden," Hal said, his rifle once more trained on Driscoll, who was letting Bert work the noose over his head.

"Please listen," Em begged. "You're making a terrible mistake. Let him go."

This time when the gun hit, lights danced inside her head and her ears buzzed. She struggled to keep her back straight, trying to see through red film.

"I'm not fighting," Driscoll said slowly, as if he were trying to explain to a dim-witted class of grade-schoolers.

Tilden and Hal huddled. Then Tilden climbed into the car and examined his options. He found the lever that moved the seat forward and when it could go no farther he sat on its edge, stretching his toes to the pedals. "Just a minute now," he said. "I've been studying these things since I was a boy. It'll come to me directly." Playing with levers and pedals, he inched the car forward—but try as he might, he could not force it into reverse. "You all push," he finally said, resigned.

After several attempts, the men managed to position the car directly under the magnificent branch. "You," Hal told Driscoll. "Get up on the nose."

While Driscoll hesitated, Tilden stuck his head out of the window. "It's called a hood," he corrected Hal. Then his voice and expression hardened. "Say good-bye to your priceless Doble, freak," he said, his eyes and voice equally hard. "You can't take it with you to hell."

The last word triggered old Fraser. "Satan's work!" he said, coming alive. "Let's smash the windows after he's hung. Burn the rest. There's a law against these devil machines."

"Not against this one." Tilden sounded quite resolute. "This one's mine. I'll drive it up the mountain tonight. It'll hold seven, eight men. Rope good and tight?"

Hal lowered the rifle to see for himself. "Nice fit," he pronounced. "But he'll need a boost up the . . . nose. Looks like even witches can't climb without hands."

The men pulled and shoved at Driscoll until he stood on the hood. His eyes, meeting Em's for the last time, held some kind of question she could not make out. His lips formed a silent name. It wasn't hers. Again, Tilden played with levers and pedals until the car slowly advanced.

"You'll want it to go in the other direction," Hal said.

"I'm trying," Tilden replied peevishly. The car rolled forward another foot. "All right then," he told the men. "I give up. This isn't like a regular car. You'll have to push it backward till his feet slide off."

The men pushed until Driscoll lost his balance and swung.

"Driscoll!" she screamed, unable to believe what she was seeing. His face! His eyes! The buzz in her ears became a loud ringing. The fresh morning colors faded to predawn gray and then darkened to a sooty black. If only she could shift things somehow, move him to a place so far away and hard to find they'd never get their hands on him again. *Make him safe!*

A jolt of current drove through her, searing her insides. With a moan, she slumped forward. Tilden's faraway voice seemed full of surprise. "Hey what—?" she though he said. "Where—? They don't even die like normal people . . ." She fainted before her face hit the dirt.

SHE CAME to on a cot reeking of mold and old urine. Her head ached. Her face felt crusty and tight. She squinted at the light coming in from a small, high up barred window. The wall under it was wrapped in spider webs drooping with dust. Then Driscoll's image appeared on the bricks. He was swinging from the rope. His eyes were no longer pleading. They were accusing, instead. She screamed.

Keys rattled. A metal door screeched open. Nev's narrow face appeared between two of the cell's bars. "So you're awake!" There was an edge of excitement in his voice. Or was it triumph? She turned away. "The sheriff's sending a message to Oren," he said. "As soon as your parents send back a description of you he'll let you go. We'll drive home in the car."

"To what?"

"You'll feel better once the drugs wear off. When your mind clears."

"Oh, give it up! My mind's clearer than yours!" She went to the bars, put her face close to his, and gave him the full blast of her anger. "The garden grows *food*. Nothing else—as you well know. And nobody can make me go back to Oren, especially you. There's nothing there for me. Never was. I belong with my new family up on the hill. I belong to Driscoll, even if he's dead."

With an ugly laugh, he said, "I was right about him. He popped like a balloon at the end. Spookiest thing I ever saw."

She stared point-blank into his lying eyes, hoping for a flicker of guilt, of shame. She found it just as he broke away from her gaze. "Why do you hate me?" she asked. "We used to be friends!"

Looking at the dusty stone floor, he said, "That's why I came, why I'm trying to help you now. Because we were friends."

"*Were* is right," she replied. "Once I thought you were an angel, but you've turned yourself into the opposite lately. You've done some terrible things. Why?"

He shook his head, looking oddly helpless. "I . . . I don't know," he whispered, backing away from the bars. A moment later the steel door clanged shut. She doubted it would open again anytime soon.

She sat on the cot and stared at the little barred window. From somewhere outside she heard faint shouting. What if she stood the cot on end like a ladder, climbed it, and tore out the bars with her bare hands? Even then, the opening would be too small for her to squeeze through.

Her gaze slipped down the blank wall and Driscoll reappeared, swinging and kicking. This time he was looking at her as if he expected her to do something. Why was she blaming Nev? It was her fault Driscoll came off the mountain, her fault for not turning him around sooner. Her fault he was dead.

Her head throbbed. Being awake was too hard to endure. She flopped onto her back, staring up at the mildewed, cracked ceiling, and sank into sleep.

Where she was free.

Her dreaming self drifted to the sidewalk in front of the store. Tilden stood on a wooden box, making a speech to all the able-bodied citizens of Yates who cared to listen. ". . . not rest until they're all hunted down like the vermin they are!" he shouted, shaking a fist. "Burn their hovels to the ground. Make them pay for what they did to my Celie!"

"Burn!" Fraser yelled from the front row, raising a bottle of beer as if it were a torch.

"Smoke 'em out!" added the lean hangman beside him, standing in the crowd's center, his gaze sweeping from face to face, gauging the mood of his neighbors.

Nev walked up behind Tilden to lend him his moral support, although no one had asked for it. "Don't leave a single stone standing!" the boy cried, his voice thin and tight. "Tear up their unnatural garden! Level the place so they won't have anything to come back to! That's how we got rid of the witch at Oren."

"Burn the witches! Smoke 'em out!" a woman shrieked from the rear.

The crowd took up the chant. "Burn the witches! Smoke 'em out!"

Nev put a hand over his mouth to hide a gloat, obviously enjoying his part. That's how he must have been at Oren—inciting, managing, stirring the mob.

Garner was way in back, his eyes darting this way and that, his cherubic mouth pinched. His mother was holding onto his sleeve, wanting him to get an education. She raised a bat with her free hand

and shrieked again, "Burn the witches! Smoke 'em out," sounding like an out-of-control Mira.

"Let's go get 'em right now!" Fraser shouted.

"Soon as it's dark," Tilden amended. "We've got to surprise them."

A wave of dissatisfied mutters moved through the crowd. Fraser took it as a vote for his side and pointed the bottle at the parked Doble. "We don't have to wait to destroy that hellish piece of work, do we? Charge, people!"

"No!" yelled Nev, who coveted the car the way he'd once coveted Thunder.

"No!" bellowed Tilden, who had already claimed it.

"Lead us not into temptation!" Fraser boomed, launching his bottle. The windshield exploded in a shower of glass.

"Deliver us from evil!" Garner's mother screeched, letting go of the boy's arm in her haste to join in the fun. She advanced through the mob, swung the bat, and shattered the rear window. While the shards yet rained to the ground, Garner leaped for the nearest alley and disappeared.

Em sat up on the cot and summoned her powers. They came easily to her. She went to the opposite wall, touched it lightly here and there, and all at once there was a low rumbling. A hairline crack appeared and widened. She could see daylight beyond. Then the wall crumbled and fell.

She opened her eyes to find herself limp on the sweat-soaked cot. A quick glance at the wall showed her that it was still solid. The glance was not quick enough; Driscoll imprinted himself on the bricks, mouth gaping as he struggled with death. She squeezed her lids shut. Through the window came distant sounds of destruction— wood against metal and glass. Let them burn the thing, too, until there was nothing left recognizable, the way there was nothing left of Driscoll except for the face now etched inside her lids, his mouth whispering that last, silent phrase. Not good-bye. Not "I love you!" Something about Bena.

That was it. His last word. Bena. Some sort of request. She remembered what he'd told her about the witch-hunt in Oren, about the doll full of pins, slashed, hung, set on fire.

Then she had it.

"Save Bena!"

She'd failed to rescue him but she would not fail him in this. Somehow, she would get out. Warn the others. Help Bena escape.

The only question was how. She hurled it at the universe, whispering, "Give me a sign."

She considered the ceiling, its flaking paint, the network of cracks. She traced each one with her gaze as they branched down the wall to where Driscoll's mouth gaped, his eyes pleading, *Save Bena!*

"You're not really here," she told him. "But wherever you've gone, know that I love you." The image faded, leaving the wall much too bare. What had they done with his body? Where was he now? Her stomach heaved. She clutched at her belly and was rewarded with a blurred band of faces flashing across the screen of her mind. Without thinking she reached for Nada's warm flank. And found nothing. Then she understood what Nada was to her and the wheel— an amplifier of power, a focusing device.

Could she summon the power she needed without the dog's help if she pretended that Nada was here? Stroke her hand over soft, slightly curled pretend-fur, feel the relaxed, happy life pulsing beneath it, the heartbeat as sure as it had always been whenever she put her ear to the dog's ribs? Ah!—now the blurred faces came clear. Ima. Tomas. Vida. The old crone, wrapped in her silken cape, smiling, expectant.

You didn't help me last time, Em silently told her.

You didn't ask.

What do I do?

Get up. Go to the wall.

Em obeyed and studied the branching cracks in the bricks. Was she supposed to copy what her dreaming self had done? Tentatively, she put out her hands and pushed. Nothing happened. Walls crumble more easily in dreams than in waking life.

Imagine it and it is, the crone said somewhere inside her.

It was as impossible a task as landing the wheel. Em turned away in defeat, hearing the witch call her name sharply.

"You're no help at all," Em said out loud. But maybe she was. What was the difference between dreaming something and imagining it? Dreaming just happened. Imagining was something that you did with conscious control. Even behind bars.

You have the power, the crone whispered inside her. *Use it. Consider the dog.*

Nada: sun-bleached floppy ears, red fur gleaming, elegant, feathered legs prancing high. Fluid grace. Nada: broken body sprawled at the end of the trail, laced with a pattern of cuts and gashes. Dying, like the wheel, like the horde's combined dreams. And yet she was whole again. Bena, bending over the dog with a face radiating pure love.

Em's gaze returned to the wall, tracing the cracks all the way down to the floor. Careless workmanship? Old age? Earthquake? She found the biggest among them and imagined it growing wider.

Look again, the crone's voice said from a great distance.

The wall was becoming a field of tiny pulsating lights. One of them blinked off and on. *Push here,* the voice said.

She pushed against a jagged brick. Nothing happened. She pushed again. Something shifted. Was that a glimmer of daylight beyond? She put a shoulder to the loose brick and heaved. It gave, sliding away, mortar crumbling like sand. Then the next brick fell, and the next, until she had made the narrowest door, fit for a dwarf. Her gateway to freedom. She stuffed herself through it and stepped over the rubble she had created into a deserted alley, moving away from the chants of destruction, the shrieking of metal.

Both the summit and the sun were obscured by thick clouds; some rays had worked their way through and were highlighting the fields, but the slopes were already plunged into deep afternoon shade. Darting from alley to alley, she came out at the first field and looked up the dirt road, avoiding the golden-boughed tree. If she ran all the way, would she get home before they came with their horses? She must.

Em ran.

CHAPTER 43

SHE RAN PAST SIDE ACHES, EXHAUSTION, collapse. When she went down for good something inside picked up her bones and ran them the rest of the way. Where the Doble had stood at the end of the road only a dry rectangle remained. Behind it, a red nose surfaced from under the trailer, cautiously sifting the evening air. Before Em could gather enough breath to speak, Nada surged out to greet her. Kneeling, Em cradled the dog's head and looked deep into her intelligent eyes. "Will you wait here and watch? Tell us when they're coming—and please stay in one piece!"

Nada accompanied her to the footpath that led through the forest and then crawled under the trailer again. The clearing was a shadow lake, the house obsidian against dusk. Em groped for the doorknob and stumbled into the living room. With only two candle stubs lit on the mantel, it was almost as dark inside as outdoors. There was no welcoming fire in the grate. She saw four indistinct shapes sitting at the table. Squinting, she counted Hertha, Anckar, Lupe and Brendan. "Something happened," she gasped, glad the gloom hid her blood-crusted face. "To Driscoll. In Yates."

"Yes, dear," Hertha said, complacently laying out rose pedals as if they were a deck of cards. "We know."

Beside her, Lupe was stitching at her embroidery frame, her nose close to the fabric. Anckar was squinting over a piece of paper at something she'd sketched. "You have to admit he *was* annoying sometimes," she muttered.

Em couldn't believe her ears.

"Too true," Brendan agreed, sanding one of his wooden spoons. "Especially when he dragged out that screechy fiddle of his." He gave Em a guileless, molasses-slow smile.

These were certainly not the reactions Em had expected. Something was wrong in this room—or maybe with her. After all, she'd had nothing to eat or drink since last night. Noticing the teapot on the table, she poured herself a cup of cold, thirst-quenching tea.

The front door swung shut behind her. It had hidden Odasan, who now advanced toward her, clutching a blade. "Don't drink that," he said, his voice rough, his eyes narrowed into unblinking black slits.

That's when she realized she knew nothing about him except that Lupe and Brendan adored him and Bena had accepted him unconditionally at first glance. "But I'm thirsty," she said, raising the cup to her lips.

The blade tapped against the rim. "Put it back down at once!" he commanded in a tone that allowed no opposition.

She yielded, spilling half in her haste. "Is that how you get when you're all out of rice?"

His teeth glinted briefly. "Here." He held out a box of matches. "Light the lamps. You'll see."

She struck a match and lit the kerosene lamps, turning the wicks up high. Hertha's rose petals were flooding the table, half of them already spilled on to the floor. Lupe's embroidery needle was unthreaded, her stabs at the framed linen pattern entirely random. Brendan was reducing the spoon handle to shavings, a pile of sawdust before him. Anckar's page was crowded with stick figures any three-year-old could have produced, and Alden, whom Em had not noticed before, sagged in his chair like a dead man, staring into the cold hearth as if it held a riddle he couldn't quite solve. Bena lay on the couch at the far side of the room, her face ashen.

"What's going on here?" Em asked Odasan in a shocked whisper.

He had his story all ready. "Right at dawn," he said flatly, "Nada started to howl. She howled so loud and so long that we all came running in here. She was pacing around and around the table. Then she dug at the door. Bena told her she couldn't go out. We were afraid she'd run off. And then Bena touched her and knew. 'Something bad has happened to Driscoll,' she said and lay down on the couch. She hasn't moved since, nor said a word. The rest of our friends fluttered around, packing their bags, ready to scatter in every direction." He waggled the knife. "I kept them together for you with this and with a calming herb in their tea."

"Drugged?" Em sniffed at her cup. "You mean Nev was right after all? Why didn't you just let them go?"

"Go where?" he asked. "To what?"

"Any place is better than here. There's a posse coming for us with guns and with clubs. To burn and to kill. Please let them out now!"

He blocked the door. "Our only way out is the wheel."

"We're not nine spokes anymore," she said with a sob. "They hung Driscoll from a tree for something he didn't do. The Doble is smashed. The town mob will arrive any minute." With a few words, she told him about her time in jail, her escape, and the danger they were now in.

A dry, rattling sound came from the couch, half cough and half moan. "They're coming for *me*. Just as well. Let it be over at last."

Em went to sit at Bena's side. "I'm sorry I was rude to you. Can you forgive me? Driscoll's last wish was that I help you escape."

"Escape to where?" Bena said. "There is no place left for me to go."

"There's up—since they're coming from below. As far as the mudpots, maybe. They'll never follow us there. And after they're done and gone we'll come back here and repair."

Bena looked at her with hollow eyes. "They will leave nothing to repair. Take the others upslope and hide in the woods. The mob will be satisfied with me—to finish what they started at Oren."

"Is she drugged too?" Em asked Odasan sharply.

"Only with fear," he said from the door. "She's lost faith in good outcomes, even between herself and me."

Em pulled at Bena's thin arm. "Driscoll's last thought was for you. Will you deny his final request?"

Bena grimaced, attempting a smile, and struggled to sit. "How can I when you put it like that?" She looked at Odasan. "I'm sorry for the harsh things I said to you after the earthquake."

331

His face gentled at once. "I've already forgotten them all."

Em went to the table and called out, "Listen up, everybody. We're climbing the mountain. Now. It'll be chilly up there. Dress warm and let's go." They regarded her with sleepy eyes but stayed where they were.

"First I must reverse the spell that binds them," Odasan told her, taking a cloth out of his pocket.

She ran to the kitchen, turned on the faucet, washed off the crusted blood, and put her head under the stream until her scalp cooled. Then she cupped her hands for a long drink. When she returned to the living room Odasan was busy going around the table, holding the cloth under his patients' reluctant noses until they gasped for air. He treated Alden last and told Em, "You cannot imagine their fear."

But she could.

She helped Odasan pull Bena to her feet. "We'll walk together, you and me," Em told her. "We'll do it for Driscoll because he loved us so much."

Bena clung to her, seeping tears. Odasan brought out his bottle of liquid rice. Unscrewing the cap, he filled it and held it to Bena's drawn lips. "Drink," he said. Glancing at Em, he added, "Sake."

It was a word as unfathomable to her as the man who spoke it.

And then a volley of barks came from below. "Nada," Bena said, downing the fiery liquid with one gulp.

Em nodded. "They're here." Her words dripped like acid into the room. As if someone had pulled a switch, her four friends at the table jumped up from their chairs. Bumping into Alden and each other, they circled the room like chickens locked in the hen house along with the fox. Then Anckar broke for the door.

Em was ready for her. "You're our guide," she told her. "Take us to where the mob can't find us."

Anckar nodded and fled outside. The others followed hard at her heels. Odasan and Em both offered Bena their arm. Then Odasan gently pushed Em's aside. "Let me. You blow out the lamps." His tone was polite, his look fierce and determined. Em squeezed Bena's hand and let him lead her away.

Nada's barking grew nearer. Was she herding the posse into the bramble sea? Em could tell from their subdued curses that the men were being slowed by raking thorns. She lowered the wicks and blew out the lights one by one, taking a last greedy look at the room she considered the home of her heart. Halfway to the clearing's upper edge, she peered down to where a flash was stabbing through the night. An instant later she heard a shot. A dog yelped once and was still. Em forced herself to keep moving.

Soon she caught up to Hertha, the last one in line. Anckar guided them on the faint path as if it were morning, though Em could barely discern the outlines of the nearest tree branch. For a while, the din of breaking glass and wild hooting competed with Hertha's labored breathing. Then the forest buffered the noise from below and Em heard only the rustling of leaves and dry sticks breaking under too many pairs of feet. Hertha clutched at her arm. "Those poor defenseless starts I planted yesterday—will they smash them, you think?"

Before Em could come up with a soothing reply, Brendan moaned and asked, "How much longer do we have to climb?"

Anckar gave a pitiless laugh. "Ten, fifteen minutes. Don't gripe."

"I can't make it that far."

"Suit yourself," she snarled, moving on.

Lupe said fervently, "You *will* make it. Don't listen to her!"

"Quiet," Em hissed. "You'll give us away!" When they stopped talking, even Em, at the end of the line, could hear Brendan's foot scrape and his teeth grind. His pace grew ever slower. She scanned downslope to see if anyone was following them but the foliage was too thick and the night too dark. She thought she smelled smoke. Hertha began to agonize over her rare treasure of seeds, so carelessly stashed in the root cellar. "Without them we have nothing," she wept softly as she blundered along.

From farther ahead, Odasan murmured to Bena, "We'll do it together, one step at a time."

Suddenly a low missile slammed into Em's knees, wedging itself between her and Hertha, who screamed and was immediately comforted by Nada's wet tongue. Amazing, how that scream rolled uphill and down. There was no doubt in Em's mind that they had just given away their position. "Anckar? Faster!" she said. Nada licked at her arm, leaving a film of foam and spittle, which Em hastened to wipe on her corduroys. "Good girl," she told the dog. "You warned us, just as I asked." *And gave us away.* But that was hardly fair since Nada had been noiseless in coming.

Then Brendan's voice floated down from above. "It's Nada. She's found us. Now we're all together again."

Together again . . . together again . . . The words rang through Em's mind like some forgotten refrain. How could they be true without Driscoll? She allowed herself a moment of searing pain and then shut it away. No time to grieve. Not yet.

THE mudpots churned and seethed as they carefully navigated around them. Each person clutched the one walking in front. They were surrounded by odd whines and whistles. The high-pitched hiss that had started during the quake sounded somewhere above. Once more scanning downslope, Em saw a single white eye glaring up at her. Driscoll's flashlight. In whose murderous hands?

"Em?" Anckar whispered. "They're getting closer. We can't stop here. We'll have to cross the scree. Step lightly, you guys. The rocks are unstable."

"Scree?" Brendan said, dismayed. "Unstable? You'll have to go on without me."

"Brendan, please try," Lupe begged.

Em felt her way along the chain of stalled climbers, brushing against Hertha's lank hair and her sweat-soaked loose gown. She grazed Lupe's bulky wool sweater, once more buttoned up to the girl's chin. Lightly, Em touched Brendan's fleecy cushion of curls, then Odasan's sinewy shoulder supporting his love, and at last Alden's slack arm.

"Huh?" he said, his mind reluctantly surfacing from elsewhere.

"It's Brendan," Em told him. "He needs your help."

"Nobody needs me," he said. "They never have."

"*He* needs you. To lean on. His foot's giving out." He continued to stand there as if awaiting some more major revelation until Em dragged him unceremoniously by his sleeve to Brendan's side, then slung the boy's arm around him. Immediately, Alden sagged under the weight. He had neither the bulk nor the inclination to handle the additional load—nor was Em capable of taking it on. In fact, she had no idea how she managed to keep moving at all.

She groped her way to Odasan's side and whispered, "I'll watch over Bena. Brendan's refusing to walk on but I know he'll do more for you than for anyone else." Pound for pound and inch for inch, the old man was the fittest among them—even without taking into account his iron will. Mutely he put Bena's hand into Em's for safekeeping, wrapping both of his around theirs before stepping away.

334

Em hugged Bena close and felt the bones of a mummy under her dress, shrinking from touch. "It'll get easier soon," Em ruthlessly lied. A gust of wind blew down the scree. Girl and woman shivered as one. It would be cold up there and none of them had brought as much as a sweater—except for enviable Lupe. Overhead, clouds swirled and shifted, allowing a sliver of moon to shine filtered light on to the vast field of stones when they were two-thirds of the way up. A gravel-sized piece rolled from under Em's feet.

"Look out," Anckar warned. "Rockslides are dangerous."

Brendan shook off the support of his friends. "Let go of me, Odasan," he sobbed, sinking to his knees. "Any minute, this whole hillside will come down on us. How can I run with this bum foot? The stones are too sharp. Leave me here—I'll find someplace to hide."

"Wait," Em told Bena. "Stay right where you are." She went to grasp Brendan's chin, turning his face downhill. "Do you see that little round eye down there?" she asked. "They've got Driscoll's flashlight, his box of spare bulbs and batteries, and no doubt his gun—and they're gaining on us. There's not a single bush anywhere near you. Where do you think you can hide from that beam? I won't lose you too! We're in this together. Whatever happens to you happens to the rest of us."

"Remember *karate-do*, my son," Odasan said, massaging the back of the boy's neck. "You can go on long after your body has given up as long as you keep your mind strong."

"This isn't exactly like doing a kata!" Brendan snapped, pulling away from his *sensei's* kneading fingers.

"Consider it number one hundred and one. *Yame!*" Odasan said, repositioning Brendan's arm around his broad shoulder. Alden grabbed hold of the boy's other arm. Behind them, Lupe whispered prayers to a vengeful God.

All at once the clouds slammed together, shutting out every vestige of light. Em felt her way back to Bena but she was gone. After fumbling around in the dark, thinking perhaps the old woman had collapsed and was lying just out of reach, Em probed past the others, feeling along the ground with both hands, then in thin air, until she finally reached Hertha, still at the end of the line. "Have you seen Bena?" she whispered, trying to keep her panic from rising.

"Someone brushed by me a minute ago," Hertha answered. "I thought it was you."

Then Em understood she could no longer keep quiet. "Bena!" she yelled, sick with foreboding. "Come back!"

After the echo died away, a weak voice from somewhere below called, " . . . too tired . . . me they want . . . leave you alone . . ." There was a shot and then a choked cry.

The clouds parted just as Odasan flung himself downhill, leaving a shadowy Lupe to take his place beside Brendan. Too slight to prop the boy up, she yanked him along by his belt while Alden and Anckar pushed from behind. Em stood alone, useless and ashamed, sure that the whole universe had just witnessed how she'd failed her best friend. The hiss from above seemed louder. The hunters below hooted and rushed toward their victim, but already Odasan reappeared at Em's side, carrying a limp form in his arms. Em stroked Bena's trailing hair, whispering, "My fault. Is she—?"

"She'll live," he vowed. "She'll do it for me. But you must buy us some time at the pass. You know that big boulder on top of the rock wall? The one that's balancing on a single point? You must make it fall into the cleft as soon as we've gone through. It'll fit like a cork in a bottle. If we're lucky it may even start a small slide."

He had to be joking. "Me?" she said. "Move that huge slab? How? With what?"

"The way you spun the wheel, Em. With your mind."

"My mind is a blank."

"Then you are halfway there," he said, shifting his burden to catch up with their friends.

Leaving her to the hunters. A much bigger target than Bena. If she let them shoot her, would it be enough to satisfy their bloodlust, or at least slow them down so that her friends could find safety? But she wanted to live. Something was up there for her, pulling her on as much as hatred pushed at her from below. Then Nada's muzzle touched her wrist. The dog moved ahead and Em followed. She stopped at the rock wall. "We need some kind of light," she told the dog. "So I can find my way to the top."

A gust tore at the overcast, sending a needle-thin moonbeam to show her some footholds. "Thanks, Nada," she said, giving credit where it was due. If a dog could shift clouds, maybe together they could roll one gravity-defying stone—which was about as likely as thinking a break into a solid brick wall. To Em's left, Odasan was carrying Bena through the pass. She watched them disappear before she concentrated on her task. The boulder didn't seem to be attached to the others except at that one point. In fact, it seemed poised to topple on its own—in a hundred years or so. She climbed up to it and tried a hard shove. On the field of scree, the flashlight beam swept from side to side. It was incredible how far their pursuers were willing to go to exterminate a few innocent vermin.

Which was the stronger force—the hate of the hunters or the combined terror of their intended prey? They might have had a slim chance without Brendan's hysterics slowing them down. She considered the immovable rock and then closed her eyes and her mind to the danger below. "All right," she addressed the place deep within her. "Now what?" But hadn't she learned that lesson with the bricks? What was it the crone had told her to do, imagine it first?

"Nada?" she whispered. Like magic, the dog appeared at her side. She put an appreciative hand on the familiar sleek neck, placed the other on rough stone, and imagined it trembling, rolling, crashing to lodge precisely where she wanted it—in the cleft. She pictured a sheet of scree breaking away from the point of impact to sweep downhill.

Out of the night came Tilden's quarrelsome voice and Nev's jeering reply. Both seemed shockingly close—until she remembered that sound did strange things on this slope. She gave Nada's neck an appreciative squeeze. "Thanks for sticking with me," she whispered, pressing her lips to the dog's forehead. A wave of love rushed through her and opened her heart wide. In that instant, the rock came alive under her palm. It seemed to stir. Something snapped. Lichen tore loose from its base. Em breathed in and out with the wind. She was the wind. She was also the boulder, falling, the rock wall it skidded across—and part of an invisible army of watchers who were watching her.

She'd sensed them for some time. Briefly, she wondered whose prey she actually was. It triggered a new kind of dread—of something immense, looming, unknown.

The flashlight arced across the sky as scree tore from under the feet of the hunters. She heard cries of pain and was almost certain that one of them was Nev's. Then all was silent except for the echo, dying away. "Corked," she said, sliding down from the wall on the uphill side. She didn't feel the least bit victorious.

"It was the earthquake," Driscoll would have explained in that skeptical, dry tone of his she'd grown to hold dear. "It weakened the boulder just as it weakened the bricks."

Nada landed beside her. "We'll catch up with the others in a few minutes," she told the dog. "I know exactly where Anckar is heading." New fear or old, Em had somewhere else to go first. She only hoped she'd gained enough time to do both.

CHAPTER 44

WAS IT ONLY YESTERDAY THAT SHE HAD come this way with Driscoll? He must have left an invisible scent trail that any good dog could still track. How could something that fragile outlive the actual man? How could things be just right one day and go wrong so fast on the next?

This time she took the ridge trail alone—if she didn't count the unseen watchers crowding close. The emerald lake below lay shrouded in night and in mist, but in her mind's eye it glowed in early-afternoon sunlight and was framed by patches of wildflowers, mighty forests, and mountain chains. She saw the gawky young girl she had been, running into the shallows with her clothes on, saw Driscoll, the better planner, strip down to his underwear before he went in after her. They splashed and played like the children they were, and then she came out, peeled off her clothes and ran off, and he . . .

And now she was in the dark, struggling for breath. His tender arms and lips, though only remembered, seemed more real than this. If she climbed down to the lake could she somehow find that slice of happy time and squeeze into it again? Reach out and touch his precious bare skin?

If she couldn't she'd just as soon keep on going downhill. Why not? The others were better off without her. She had failed them too many times. She had promised Odasan to take care of Bena, then let her slip away. She promised Driscoll to lie with him on the couch, but instead had watched him . . . had seen . . .

She collapsed, whimpering, overtaken by a grief so immense that she felt she would die from it. Good. Let it be over. There was not one reason to keep breathing. Kneeling, she tilted her head at the sky and shouted, "Let there be an end to my miserable life now!"

In the next instant some huge thing swooped at her like a giant bird and tore her out of herself. Her body slowly crumpled to lie prone on the trail. The rest of her writhed and screamed while the thing carried her higher. A compelling voice thundered, "Cease!" and she did.

And then she was lifted, not into the sulphurous clouds but to somewhere beyond. And the higher she rose the more she seemed to expand toward some clear, radiant place that was lighter than air, than thought, until she towered over the world and watched it fall away below her. Countless invisible arms, infinitely tender, reached out to embrace her and pass her along. Waves of well-being bathed her from every side. At last she was enveloped by a being of crystalline light. It permeated her and filled her with unspeakable joy. The voice spoke again, more gently, "Beyond your illusion of fear there is this. Always and only this. Welcome to your true home."

Her human eyes were not made to see it, her everyday mind could not grasp it, but her core knew that this non-physical place she was in was the center of everything, everywhere, and thus the most real place of all. The being of light knew every thought she'd ever had, knew her most shameful secrets, and yet it loved her just as she was. In its ever-observing invisible eyes, every move she had ever made was the right move. To it, she could never fail. It was wherever she went, cheering her on.

Far below, her human friends toiled over frozen wasteland toward some bad end, trapped by their own despair. Anckar was still in the lead. Odasan, with his precious bundle, was close behind her. The rest of them crowded around Brendan, the greatest resister of them all, coaxing, pulling, supporting. She leaned toward him, wanting to share her joy, tipped too far, and found herself in his paralyzed mind, looking at the world out of eyes that recognized only darkness and shadows. She felt the heavy sensation of being utterly lost and alone. Then loving invisible arms righted her again, pulling her back to the light. But she could not ignore Brendan's need. "In their hearts, they are calling me," she said. "I want to go to the finish with them, whatever it is. As you love me, guide me to that. Guide us."

No sooner had she spoken that the light dimmed, the arms opened, and she drifted faster and faster back to that lonely place of no hope. She awoke on the trail and felt herself glow. Nada was lying beside her. Their eyes met. "You're from that bright place, aren't you?" she told the dog. "And the joy filling me now is what you feel every day."

Nada closed her eyes. When she opened them again they shone in the dark. "Come," Em told her. "Let's catch up with our friends and tell them the truth of things."

Soon she could smell their panic. It thickened around her and seeped into her bones along with the cold, congealing her blood. Her thoughts became clumsy and slow. What was it she wanted to say to them? It was no longer clear. By the time she came to Brendan and his hapless assistants it was entirely gone. Her dread rose to match theirs. Between them, they were trying to support those parts of the boy that no longer worked while he struggled against them.

He managed to shake them all off. "Don't move me!" he sobbed through clenched teeth. "I have the right to give up!"

"Yes, you do," Em told him, at last stepping into the space that had been waiting for her—in front of the boy. "So give up already. Right now. Put your arms around my neck and hold still." Something in her voice made him obey. He hung on her back like a sack of scrap metal, his forearms tight against her windpipe until the others braced him from behind. Em focused on the shadowy house-with-no-roof, which looked like a murky, flat-topped hill in the distance.

She took one small step toward it. And another. And another. "You are light as a feather," she said in a whisper, adjusting his arms. "As a snowflake. Why, you weigh no more than a kite sailing the updrafts. Feel that power? That's all of us, working together. You have no idea how many we are."

Odasan and Anckar were waiting for them at the foot of her cliff-wall. Even though the old man still carried Bena he looked as fresh as if the journey had yet to begin.

"Is this our hiding place?" Brendan asked, his voice brittle.

"It's the rear of my castle," Anckar told him. "Let's go around to the front so we can't be seen from below."

They were almost safe. If they could keep quiet there would be nothing to give away their location. Whoever heard of a hollow hill?

"It's easy from here," Anckar said when they arrived at the uphill side. "I'll go first." She climbed effortlessly, pausing to point out the most prominent footholds. While Em considered how best to proceed with Brendan's weight on her back, he released her.

"I can do it myself," he said. "I can lift my own weight." He hoisted himself up with his muscular arms.

Odasan entrusted Bena to Em and climbed to the rim. The others stationed themselves at various ledges and passed Bena from one loving pair of arms to the next until Odasan, reaching down, could lift her the rest of the way. Soon they were all sitting beside him, staring into the black pit beneath their feet.

"I've done this lots of times in the dark. Like so," Anckar told them, sliding down into the hole. Odasan followed and stood on the moss-encrusted floor with his arms raised. Em lowered Bena toward him. And then they were all inside together, stumbling over the uneven ground, brushing against one another and along the castle's wall—until Lupe gave a terrified scream.

"There's something in here," she blubbered. "Big and hairy. I think it's alive!"

A bear? Perhaps it would do them the favor of eating her first.

"Nobody move," Anckar hissed. "I've got a candle in my camping stash."

Nada gave a soft whine while Anckar fumbled at the niche where she kept her supplies, struck a match, and lit her stub. By its unsteady flame they saw a long, sleeping form curled against the wall. Nada was licking his beard with devotion.

Driscoll.

How could this be?

Em had the dizzying sensation of being on a swing with her eyes closed, soaring, plummeting, and soaring again.

"You told us he was dead!" Anckar said.

"I saw him hanged," Em whispered, hunching over his face. "Look, that bruise on his neck. It's from the rope. And see, his hands are still tied."

She had Odasan's full attention. "What were you thinking when you saw him hanged?" he asked.

She tried to remember. "I wanted to make him safe." Spilling tears onto Driscoll's dirt-streaked cheek, she repeated, "More than anything, I wanted to make him safe."

"And so you did." Odasan shifted his load, supporting Bena's limp head against his shoulder. "Just as you collapsed the brick wall and made the boulder fall at the pass. Your power is increasing—or maybe you're fighting it less."

Anckar swiped at her eyes. "Actually, I'm glad he's here with us. Truth be told, he kind of grew on me." She produced a knife and sawed at the twine binding Driscoll's wrists.

Odasan lowered Bena to the mossy ground and sat, his arms wrapping around her. Brendan braced her from the other side. "Do you think Em has enough power to get the energy wheel out of here?" he asked the old man.

"I don't know," Em answered for herself, drying Driscoll's beard with her sleeve. "The things I've done so far only work when I'm half frightened to death."

Anckar's blade nicked a wrist, drawing blood. Driscoll mumbled and stirred but slept on as she brushed off the cut twine.

"If you need something else to be scared of you've come to the right place at the right time," Odasan told Em. "Hear that hiss? We're sitting on top of an erupting volcano. In a few minutes the ground under us will be blown to bits."

If he was right they'd be blown to bits right along with it, for not one of them had the strength or will left to escape this final trap. Besides, where would they go?

Brendan gave Odasan a suspicious look. "You know too much. About everything. Who are you anyway?"

The old man chuckled. "Just one of the spokes, my son. And no matter what I know or don't know, the only way out for us is the wheel."

The hiss *did* seem to be getting louder. Em upended a flask Anckar supplied, splashed Driscoll's face, then wet his parched lips. He swallowed and opened his eyes. "Em?" he said hoarsely. "Is this just my dream or are you dreaming it, too? In mine I've been calling and calling. This place may be safe, but not for a man without hands!" He raised his to prove the point, and seemed astonished to find them unfettered.

Laughing and crying at once, Em held him close. A surge of pure love streamed through her, matching what she'd felt on the ridge. "Who cares who's dreaming this dream?" she said, helping him to sit with the others. "As long as we're in it together. Are you ready to fly?" It was worth one last attempt. If Odasan was right the next minute would bring total annihilation—or complete success.

Somehow they managed to form an ungainly circle. Fortunately, they had rehearsed well. Their hands linked with no hesitation. Em closed her eyes, waiting to sing the note that was the sum of their vibrations. The ground began to throb under the moss. Then a light played over her face.

"It won't work, you know," a boy's voice called from the rim. "Not without me." The flashlight beam spot-lit each of their faces as they stared up in disbelief.

"Nev!" Em gasped. "What do you mean? It's your fault we're trapped here."

"So it is. It was me who led you to Nada and to the mountain. It was me who fixed it so Bena and Driscoll couldn't return to their old lives. I'm the one who stopped you from settling for less than we planned. Step by step, I pushed you to this place and this time. After your rockslide knocked me out I finally remembered my part in all this."

In the stunned silence that followed, time itself seemed to pause. Then Odasan said, "He is like the yeast that makes bread rise."

"Our own catalyst," Driscoll supplied, fingering his bruised neck. "A bit over-zealous, don't you think?"

"Nev is our tenth spoke," Odasan said firmly. "And Em was right to say he was not coming to join us. He had another role to play first, one that was absolutely essential in our scheme. It's easy to accept people who appreciate us. But more often than not our worst enemy is an old friend from the before-time who has come to teach us to love those we hate. We're getting a bit better at it. Now will you kindly make room for Nev in our circle?"

Alden moved away from Em and sat tall. "I was right too. It was me who drew him in . . . but skewed, somehow."

Nev slid to the bottom and wedged himself into the place that had been waiting for him. "Celie?" Em asked in a whisper, and had a mental glimpse of Nev and the girl riding through the night. He ducked for a branch; she didn't.

"Mending her head in some hermit's cabin. She refused to get back on the horse," Nev whispered back.

Then Em heard a metallic click from above, followed by a small explosion. A split-second later a bullet slammed into the wall behind Driscoll. Nev trained the flashlight upward. It illuminated a rifle barrel pointing at them from the rim, and Tilden's flushed face.

"Never did trust you a lick, Nev!" the pharmacist yelled over a fast rising, deafening hiss. "I found me a whole snake pit! Don't even need to aim!"

Em thought that unlike his wife, Tilden had at least tried to be kind. His murderous rage was no more than a father's devotion turned inside out. Nev tossed the flashlight straight up. Then these things happened at once:

The flashlight struck the rifle,

the earth heaved,

the hiss grew unbearably loud,

and Nev's hands completed the wheel's power circuit.

Singing her note, Em wished Tilden out of harm's way. The wheel spun. The ground ripped. The wheel disappeared along with the top of the mountain.

Or so Tilden thought as he jack-knifed awake in his bed from some horrible dream, fully clothed and booted, minus the gun. Somewhere within a voiceless voice told him that all was well with his Celie and that he'd hear from her soon. He chose to listen.

CHAPTER 45

THERE WAS A BIG PARTY on the deck of Driscoll's round house that night. Every room was filled with music and laughter as new friends greeted old.

Nada kept herself busy weaving in and out of the crowd. For a while she sat among cheering onlookers as Brendan and Lupe improvised on the dance floor. Then she moved on, brushing against the silken robe that belonged to the ancient crone, in deep conversation with Odasan. He kept an arm firmly around Bena's shoulder as she sat beside him. And she was beaming at Ima and Vida who were bringing her casserole tidbits from the nearby table.

Next, Nada accompanied Tomas and Hertha as far as the garden gate. Returning uphill, she stopped to watch Nev who was standing on the edge of the meadow, forehead to forehead with a tiny, impossibly long-legged black foal. It held very still while he wept for all he had lost and found.

When the dog rejoined the throng on the deck Driscoll had just discovered his fiddle—or a near double—casually propped against the porch wall. While he tested the strings Nada settled herself comfortably at Em's feet. As soon as Driscoll tucked the fiddle under his chin it became a magical violin, playing a tune both slow and achingly sweet. Anckar and Alden sat shoulder to shoulder between

347

two posts of the railing, swaying along.

Leaning a hip against the banister, Em gazed down at the smooth, silvered lake and launched her voice across to the valley beyond. She lifted it higher and higher, past friendly dark slopes to where a perfect round moon met a divinely symmetrical peak capped by a white crown . . . and let it soar free.